The Scourge Incursion

LEGENDS OF LAIRHEIM

BOOK 3

Also By Tora Moon

Legends of Lairheim (Science-Fantasy)

Ancient Enemies (Book 1)
Ancient Allies (Book 2)
The Scourge Incursion (Book 3)
Exile's Vengeance (Book 4)
Redemption - A Novel

The Sentinel Witches (Urban Fantasy)

Crossroads to Destiny (Book 1)
Descent Into Darkness (Book 2)
Well of Sorrows (Book 3)

Indie Author Guides

Business & Accounting for Authors
Business Plans for Authors (forthcoming)

To get an up-to-date listing of all my books or to purchase visit
ToraMoon.com

LEGENDS OF LAIRHEIM

THE SCOURGE INCURSION

BOOK 3

TORA MOON

Lunar Alchemy Publishing

ACKNOWLEDGMENTS

An author may sit alone at the computer, but no book is completed without help. My sister, Angelique, is my greatest supporter, cheerleader, and encourager.

Thank you to all the authors I've had the pleasure of reading their stories and making me want to tell my own. Without story, this world would be a much poorer place.

And especially to my daughter, Sasha, you have made me become a better person by being your parent. I couldn't have asked for a more amazing daughter. You believe in me, even when I struggle with my self-doubts.

Thank you to all my readers. Thank you for spending time with my stories and letting me be a part of your life. I hope you love them as much I loved writing them.

*To my daughter, Sasha.
Thank you for believing in me. I love you.*

EXTRAS

The world of Lairheim isn't a re-imagining of Earth. It has its own culture, language, and landmasses. I've created several extras and resources to help you enjoy this fantasy world more. You can find these on my website at: ***ToraMoon.com/Legends-Extras***.

Extras you may like:

Pronunciation audio - While the appendix includes a cast and glossary, fantasy names and words can be difficult to figure out how to say. I've recorded audios for each name and Posair word.

Maps - There is a map at the beginning of the book to help you orient into the world of Lairheim. A black and white pdf map is available to download for free. Or if you love maps, I've created a beautiful, hand-drawn, color map you can purchase.

Merchandise - I've created some fun merchandise centered around the books and the world of Lairheim. Check them out in my shop!

MAP OF LAIRHEIM

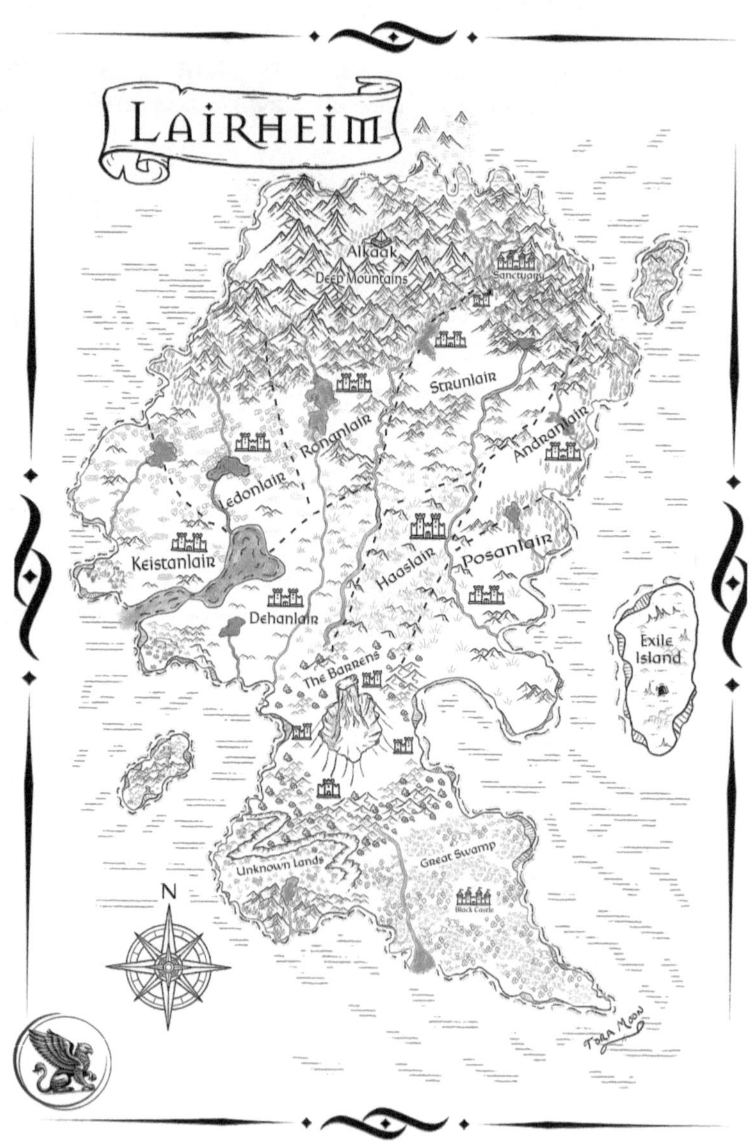

Prologue

Water dripped, a slow, annoying sound, forming a forest of stalactites and stalagmites in the cave. Over the years, she'd come to hate the sound. It had become one more thing to add to the long list of crimes against her people. When she'd first arrived on the island, the huge pillars were small nubs.

During the first few years of their exile, hope filled her people that they could break the magical barrier and return home. They'd thrown their magic against it, but with little life on the island to fuel their death magic, the attempt had only weakened them. Hunger set in. Before her exile, she created pets and left them in her homeland to wreak havoc and death on her enemies. Later, in a desperate move, her people pooled their magic and created a device to allow them to gather the death energy dealt by these pets upon their enemies. The effort cost them most of their remaining power, leaving them barely alive. Because of the barrier, the energy gathered from the device wasn't much, but it was enough for them to survive. It was fitting their enemies should feed them in their exile.

Slowly over the centuries, as slowly as the water dripping from the cave ceiling formed the large stalactite in the center of the chamber, her people regained their strength. Until at last, they were once again strong enough to attempt to break the barrier that held them captive.

This time, their efforts were rewarded with a tear, just a small one, in the barrier. More nourishment than ever before flowed to them from their pets. They feasted in gluttonous abandonment, reveling in the windfall. But before they could rip the barrier apart, something happened to their pets, and their flow of sustenance dwindled back to a trickle.

She lamented the injustice of it all, as the formations in the cave grew larger and larger, until the fires of fury burned hot in her breast. Finally, she bent her attention back to escaping. She found a way to manipulate and change one of her pets to give it new abilities. This allowed her to control it and to experience the outside world through its senses.

Shock and dismay filled her the first time she looked upon the land of her birth. Her hatred burned hotter. Her enemies thrived while her people clung to life by the barest thread. It gave her the will to continue where some of her fellows languished into their final sleep.

She lifted the heavy apparatus and put it on her head, her shoulders aching from its weight. But she was the only one with the strength to use the device that connected her to her pets, no matter where they were on Lairheim. The close, dank cave receded, and she entered a world of bright colors and life. It had been ages since she'd seen the sun with her own eyes. A thick fog perpetually covered the island. The new pet gave her control over the others, and under her direction, they were once more effective killing machines.

Life flowed through them and into the device, which converted it into globules of pure death magic. The bowl filled. Her people ate and grew strong.

Soon. The end of their exile was so near. She could feel it in her flesh and bones. And then hell hath no fury like a woman seeking revenge.

The Posairs would pay.

Chapter 1

Rolstrun - 34 de Sandar, 1075

Petrified wood pebbles skittered across the black sand-glass, away from the hooves of the plodding horses. They were as exhausted as the men and women stationed at the northern guard post. They trudged home after their most recent battle to keep the Malvers' monsters hatched in Shandir's Crater from leaving the Barrens. Ahead of them, the fortress rose above the stark landscape. Pink tinted the sheadash stone walls in the fading sunlight.

"Almost home, boyos," Maheli said, her voice muffled by a scarf over her mouth.

"Thank the Goddess." Rolstrun squinted against the dust kicked up by the horses' hooves. He glanced at his guard-pack alpha. Sweat plastered her short, curly hair to her head. Gray tinged her normally pale, creamy skin around the wound on her cheek where monster ichor had spattered it. Pain dulled her light green eyes.

"That doesn't look good, Alpha," he said. "It's a good thing we're close. Faelyn needs to remove the poison."

She touched the acid burn and hissed. "I may have to give in and have one of the girls cauterize it for me. It'll teach me to duck faster."

"Could be you're growing old and slow."

"Pfft." She waved a hand at him. "We're all getting slow. After fighting every day since the middle of Neydar, and sometimes several times a day, against these new control-janacks, we're all tired. We need a few days off. A chedan would be wonderful!" She sighed wistfully and hunched lower in her saddle.

The black ironwood gates stood open, waiting for the fighters to return. Bands of helstrim, the same alloy used to create the Reds' helbraughts, strengthened the wood. The Reds could extend their magic through it and into the gate—if the need should arise—to protect the fortress from attacking Malvers' monsters. But so far, even with the increased activity, the monsters had steered clear of the edifice. The tired horses picked up their pace, knowing their stables were close at hand.

Rolstrun grabbed the reins of Maheli's horse when they were abreast of the infirmary. "Go see Faelyn," he said gently.

Maheli nodded, slowly climbed off her horse, and limped into the infirmary.

Once inside the stables, Rolstrun slid off his horse and shook the black sand from his hair and shoulders. He reached up to rub his eyes and stopped, knowing from experience how painful it would be. Fine particles of glass made the sand. He plodded to a bucket of water by the door and washed the grit from his eyes. Finished, he unsaddled Brishna, led her to her stall, and filled her manger with hay.

"Soon, girl, we'll be able to get out of this hell-hole and go home." He slapped her golden-brown shoulder. A coughing fit racked him. Fighting in the clouds of sand irritated his lungs. Still coughing, he poured fresh water into Brishna's bucket, then hurried to do the same for Maheli's horse. The horse-master would groom them later.

His feet dragging in the dust, Rolstrun trudged to the pack house and down the winding stairs to his favorite place: the bathing room. He stopped on the threshold, breathing in the steamy air until his cough eased. His pack mates had already scrubbed down and were soaking in the deep redwood tubs. He gazed longingly at the steaming water, but both Faelyn and

Maheli would skin his hide if he tracked Barrens' glass into them. They worked hard to keep the water clean and hot, but the black dust permeating everything made it an uphill battle.

Rolstrun quickly stripped out of his filthy clothes. He walked to the tall tank tub with a big, wide spigot on a pipe extending out the top and a chain hanging next to it. He stood under the spigot and tugged on the chain. A lever lowered, and water swooshed out, like a mini waterfall. He sighed as the water sluiced the black dust from his body. Only after washing thoroughly did he finally make his way to the soaking tubs.

"Ho, Rolstrun, come join us." Calistrun waved. He ran a hand through his wavy reddish-gold hair he wore long down the middle of his back. His blue-green eyes crinkled with a smile as he tossed his arm around Alestrun's shoulders, and pulled Myndera, who snuggled against his other side, closer. The handsome man never lacked for lovers.

Alestrun had pale green hair and yellow-green eyes, and he was broader and shorter than Calistrun. Myndera smiled and beckoned for Rolstrun to join them as well. Her long maroon hair hung in curls around her heart-shaped face, and her brown eyes were ringed with yellow.

Beside her lounged Laean. Rolstrun's breath caught at her beauty. She had an unusual shade of rose hair and amber eyes. She was the right height to fit under his chin. As a fighter, she was all lean muscle, except for her abundant bosom, which swelled above the water. Rolstrun's belly clenched, and he hurried into the tub, sliding over the top of Laean's body, kissing her deeply. He had never expected the beauty to fall for him. Moving so he could hold her in his arms, he propped his back against the tub, and after a while, the heat and good company helped him relax.

"Only three more chedans," Myndera said, "before we can go home. I, for one, will be glad to get out of this black dust. It gets everywhere—and I mean everywhere."

"Do you think the new control-janack is in the nests at home?" Laean asked.

"Goddess, I hope not." Alestrun rubbed his upper arm. A few days ago he'd landed wrong as he jumped to avoid a flaying tentacle and had broken it. Faelyn had healed it, but it still bothered him. With as many injuries as the pack suffered recently, Faelyn was hard-pressed to fully heal them all.

"Or if there are, hopefully someone has found a way to kill it besides exploding the damn thing." Calistrun grimaced. "I'm sick of ducking monster debris."

Rolstrun grinned and shrugged. "Well, if you ran faster..."

"And risk Myndera? Never!" Calistrun kissed her. "She's usually the one riding the bucking control-janack to explode it."

"It keeps getting harder," Myndera said. "They seem to know what I'm doing. The other monsters are simply mindless hunger, but the control-janacks are intelligent."

Rolstrun nodded in agreement. He'd sensed the same thing. He thought about his friends back home and smiled. "If these things are at home, I bet Rizelya's in the thick of it. If anyone could find a better way to kill them, it would be her."

"Or one of her followers..." Alestrun paused, his forehead wrinkled. "Say, do you remember Eiden? The Yellow Rizelya taught how to fight?"

The others joined Rolstrun in nodding. "Yeah, what of it?"

"I practiced with her once, just to stop Rizelya from nagging me. The girl developed a way to direct cold air and was experimenting with making a cold-air shield. Brilliant, if you think about it. The control-janack, like the regular janacks, senses our body heat. What would happen if it couldn't?"

"We'd be able to get to the control-janack much quicker and end the fights easier." Rolstrun frowned. "Too bad we don't have anyone with enough Yellow Talent." He turned and looked intently at Laean and her amber eyes.

"What?" Her eyebrows creased, then her eyes widened. "You mean me?"

Rolstrun nodded.

"Sorry, I haven't tried anything like that before. I'm stronger in Brown Talent than I am in Yellow. Dehali had just agreed to work with me when I was selected for the guard-pack."

Rolstrun fingered a strand of his own red hair striped with yellow and closed his amber eyes. He rarely lamented the loss of magic. If he were a woman, he'd have plenty of Yellow Talent to do anything he wanted with air magic—like form cold-air shields. But the Posair men had exchanged most of their elemental magic for the gift of shapeshifting.

He concentrated and felt his unused Yellow power stir inside of himself. He let it grow, opened his eyes, and released the energy. A small breath of wind blew across the water, not even strong enough to cause a ripple. He snorted at himself. *Little good that will do.*

A loud rumble startled everyone. Calistrun stared at his belly and laughed. "Enough soaking. My stomach's complaining it's too empty." It grumbled again.

Laughing, the friends climbed out of the hot water, dressed, and headed upstairs to find dinner.

Later that night, his stomach comfortably full, and his body languid from making love to Laean, Rolstrun let his mind drift. The tutors had instructed the boys in the keep the bare minimum about their Talents. He had sufficient Red to be dangerous with his fire magic, so he'd been taught how to control it. His teachers deemed his Yellow air magic to be so little as to be useless. Once he'd made his first shift to wolf cub at six, he'd never thought about his other magic again. Until now.

There had always been enough women with the various Talents to take care of any tasks requiring magic. The guard-pack made do with what they had, and the few women provided the little luxuries, like the hot water in the bathing room. For most men, their magic manifested as a natural ability in the areas ruled by the Talent. Such as Teledon, who had Green and Yellow Talent and was a great chef. Rolstrun didn't know any males who actively used their magic besides to shapeshift.

He knew of only one man who did—Blazel. He recalled the wonder he'd felt when he saw fire dancing on Blazel's palm. Sure, the Reds did it all the time, but it had been the first time he had seen a man tame fire.

Rolstrun rolled onto his back and held out his hand, palm up. Staring at it, he reached for the magic he used to change his shape. This time, he concentrated on accessing his fire magic instead. Warmth seeped into the soles of his feet, and as he inhaled, the heat flowed up his legs, through his belly, and into his arms. His eyes widened in surprise as a tiny spark flickered in the center of his palm. It only lasted a moment before it faded. With his next exhalation, let the magic go. The room reeled, and he closed his eyes against the vertigo.

A quiet excitement in him grew. He'd created a spark!

He turned onto his side and gazed at his lover. *Would she teach me to use my Talent?* He shook his head at his folly. But when he returned home, he'd seek out Blazel—even if he had to track him down in the Deep Mountains. His eyes drifted closed as his thoughts circled around Blazel. *Has he made it to the Sanctuary yet? Will the Supreme send us help?*

Fire streaking from the sky filled Rolstrun's dreams. The land burned, and rivers of blood flowed, soaking the earth. Blazel's voice whispered, "The madness comes."

Rolstrun jerked awake with the blankets stuck to his sweaty body. His heart beat a fast staccato in rhythm to the word "madness" reverberating in his mind like a pealing bell.

Rolstrun - 35 de Sandar, 1075

The next morning, Rolstrun sat at the table, his head propped up on his hand, idly stirring his porridge.

"Hey," Laean said, bumping his elbow gently. "What's wrong?"

"Huh?" He blinked a few times, then rubbed his gritty eyes. After the nightmare, he hadn't gone back to sleep. Every time he'd closed his eyes, he'd seen fire and blood.

"You're not eating." She put an arm around his shoulders and leaned against him. "It isn't like you to not eat, so something must be wrong."

"Just didn't sleep well last night. Nightmares..." He shuddered.

"Want to talk—"

"No," he cut her off. As daylight had finally swept away the dark, he'd decided not to say anything to her—or the other Reds—about men using their Talents. His attempt resulted in nightmares about fire streaking the sky, the land burning, and blood flowing like rivers. He could still hear the echo of Blazel's voice whispering, "The madness comes."

"Bro, you look awful." Calistrun set a big bowl of porridge and a pot of taevo on the table. He ran his hand through his long hair as he sat down. "Did you two play all night?" He waggled his eyebrows and leered at Rolstrun and Laean.

Laean gasped and stammered while turning a bright red.

Rolstrun grinned. "More than you did, I'd wager."

"You'd win." Myndera stood behind Calistrun and yawned before sitting next to him on the long bench. "I'm too exhausted to do anything besides sleep."

"Do you think we'll get today off?" Alestrun juggled two bowls of porridge. He slid one in front of Myndera before seating himself on the other side of Calistrun.

"Not likely." Rolstrun sipped on his mug of taevo, letting the stimulating drink revive him as his friends' talking washed over him in comforting waves. He'd taken only a few bites of his now-cold porridge when the bell clanged. His spoon stilled in midair as he listened, then sighed. The pattern wasn't for their group. "Maybe we will get a day—"

The bell rang again, this time five short clangs and three long.

"Damn, that's us." His spoon clattered to the table. He quaffed the last of his taevo before grabbing Laean's hand and running out the door.

By the time they reached the stables, another team was called to action. The first team had moved their horses into the courtyard and were cinching girth straps. At a command from their pack alpha, they stepped into the stirrups and swung into the saddle. A few moments later, they picked up provisions from Faelyn and rode out through the gates. Rolstrun and his team hurried to saddle their horses, and within a quarter octar, they too were cantering away from the fortress.

Myndera led them southeast. After riding for several measures, a plume of dust marked the passage of the Malvers' monsters. Unlike at home, where there were specific nest sites, here in the Barrens, the monsters formed at any time, and anyplace, to speed across the Barrens toward life.

A measure from the approaching monsters, the fighters stopped. A Red and her male partner would stand guard over the valuable horses. The woman gripped her helbraught in readiness, her lips pulled in a grim line.

The rest of the women stalked toward the monsters, leaving the men behind to change. Rolstrun reached for his magic to shift into his warrior form, a perfect blend of wolf and man. His bones lengthened, his muscles bulked, his face changed shape into the muzzle and jaws of a wolf. His red hair streaked with yellow translated into yellow-striped red fur. He flexed his hands, which now had six-inch claws, long and sharp enough to slice through the monsters' thick hides. He stood and stretched to his new full height of nearly seven feet. Shaking his fur, he rid himself of the last tingles of the change and lifted his head to howl. Other men answered him with their own howls, all now in their warrior forms.

Calistrun led the pack of men, their long strides quickly catching up to the women, who had stopped, spreading out into a wide semicircle. Their helbraught blades glowed red from their fire magic. Rolstrun loped to stand beside Laean near the center, flexing his claws and twisting the kinks out of his neck.

The first brecha came into sight. It lumbered on its four feet, the front claws curled under to run on its knuckles. Brechas didn't have any eyes or ears, only a huge mouth full of sharp teeth and over-sized nostrils to scent their prey. It ran in a direct path toward them, and two women blocked a barrage of poison-tipped spines released from the brecha's back with their helbraughts.

Behind it, two large janacks rolled forward on their tentacles, each flanked by six brechas. The women on the circle's outer edge calmly tipped their helbraughts, touching the ground with the blade's tip. A thin line of fire zipped between the lumbering brechas and the janacks.

Warriors raced to engage the monsters as flames flared up to surround the warriors and their chosen monsters in a fire-ring. Jorstrun, an older fighter, raked his claws across a janack's tentacles, ripping out chunks of flesh. A tentacle reached behind him and wrapped around him, dragging him toward the janack. Its enormous maw gaped open, and saliva dripping through sharp teethed hissed on the ground. Two warriors leaped onto the tentacle, stopping its upward movement, while a Red hacked at it with her helbraught. With a screech, the janack dropped Jorstrun, who rolled away from the fight.

Rolstrun let go of his held breath and craned his head, rising on his toes. He settled back when he didn't spot a dreaded control-janack in the group of monsters racing toward them. The next group of fighters faced the new monsters.

Perhaps there won't be a control-janack, Myndera said in mind-speech. She continued to stand in readiness, eyes scanning the horizon, helbraught held across her body.

We're not that lucky. Alestrun pointed with his claw.

A gigantic janack rolled into view. Its size and a long protrusion covered in disk-shapes rising above the heat stalks differentiated it from the other janacks. It seemed to watch the battle's progress. Before it changed direction, Myndera raced toward it, followed closely by Laean and the few Reds not already fighting, their helbraught blades blazing.

Calistrun, Alestrun, and Rolstrun ran straight for the control-janack, reaching it before the women did. Rolstrun leaped at a tentacle. His outstretched claws penetrated the hide, slicing off a chunk of the tentacle and releasing venom into the monster. The men continued to harass the janack, causing damage whenever they collided. It took copious amounts of the men's venom and time to affect the enormous creature.

A red ball of leather rolled by Rolstrun. A rose braid thunked the hard dirt and stopped at the edge of the fire-ring. He stepped back and helped Laean to her feet.

"You hurt?" he asked, a growl in his voice.

She rubbed her shoulder. "Damn thing caught me and tossed me around. But I'm okay." Her eyes narrowed, and she tightened her grip on her helbraught. "Look! Myndera's on its head. Let's keep it busy." She raced back to the janack, Rolstrun at her side.

Together, they attacked the janack. Laean slid under a tentacle, her helbraught slicing into it, while Rolstrun struck it from above. Their combined efforts sheared the tip of the tentacle away. A few moments later, Myndera yelled, "Run!"

Rolstrun and Laean sprinted to the edge of the fire-ring. He curled into a protective ball around her as her shield surrounded them. Monster debris hissed all around them, vaporizing as it hit the shield. He kept his head tucked until the sound faded, then he slowly stood.

Monster bits littered the ground, but no more fell from the sky. The final brecha shuddered as the warriors' poison finally brought it down. The battle over, the fighters tended to their minor injuries. No one had been killed. A lucky day.

Rolstrun stood guard while the Reds burned the monster's remains to ash. He uneasily scanned the skies, remembering his nightmare. Only a few fluffy white clouds marred the clear blue expanse. He turned his attention to the north and slumped in relief when there wasn't anything but clouds in that direction, either.

They had nearly returned to the fortress when Myndera sat straight in her saddle. Her eyes slightly glazed as she mind-spoke with Maheli. After a moment, her shoulders slumped, and when she faced the fighting-pack, bleakness lined her face. "We're to go northeast. Another nest has broken out."

Rolstrun grumbled, but turned his horse around to follow Myndera back into the Barrens. He nibbled on the travel bar in his pack, wishing he had some fresh meat or even fruit. Until they finished their rotation and they could leave the crater, he wouldn't enjoy that luxury. *Only three more chedans. The time can't go fast enough.*

The farther north they rode, the more ants of anxiety crawled under his skin. He couldn't keep from scanning the sky.

Laean reached over and grasped his hand. "What's wrong with you? You keep watching the sky, and you seem jittery."

Rolstrun dragged his gaze away from the heavens. "Nothing. I just had a bad dream last night." He paused and took a deep breath. "I dreamed about Blazel. Do you remember him?"

"Of course. How could I forget?"

"Hey, bro, did you mention Blazel?" Calistrun's eyebrows furrowed in puzzlement. "Why?"

"I was wondering if he made it to the Sanctuary yet." Rolstrun tried to make his voice light.

Calistrun leaned in close and lowered his voice. "Did you dream about him? Did you see fire in the sky?"

Rolstrun gaped as he nodded. This was strange.

"Keep your eyes on the sky..." Calistrun whispered.

"...madness is coming," Alestrun finished.

Both Calistrun and Rolstrun gave Alestrun shocked expressions. He shrugged. "Yeah, I dreamed the same thing."

"I wonder how many others did." Rolstrun turned to Laean. "Did you?"

She shook her head. "No, not that I remember."

Rolstrun had a feeling only the men who'd been friendly with Blazel had had the dream. He remembered the streak of gray in Blazel's hair. *That must explain it. The Grays are the mind-workers.*

"There are the monsters!" Myndera's shout tore him out of his reverie, and he poured all of his attention into fighting.

Rolstrun - 35 de Sandar, 1075

Rolstrun stumbled with fatigue after finishing their third battle for the day. If they had another one, he didn't think he had the strength to shift to his warrior form. Brishna whinnied at him as he approached. Black sand dust of the Barrens dulled her golden-brown pelt with its fine, dark stripes. He pulled out his canteen, poured water into the wide lid, and held it out for her to drink. She greedily slurped up the water.

"Finally, we can return to the fortress." Alestrun drooped against his horse. "Goddess, I'll be glad when we can go home."

"That makes all of us," Myndera said, limping as she joined them. She waved away Alestrun's frown. "It's nothing. I landed wrong jumping from the last control-janack." She also pulled her canteen off her horse and gave it a drink.

The rest of the fighters were doing the same. All their horses were plains-bred and were as much partners as anyone else in the pack. Even though the men could, if they weren't so tired, shift to their wolf forms and travel in them, the women couldn't.

Myndera shook out the last drops of water before screwing the lid back onto the canteen. "We might make it back before it gets too dark."

"They better save us food," Calistrun grumbled. "I'm starving—even if it will be just stewed journey rations."

Rolstrun chuckled as he put his foot in the stirrup.

BOOM!

Brishna whinnied in fright and lunged away from him. His foot dropped painfully to the ground. He had enough presence of mind to keep hold of Brishna's reins.

"What in the seven hells was that?" Myndera swore.

Rolstrun glanced up, and his mouth dropped open. He swallowed hard. "Look!" He pointed at the red comet streaking through the sky—from the north. The horses shrieked, and for the next several milcrons, the fighting pack worked to calm the terrified animals. Rolstrun exchanged a glance with the other men. Together, they said in hushed tones, "Fire in the sky. Madness comes."

"What?" Myndera's eyebrows pulled together in confusion.

"It seems we all had the same dream," Calistrun said. The men nodded.

"Blazel told us when there is fire in the sky, the madness is here." Rolstrun continued to track the fireball.

"What madness?" Myndera asked.

"I'm guessing we'll find out sooner than Blazel." Rolstrun pointed.

An enormous metallic object filled the sky. Two dozen smaller objects broke away from it to fly in front and alongside it. The large object hovered over the crater for a long moment before it dropped to land next to the eastern rim. Even from thirty measures away, the setting sun glinted off its surface. The oblong ship appeared to be a hundred feet high and at least a measure long. Terror zoomed up his spine.

"Let's go!" Myndera ordered.

Rolstrun leaned over his horse's neck as they ran. Sweat dripped into his eyes. Fear of what they would find made Rolstrun's hands clammy. *Dear Mother, Warrior, and Crone, keep our people safe.* His prayer became a chant as they raced across the Barrens back to the fortress.

Rolstrun's fighting pack barreled through the wide-open gates. The courtyard writhed with angry and frightened people. His pack was the last to return for the day. The uproar made his horse shy, and it took all his skill as a rider to stay in the saddle and calm her down. Lather covered Brishna, and she blew great gusts of air. She deserved a good rubdown and some hot mash. Instead, Rolstrun climbed off and led her around the courtyard's perimeter, his attention on the commotion.

The alphas, Maheli and Bohandran, stood on the steps of the keep-house nose to nose, angrily shouting and gesticulating. Rolstrun frowned at the unusual behavior. They never argued in front of the pack.

"We don't know what that thing is," Maheli ground out. "It will be safer to stay away from it."

"We should send a team to investigate precisely because we don't." Bohandran scowled at her.

The crowd shouted angry retorts, individuals supporting one stance or the other. Rolstrun was as curious about the object as anyone else, but he agreed with Maheli. The fireball gave him the creeps, and he couldn't dismiss his nightmare. Still listening to the argument, he led his now-cooled horse to the stables and gave her the most basic of care. He returned as Maheli gestured for the crowd to be silent. A wave of alpha power enforced her command.

In the quiet, Maheli's voice rose in frustration. "We barely have enough fighters to keep the Malvers' monsters under control. We don't have anyone to spare."

"I know. But if this thing means to harm us, we need to discover it sooner rather than later. If we have some idea about what it is and why it's here, we'd be in a better position to protect ourselves." Bohandran stepped back, and his face softened. "Maheli, all I want is for our people to be safe. I feel it in my bones. We're in danger."

Calistrun pushed to the front. He shoved his hands onto his hips, his stance wide. "Maheli, listen to him. That thing brings nothing good."

She turned to him, her forehead crinkled in confusion. "Why do you say that, Calistrun? How do you know?"

He turned, scanned the crowd, and received nods. "I, and every male here, had nightmares last night with a fireball, exactly like what we just witnessed. It brings destruction to our land and our people."

Maheli gazed quizzically at Bohandran.

He nodded. "Aye, I dreamed the same thing. Although, I wasn't aware others had as well. It's why I am so insistent we must prepare for the worst."

"And what is that?"

Bohandran's shoulders slumped. "A new menace is threatening our survival."

Maheli sagged as the realization hit. She closed her eyes for a long moment. When she opened them, sadness pulled her face into a grimace. "Choose a small team, but only volunteers." She turned and made her way into the keep-house, her steps plodding, and her shoulders stooped with worry.

The crowd broke up into smaller groups, and Rolstrun caught up with his friends. He rubbed his itchy scalp and wished he could wash away the grime. His stomach knotted. Whether from hunger or fear, he wasn't sure. Probably both.

"Are any of you going to volunteer?" Calistrun asked, looking around the small group.

Rolstrun ignored the expectant looks from his friends. Instead, he tipped his head back and gazed at the sky for a long moment. He finally turned his attention back to them and shook his head. "Our duty is to protect the land from monsters escaping the Barrens. There's a good reason we're here. Whatever this is, I trust the Goddess will provide us a way to fight it. She did when the monsters appeared."

"I wish we had a White Priestess here." Laean hugged herself. "The Goddess would tell her what we're facing."

Rolstrun put his arms around her. She leaned into his chest, and tremors ran through her body.

"It's been too long since we last attended temple services." Longing tinged Myndera's voice. Her eyes narrowed, and she tipped her head to the side. "Isn't there a temple here? I've been too busy and exhausted to even search for it."

"Yes..." Alestrun tapped his chin, turning in a slow circle, his eyes distant. "There's one... there." He pointed toward a small building.

Rolstrun hadn't ever been in it. He scratched his head again. "The temple is in there?"

Alestrun nodded. "I explored it when we first arrived."

"I would like to get cleaned up before going into it." Rolstrun rubbed his hair, and black dust flew around his shoulders.

"The Goddess doesn't appreciate dirt in Her sanctuaries." Laean grinned at him.

The friends made their way to the bathing room. No one lingered in the hot tubs. Word passed around the keep, and by the time they strode to the temple, a large group joined them.

The door swung open to reveal an antechamber with small cubbyholes. Silently, they removed their boots and filed into the sanctuary. An altar stood in the center of the room. Murals of the Goddess in Her phases decorated the walls. Light streamed in from the open door. Rolstrun opened a cabinet and quietly handed out candles and sticks of incense.

The Reds in the group lit them, and soon the sweet fragrance of kehani flowers and the tang of frankincense filled the room. Rolstrun sighed deeply as the sacred fragrances soothed his mind. Even though they didn't have a priestess to guide them, they had attended ceremonies all their lives and knew the forms and prayers. The Goddess's presence seeped into Rolstrun's soul, bringing with it serenity and hope.

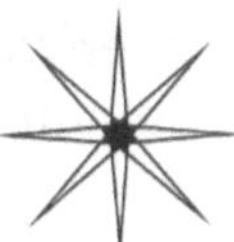

Kaieli - 35 de Sandar, 1075

Kaieli stood in the open gate of Posanreande Keep, overlooking the scrub lands, so unlike the forests of her home. The tips of the few trees beyond the sheadash stone walls provided the only green for measures. Gray sagebrush pocked the ground, surrounded by sand littered with black sand-glass. Ten measures southwest lay the Barrens, an area of utter desolation. It wasn't a desert. Deserts held life.

On the same horizon, the lip of Shandir's Crater dominated the landscape, a relic of the Great War. In a desperate attempt to end the conflict, the White Priestess Shandir had gathered all the magic around her, both from the Posairs and from the land. When she unleashed the tremendous force, only a vast, deep crater, and the Barrens remained of the lush forest. The land on its perimeter still suffered. Wells and springs provided the only water in the area.

Posanreande Keep existed in this desolate landscape to protect the rest of Lairheim from any Malvers' monsters escaping the guard-packs near the crater. Even one monster left alive wreaked devastation on the land, animals, and people. The symbiont monsters, the janack and its attendant brechas, had appeared not long after the end of the Great War a thousand years ago. Since then, the Posairs battled tirelessly against the monsters for survival. Until recently, they'd managed to keep the monsters in check.

But a little over a lunadar ago, Kaieli rode with her heart-sister, Rizelya, to what was supposed to be a routine clearing of a monster nest. Instead, the fighters discovered a new janack. Kaieli shuddered when she remembered running to the killing field to find Rizelya lying pale amid monster debris. During her encounter with the new beast, something had drained Rizelya's magic reserves to a dangerous level, and she had almost died. Afterward, every time Rizelya engaged a control-janack, she suffered visions of a strange woman.

Rizelya and Kaieli's lives took different paths several chedans ago. Rizelya rode north to the White Mountains and the Sanctuary to ask the Supreme about her visions. Kaieli traveled south to fight a plague.

Kaieli shifted to lean her back against the open gate's threshold, gazing to the north. *Has Rizelya reached the Sanctuary? Hopefully, the Supreme can help Rizelya with her strange visions.* Kaieli longed to return home to the lush lands of Strunlair Province. Silent tears streamed down her face. She couldn't go home. The people in this Keep needed her.

Behind her in the courtyard, the White Priestess burned another body ravaged by the strange plague. Posanreande Keep was the hardest hit in Posanlair Province. They had burned nearly sixty people before Kaieli had arrived, and they'd burned another dozen in the past ten days. The keep couldn't survive if any more people succumbed to the disease.

She'd left Strunlair Keep four chedans ago, certain she could heal this plague. Her dark brown, almost black hair and blue-gray eyes made her among the most powerful Browns in all of Lairheim, and her healing abilities were legendary. Where other healers failed, Kaieli succeeded—until now. She snorted at her hubris. The burning body attested to her failure to cure the disease. It resisted everything she did, magically or otherwise.

She dreaded when the Reds left to battle the monsters because every time they came back, one or more of them became ill. And more people in the keep would contract the disease. *If only I could go to a battle and collect monster bits to study, or better yet, dissect one.* Kaieli rolled her eyes at the unlikely event. The Reds burned any monster corpses to prevent the malignant magic creating them from spreading. *I know there's a connection between the monsters and this plague. I wish Rizelya were here. She'd help me. But she isn't, and this keep isn't as open-minded as home.* They wouldn't risk a healer as valuable as Kaieli going into danger.

"You can't help them waiting here." Faliciden, a healer from Posanlair Keep, joined Kaieli at the gate. Faliciden had strong Green and Brown Talent, as attested by her evergreen hair and dark brown eyes. Together, the two gifted healers fought the plague.

"I know." Kaieli sighed and wiped the tears from her face. "They should be back soon. It's getting late. We've finally identified the early symptoms. Perhaps if we catch it as soon as someone contracts the disease, it will make a difference."

"We can only hope." Faliciden gave her a wan smile, then turned to gaze out the gate. She lifted a hand to shade her eyes from the lowering sun. "They're almost here."

A plume of dust hung in the air, heralding the return of the fighters. Kaieli bounced on her toes. She prayed she'd find some way to help the people with the disease. Especially the children. They suffered the worst.

Over the years, she had watched many patients die and hadn't experienced the grief of their loss like their loved ones. She had enough Gray Talent to understand death wasn't to be feared, but was a joyful experience as the soul rejoined the Goddess.

But this plague was different. While at Posanlair Keep, waiting to travel to this small keep, Kaieli witnessed a patient die from the disease. Kaieli waited expectantly for the soul, now in peace, to cross the veil and rest with the Goddess in the Summerlands. Instead, the soul had writhed in continual pain, unable to cross the veil, hanging in a state of tortured limbo. It took the efforts of both a White and a Gray Priestess to heal the poor soul and escort it across the veil.

There wasn't any such relief for the people who died from the plague here, which only housed a White Priestess. Women with Gray Talent were so rare, they were only stationed in the Clan Keeps. Unfortunately, Kaieli's minuscule Gray Talent wasn't enough to assist in the soul healing.

The fighters rode slowly through the gate, dragging with fatigue. Kaieli searched each face for the first symptoms which showed within an octar after infection. She slumped when no one had red splotches on their cheeks and a runny nose.

"Let's go in and attend to our patients." Faliciden put an arm around Kaieli's shoulders, and they turned from the gate.

BOOM!

Kaieli ducked as the noise split the air. A red comet burned on the horizon. Horses shrieked in terror. Fowl squawked. Everyone in the courtyard stopped in their tracks and stared. Those inside streamed out of buildings, loudly inquiring about what had happened.

The gathering crowd watched the fireball, growing more terrified when it seemed to be heading directly toward them. Kaieli tracked its progress, unable to drag her eyes from the baleful light streaking across the sky. Her uneasiness increased as the red tail of the comet grew brighter in the darkening sky. She clapped her hands over her ears as a strident shrieking sound echoed off the keep walls. Before it faded, Kaieli bent over, lifting her shirt over her nose, gagging at the harsh odor.

A few moments later, a humongous shiny metallic object—at least ten measures wide—dropped out of the sky, followed by several smaller objects. They zoomed toward the crater and landed deep in the Barrens.

"What was that?" a young woman asked, a baby in her arms. Others in the crowd repeated her question.

Kaieli pushed her way through the crowd and to the keep-house.

On the porch, the keep alphas, Kothera and Kederposan, stood opposite each other in a heated discussion. Kothera, a small woman with pale red hair and brown eyes, punctuated her words with angry gestures. Kederposan scowled at her and ran a hand through his long red hair and bushy red beard before crossing his arms belligerently across his chest. The large man towered over his co-alpha.

The crowd surged toward the porch and the alphas, with the various speculations about the fireball growing louder.

"Quiet, people!" Kederposan bellowed.

The crowd fell silent, waiting.

"None of us know what that thing is," Kothera said. "We're the closest to the Barrens, so we'll send a scout-pack to investigate. Once we find out more about it, we can decide what to do. Go back to your duties."

As the crowd dispersed, Kaieli walked to the infirmary, one eye on the sky. She rubbed her arms as an ill foreboding filled her.

Chapter 2

Kaieli - 36 de Sandar, 1075

Treana coughed. The little girl's chest heaved with strain, and blood trickled from the corner of her mouth. Red sores, seeping pus, splotched her pale face. Dark bruises circled her sunken eyes. Her once bright gold hair hung in limp strands.

Her mother continued stroking her hair even when the coughing fit stopped. "Is she going to die?" Hope filled Jaelena's eyes while her voice cracked with loss.

Kaieli strode to the bedside. "I'm doing all I can to prevent it." She focused on her patient, using the time to blink away her tears.

The little girl's symptoms were the final stage of the plague. Another twenty people lay in the sick room, all in various stages, battling the dreaded disease. Even with the excitement of the fireball crashing into the Barrens last night, the ill still needed to be cared for.

Kaieli put her hands above Treana's chest. She called to her magic, and the power of Earth. Warmth crept into the soles of her feet, quickly flowing to her hands. Bronze-gold light radiated from her palms to cover the little girl. Treana's breathing eased for a moment before another coughing fit racked her frail body. When it subsided, Treana wheezed, and her chest rattled.

Kaieli swore—then prayed. *Sweet Goddess, help me find a way to heal your people. What can I do? What haven't I tried?* Avoiding Jaelena's eyes, Kaieli turned away from the girl and beckoned to Faliciden.

"Do you have the poultice ready?" Kaieli held out her hand.

"Yes. Here it is. I've charged it."

Faliciden handed Kaieli a tightly wrapped bundle, slightly smaller than the little girl's chest. Magic thrummed from it, and Kaieli closed her eyes to add her Brown magic to Faliciden's Green. They'd found the combined powers helped ease the plague victims' suffering. The disease had hit this little girl the hardest. The sight of the ravaged face broke Kaieli's heart. In desperation, she accessed her Blue and Gray Talents, adding them to the poultice. Gently laying it on Treana's chest, she said a prayer, hoping against hope to save the sweet life.

"This should help her," Kaieli told the mother.

She turned away, unable to witness Jaelena's anguish as she watched her child in pain and wasting away. The rattling in the little girl's chest stopped. Kaieli whirled around, putting her fear behind her healer's mask.

"She's breathing normally!" Jaelena exclaimed.

Kaieli exchanged a look with Faliciden. The poultice only eased the congestion. It didn't cure it. Together, they bent over the little girl. Easy breaths rose and lowered her chest with only a faint rattle lingering. The sores on her face weren't as red, and the pus was drying even as they watched.

"You did it! You healed her," Jaelena wept.

Faliciden grasped Kaieli's arm and dragged her from the sickroom.

As soon as the infirmary door closed, Faliciden whispered, "What did you do differently?"

"I don't know!" Kaieli paced the hallway's narrow confines, nibbling her lip while recounting the incident in her mind, thinking furiously. She whirled to face her friend. "I added my Blue and Gray Talents to my Brown."

"Brilliant idea! Do you think she's cured, or is this just a lull before she passes?"

"Hopefully, she's cured. I don't know why this would work when everything else we've tried hasn't."

"Perhaps it's the Gray magic. This plague causes a disconnection between the body and the soul. Maybe you healed the rift." Faliciden shrugged.

Kaieli rubbed her face, trying to relieve some of the strain from the last few chedans. "I'm not much of a Gray. If this is the answer, we need to get a Gray Priestess here immediately. But before we cause an uproar, let's test this on another patient."

Faliciden nodded and hurried to the stillroom to prepare a fresh poultice.

Kaieli moved through the infirmary, checking each patient, evaluating the stage of the plague they were in, searching for a good test subject. While the highest concentration of patients was fighters, the disease attacked every segment of the population. When it struck the Reds, they died within a few days, whereas the other Talents lingered for a chedan, sometimes two, before they finally succumbed to it. The young and old suffered the worst. She hadn't saved a single patient.

She stopped at the bedside of an old woman, well past her century mark. Paena's pale red hair had faded to pink, and wrinkles covered her face. She had survived many battles with the Malvers' monsters, but even with all her courage, she was losing the war with this illness.

Paena opened her eyes and reached for Kaieli's hand. "I heard the commotion. Is it true you healed Treana?"

"It's too soon to know if she's going to recover, but she is breathing better."

"Thank you." Paena spasmed with a coughing fit, curling around herself and holding her chest. Blood spattered her handkerchief.

Kaieli sent healing energy to support the old woman's lungs.

Finally, Paena's coughing stopped. "She's my great-granddaughter. My grandson, her father, died last winter when a group of monsters escaped the Barrens and attacked our keep. Her mama doesn't need any more grief."

In the larger keeps, the entire pack raised the children in crèches. The Reds, like her heart-sister, Rizelya, never spent much time with their birth parents. The other Talents, though, had close ties to their direct family lines. Paena lived long enough to leave the fighting-packs and help raise her grandchildren—and their children.

Kaieli decided to make Paena the test patient. She hadn't progressed as far as her great-granddaughter. Even if the charged poultice didn't cure her, it should ease her suffering. Kaieli motioned to Faliciden, who hurried over with the bundle of herbs in her hands. She didn't question Kaieli's choice.

"I considered what you did," Faliciden said, "and I added my Brown magic along with the little Red I have. It certainly can't hurt."

The light shone on Faliciden's eyes, highlighting the pale red ring around her dark brown eyes. Faliciden's Red Talent was minuscule, but she did have some.

Kaieli studied the bundle, frowning. "My Talents are Brown, Blue, and Gray, while you have Green and Red. Only Yellow and White are missing for all of the Talents to be represented in charging the poultice. Perhaps we need the power of all the Talents to drive this disease from the bodies and souls of its victims."

"But no one has all the Talents," Faliciden scoffed. "There are stories of Blacks from the time during the Great War, but they're just stories."

"We don't need a Black. We can combine our Talents." Kaieli hurried from the infirmary with Faliciden on her heels.

"Where are you going?" Faliciden called.

"To the temple." Even a keep as small as Posanreande contained a temple staffed with a White Priestess. Kaieli burst into the temple. "Where's the White Priestess?" she shouted.

"I'm here, child." A woman passing from her middle to her elderly years stepped from behind the altar. She had snow-white hair and light yellow eyes.

Kaieli silently whooped. Loshera was both a White and a Yellow. They didn't have to search for anyone else to help them.

The priestess drooped, sadness filling her eyes, and she put a hand over her face. "Please, no more deaths. I was praying to the Goddess to have mercy on our small keep. She did not hear me."

"But she did!" Kaieli gently touched Loshera's hand. "I'm here because I need your help to save them. We think we have to use all the colors of magic to save them. You have the two Talents we're missing." She indicated herself and Faliciden.

"Of course, I'll help," Loshera said. "What do you need me to do?"

"Help us charge a poultice," Faliciden said.

"I can do that. Where is it?"

"Come with us to the infirmary," Kaieli urged. "If this works, we'll need to charge more."

When they arrived back at the sickroom, blood dripped from Paena's nose and mouth. She eyed the priestess. "I didn't think I was that close to dying." Her voice was hoarse from coughing.

"The Goddess would welcome you home with open arms." Loshera gently patted Paena's arm. "But today isn't the day. We've lost too many good people."

Faliciden held out the poultice. Kaieli and the priestess laid their hands on it. Kaieli closed her eyes, concentrating on filling the bundle of herbs with her healing Brown magic. She also allowed her Blue and Gray to flow into it. As she did, she detected the other women's magic.

Faliciden's Green swirled and intertwined with her Brown, and together, melded with Kaieli's. Loshera's Yellow danced around the column of growing power before joining it. A spark of Red, the fire magic, ignited the rest, setting the pillar ablaze with light. A rainbow of colors danced. The powers were still separate and distinct until the priestess's White Talent surrounded them, and they merged, bursting into a pure, white light.

Kaieli directed the power toward the poultice. Instead, it leaped above their heads, growing into a huge pillar with heat pouring off it. Her eyes flew open. The power had materialized into a physical form.

Multiple streams of light, like fingers, emerged from the pillar and reached out to touch each patient in the room. Paena gasped. Her back arched, and her eyes rolled to the back of her head. The light expanded to envelope her body, encasing it in opaque white light. The light cocooned all the sick, even little Treana. Kaieli stood mesmerized by the miracle. She could still feel Faliciden and Loshera's hands in hers, but couldn't see them.

The light expanded until it enfolded Kaieli in it. Love washed over her, and her exhaustion fell away. The little aches and pains she usually ignored disappeared. New energy and strength flowed through her veins. She watched in wonder as the small cut on her hand faded. *If this is what happens when the Talents combine, why has no one tried it before?* After a few moments, the light faded and Kaieli took a deep breath.

Shaking her head to clear it, she returned to her full senses. *How did the miraculous energy affect my patients?* She knelt beside Paena's bed. The old woman's eyes were closed, and her face was peaceful, devoid of all traces of the plague. Kaieli lightly pressed on Paena's neck and choked back a sob. The old woman hadn't made it.

Don't be sad for me.

Kaieli put a hand over her heart. It still shocked her whenever a newly departed soul spoke to her. It didn't happen often.

Paena's ghost hovered above her body. *It was my time, and now, because of you, I can cross the veil and return to the Goddess's arms. My great-granddaughter is well. Thank you.*

Kaieli spun around. Treana sat up and loudly announced she was hungry. When she turned back, Paena's ghost had vanished. Her heart lightened. She'd rather Paena's soul cross the veil than stay too long as a ghost. Souls who stayed too long became lost and caused problems such as hauntings. Once they did, it took a strong Gray to help them cross over. Kaieli wasn't strong enough to help them.

The two healers shook off their daze and walked around the room, examining their patients. In every case, all symptoms of the plague were gone, as well as any other health issues the person suffered. Kaieli and Faliciden's scans showed the people were completely free of the disease.

Kothera rushed into the room, looking both anxious and stunned.

"What happened here?" Kothera's hands flew to the sides of her face. "I was outside when a white light burst out of here and surrounded me. When it left, I felt amazing. I had the sniffles, and now they're gone. Everyone else in the keep had the same experience. What did you do?"

Kaieli's eyes widened. Both Faliciden's and Loshera's faces reflected their shock at the news.

"We did a healing for Paena," Kaieli said. "It somehow expanded to heal everyone here of the plague, but I wasn't aware of it extending to cover the whole keep. Did either of you?"

Faliciden shook her head, but the priestess appeared thoughtful.

"The plague's gone?" Kothera surveyed the room. Slowly grinning as more patients sat up. Treana still complained about being hungry, while her mother alternated between hugging her and gazing into her face.

"I sensed the Goddess's hand in our working." Loshera put an arm around the stunned alpha. "The Goddess truly worked a miracle if she healed everyone in the keep."

More people wandered into the infirmary, dazed. Joy brightened their faces when they saw their loved ones healthy, who moments before, had been knocking on death's door. The room soon filled with laughter and joyful shouts.

"It is as I suspected," Loshera said with a wide smile. "This keep has suffered much. The Goddess brought healing of the heart as well as the body." She turned to Kaieli, took her hands, and bowed. "We are grateful you came to our small keep. Without you, we would have lost more of our loved ones."

"You were as much as part of this as I was," Kaieli sputtered.

"Ah, but you were the one the Goddess blessed with the insight of how to heal this dreadful plague."

Kaieli bowed her head, pleased the Goddess had answered her prayers.

Kitchen staff hurried in with platters of nourishing soups, and a festive air filled the infirmary. A smile slowly lifted Kaieli's lips at the wonderful sight of her previous patients eating with their packs. They didn't need her now.

She slipped outside into the cooler evening air and walked to the center of the courtyard. Leaning her head back, she gazed at the night sky. Kelar, the largest moon, was just past full. A huge shadow passed over the moon. Kaieli shook her head and looked again. She glimpsed a huge, winged body with a long tail trailing behind it. The shadow flew northwest in the direction of the vast plains. Behind it, a smaller shadow followed. Awe filled her rather than fear as the two winged from view.

The shapes reminded her of her favorite story—the one where mystical Gryphons saved the hero, Shandir, from the clutches of Mordar. *Did I just witness another miracle? We believe the Gryphons to be extinct. No one has seen any since the end of the Great War. Why are they here? Are they friend or foe?*

Rolstrun - 36 de Sandar, 1075

Rolstrun stood on the keep-house porch, leaning against the railing and sipping a mug of taevo. After the ceremony, he'd slept the best he had since coming to the Barrens. In the courtyard, three men and one woman clustered around the alphas, receiving final instructions. Maheli pulled each one into a hug, and Bohandran awkwardly patted their backs. After saluting, the volunteers climbed onto their horses and trotted through the gates.

The bell clanged, calling Rolstrun's pack to work. He quickly drained his mug and ran to the stables. Within a few milcrons, he and his fighting-pack rode out the gates. He hoped this day wasn't as bad as the last one.

The control-janack finally exploded. Rolstrun bent over, his hands on his knees as he gasped for breath from the drawn out and nasty battle. He winced as he stood straight, hugging his ribs where a janack had slammed him. Tears sprang to his eyes at the devastation. Jorstrun's head was caved in, and brecha spikes protruded from his back. He had recently moved into their fighting-pack, and now Rolstrun wouldn't have a chance to know him better. He howled in grief when he saw his mentor, Molstrun's, body. No longer would he chide them as they practiced while he soundly trounced them. Rolstrun would miss the older man.

"Please, no, no!" he cried as he ran stiffly toward Laean. Blood seeped into the black sand from the deep gashes on her leg and on the back of her head. Already, bruises purpled the right side of her face. "Thank Goddess," he breathed when he found her weak pulse. Shifting back to his natural form, and running hunched over to protect his cracked ribs, Rolstrun grabbed the first-aid pack from his horse.

Rolstrun glanced up at the rumbling sound overhead. A much smaller vessel than the original one zoomed past, heading northeast. Light glinted off the dark metal when it turned due east and out to sea.

A moan recalled him back to his surroundings, and he hurried to Laean. He gently placed a pad over her head wound to sop up the blood. The gash in her leg wasn't turning gray, indicating the absence of monster poison. When he finished field dressing her wounds, he gingerly stood.

Calistrun clapped a hand on Rolstrun's shoulder. He couldn't stop the hiss of pain.

"Bro, you don't look so good."

"Cracked ribs." Rolstrun grimaced. He gazed east, in the direction the vessel had taken. "Why is it going there? The ocean is empty of any landmasses."

"So we've been told." Calistrun pulled on a long lock of hair and bit his lower lip. "Whatever—whoever—is in that big ship hasn't made any effort to contact us. I'm worried they aren't here to make friends."

"I agree. Until the scout party returns, we won't know what the invaders want." Rolstrun shrugged, growling as the movement jarred his ribs. "Come on, help me with Laean. The Reds are done burning the monster remains."

As they rode to the fortress, Rolstrun kept a watch on the sky and urged Myndera to hurry. The petrified boulders strewn across the Barrens provided little shelter to protect them from an overhead attack. Rolstrun said a fervent prayer of thanksgiving when they crossed through the fortress gates.

Rolstrun - 39 de Sandar, 1075

Three days later, Rolstrun and his team trudged into the dining hall after the morning's battle. He stopped at the threshold in surprise. Every fighting-pack filled the hall for the midday meal—a rarity these days, as they struggled to keep the increasing number of monsters from escaping the Barrens. The brutal fighting had taken a heavy toll on the guard-pack. Fresh burns marked the faces and arms of several Reds from monster ichor. Rolstrun wasn't the only one moving stiffly from broken ribs. At one table, a fighter snoozed with his head propped on his hand, with his meal unfinished. A pack-mate quietly removed his plate, while another gently shook him awake and helped him stagger from the dining hall. At another table, grief lined the faces of the fighters. Three of their pack had been killed. The Keep Alphas, Maheli and Bohandran, had dark circles under their eyes, and their cheeks sagged from exhaustion from directing the battles and trying to keep their people alive.

To make things worse, Maheli hadn't received any word from the scout party. They should have returned already. She couldn't contact them because the black dust interfered with the mind-link after more than a measure.

As Rolstrun filled a plate with food, several older, more experienced fighters commented on how they'd never seen so many injuries, or deaths, during a guard rotation before. Laean, who'd been out of action while her injury healed, waved from a table she'd saved for them. He put his food down, leaned over, and kissed her in greeting.

"You're all back," she said in relief. "No one hurt?"

Rolstrun shook his head, wincing as he sat. His cracked ribs still caused him pain, especially after the morning's battle. "This nest was small, even smaller than normal."

"And there was only one nest," Calistrun added.

"Strange." Laean poured taevo in cups and passed them around to her friends.

"It is," Myndera agreed. Nodding thanks, she took the proffered cup. "Even stranger, there wasn't a control-janack with them."

"Your nest didn't have one either?" Maheli said, stopping at their table. "That makes it unanimous. None of the nests today contained a control-janack. I don't like this. However, I'm not going to complain. We could use the respite."

She put her fingers to her mouth and whistled. "Listen up!"

The room quieted.

"It seems like the monsters are taking a break, thank Goddess. Whatever the reason, we'll take advantage of it. After you eat, go get some rest. I'm sure they'll be back to 'normal' soon enough."

Rolstrun cheered with the others. He bolted down his food— he wasn't going to waste his rest time eating—and then helped Laean to her feet. Together, they walked to the small room they shared. He stripped off his grimy clothes and stretched out on the bed with a deep sigh. Laean snuggled next to him, her head on his chest. He wrapped an arm around her and pulled her close.

"Do you think we'll make it back home?" Laean asked. "You've heard the older fighters. It's never been like this before. So many of our friends have died."

"Yeah, we'll make it home. We only have a few more chedans of our rotation left. We can hold out until then. I'm more worried about that humongous ship and what it means. If whoever is in it is here for peaceful reasons, they'd have tried to make contact by now."

"How do we know they haven't? They could have contacted the eastern fortress. It's closer to them than we are."

Rolstrun shrugged. "We don't. But I can't forget the nightmare I had before it arrived. There was so much blood and death in it. I'm afraid of what it portends." He kissed her forehead and ran his thumb along her jawline. "No matter what happens, I'm glad you're here with me."

She lifted her head and kissed him. "Me too." She laid her head back on his chest and made slow swirly patterns in his chest hair with her fingers. Her movements slowed until they finally stopped, and her breathing deepening as she fell asleep.

Rolstrun kissed the top of her forehead again. He cared deeply for Laean, but he wasn't sure if he loved her. He wondered if they'd stay together when they returned to normal life at Strunland Keep. His eyes drifted closed, his exhaustion pulling him into sleep.

The walls shook. Alarm bells clanged.

Rolstrun jerked awake, still groggy. A muted boom preceded another shake of the building.

"What's happening?" Laean cried out, sitting up.

"I don't know."

All the grogginess left him as he grabbed his clothes in the dim light. Night had fallen while he'd slept. Opening the window, he leaned out and gasped. "Holy Warrior!"

"What is it?" Laean scrambled next to him.

Rolstrun gaped, pointing. Light pulsed from the large ship hovering above them. He threw a hand over his eyes at the brightness. The cobblestones in the courtyard disintegrated from the blast. A metallic ball slammed into the side of the building just below them. The impact rocked the building.

He quickly pulled his head back in as a flurry of stone shards flew everywhere. "We're under attack! Hurry!"

"I'm ready." Laean's helbraught blade glowed. Her limp nearly disappeared as they ran down the hallway and stairs, toward the sound of curses and fighting.

Outside, they stopped short. Light from the attacking ship provided enough light to make out the black-robed and hooded insect-like beings filling the courtyard. The alien blocking their exit stood as tall as a man in warrior form. The alien had a long face, big eyes, and an elongated snout. A forked tongue flicked from its tiny mouth. Fine scales covered the gray-green skin. It, like its fellow invaders, carried long, thick sticks that spit small projectiles.

Calistrun ran past Rolstrun into the courtyard. The alien pointed its stick at Calistrun and fired. The projectile hit Calistrun, knocking him down. He didn't get up. With a roar, Rolstrun shifted into his warrior form and raced toward the invader. Rolstrun jerked his head as a whine whizzed past his ear. When the stick fired again, a trail of light preceded the projectile. He dodged as a blast of fire warmed his side. The invader dropped the stick when it burst into flames. Rolstrun took the opportunity Laean had given him and crashed into the invader.

Rolstrun slashed at the robes, searching for a throat to tear out, but the cloth entangled his claws. Swearing, he pulled back. Laean surrounded the three of them in a fire-ring. The invader snapped harsh, unintelligible sounds when he attempted to cross it. His robe smoked where it touched the fire before it burst into flames. Using a knife, it quickly cut away the burning parts of its robe. Rolstrun sneered at the small knife. It couldn't match his claws or Laean's helbraught blade. Together, he and Laean attacked the invader, using techniques honed by years of fighting Malvers' monsters. Rolstrun attacked the invader's long snout. It jerked away, right into Laean's helbraught. The long blade skewered it. Purple blood gushed from the wound.

When the invader stopped twitching, Laean dropped the fire-ring. She immediately crumbled to the ground with a cry as a projectile buried into her back. Rolstrun shifted into his natural form, and with shaky hands, checked her pulse. He let out a breath of relief when he found one. He didn't hear the projectile until it slammed into his shoulder. Pain exploded. Yelling in rage, he surged to his feet. A projectile punched into his lower back and another one bit into his chest. His eyes clouded over, and his legs gave out. Consciousness left him as he collapsed.

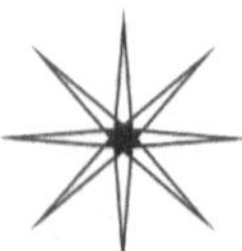

Kaieli - 39 de Sandar, 1075

Laughter from children running and playing in the courtyard filled the keep. Kaieli stood on the steps of the infirmary watching them, and a smile fluttered across her face when Treana ran past, kicking a ball. Three days ago, she'd been on her deathbed. Now, she played as spryly as the other children. In fact, since the healing light had covered the keep, no one had any ailments at all. Kaieli felt a bit superfluous with everyone so healthy. But the keep alphas refused to allow her to leave until they were sure the plague was completely gone. After all the deaths, she didn't blame them.

Until they released her, she contributed by making and distilling more healing potions. She'd worked all morning in the stillroom and had come outside for a break from the hot room. Kaieli took a breath of fresh air and stretched. Sighing, she turned to return inside when a now-familiar loud, whining sound came from the crater. Four small ships rose from the crater's depths, scattering to fly in low, sweeping arcs over the Barrens. One headed toward them.

The children stopped their play to gape at the machines. The adults working outside joined them. Until a few days ago, nobody had ever seen such mechanical contraptions. They gave Kaieli the creeps. Her Gray Talent allowed her to read souls enough to know the basic personality of her patients. But when she'd tried to scan a ship, the only thing she'd sensed was a hungering menace. She wanted to run as far and as fast as she could from them.

"Quickly, children," she yelled, "go inside and hide." She didn't want them anywhere near the evil creatures.

All the children, except Treana and her older sister, Dreana, followed her orders and ran into the nearest pack house.

"Come on, Treana." Dreana tugged on her sister's hand. "Healer Kaieli wants us to go inside."

"I don't want to go inside." Treana pouted, pulling her hand away and crossing her arms. "Why can't I play? I'm tired of being stuck indoors."

Kaieli hurried to the children and picked up Treana. "You can play later."

As Kaieli reached for the infirmary door, a loud roar echoed off the keep's stone walls. The machine flew low over the keep before climbing into the sky again. It sped away toward the eastern fortress on the crater's rim.

"Oh, that doesn't look good," Faliciden said. She took Treana from Kaieli's arms and shooed the two girls to their pack house. "It's Posanlair Clan's turn to guard the crater's east quadrant, and I have friends there. I hope nothing happens to them."

"Same here," Kaieli said. "My keep, Strunlair, is guarding the northern fortress. My friend Maheli is the alpha of the guard-pack. She's cunning and strong. They'll be fine." Kaieli hoped they would be, but fear skittered across her heart at the thought of those four ships: one for each fortress.

Late the next afternoon, while she ground herbs and mixed them into various remedies, she paused at the clatter of hooves and panicked chaos.

"Oh, no! Now what?" Kaieli quickly dried her hands.

"Kaieli! Faliciden!" Kederposan shouted. "Hurry, we need you."

Faliciden's eyes widened with worry as the two healers ran outside.

A fighting-pack, returning from battle, filled the courtyard. Horses stood with their reins dropped to the ground, while their riders milled in confusion around a knot of fighters, many of whom had minor injuries. When a scream of pain pierced the air, Kaieli elbowed her way past them.

A woman lay in the center of the crowd, a gash in her thigh. A tourniquet had stopped the bleeding, and shock glazed her eyes. Next to her, blood gushed from an older man's left eye. But the screaming came from another young woman, barely old enough to fight, who had acid burns along her right side. The monster's ichor had burned too much of her body for the usual first-aid treatment of using a helbraught's fire to neutralize the acid. If left untreated, the toxin in the ichor would become a lethal poison. The toxin inflamed Anyola's wounds and turned the surrounding skin a sickening gray. Kaieli wrinkled her nose at the rotting stench wafting from the wounds. Of the three injuries, hers was the most serious.

Kaieli motioned Faliciden to take the bleeding man while she dealt with the monster poison. Kneeling next to the young woman, Kaieli ran her hands in the air over the girl's injuries. Beautiful bronze light poured from her hands and covered the wounds. The light slowly deepened to a dark, mud-brown as it drew the poison from Anyola's body. She had to make several passes to get it all out, but at last Kaieli made a circular motion, gathering the noxious energy into a tight ball. One of the Reds stepped forward with her helbraught and sent a tendril of fire to the ball. It flared and fine ash trickled to the ground.

"Take her to the infirmary," Kaieli ordered, sitting back on her heels. "The other healers can treat her burns." Several strong men carefully lifted Anyola and carried her away.

Kaieli turned to the woman with the injured leg. Scanning Detheren with her magic, Kaieli drew in a sharp breath. The gash had barely missed the femoral artery, but had sliced into the bone. Luckily for Detheren, it was a clean cut. Closing her eyes, Kaieli concentrated on reconnecting the muscle, veins, and bone. Then she knitted the skin back together. It would scar, and Detheren would need to stay off of it for a few days, but she'd survive.

"Will Detheren walk?" Kothera had arrived sometime while Kaieli was working.

Kaieli nodded. "Eventually. The bone is weak from the slash. She needs rest and fluids."

Several men stepped forward and carried the woman to the infirmary. Warriors had already taken Faliciden's patient away. Blood soaked the ground, turning the cobblestones red.

Kederposan turned to Nelieh, the squad-pack alpha of the fighters. "What happened? Why are so many injured, and so badly?"

Nelieh looked down and toed a stone with her boot. When she raised her head, fear shone in her eyes. "I haven't seen anything like it. Not even Paena's stories about how awful the battles were before the Zehis method were close to what we faced. Instead of a janack or two and their attendant brechas, there were five! It took all our skill—and quite a bit of luck—to kill them. To get them all, we had to spread out too much. A group of them went after our horses. We lost four and another two are lame."

"We'll have to send more than one fighting-pack out at a time," Kederposan said.

"After the plague, we barely have enough fighters as it is." Nelieh gripped her helbraught and leaned on it. "The scout-pack we sent to the crater hasn't returned. Something bad has happened to them. I feel it in my bones. Have you heard anything from them?"

Kothera shook her head. As the keep alpha, she could communicate with her people using mind-speech, even at a distance.

"No, the crater is beyond my reach." Kothera gazed southward, toward the crater, with a frown. "I haven't heard or sensed them for a few days. I'm afraid they're hurt—or dead."

Kederposan scowled at the open gate. "The guard-packs at the crater are supposed to stop the monsters before they can leave the Barrens. We shouldn't be fighting a whole nest or two. I'll have words with the alpha!"

"I don't think they're being lazy," Kaieli interjected. "Maheli would never allow a full nest to escape, and I doubt the alpha at the eastern fortress would either. The only way it would happen is if the entire guard-pack can't fight. Yesterday, one of those strange ships flew toward the fortress."

Kothera put a hand over her face and groaned. "And now today we have whole nests roaming free. How many have we missed?"

"We don't know anything has happened to them for sure," Kederposan argued.

"You can't honestly believe that!" Nelieh's knuckles whitened as she gripped her helbraught tighter. "The mob we just fought tells me the guard-packs are in trouble."

"I agree," Kothera said. "We need to tell the Clan Alphas about this and request more people. We're dangerously short on fighters as it is after the plague killed so many."

She turned on her heel and stomped to the keep-house. Kederposan shrugged and followed her. Kaieli contemplated the blood-soaked cobblestones, rubbing the chills from her arms. It seemed to be an omen of things to come.

Chapter 3

Rolstrun - 39 de Sandar, 1075

Jostling roused Rolstrun, and his breath whooshed out as he landed on a hard, cold surface. Every muscle in his body ached, and pain flared where the projectiles had hit him. When he tried to move his hand, it quivered, not responding. He couldn't move his legs, either. His stomach plummeted, and heat washed over his body.

When he was little, he'd seen a warrior who'd been paralyzed by a broken back. He hadn't lived long. Squeezing his eyes shut, Rolstrun tried again. First, his little finger moved, then his thumb, until finally his hand obeyed the command. Concentrating on his toes, he willed them to move. When they did, tears trickled from the corners of his eyes.

Carefully, he felt his chest. His fingers encountered the wetness of blood, but not as much as he'd expected. Bodies thudding to the ground caught his attention. He wasn't alone. In the dim light, the robed creatures entered the enclosure, carrying burdens over their shoulders and dropping them unceremoniously. Someone shouted, and Rolstrun cheered inwardly, recognizing Bohandran's voice. He cringed at the loud striking sound, abruptly ending the shouting. Eventually, the invaders stopped coming in, and a door slid shut.

Darkness descended. The floor rumbled below them, and a strange sensation of rising made Rolstrun clutch at the floor. The slick surface didn't provide any purchase for his questing fingers. He pushed to a sitting position and gasped at the blinding pain in his head and chest. He dropped his head to his knees, gritting his teeth against his heaving stomach. After several milcrons, the pain receded.

"Who is still alive?" Maheli said in the dark. A pale light rose above her, just enough to dispel the heavy darkness.

"Myndera," a voice trembled.

"Alestrun."

"Faelyn."

"Rolstrun," he added his voice to the others. He nearly sobbed when Laean spoke up. Name after name was spoken, and some had to speak for their still-unconscious neighbors, until at last no one else lifted their voice in the darkness. Out of their complement of 150, they'd lost 25.

"Thank Goddess so many of us survived," Maheli said. She switched to mind-speech. *Be careful until we know more about these invaders. If they wanted us dead, we would be. At the first opportunity, escape. Get word to the others, to the Supreme.*

Rolstrun agreed with her. His head still ached. The places he'd been hit throbbed, and his body trembled. Who were these invaders that could so easily capture a garrison of seasoned fighters?

A short time later, they descended. The ship bumped to a stop, and the low-pitched humming stopped. Rolstrun pushed to his feet. He refused to cower before his captors. The rustle of clothing told him the others also stood. He blinked and put a hand over his eyes when the lighting overhead brightened. Finally, he could clearly see his pack-mates.

A tall being entered, different from the species that had attacked the fortress. It had lime-green skin, pale green hair, and light yellow eyes. Baggy gray coveralls covered its reed-thin form.

A large group of the black-robed insect-like creatures stood in the opening, each carrying a projectile stick. Rolstrun rubbed his still-throbbing chest and cowered away from them.

They pushed their way in, forming a barrier, and pointed their weapons at the crowd.

"The Scourge have arrived," the green person said, its voice easily reaching the far corners of the hold.

Rolstrun blinked in surprise at the perfect, unaccented Posarian.

"There can be no resistance." No emotion showed on the green alien's face. "The great Ke-ke-tak, commander of the Scourge, has been lenient and allowed you to live. He now owns you, body and soul. Please him, work hard for him, and you will continue to live. Refuse to work, try to escape, or fight your new masters, and you will die." He paused, and sadness flitted across his face. "You will suffer a long, slow, painful death. The Scourge do not tolerate resistance. You will now be processed into the service of the Scourge. March out in single file."

The crowd undulated, and Maheli stepped out. She was tall for a woman, nearly six feet, but next to these creatures she looked small. Dirt dulled her fiery red hair, and blood trickled down the side of her face.

"No one owns us." She thrust out her chest and crossed her arms. "We are free people. The only one we serve is the Goddess. She will stop you."

"Your deity can no longer help you." The green alien shook his head. "Others have relied on their deities, but the Scourge are stronger and have defeated all who came against them. You are not the first, nor will you be the last, people to be conquered by them. Many worlds, many species, now serve the Scourge or lie dead under their feet. Do not let this happen to your world." He bent at the waist until his face was close to Maheli's and lowered his voice. Rolstrun strained to hear him. "Be smart, lady. Keep your people safe. Now is not the time to fight." He straightened and inclined his head at the waiting Scourge. "Order your people to come peacefully. Otherwise, they will open fire, and this time their weapons will kill rather than sedate."

Maheli studied the invaders. Her shoulders drooped, and she nodded. Her voice dripped with defeat. "Go quietly with them. Now is not the time to fight." She echoed the green's words, but her mind-speech was defiant. *Another day, after *we've rested, we will fight and throw these invaders back to the world they crawled from.**

May it be so, Rolstrun prayed. Meekly, he fell into line and trudged into captivity.

Rolstrun - 40 de Sandar, 1075

As Rolstrun plodded from the ship to a large tent, he shivered in the gray light of predawn. A new day, a new life, but not one he'd choose for himself.

Black-robed invaders lined the perimeter of the tent, each holding a projectile weapon. A whip coiled at each one's waist. They appeared hunched over, with a hump on their back rising over their heads.

Inside the tent, Rolstrun counted six different species besides the translator and invaders. Proof the invaders had indeed conquered many worlds.

The green being stood on a raised platform. "I am Flo'kik, a translator slave. Before you can work for the masters, you must be processed. I remind you, resistance is not tolerated. The Scourge will kill any who attempt to escape and punish their compatriots. You will be injected with a tracker containing an explosive. The masters can remotely activate it if you run. You are no longer free individuals. You belong to the Scourge. All these others—" he waved an arm, indicating the various species standing at attention "—have been captured and subjugated by the Scourge. Many worlds have fallen to their conquest. Yours is simply the latest. If you think you can overthrow the Scourge, be warned. My race was the first to fall. That was over four hundred cycles ago, and we still remain slaves."

He said something in another language, and a group of golden-skinned aliens with golden hair and eyes raised their hands. They could pass as Posairs, except for their coloring and the sharp fangs peeking from their mouths. They waited at the first three tables, holding smaller baskets on them. Several tall, round bins stood behind the tables.

"That is the first station. Start there. Do not skip any positions. Doing so will result in punishment. Any who are female, go to the left. Males form lines at the other two tables in an orderly fashion."

Rolstrun craned his neck, groaning at the numerous stations they'd pass through designed to reduce the proud Posairs to lowly slaves.

Bohandran, as alpha, stepped up to the table first, his head held high. A golden-skinned alien placed his personal items into a basket, then mimed taking off his clothes. These were tossed in the tall bins. When Bohandran stripped, the aliens sucked in a breath at the numerous scars covering his body. When Maheli took off her shirt and revealed the large acid-burn scar on her ribs, shocked murmurs rippled through the assembled slaves.

None of the aliens, except Flo'kik, spoke their language. When they did speak, it sounded like each species spoke in their own language. Through pantomiming and exaggerated gestures, they directed the Posairs on what to do.

At the next station, Rolstrun stepped into a small cube. A black-skinned alien with a long, narrow face, bulbous lips, and slits on the side of its neck prodded him into a machine. He squinted at the bright light that slowly moved from the top of his head to his feet. Something pricked his wrist, and a tube sucked out a small amount of his blood. The alien grabbed Rolstrun's face and forced his mouth open, then stuck a swab in it, making him gag. Rolstrun yelped in outrage when the alien groped his private bits. After more poking and prodding, the alien released Rolstrun from the cube.

When he stepped out, only men plodded through the various stations. Rolstrun craned his neck, standing on his toes, searching for the missing women. A curtain on the east wall sectioned off the tent, and he glimpsed Laean through a crack tying it together.

Laean, he called out in mind-speech, *are you and the others okay? They haven't hurt you have they?*

No. We're okay. If you call being treated like breeding multas okay, she huffed. *They've thoroughly poked and prodded us, including our private parts. They even examined our teeth!*

Relieved the women were safe, Rolstrun plodded to the next station, which held tables piled with ugly orange fabric. He hoped it was clothes, even if it was the hideous coveralls all the slave aliens wore. Normally, nudity didn't bother him, but he didn't like the looks the other slaves were giving him. Rolstrun rubbed the chill from his arms. Golden-skinned, fanged aliens handed him a piece of the fabric. Shaking it out, he discovered a coverall. He grimaced at the ugly slave's uniform. The aliens showed him the mechanism on the collar that allowed the uniforms to fit the varied heights and body types.

At the next place, hairless men with big noses, full lips, and rolls of fat shaved the men's hair close to their scalp. Rolstrun breathed a sigh when he ran his hand over his new-shorn head, and discovered he still had hair, albeit extremely short. He'd never seen a bald man. The Posairs' hair and eye color indicated their Talents. He didn't know what would happen if they lost all their hair.

Bro, you look strange without hair, Rolstrun said to Alestrun.

No more than you. Warrior forbid we can't access our Talents because of this.

Calistrun absently rubbed a hand on his thigh where he'd been hit. *I'm not going to try where they can see us. Whatever they use in those weapons hurt.* In a familiar gesture, he ran his hand through his hair and stopped. *Those damned invaders! It took me forever to grow my hair that long. What are the girls going to do now they can't run their hands through it?*

Rolstrun chuckled quietly and moved forward.

A small, delicate woman with fine blond hair and pale white skin gestured to his arm. He held it out, and she put a cold metal object over his upper arm. A moment later, he jerked at the sharp jab. When she removed the device, a small lump lay under the surface of his skin. *It must be the tracker the translator mentioned.* Rolstrun ran a finger over it and shuddered at the alien technology in his body. Hopefully, their healer, Faelyn, could find a way to remove the things or disable them.

Still rubbing his arm, Rolstrun entered a partitioned-off section. Bohandran, as the first to be processed, stood in the area with his hands grasped behind his back. He glanced over his shoulder at Rolstrun when he entered, then returned to staring at the back of the tent.

When a slave handed Rolstrun a small cup of water and a third of a travel bar, he raised his eyebrows at the familiar food. The invaders had raided the fortress's food supplies. He frowned at the bar, wishing for something more substantial—or at least the whole thing. The light in the tent had brightened while he meandered through the stations, and Rolstrun estimated it nearly was mid-day. His stomach growled. Lunch yesterday was a long time ago, and the small amount of the travel bar wasn't enough to assuage his hunger. He rubbed at the dried blood caking the side of his face, grimacing as it flaked off. The invaders hadn't allowed them to clean up. Done eating, he stood waiting for what would happen next.

As other men finished with their processing, they entered the enclosed area.

"Have any of you heard from the women?" Calistrun asked, nibbling on his travel bar.

"I talked to Laean earlier," Rolstrun said. "She and the others are okay."

When twenty men stood warily waiting, an invader with a yellow-edged black robe stomped through the opening Bohandran had been watching. Following closely behind him, another slave, who seemed to be the same race as the translator, only with dark blue skin, stepped into the waiting area. The invader barked an order.

"I am Vy'shol," the translator slave said. "Follow the overseer. He will take you into the crater, where you will dig the nucla."

Bohandran growled, stepping forward. "We can't go into the crater. It's a death sentence for us."

Vy'shol backed up, her forehead crinkled in confusion. "But don't you live on the edge of it in your fortresses?"

"Only for a short time. Then we must leave or we become sick from the crater poison."

"Do you know what causes the sickness?"

"Malignant magic."

Vy'shol laughed. "Magic? Ha! You just don't want to work."

"Magic is real. It is part of our lives." A shimmer around Bohandran heralded the beginning of his shift.

No! Maheli shouted in mind-speech. As his co-alpha, she must have sensed Bohandran. *No, Bohandran, don't shift here, now. It's too dangerous. They'll kill you. We need you. We need you to lead.*

The shimmering stopped. Bohandran shook his head, grimacing in anger. *We must kill these invaders.*

Yes, we must. But right now we're outnumbered, and without our helbraughts, their weapons are superior. Wait until the time is right, Maheli pleaded.

I will wait, but only for a little while, Bohandran conceded. He glared at the black-robed invader. "We will do as you say, for now."

"Sir, remember resistance is not tolerated," Vy'shol said. "I also must remind you, the masters hold your womenfolk. It will be they who suffer first. The masters need workers, not breeders."

"You threaten our women?" Bohandran roared.

Vy'shol stepped back, cowering, a hand upraised for protection. "I beg you, please don't make a scene." She glanced at the invader.

It raised its weapon, a chittering sound came from its back, and the lump under its robes moved.

Bohandran backed up, his eyes wide in fright. Rolstrun covered his mouth with a hand.

Vy'shol straightened and stepped in front of them, speaking to the invader. It protested, but lowered the weapon, and its back stilled.

The translator turned back to the men. "It is not I who will harm your people. But the Scourge? Yes, they threaten all of you. If you wish to survive, do not provoke them. Him—" she pointed at the overseer "—he'll only eat your emotions. But Ke-ke-tak?" She shrugged. "He'll eat you with the slightest provocation, or simply because he's in a bad mood."

"Eat?" Rolstrun asked.

"Eat. First, he'll drain your emotions, then your blood. When he's done, he'll toss you to his troops, who will eat your liquefied organs."

The invader said something, sounding angry.

She gestured to the tent door. "Go. I've kept you long enough." Before Bohandran passed through, Vy'shol stopped him and leaned in close. "You seem to be the leader of these people. Pass the warning along to them."

Bohandran nodded and stepped out through the tent flap. Rolstrun followed closely after, pondering the translator's warning. *Why are they helping us?*

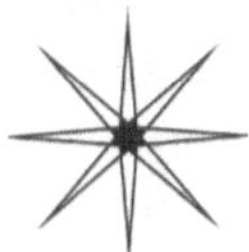

Rolstrun - 40 de Sandar, 1075

Rolstrun stepped outside the tent, blinking from the bright sunlight, and looked around, trying to gain a sense of where they were. The slave camp squatted on relatively flat ground near the crater's rim. Based on the sun's direction, they were several measures south of the eastern guard fortress. Everywhere else had a steep slope up to the crater's edge.

He tipped his head back, allowing his gaze to travel up the sides of the monstrous ship looming above them. It stood over three hundred feet high and covered nearly a measure of ground. Parked next to the behemoth were two medium-sized ships, two large ships like the one he'd been on, and twenty-four small ships. A team of fifteen invaders climbed into one of the small ships and, moments later, it zoomed out of sight.

Along the side of the mother ship, six hatch type doors stood open with ramps extending from them. A steady stream of invaders trundled down the ramps. Most appeared groggy and their movements were jerky. Rolstrun gulped at the large number of the insect-like creatures. Already, more invaders roamed in front of the ship than all the people in Strunland Keep, and they kept oozing from the ship. *Goddess help us! How can we fight off so many?*

The invaders all wore the same black robes, except different colors edged some in what seemed to denote a type of hierarchy or ranking. The invaders wearing robes with bronze, silver, or gold edging received the greatest deference. Those wearing yellow-edged robes, like their overseer, barely received a salute from those without any edging, and hardly an acknowledgment from those with other colored edgings.

Other aliens, also dressed in the orange slave coveralls, emerged from a wide hatch at the tail end of the ship. They carried loads of supplies or pushed carts filled with various materials. Rolstrun whipped his head around at the sound of banging and a strange, high-pitched whine. A swarm of slaves worked on constructing a structure. A contraption spat out an ugly beige material between tall poles, which formed a solid surface as it dried. Behind it loomed a long, two-story building already finished. The groggy invaders streamed into it.

Rolstrun jumped at a sharp command from the overseer and hurried back in line with his friends as the invaders herded them toward the crater. Rolstrun's heart pounded, and he wanted to run in the opposite direction. The guard-packs told horror stories of what happened to people when they went into the crater.

Steady, Bohandran said, putting a touch of alpha power in the word. *Don't run. We'll find a way out of this.*

Rolstrun glanced around. He wasn't the only one terrified of where they were heading. He breathed in deeply for several breaths, trying to calm himself, but his legs trembled as each step took him closer to the crater rim.

Five more invaders joined the escorts for their group, holding their weapons in a ready position to discourage escape attempts. In front of them, a giant, hairy alien, carrying a large load of metal poles in its four arms, tripped on a chunk of petrified wood. Its load flew into the air, and its wind milling arms struck a passing invader, knocking him to the ground.

The invader shouted in outrage as it struggled to its feet. Two of the lower-ranking soldiers rushed to help the downed officer. Brushing the sand off his bronze-edged robes, the officer stalked toward the cowering slave. Two appendages slithered from his robes, stretching above his head. More invaders surrounded the slave, crowding for space until Rolstrun couldn't see the slave anymore. The officer plunged the extra limbs down. Agonized screams tore through the air. After several long milcrons, the invaders stepped away, returning to their duties.

Rolstrun shuddered at the desiccated body and put a hand over his mouth to keep from vomiting. *Oh, Sweet Mother! That's gross.*

We just had a demonstration of our captors' feeding. Disgust filled Bohandran's mind-voice.

The overseer smirked at them as he motioned for them to continue to the crater's edge.

Rolstrun hadn't been this close to Shandir's Crater before and gaped at its immensity. The crater was over 45 measures across and 1,000 feet deep at the center. His heart raced with terror as he took in the black rock stone pillar rising from the center like a misshapen altar. It soared 1,200 feet high and spread to 1,500 feet wide at its base. It gradually tapered to 300 feet in circumference at its flat top. He'd seen the tip of the pillar from the fortress, but hadn't appreciated its enormity.

Rolstrun squinted at the movement on the pillar, trying to decipher what made it appear like ants crawling all over it. A rumbling sound drifted to them. The sides of the crater glistened like the black sand-glass of the Barrens. Rope and metal ladders dangled over the edge. Vertigo hit him as he looked down the thousand feet or more to the crater's depths. Rolstrun hated heights.

The overseer gestured, and Bohandran slipped over the side, climbing carefully down the ladder. When Bohandran's head disappeared, the overseer poked Rolstrun's back with his weapon and barked a command. Swallowing hard, Rolstrun gingerly turned around, gripped the ropes, and reached with his foot for the first rung. The ladder swayed slightly, and his foot slipped off. He stifled a scream as he fought to find the rung.

The overseer said something and raised his weapon to hit Rolstrun.

"I'm going! I'm going!" Afraid the overseer would knock him off to fall to his death, Rolstrun frantically climbed down. He kept his eyes focused on the rope. Half an octar later, Bohandran finally told him he'd reached the bottom. He forced his fingers to release their death grip on the ladder and stepped away from it. His legs buckled, and Bohandran grabbed his arm to keep him upright and moved him out of the way of the next man coming down.

"Thank the Mother that's over!" Rolstrun made the mistake of tipping his head back and raising his eyes and saw how far he'd climbed. It hit him he'd have to make the climb again to get out of the crater. Groaning, he bent over, his hands on his knees, and retched. *Maybe I'll just stay here.*

The others soon stepped off the ladder and stood waiting uneasily.

Rolstrun jerked his head up at a buzzing sound over their heads. The overseer stood on a metal platform that was slowly dropping into the crater. His hand was on a stick attached to the front center of the platform, and on the underside, two spinning disks provided propulsion. The buzzing sound stopped as the platform touched down. The invader stepped off the platform and folded it into a square, which he tucked into a pouch on his back. Rolstrun wished he could descend into the crater so easily. The overseer said something, motioned for them to follow, and started walking toward the activity at the base of the pillar. After a few steps, he looked over his shoulder, shouted at them, and fired his weapon.

Dirt flew at their feet from the projectile's impact. Rolstrun and the others hurried to follow him. Another of the hairy giants passed them, pulling a train of wheeled carts filled with shiny black rocks. Waves of malignant magic rolled off them.

"What do they want with this nasty stuff?" Rolstrun rubbed his arms to rid them of the evil magic's sting.

Bohandran shrugged. "We'll find out soon enough."

Rolstrun - 40 de Sandar, 1075

A miasmatic fog swirled around the pillar's base. Rolstrun threw an arm over his mouth and nose to keep from breathing it in. The beautiful golden-skinned aliens worked next to short, heavy, hairless aliens, swinging pickaxes and other unknown tools to break the solid rock. Tall, dark-skinned aliens with broad, spatula hands shoveled the pieces into waiting carts. They had already dug a ten-foot wide shelf into the pillar.

The overseer led them away from this activity, farther along the pillar. A chunk of rock crashed to the ground. Rolstrun gaped at the Posair man dangling from a rope above them and digging into the pillar. Several more wore harnesses as they hacked at the rock. Below them, more Posair men swung pickaxes while others shoveled the debris into carts. *Where did the Invaders take them from?*

The overseer led them to a pile of tools and pointed at it, then at them. A man with dark red hair streaked with thin yellow stripes stopped working and leaned on his shovel handle.

"You better choose your tool quickly," he said. "If you don't, the Warrior-damned assholes will kill you."

Rolstrun, Calistrun, and Alestrun picked up shovels. Bohandran grabbed a pickax and considered it while glaring at the invader.

"I wouldn't, Bohandran," the man warned.

Bohandran's eyes narrowed in defiance, then widened. "Nederposan? What are you doing here?" He tossed the ax over his shoulder.

"Working. So should you." He picked up his shovel and returned to his digging.

Bohandran nodded and found a spot on the pillar near Nederposan. Rolstrun shoveled the rocks broken from the pillar into a cart. The others in their group settled into work nearby.

"These are my pack-mates." Bohandran introduced everyone. "We were guarding the north fortress when they captured us. What about you?"

"Guarding the east fortress. When did you give up on your little keep and join the Strunlair Clan?"

"A few years ago. I'm now a pack alpha. How long have you been here?"

"Three days. Long enough to get blisters." He put down his tool and rubbed his hands. "The invaders captured the eastern fortress first. I've met people here from the southern and western fortresses. Your group is the last of the fortresses to fall. Did they capture all of you?"

Bohandran nodded, swinging his pickax. "Those they didn't kill first. But there were surprisingly few deaths."

"Not so surprising. They want us alive. For workers. For food. You do know what they eat, don't you?"

"Yes, Goddess, help us," Rolstrun said with a shudder. "One of them killed a hairy alien just before we climbed down."

Bohandran slammed his pick into the pillar, breaking off huge chunks of rock. "We have to find a way to get out of here. This stuff will kill us, or worse, if we stay too long."

"We've all heard the stories," Nederposan agreed. "But how are we going to escape? They've taken away the women's helbraughts, and they whip or shoot us anytime we try to shift. Their weapons are superior to our claws and fangs."

"We'll find a way." Bohandran paused, staring hard at the guard. "I'm sure others saw that fireball, and without us stopping the monsters from crossing the Barrens, they'll soon overrun the rest of Lairheim. Someone will come eventually to find out what's wrong."

"Hopefully, they bring an army with them."

"Goddess, Nederposan, you're not suggesting war, are you? The Great War nearly destroyed us. Only Shandir's sacrifice ended it."

"I'm afraid we'll need that kind of magic to free our world of these invaders."

A whip cracked across Bohandran's shoulders. He turned and snarled, baring his teeth at the guard. The guard's beady eyes narrowed, and he lifted his whip and swung, but instead of hitting Bohandran, the whip slashed Rolstrun's face. Blood dripped from his forehead and cheek. The whip flicked again, hitting his chest. He instinctively curled into a ball, his arms over his head. Two more slashes seared his back. He fell to the ground, writhing from the burning pain.

"Kneel, Bohandran, or he'll kill Rolstrun! They won't punish you. They'll choose someone close to you. It increases the emotions they feed on."

The whipping stopped. Rolstrun opened his blurry eyes. Bohandran knelt with his head bowed in submission. The guard nodded in satisfaction, coiled his whip, and hooked it on his hip. He stepped forward, a hand stretched out toward Rolstrun, who was still curled on the ground. Rolstrun bit the inside of his cheek, swallowed the pain, and struggled to stand. He stared at the guard while taking deep, long breaths until his mind calmed and the pain receded.

The guard snarled something and withdrew his hand.

"Turn your back on him and return to work," Nederposan advised. "Once you do, he'll leave us alone for a while. Rolstrun, I know you're hurting, but you have to finish your shift. If you don't, they'll kill you."

Bohandran helped Rolstrun to the rubble pile and handed him the shovel. "I'm so sorry. I didn't mean for you to get hurt."

"You're the alpha. I'd rather take the beating and have you stay strong." Rolstrun dug into the pile, carefully lifting a load. A groan escaped him before he bit his lip. The guard glanced his way, its tongue slithering in and out, until he shoveled several more loads without making a sound.

They worked with few breaks and even less water. By the time the overseer motioned for them to follow him, blisters covered Rolstrun's hands and black dust caked the whip cuts. Bohandran had to help him climb the rope back out of the crater. When they reached the top, darkness had fallen. The invaders marched the men through the camp and pushed them into a cage. Rolstrun was dimly aware of the women from his pack huddled inside of it as he stumbled in. Laean let out a cry of dismay and ran to his side. He gasped in pain as her touch opened a wound on his back.

"Hurry, Faelyn," Laean cried. "He needs help."

Rolstrun's knees gave out, but before he could hit the ground, Bohandran caught him up.

"Bring him back here," Faelyn said.

Bohandran carried him to the rear of the enclosure and carefully laid him face down on a thin pallet.

Faelyn knelt beside him and gently touched his shoulder. He screamed as her touch reignited the pain. "Shh..." she crooned. A moment later, he fell into unconsciousness.

Chapter 4

Kaieli - 42 de Sandar, 1075

Kaieli awoke early. Dawn was still an octar away. She listened to the soft sounds of Faliciden snoring, wondering what had woken her up. Throwing back the covers, she sat up to go to the necessary room. She paused at the quiet murmuring outside her window, then padded to it. Kothera and Kederposan stood in the courtyard below, speaking with two men. Kothera held out a message cylinder, and the taller man took it, slipped the thong over his head, tucking the cylinder into his jacket.

"Go in safety," Kothera said and kissed each one on the forehead.

The men nodded, shifted into their wolf forms, and loped through the open gate. The guard shut the gate with a low bang.

Her forehead resting on the cold pane of glass, Kaieli fervently prayed they would make it to Posanlair Keep and help would come. The few fighters remaining in the small keep couldn't hold the monsters at bay.

Just yesterday, a brecha escaped the fighting-packs and slaughtered several multas in the pasture near the keep. With all the able-bodied warriors out battling monsters, it left only the old and injured to stop the brecha. Larenposan, frail with age, fought the brecha. His only help came from three boys not old enough to shift to their warrior form and Anyola, the young woman treated for acid burns. Even though her wounds still wept fluid, the young woman forced herself out of bed to combat the brecha. New respect for the fighters blossomed in Kaieli after watching an old man, three boys, and an injured woman kill the brecha.

Thinking about them, Kaieli hurried down the stairs to the infirmary. She checked first on Larenposan. His shallow breathing assured her he still lived. She gently flowed healing energy into him, but she doubted even with all her skill and power he'd last the day. A few beds down, Anyola slept fitfully. The burns had broken open when she'd fought. Kaieli bent over her, frowning. They needed fighters such as Anyola healthy. Kaieli accessed her Talent. Her hands glowed bronze and where she touched Anyola's burns, the skin regenerated. Not even scars were left behind.

Kaieli's vision blurred, and the room spun. Any healing of injuries caused by the Malvers' monsters took more power and energy than normal wounds and illnesses. Anyola sighed softly in her sleep and turned onto her side, her head cradled on her hands. Kaieli smoothed the woman's brow, smiling. The expended energy was worth it to save the young woman.

The rest of the day flew by as fighters returned from monster battles with injuries, keeping Kaieli busy. By afternoon, Anyola recovered enough to leave the infirmary. And when Kaieli made her final rounds for the night, Larenposan still clung to life.

Noise and screaming woke Kaieli from a deep sleep. Her teeth hurt from the unusual low humming sound. Throwing on the clothes she kept by her bed for emergencies, she rushed to the window. A bright light filled the sky, and the keep gates hung on their hinges, while in the courtyard warriors fought strange people. She couldn't make them out clearly through their loose, flowing black robes. She extended her Gray Talent and recoiled from the slimy feel of the invader's energy.

Tight beams of light streamed from the sticks the strangers held. She covered her mouth in horror when blood bloomed on a warrior's chest in several spots. He sagged to the ground, and Kaieli sensed his soul depart his body. Two others lay quiet with their limbs in awkward positions.

Doors crashed open and invaders, wearing black robes, entered the buildings, including the temple. A few moments later, two invaders dragged out White Priestess Loshera. She hung limply in their grasp, but her chest rose in frightened gasps. Kaieli rushed down the stairs and stood in the infirmary doorway, unsure how to protect her charges, but determined to find a way.

Faliciden joined her, breathing raggedly. "Can we form a barrier?" Her long hair was mussed from sleep, and her clothing was in disarray.

"Let's try."

They stood on either side of the doorway. Kaieli calmed her mind, accessed her pool of magic, and drew upon all the aspects she held. Gray and blue lights laced the dark brown energy streaming from her hands. Faliciden added her Green and Brown magic. Kaieli wove it into hers, like the warp to her weft in a woven fabric. The space in the doorway shimmered, then became opaque. Kaieli slowed her breathing and tilted her head to listen.

The outer door smashed. Heavy footsteps scuffed the stone floor. Several voices spoke in a harsh, guttural language. Then came a click and a soft pop, followed by a bright light.

The shield flickered transparently for a moment. Kaieli gaped at the long, gray-green face with wide, big eyes. A forked tongue slithered from its tiny mouth.

Terror rooted her to the spot. Her body shook.

"What... what..." Faliciden stuttered.

"I don't—"

Another flash of bright light hit their shield, making it momentarily translucent.

"I think we just found out who was on that ship."

Frantically, Kaieli added more energy to the shield. It trembled as it took another hit, and another. Each hit drained her reserve more. Faliciden screamed, grabbed her head, and slumped to the ground as the attack depleted her magic. Kaieli gritted her teeth, tears streaming down her face, as she desperately pushed all she had into the shield.

Another bigger, brighter flare of light hit the shield. She lost her hold on it and collapsed into a huddle on the ground as the last tendrils of the shield dissipated.

An invader stepped through the door and kicked her. She curled into a protective ball, expecting more blows. But instead, she heard a hissing sound. She peeked under her arm. The invader's forked tongue lapped at her exposed skin. Her stomach rebelled, and she struggled to keep from vomiting. After an interminable amount of time, it withdrew. A cold, four-fingered hand clutched her shoulder and dragged her to her feet.

A sob escaped her when an invader moved away from old Larenposan. His empty, terrified eyes stared at the ceiling. His skin was pallid from blood loss, and his chest gaped from a nasty, tearing wound. Staring in wide-eyed shock, Kaieli couldn't believe they had killed a harmless old man.

A jerk on her arm brought her back to her senses. As the invader dragged her out, she noticed the other two seriously injured had the same wounds as Larenposan. Ahead of her marched the rest of those who had been in the infirmary.

Out in the courtyard, the invaders herded Kaieli and the others into a tight knot. Women and children cried. Men lay in a heap. Dazed, Kaieli assured herself they were only unconscious, not dead. None of the Reds still standing held their helbraughts. An invader negligently tossed a helbraught on the already large pile of weapons. Two others dragged Nelieh to the group and dropped her. Kaieli couldn't hear any more fighting.

They had lost.

From the direction of the stables and pastures came the ruckus of frightened and hurt animals. Tears ran down her cheeks as the sounds grew quieter and quieter, until after a long time, they finally silenced.

"They killed the livestock." Kothera's voice trembled in shock. "Why would they kill innocent animals?"

Kaieli shrugged. *Why are the invaders doing any of this?*

"Dreana! Dreana!" Jaelena called in a frenzy as she moved through the crowd, tightly holding Treana in her arms. At last she reached Kaieli. "I can't find Dreana anywhere. I've asked everyone else, but no one has seen her. Have you seen her?"

Kaieli shook her head and frowned. "No, but I haven't seen any children killed. When did you see her last?"

"When I tucked her in for the night. I'm so scared."

"Maybe she found a hiding spot in all the chaos," Kaieli suggested.

Jaelena's face brightened with hope. "She sometimes sneaks into the kitchens late at night for a drink." She turned to go back to her pack-house, only to be blocked by an invader. It pushed her with its stick-weapon, making her stumble. Kaieli caught her before she hit the ground.

A tall, thin being with pale blue skin, darker blue hair cropped close to its head, and pale blue-green eyes climbed the steps to the keep-house. A small, gold hoop glinted in its nose, and it wore shapeless gray coveralls. The alien's strangeness and calm demeanor caught the Posairs' attention, and they quieted. Nothing physical about the person suggested its gender. Kaieli probed carefully with her Gray Talent, and its aura and thought patterns led her to believe it was a male. She relaxed when she sensed he didn't want to harm them, but would do what his masters ordered.

"The Scourge have arrived." His voice echoed in the courtyard.

Kaieli's forehead crinkled at his perfect command of the Posarian language.

"There can be no resistance. You are now slaves. The Scourge owns you, body and soul. Work hard, and you will live. Resist and you will die. A long, slow, painful death. Come with us peacefully. Otherwise, they—" he pointed at the black-robed figures surrounding the crowd, projectile sticks directed at them "—will open fire and kill you where you stand."

Kothera stepped forward and took in the ring of armed invaders. She sighed heavily, her shoulders sagged, and defeat clouded her eyes. "We must do as they say. We are outnumbered." She lifted her head, and her eyes glittered with steely determination. "We can't fight them as we are now."

Kaieli sensed the unspoken promise that Kothera would find a way to fight for the safety of her people.

The spokesperson nodded once in acceptance. "Follow the one on the sheezet." He pointed to an invader sitting on top of a large, lizard-like beast, which stood nearly erect on its thick hind legs. The forefeet were much smaller. Sharp horns jutted from its head.

Slowly, Kothera led the people of Posanreande Keep through the gates.

Jaelena held back. "I can't leave without Dreana!" she whispered frantically to Kaieli. "Here, take Treana for me." She thrust the child into Kaieli's arms and ran toward the packhouse.

Crack!

A whip snaked out, catching Jaelena by the throat, stopping her in her tracks. The invader tugged, dragging her to her knees. She clawed at the whip as her eyes bulged. The blue alien rushed over and said something in the invader's harsh language. The invader holding the whip shrugged and released Jaelena. She gasped for breath, tears flowing down her face, her eyes locked on the building Dreana might be in.

The blue alien stood over Jaelena. "You are lucky he didn't kill you. Is whatever you're trying to save worth your life?"

"My daughter is missing. Please help me."

Sadness filled the alien's face. "It would be more merciful for her to stay missing than to be found and taken by the Scourge. Do you not have another child?"

Jaelena nodded.

"Take care of her. Protect her. She needs you now more than ever if she is to survive the upcoming ordeal." He helped Jaelena to her feet and escorted her to Kaieli.

Treana, wide-eyed with fright, nearly leaped from Kaieli's arms into her mother's embrace. Together, they walked to the gates. Kaieli couldn't help glancing back over her shoulder. A piece of torn fabric flapped in the slight breeze. A doll dropped in the chaos lay forlornly by the keep-house stairs. Blood blackened the courtyard cobblestones, and the bodies of the fallen sprawled on the ground. Kaieli resolutely turned away from the carnage. She wondered if anyone would see their home again.

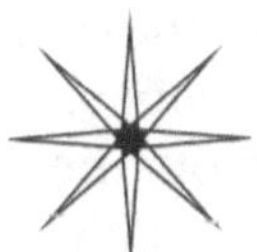

Kaieli - 43 de Sandar, 1075

Daylight brought with it new horrors. The invaders led Kaieli and the other captives southeast, directly toward the Barrens. Most of the Posairs wore light night clothes for comfort during the hot summer nights, but they provided little protection against the blazing sun. Their skin turned red and blistered. Kaieli was unfamiliar with the scrubland and didn't know which plants could be used to relieve the agony of sunburn. Few people had had time to put on shoes, and the rough ground tore up their feet. Kaieli fared better than most, though. She'd dressed and put on her boots before being captured.

Mid-day came and went without the invaders stopping. The invaders passed a water-skin to the prisoners as they walked. Kaieli sipped, grateful for the moisture, then handed it to Jaelena, who limped, carrying Treana. Neither of them had shoes. She passed the water-skin down the line of marching people snaking behind them. They left a trail of bloody footprints. If those without footwear didn't receive something soon, they wouldn't be able to walk. Someone handed her a travel bar, and she absently broke off a piece, tucking the rest into her shirt while wondering how to convince the invaders to stop. Maybe the man who spoke their language would help. She raised onto her toes and craned her neck, but couldn't see him.

She whirled around at the sound of a cracking whip. Metherposan's back arched, and a ripple under his skin precipitated shifting. The whip hit again, stopping the change. The invader riding atop his beast swung the whip again from his higher vantage point. A red welt sprung wetly on Metherposan's back, and he screamed in pain.

The invader's tongue slithered out of its small mouth. The lump on its back seemed to move, and an eerie, dry chittering sound came from under its robes.

Metherposan cowered on the ground on his hands and knees. Kaieli rushed to him, glaring at the invader. It barked harsh, guttural words at them.

The blue man hurried down the line to the disturbance. He paused, a perplexed look on his face when he reached them. He and the invader exchanged a few words, and the invader backed his mount a few steps, his whip held menacingly in his hand.

"Resistance is not tolerated," the translator said, scowling at them. "The next time he resists, the masters will kill him."

"He wasn't resisting." Kaieli moved to stand protectively over Metherposan, who lay curled on the ground, holding his ankles and moaning. She pointed at his shredded feet, blood oozing from the numerous cuts. "Look at his feet. He can't walk any longer. He isn't the only one. Can't you stop this abuse?"

"I can do nothing. I am a slave like you." He tilted his head toward the invader. "They are the masters."

"Please, we need to rest. We can't travel without food or proper shoes and clothing. From our direction of travel, I assume you are taking us to the crater. Nothing grows there, nothing lives there. We need supplies or we will die. Surely the masters would prefer us to be healthy and productive."

"The Scourge soldiers loaded the transport ship with supplies to take to our compound. But do not expect much. You will only be given just enough to keep you alive to work."

"We can't make it there in one day. It's too far."

"It is known. We will stop for the night." He gazed toward the west, a hand shielding his eyes. "They should call a rest break soon."

"Thank you."

He turned away and took a few steps toward the front of the line. He shook his head and spun on his heel to face Kaieli again. "Lady, you were brave, but foolish, to try to protect your friend. May I have your name?"

Kaieli's eyebrows raised. "I am Kaieli."

"I am called Tre'nok." He bowed slightly with a flourish of his hand in front of his face. "I will ask about the clothing, but do not expect kindness from the Scourge. It is not in their nature." He strode away.

Kaieli bent over Metherposan, ignoring the invader who still watched them, whip ready to strike. With her back to the invader—she didn't want him to profanc her gift from the Goddess—she drew upon her Talent and healed the welts on

Metherposan's back. "Walk as if you still hurt," she whispered to him. "They enjoy inflicting pain."

Metherposan nodded as he struggled to his feet. "I can do that. My feet are killing me."

The invader motioned to them with the whip to get moving. Kaieli wondered if Tre'nok would do as he promised. She continued walking, dragging one foot in front of the other. Whenever she'd had to travel in the past, she'd ridden a horse, not walked, and wished she rode her horse now. She bit back a sob, remembering the dead animals in the pasture. The heel of her left foot had a blister, and her legs ached. The sun beat down on her, giving her a headache. A coughing fit hit her from the dust kicked up by so many feet.

"Kaieli! Kaieli!"

She raised her head at the sound of her name. "Here," she called.

"Come quick!" Baerenposan, one of the young men who'd fought with Larenposan, skidded to a stop in front of her. "Detheren needs your help. The gash on her leg opened. It's bleeding badly, and she fainted." He said the last in a low, scared voice. He tugged on her hand. "Hurry, those creatures are standing over her. You have to stop them."

Forcing her tired legs to a run, Kaieli followed the boy. Two creatures bent over Detheren, making hissing sounds. The humps on their backs appeared to be growing taller. One of them kicked the downed woman in her ribs, and she moaned weakly.

"Hey! Stop!" Kaieli yelled. She dropped to her knees next to Detheren, and scanned her, relieved to detect her heart beating a faint, thready rhythm. Kaieli moved her hands toward the injury, swearing. The walking had undone all the work she'd done a few days ago to heal the gash from the Malvers' monster.

A third invader joined the group, pushing Kaieli to the side. She landed hard on her butt, her breath whooshing out of her. Gasping, she rolled to her feet. This one was taller than the other two, and silver edged his black robes. The other invaders dipped their heads and pounded a fist on their chests in deference to him.

After a short conversation, the first two invaders bowed, then knelt, jerking Detheren's arms and legs into a spread-eagle position, and held her against the ground. The leader towered over her, his black robe fluttering in the breeze. His lump visibly grew until two thin appendages extended above his head. In a swift move, he jabbed the sharp points into either side of Detheren's neck. Her body jerked, quickly stilling as a tube connected Detheren and the invader in a grotesque parody of an embrace. Kaieli gagged at the sucking sound it made, while the two lower-ranking creatures holding Detheren let go and gazed on hungrily.

A blur of fur rushed at the invaders. One flung out an arm, caught the wolf cub, and tossed him to the ground. He rolled to a stop at Kaieli's feet. Baerenposan shifted back to his human form, holding his head.

Detheren was dead. Only a dry husk remained. All her blood, organs, and muscles were gone.

Kaieli turned away and spewed the contents of her stomach. *Oh Goddess. Oh Goddess. He ate her!*

At last she stopped heaving.

"Kaieli, Lady, you must get up now." Tre'nok's voice penetrated her misery. Her anger flared at his placating tone.

"You!" She rushed him and struck his chest with both hands. "Why didn't you stop them? What are those things? It... it ate her!"

Arms folded around her. "I know. It is what the Scourge do. It is good you have seen this now."

She pushed away from him. "How can it be good?"

"There will only be more. It is how the Scourge eat."

"What?" Kaieli eyes were so wide they hurt. "They eat people?"

"Yes. Emotions and blood also provide sustenance." His much greater height made it easy for him to tuck her into his shoulder. "Shh... Lady Kaieli," he whispered. "Calm yourself. You are feeding them now with your distress."

She peeked under his arm and shuddered.

Five invaders stood in a ring around them, tongues rapidly flicking out. The closest one touched her shoulder. She jerked away from the cold touch.

Taking deep breaths, Kaieli pushed away the horror. She focused instead on the Goddess in Her Mother aspect, letting the love and comfort of the Mother flow into her. When she reached a state of serenity, she stepped back from Tre'nok. The invaders had departed.

Awe and respect filled Tre'nok's face. "There are not many species who can close off their emotions so completely. Can others do this?"

Kaieli shrugged, thinking furiously. White Priestess Loshera would know how to call upon the Goddess and could teach everyone. The Goddess's presence had brought Kaieli the serenity she needed to block the invaders.

The invader who had eaten Detheren barked something at Tre'nok. He stood with his head bowed and his hands clasped behind his back. When the invader strode away, Tre'nok raised his head, put something up to his mouth, and spoke. The device amplified his voice so everyone could hear him.

"The honorable Se-ka-tak, captain of this pod, is feeling gracious and has called for a break. You may rest for a single chime. Be aware if you fall behind or are weak, you will provide a different service to the Scourge. You will become their nourishment. Take your ease and be ready to move when the horn sounds."

The break wasn't nearly long enough. In less than half an octar, the invaders pushed the Posairs to march again. Before they stopped for the night, four more people collapsed from the relentless pace, and the invaders killed them. Kaieli and Faliciden visited every person, treating their wounds and lending them strength.

Kaieli plopped onto the ground, worked off her boots, and stared at her swollen, blistered feet. Silent tears dripped down her face. She didn't have any energy left to heal herself. She curled onto her side and slipped into sleep while praying for deliverance.

Kaieli - 44 de Sandar, 1075

The morning dawned with the groan of the invader's horn. Kaieli moaned as her stiff body protested. Half of a travel bar and water broke her fast.

Invaders in plain black robes walked through the crowd of Posairs, handing out stacks of ghastly orange fabric to each person. Kaieli easily deciphered two of the items in the stack. One was a type of cape with a slit in the center, and the other was coveralls similar to what Tre'nok wore. Although, the coveralls appeared like they'd drown her. Kaieli held up two squares, turning them this way and that, trying to figure out what they were.

Tre'nok came up behind her, laughing softly at her confusion. "Footwear. Here, put one foot into the center, and touch this button. It will mold to your feet."

"My boots are still good," she said. "But Metherposan needs them. Can you show him?" Tre'nok agreed, and she watched in fascination as Metherposan stepped on a square, and gingerly touched the blue button. The material reshaped to cover his foot and ankle. He stamped on the ground, sending a puff of dust into the air, making those around him cough.

"Hey," he said when he stopped coughing. "They're hard!"

"Just touch the button again to take them off," Tre'nok said. "The overalls will also conform to your size. Put them on. You too, Kaieli."

"But my clothes are fine," she protested.

"It does not matter. The coveralls are the slave's uniform, and the masters require all their slaves to wear them."

Fuming, Kaieli stepped into the coveralls. As she'd feared, the legs and sleeves were too long and hung off her hands. Metherposan held his coverall in front of him, frowning at how small it was. Tre'nok reached over and touched a button on the collar, and Kaieli's coveralls shrunk to her size.

Dubiously, Metherposan stepped into the legs and pushed the button. The fabric stretched until he could pull it over his shoulders. When he had them on, they adjusted themselves until they fit him.

The fabric was surprisingly light and stretched with her movements. Not needing the cape at the moment, she tied it around her waist. She tucked the unused foot coverings into her belt. Wandering through the group, she showed others how to use the unusual attire. Soon everyone had decent, if ugly, footwear and clothing.

A horn blared. The guards cracked their whips, and the Posairs stumbled into line.

Once her muscles warmed up, Kaieli found the walking easier than the previous day. Jaelena walked beside her, with Treana skipping in front of them. A smile curved Jaelena's lips as she watched her daughter.

"Thank you, Kaieli," she said. "I wouldn't have her now if you hadn't saved her from the plague." Her eyes flitted to the side as an invader rode by. "Although, I'm not so sure this is better."

"If there's life, there's hope," Kaieli assured her.

"Please, Goddess, I hope Dreana's all right." Jaelena grasped Kaieli's arm. "Do you really think she hid someplace and is alive? She's still a little girl. The damned invaders killed all the horses. She won't have a chance to reach the nearest keep."

"Kothera and Kederposan sent messengers to Posanlair Keep. I saw them leave. Somebody should arrive at the keep soon and help her." Kaieli said a prayer, hoping her words were more than empty comfort to a scared mother. They walked on in silence.

By mid-morning, the irrepressible energy of the children reasserted itself, and the sound of their laughter lifted her spirits. They played tag and ran alongside the marching adults, falling back in line whenever an invader approached. The adolescents began to venture farther away, challenging each other to test the limits of their confines. A shout of alarm rang out, and the awful horn blared again as a ruddy wolf streaked from the line of marchers.

"Go, Serenposan! Go!" his friends cheered him on.

A mounted invader chased the young man. Kaieli silently urged him to greater speed as the gap between them continued to widen. The invader lifted his weapon and fired. The crackling light zipping from the weapon silenced the watchers. A moment later, the wolf yelped and dropped like a stone to the ground. Cries replaced the cheers. The invader rode to Serenposan, tossed him onto the beast, and returned. Kaieli let out her breath when she saw his chest rising and falling.

The invaders rained their whips indiscriminately on the crowd. Kaieli ducked with the others, protecting her head with her arms and yelped when a whip caught her arm. The officer, Se-ka-tak, stalked to the prisoners and singled out every fourth person regardless of gender, skipping over the small children. Soldiers forced the chosen to the front.

Tre'nok, still out of breath from his run to catch up with the officer, translated the orders.

"You were warned not to run, not to escape," he said in a monotone voice. He'd wiped any emotion from his face. "Resistance is futile. We will catch you every time. Our weapons are superior to yours. Our technology trumps your magic. We are now your masters. The misdeeds of one will be punished by the many. Perhaps you do not fear us enough. Learn to fear."

Captain Se-ka-tak nodded to his waiting troops. They fired into the selected people, yellow and blue light flashing from the weapons.

Yellow light hit about a quarter of the group. No visible wounds appeared, but they gasped for breath and grabbed at their throats. Foam dribbled down their chins, their faces turned blue, and they eventually fell motionless, dead. The invaders dragged them to the side, forming a pile. The blue light had struck the remaining people, who screamed and danced in agony for long milcrons until they finally crumbled to the ground, their chests heaving.

These also didn't have any easily discernible wounds. Kaieli moved to go help them.

"No, do not move." Tre'nok grabbed her arm and held her back. He had slipped to her side once the shooting had begun. "Do not speak. The punishment is not over."

She wondered why he was explaining it to her, rather than Kothera, who was the alpha.

Screaming on the inside, tears streaming down her face, Kaieli watched helplessly as the invaders methodically beat every third woman left alive in the selected group. The Posairs fought for survival against the Malvers' monsters, but they never deliberately harmed each other. Even the Malvers' monsters didn't torment their victims as these creatures were doing. Kaieli's mind went numb, unable to cope with the cruelty she was being forced to witness. It seemed like octars passed before they finally stopped. She hoped the atrocity was over.

Her shoulders sagged when two invaders dragged Serenposan, who was now awake and struggling, to the officer.

Slowly and carefully, so all could see, he extended his feeders and plunged the sharp points into Serenposan's neck. A tube snaked from the invader's upper chest and buried into the center of Serenposan's chest. Terror and pain filled the young man's face as the invader sucked his life from him.

At the officer's order, the troops fell on the bodies and gustily slurped them dry.

While others retched, Kaieli pursed her lips tight and stared at the captain. She hoped he choked on her hate. She had never hated anyone or anything in her life like she did now. As a healer, she valued life, but as the invaders tossed another corpse aside like trash, she vowed she'd find a way to kill these monsters.

As soon as the feeding frenzy ended, the officer ordered the march to continue, not giving the beaten women much of a chance to recover. A measure later, they trod from the scrublands to the Barrens black sand-glass glittering in the sunlight.

Kaieli lost her footing as she slid on the slick sand, along with many others. Petrified wood banged her toes. Jumbled piles of boulders blocked their way, forcing the group to snake around and through the mess. In some areas, walking in a straight line was impossible. Even through the thick fabric of the coveralls, Kaieli's legs and arms bled from numerous nicks as the sand-glass splintered under their marching feet. The black dust covered everything, seeping into her clothing and making breathing difficult. The further they marched into the lifeless expanse, Kaieli's spirits descended deeper. Escape now seemed impossible. Even if they did, how would they survive in the Barrens?

Chapter 5

Rolstrun - 45 de Sandar, 1075

Sweat dripped from the end of Rolstrun's nose. The sun blazed high in the sky. Even the huge pillar didn't provide any shade as he and the other Posair men hacked at it. He wanted to roll his coveralls down to his waist in the heat, but the constant threat of being whipped made him keep it on. His back still hurt from the whipping he'd received the first day.

Rolstrun whacked the rock and coughed as black dust rose. He covered his mouth and nose with the crook of his arm, wishing for a scarf or even a scrap of cloth to use as a mask. The hateful coveralls couldn't be torn, and the invaders had taken all their previous clothing. Constantly breathing the dust, filled with malevolent magic, played havoc with the men's health. As each day passed, he and the other men found it harder and harder to mind-speak. Fear swept through Rolstrun. *Is it the first symptom of crater sickness?*

He swung his pickax as the stories of the ill-fated force nibbled at his mind. *They spent six lunadars in the crater. We've only been here for a few days. Surely, it can't be affecting us so quickly!* Although no one knew when the first team fell ill or when they couldn't access their gifts anymore.

Last night, Laean tried to seduce him, but he couldn't bring himself to make love to her. The invaders had confiscated the herb the women used to keep from having any unwanted pregnancies, and the fear of horribly deformed children kept his libido in check. He couldn't imagine a child surviving the brutal conditions of the slave camp. Besides, Laean was still recovering from her head wound. Instead, he'd held her in his arms, listening to her soft weeping. After she'd fallen asleep, her pain-filled moans and her rattling chest worried him. Faelyn's attempts to heal her had all failed.

The sun finally dropped, and a cool breeze dried the sweat on Rolstrun's face. A horn blared, announcing the end of their shift. He sighed, dropping the ax in the tool pile as he trudged to the ladder. Gazing up, he grimaced at the long climb out of the crater after an exhausting day of digging. He concentrated on placing each foot carefully on the narrow rungs. A scream broke his concentration. Horror filled him as a Posanlair man fell from a ladder. He turned his head away from the body shattered below on the rocks. After wiping first one sweaty hand on his coveralls, then the other, he resumed his climb.

Rolstrun finally crawled over the crater rim and lay panting until he had to move to allow the next man off the ladder. Each day, when he returned to the top, he marveled at how much the invader's camp grew. The compound now consisted of twenty-five long buildings housing the invader's various alien slaves. The soldiers bunked in fifteen three-story buildings, with more in the process of being built. Thirty pens squatted nearby, filled with the strange lizard-like beasts the invaders used for mounts. Invaders marched or practiced with their weapons in an area left clear. Rolstrun had once traveled to Strunlair Keep, the largest keep in Lairheim. This compound was already twice as large, and when they finished building, it would be four or five times larger. Rolstrun trudged toward the slave cages on the far side of the cleared area. How could his people win against such a greater force?

He kept his head down, ensuring he didn't make eye contact with one of the officers. He'd seen a Dehanlair man lock eyes with an officer with silver-edged robes. The invader had whipped the man and burned out his eyes before consuming him.

The group turned down the walkway leading to the cages, and Rolstrun risked gazing longingly at the edge of the compound a few hundred tantalizing feet away. Freedom appeared so close. Maybe if he sprinted, he could make it.

A Keistanlair man broke from the ranks, running full-speed toward the Barrens. The invaders guarding them gaped at the escapee, then talked excitedly between themselves. He'd run about a measure when a bright flash of light surrounded him. The next moment, he exploded.

Rolstrun whirled to the side, vomiting. His stomach clutched again at the sound of other men retching. Finally, he stood, wiping his mouth. The voice of the translator during the induction floated in his memory, telling them they'd be injected with an exploding tracking device. They'd just seen proof of it. Rolstrun rubbed his upper arm where they'd jabbed him during the processing procedures. He shivered in fear as he detected an unfamiliar bump under his skin. One of their guards tucked several small objects into his robes that his companions grudgingly handed to him. He noticed the men frozen and gaping, and he gestured angrily at them to move into their pens.

Numb, Rolstrun stumbled after the other men into the cage.

"What happened?" Maheli asked as soon as the cage's gate slammed shut.

"A Keistanlair man tried to escape," Bohandran said quietly. His face was pale, and his hands shook. He led the group to the back of the cage, away from the guards. "The translator didn't lie. The invaders injected us with a device that will kill us if we try to run. Here, feel." He held out his arm, pointing at his biceps.

Maheli touched his upper arm. Her eyes widened as she felt her own arm.

"We have it too." Her shoulders slumped. "How can we escape now?"

"Can Faelyn remove it?" Rolstrun suggested.

Faelyn made her way through the crowd. "I heard what happened. Maheli, hold out your arm."

Maheli did so while Faelyn focused on a slight bump. Now he knew what to look for, Rolstrun could see it. Bronze light surrounded Maheli's arm, outlining the device. Maheli groaned, biting her lip. The light intensified. Maheli cried out, and her eyes rolled to the back of her head.

Faelyn quickly stopped working and gently lowered Maheli to the ground. "I can't remove it without killing Maheli. At least not by myself. I'd need another powerful healer, like Kaieli."

Maheli moaned and sat up, then hurried to put her head between her knees. After a long moment, she raised her head. "That hurts like the seven hells. Not only did it hurt where the device was, but my head felt like it was going to explode. It still does." She groaned and put her head back down.

Laean came to stand next to Rolstrun, fear in her eyes. He wrapped his arm around her shoulders and pulled her close. He held her for a long time.

"Food is ready," Myndera said into the quiet. "It isn't much, but it's hot."

After the recent events, Rolstrun's appetite fled, but he knew he had to eat. He wouldn't let the invaders win by giving up. Together, he and Laean joined the line for the thin soup.

Later that night, as he lay on his pallet looking up at the stars, he rubbed the bump on his arm. Would he ever escape the horror his life had become?

Kaieli - 45 de Sandar, 1075

Throughout the next day, the elderly collapsed, one by one, from the harsh conditions. Kaieli made herself watch each and every one of the fallen be eaten by the invaders, feeding her hate. It kept her moving when she wanted to give up. When a sick toddler died and the officer tried to consume the child, a frenzied, angry mob of Posairs, unconcerned with their own safety, attacked him. It took killing several Posairs for his troops to push them back.

Late afternoon, Kaieli wrinkled her nose as a stench rolled over them, carried on the breeze.

Kederposan lifted his head, sniffing deeply. "Monsters!" he shouted.

Tre'nok raced to them. "What's happening?"

"Didn't you hear?" Kothera snapped at him. "Monsters! Let us fight, or we'll all be dead." She turned her back to him. "Form up." She yelled. "We protect our innocents."

Kederposan, Metherposan, and the other men shifted into their warrior forms. Snarling and howling, they pushed the women, children, and the few remaining elderly into a tight group. Kaieli glimpsed the men pacing outside the circle.

Kothera cursed the invaders for taking their helbraughts. "Reds," she shouted, "form a ring around the noncombatants! We can still access our fire magic, even though we don't have our helbraughts to direct it."

Kaieli wasn't sure how she could help, but she joined the women with other Talents as they formed a second ring around their weakest members.

Invaders rode by and cracked their whips at the men, who snarled at them, but didn't break formation. The invaders' beasts appeared to smell the monster stench as they bleated, bucking and pulling against the reins, making their riders work to stay in the saddle. The captain barked an order, and Kaieli cursed when two invaders turned back toward the Posairs, weapons held ready.

Tre'nok squeezed his way through the center group to stand next to Kaieli. His light yellow eyes stood out against his now paler blue skin. "What are you afraid of?" he asked.

The stench grew, and a rumbling reached them. Spines appeared over the low hill.

"That." Kaieli pointed. "A nest of Malvers' monsters is loose."

A brecha ran toward them at full speed. Large, sharp teeth dripped saliva that hissed when it hit the ground. Its nostrils flared as it caught their scent. Five more brechas crested the hill, followed by a janack trundling on its tentacles.

Tre'nok screeched, ducked, and threw his hands over his face.

A sheezet reared, its rider falling to the ground. He quickly scrambled to his feet, grabbed his weapon, and fired. The lead brecha jerked from the impact but kept on running. The captain barked an order, and his foot soldiers formed a line in front of those mounted. Their weapons whirred as a barrel on the bottom spun. The troops fired again, bright lights streaking from their weapons. The brecha jerked again, then screamed. Holes appeared in its hide, expanding until they combined, and the brecha exploded. The invaders kept firing.

A mounted rider charged away from the group, toward the monsters, yelling as he brandished his weapon. The janack's tentacles stretched over the brechas and reached for the solitary invader, plucking him from his beast. Yelling and screaming, the invader shot into the janack. Another tentacle slid behind him and knocked the weapon from his hands as the monster inexorably carried the invader to its mouth. A moment later, purple blood flowed from its maw.

Metherposan stepped away from the circle, his claws flexed.

"No!" Kothera yelled, adding alpha magic to the order. In mind-speech she added, *We fight only if we must. Let the monsters take care of the invaders for us.*

Growling, Metherposan returned to the circle, pacing. Not long after, a brecha evaded the invaders and barreled toward the Posairs. He and Kederposan leaped forward. As the taller of the two, Metherposan used his claws to shear the spines off the brecha's back while Kederposan disemboweled it.

Kothera ordered the Reds to hold hands. With their combined magic, she guided them into forming a thin fire-shield around the women and children they guarded. A barrage of brecha spines sped toward them. Kaieli squealed in fright as she ducked, expecting a spine to impale her. But the spines sizzled to ash when they hit the fire-shield.

Another brecha galloped toward the group, spittle flying from its sharp teeth, and sand-glass spraying from its clawed feet. She stood transfixed as death stalked her. She'd attended many monster battles with her heart-sister, Rizelya, but she'd always stayed far away from the fighting, only approaching the battlefield after the monsters were dead. This was the closest she'd ever come to a live Malvers' monster. A small red-brown ball of fur bowled into the brecha, knocking it to the ground and to a waiting warrior, who decapitated it. The fur-ball stood and shook its wolf form.

"Baerenposan!" she cried. "What are you doing out there?"

The boy yipped at her, then turned back to the monster battle. He wasn't old enough to shift into his warrior form yet, but that wasn't stopping him from doing his duty to protect his people. Tears pricked Kaieli's eyes. If only he survived this ordeal, he'd become a powerful warrior.

Soon, only the janack remained. The invaders concentrated their weapons on it, firing at it repeatedly with the bright light-type projectiles until it finally exploded.

Kothera turned away, disappointment clear on her face, and joined Kaieli and Tre'nok. "Damn! Only two invaders died."

Tre'nok watched the last monster bits drift to the ground. "You fight those? All the time?"

Kothera nodded. "This was a small nest, with only six brechas and one janack. We were lucky there weren't more."

The exploded monster bits weren't enough for the invaders to try to eat. The captain took out his frustration by killing one of his own men, who hadn't moved out of his way quick enough. After the battle, outriders scouted the trail ahead, and the group didn't encounter any more monsters.

The next two days passed in a blur of marching misery. Dread filled Kaieli as the crater mound drew closer and closer with each measure she walked. The big ship glittered in the harsh sun, acting as a beacon. Five days after being captured, the people of Posanreande Keep reached the crater late at night and the invaders herded them into pens. Corpses littered the trail behind them.

Rizelya - 46 de Sandar, 1075

Rizelya and Blazel raced across the Sanctuary grounds toward the Gryphon's housing. She and her friends had returned from their quest to the Deep Mountains yesterday. They'd accomplished their mission of finding the legendary Gryphons. Prince Moraak led three flights of Gryphons out of the Deep Mountains and into Posair territory for the first time since the Great War. The comet streaking through the sky, bringing an unknown invader into their world, had convinced Moraak's father, King Zorlaak, to tentatively renew the ancient alliance between Posairs and Gryphons.

Now, she and Blazel were heading on a reconnaissance mission with a small flight of Gryphons to Shandir's Crater, where the aliens landed. After Sheekeek's, a Gryphon mystic, vision, both the Supreme and Prince Moraak wanted information on what the invaders were doing. His words haunted Rizelya, pushing her to run faster. *They rape the land. Keeps slaughtered, survivors enslaved. Madness is here.* Had the invaders already captured her people?

The pack of food and water skin bumped against her back. The Barrens, where they were going, didn't hold any life. Rizelya swiped at the sweat coating her face. Even though early summer reigned, Graak, Blazel's friend and the leader of this mission, insisted she and Blazel wear winter clothing.

When they arrived, the talon of Gryphons were filling water bags from the fountain. Rizelya's eyebrows rose in curiosity at the modified saddles Glork and Graak wore on their backs. Both Gryphons stood over six feet at the shoulder. Graak, the larger of the two, was nearly fourteen feet long, while Glork was about a foot shorter. The saddles were longer and flatter than those made for horses, and fit along the Gryphon's upper back. Straps, similar to a girth strap, led from the seat on either side of their wings and under their bellies. Lines attached the saddle—or was it a harness—to the leather collars they wore.

Rizelya had ridden Glork once before, but only to reach Alkaak, the Gryphon city, located on a high cliff. At the time, she'd sat on his shoulders in front of his wings. This ride would be much longer. She hadn't relished the idea of riding him the length of Lairheim with only her legs gripping his shoulders to stay on. While she appreciated the addition of the saddle, it didn't appear like it'd be comfortable sitting on.

"Hello, Glork." Rizelya bowed to the Gryphon. "Thank you for allowing me to be your passenger."

The brown and white Gryphon ducked his head, and tucked his white striped, brown wings closer to his creamy tan and brown feline body. *My pleasure. The saddles will make the long flight to Shandir's Crater more comfortable for both of us. Put on your hat and gloves, and fasten your coat before buckling in. As high as we'll fly, you'll get cold.* He crouched low for her to climb on his back.

Rizelya frowned at the multiple straps with buckles hanging from the saddle. The flatness and position of it made her wonder where her feet would go, or if they rested on the Gryphon's wings.

"What do I do?" she asked, confused by the strange contraption.

Blazel shrugged. "I don't know. When I stayed with Graak as a teenager, he didn't have one of these."

The harness is what your ancestors used when we fought with them during the Great War, Graak explained. *We discovered them while exploring the house. It's a good thing too. Otherwise, Blazel, you'd fall off.* He warbled a chuckle, making his sandy brown feathers jiggle.

"Hey, that only happened once!" Blazel protested, scowling at Graak. "And you didn't warn me you were going to fly a loop."

Broogk stepped forward. *Here, I'll help you. We also found instructions with them.* His front talons, with four "fingers", were as dexterous as Rizelya's hands.

Together, they figured out how to strap a person onto the Gryphon saddles. By the time they were done, Rizelya felt like a bird trussed up for roasting. Her legs were tucked up on either side of Glork, and she laid on her tummy. Her feet rested on Glork's back, next to his wings. She had limited room to sit up into a crouch. Riding a Gryphon was nothing like riding a horse!

Once Rizelya and Blazel were securely bound in the harnesses, Graak gave the order to fly. Glork's leap into the air snapped Rizelya's neck back. His wing's powerful downstroke flung her forward again.

Relax and lay forward, Glork suggested. *Rest your head on my shoulders.*

Rizelya did, and the jerking motions of Glork's pumping wings smoothed. The Gryphons climbed higher before leveling out, and Rizelya was glad Graak had insisted she wear warm clothing.

Far below them, the land passed quickly. The Storengher River sparkled in the sun. Rizelya experienced a moment of homesickness as they flew over her home, Strunlair Keep. What had taken her days to traverse, the Gryphons covered within a few octars. At noon, the Gryphons spiraled down to the plains for a break.

Rizelya carefully slid off Glork, keeping hold of the riding straps. She groaned, shaking her arms and legs to return the feeling to them.

Blazel hung onto Graak's saddle, wincing. "My butt and thighs hurt in ways I never thought possible. I feel like I've been doing squats for hours."

Rizelya laughed. "Yes, this will take some getting used to." She dug a piece of dried meat from her pocket and chewed it while walking in circles and stretching. All too soon, Graak announced the end of the break. This time, Rizelya found buckling into Glork easier and didn't tighten them as much, giving herself more movement.

The sun sunk low on the horizon when Graak descended again. He landed near the Storengher River, right before it disappeared beneath the Barrens. The black sand-glass glittering in the fading light created a stark demarcation where the plains stopped and the Barrens began. Blazel cleared the grass and carried rocks from the riverbank to build a fire ring. Rizelya wandered the riverbank and found several large pieces of driftwood. They soon had a fire to push back the night.

The river's rocky shore wasn't a comfortable place to sleep, but it provided fresh fish for the Gryphons. Glork carried a large trout, still flopping wildly, in his beak, and dropped it next to Rizelya. He sauntered back to the river before she could thank him. She wrinkled her nose at it. "Do you really want me to cook this?" She fully admitted she wasn't the best cook.

Blazel chuckled. "Not if we want it edible." He quickly cleaned, seasoned, and thread the fish on a stick, placing it over the fire. He mixed a batch of pan bread to go with it. "Can you watch this? I need to stretch."

Rizelya nodded. She could do that much cooking. Blazel wandered to the where the plains met the Barrens, and stood a long time gazing into the bleakness. Rizelya hadn't been here before, but she remembered his stories about running through the Barrens alone. She shivered at the thought, grateful they had the Gryphons to carry them over the barrenness.

What would they discover there? Her pack-mates guarded the northern fortress. Maheli, the guard alpha, had mentored Rizelya over the years, welcoming her when others considered her too young to become a fighter. She knew every person at the fortress, and they were excellent fighters. Surely, the invaders wouldn't be a match for their prowess. Rizelya couldn't imagine the fortress guards being captured and enslaved.

Blazel - 47 de Sandar, 1075

Blazel groaned as he crawled from his bedroll. Every muscle hurt from the unusual ride on Graak. He didn't look forward to another day trussed up like a bird. But they had to know what the invaders were doing. After a hasty breakfast of dried meat and taevo, he and Rizelya climbed back on the Gryphons.

They had only flown a short time when Rizelya cried out, and her face was white with fear. "Oh, Sweet Mother, no!" She pointed below them.

Two janacks and six brechas trundled from the Barrens and into the plains. He searched, but there weren't any fighters on the ground.

"We can't let them get away," Rizelya shouted. "Glork, take me down."

Glork complied. Rizelya's helbraught glowed. A moment later, a stream of fire shot from the blade and arced to surround a brecha. It burst into flame and quickly disintegrated. Broogk screamed in anger, flames erupted around him, and he dove at a janack. The monster instinctively reached out a tentacle to yank him from the sky. It jerked away from the heat, but not before fire engulfed the tentacle and raced toward the bulbous body. Screeching, Gryphons dove and darted at the monsters. Blazel gritted his teeth at his uselessness and inability to fight the monsters with tooth and claw like he normally did. Rizelya and the Gryphons swiftly destroyed the beasts, leaving only smoking piles of ash. A breeze carried the ashes back into the Barrens.

We haven't fought this type of creature before, Graak said, winging higher. *This is good practice for us.*

"But it's difficult for me to sit and only watch," Blazel grumbled.

Rizelya gave him a rueful smile. "Since your focus isn't on fighting, your job is to make sure none of them escape."

"I can do that. But I don't like this. Something is wrong. When I crossed here before, the guard-packs were all over the monsters—"

"We're a long way from the crater—"

"Rizelya, it didn't matter how far the monsters ran. The fighters chased them until they caught them."

Her eyebrows crinkled in worry.

They fought four more battles without a single fighting-pack on the ground. Graak finally approached the northern fortress, where Blazel had met the Strunlair guard-pack and Rolstrun, the first Posair male to accept him.

Blazel's heart lodged in his throat at the gate hanging open and the lack of sentries standing on the wall. An eerie silence filled the fortress.

"No, no, no!" Rizelya fumbled out of her saddle harness. "Maheli! Rolstrun! Bohandran! Where are you?" She ran into the Keep-House, with Blazel on her heels.

The only sound was their boots echoing on the stone floors. Small holes in the walls and the overturned furniture pointed to a struggle. But there weren't any bodies until they entered the stables. A few horses had escaped, but those caught in their stalls had been slaughtered. Whatever had killed them had left only dried husks behind. Blazel ran outside and heaved. *Who would kill horses?*

They found the same thing at the other fortresses. With heavy hearts, Graak led his flight into the upper atmosphere, catching the thermals and resting. They flew farther south. Even from their height, they could clearly see the wound in the earth. Shandir's Crater. An ugly, oblong object squatted on its rim. Blazel gaped at the size of it.

Graak sent Baekeek, a fast-flying owl-type scout, down to the crater, while they continued to circle high above it.

There's activity in the center, Graak explained, his long-distance sight much better than Blazel's.

Baekeek circled the crater once before he dove. Blazel gripped the riding strap as he waited, his fingers hurting with the pressure.

Suddenly, loud pops rent the air, and with a screech, Baekeek zipped out of the crater, his flames extending several feet away from him. As he gained altitude, he wobbled, and his flames sizzled out. Two of the larger Gryphons dove and came up under the injured scout, supporting him with their wings. Graak began to descend.

"No! His injury will get infected if we land in the Barrens," Blazel said.

Graak grumbled, and with a squawk, directed the others to keep flying and to stay together. They caught a thermal that carried them quickly out of the Barrens. Blazel kept glancing over his shoulder, afraid of pursuit. He didn't relax his vigilance until they returned to the edge of the plains, where the black sand-glass met scraggly bushes.

The injured scout keened in pain. Blood covered his left wing where something had punctured a hole in it, and his feathers around it were scorched. His flaring had sealed the wound's edges, although blood still oozed from its center. Baekeek screeched as Graak examined the injury.

Grimacing, Blazel stomped away from the injured scout and to the edge of the Barrens. He scuffed the toe of his boot into the black sand. A few moments later, Rizelya threaded her arms around him and laid her head against his back. He pulled her hands tights against his chest.

"How can we fight these invaders when they're able to shoot a Gryphon from the sky?" Blazel said.

"We'll find a way. We've survived the Malvers' monsters, so we can survive against this." She scooted around until she faced him.

Blazel held her for a long time, staring out at the Barrens. His gaze swept to the boundary marking life and death. He squinted, trying to make sense of what his eyes were telling him. Letting go of Rizelya, he crouched to examine it closer, scowling. Still confused, he followed the beaten, compacted glass for several paces into the Barrens. He turned and walked along the trail back into the scrublands. Rizelya paced behind him.

"What's wrong?" Rizelya asked.

"A large group of people marched through here. And see here." He pointed to the strange track. "This must be an invader's print. I believe we're in Posanlair Territory, and if so, there's a minor keep in the direction the tracks are coming from."

"Warrior, take them!" Rizelya slammed the butt of her helbraught on the ground. "We have to go and search for survivors." She turned to run toward to the Gryphons.

He reached out a hand and stopped her. "We'll have to wait until morning. By the time we get back up in the air, it will be too dark."

Rizelya glared at the setting sun and swore again. She stalked toward their camp.

Blazel studied the tracks once more before following her. Bile burned his throat. He doubted they'd find anyone alive at the keep.

Rolstrun - 47 de Sandar, 1075

Rolstrun and his work group filed in line for their noon ration of water. He brushed the black dust from his hand before reaching for the metal cup. It didn't do any good. The dirt from the pillar felt embedded into his skin. *Why did the invaders want the awful stuff?* He handed the cup back to the golden-skinned alien, who he'd learned were called Vhelopsi, with a nod of thanks.

The Vhelopsi gave him a small smile, the tips of his fangs peeking out. If not for the fangs and their coloring, the Vhelopsi could pass for Posairs. Unlike the tall, dark-skinned Gheethong, who had slits on the sides of their necks for breathing and wide, spatula-like hands, or the giant, hairy Hap'thez. Rolstrun discovered most of the slaves brought with the invaders were friendly and likable, except for the dreaded Kaigor.

The short, squat, brutish creatures made up for their short stature with their meanness. He'd seen one beat a Gheethong to death for some perceived slight. Everyone gave the nasty Kaigor a wide berth whenever possible. The invaders encouraged their aggressive behavior so they could feed from the terror and pain the Kaigor caused. Before they'd climbed down into the crater, a Kaigor had forgotten itself and slammed a fist into a guard. Within moments, soldiers had bound the slave, and Commander Ke-ke-tak had slurped up the Kaigor's mind and blood.

No one was safe from the invader's hunger. Rolstrun said a prayer of thanksgiving. So far, the invaders hadn't eaten any of his people. Although it seemed longer, he'd only lived in this hellhole for nearly a chedan. Hope still burned in his heart that his people would rescue them. It took several chedans to travel from the northern mountains to Shandir's crater in the southernmost part of Lairheim. He could wait. If he kept his head down and didn't draw the commander's attention, he might still be alive when rescue arrived.

Twilight sunk the crater with gloom when the horn announcing the end of their shift blared. Rolstrun gratefully put down his tools and tromped wearily to the water barrel. The invaders allowed the men one small cup of water before being herded up the ladders. Rolstrun stood in line, waiting for his turn. He yawned and stretched, leaning back, and stopped, stunned. He shook his head and gazed back up into the sky. The object appeared different from the invader's small ships. No metal glinted in the setting sun, nor did he hear the low rumble of machines. The speck reminded him of a bird, but for him to see it that high overhead, it'd have to be huge. It dropped lower, and now others were watching it.

"That isn't a bird," Bohandran said. "It's too big."

"I see paws and a tail." Wonder filled Rolstrun's voice. "It looks like... like the Gryphons I've seen pictures of on ruin walls."

"But they're supposed to be extinct," Calistrun protested.

The invaders noticed the creature, too, and several loud pops sounded as they fired their weapons. Flames covered the creature's body, but not before a projectile pierced it. It screeched, and the pain-filled sound reverberated on the crater walls, amplifying it. It flapped its wings and quickly flew away, directly into the setting sun.

The invaders cheered.

Rolstrun's heart soared with hope as the creature disappeared. "Do you think it saw us? If a Gryphon is flying here, maybe it means someone knows we're trapped here. All the stories say they were our allies during the Great War."

"It doesn't mean they are now," Bohandran grumbled. "Until we know for sure, we can't assume it was a Gryphon, or that help is on the way. We have to plan our own escape." He turned and climbed the rope ladder.

The invaders were rushing around the camp when Rolstrun poked his head over the edge of the crater. Incandescent lights on tall stands lit the compound, pushing the growing dark into submission. The commander, his gold-edged black robe flaring behind him, strode to a waiting ship and shouted orders.

Rolstrun prayed the Gryphon—if that had been one of the legendary creatures—reached cover before the invaders could find it. The hatch clanged shut, and the ship lumbered into the sky, awkward and graceless compared to the Gryphon. Extra guards watched the skies from the perimeter, lights sweeping the darkness overhead.

Chapter 6

Kaieli - 48 de Sandar, 1075

A blaring horn shattered Kaieli's sleep. When they'd arrived late last night, the invaders had herded them into a large cage. Against all logic, the slave pen gave her a sense of security, and combined with the physical and emotional exhaustion of the past few days, she'd slept deeply. She stood, shook the ever-present black sand from her clothes and hair, and yawned. Fingers of early morning light crept into the cage. Movement near the gate caught her attention.

"There are other Posairs here!" someone shouted.

Kaieli rushed forward to stand next to the metal mesh.

Haggard men tromped by, black dust coating their downcast faces, making it difficult to clearly see their features. A few stole glances at them. Their eyes widened and mouths dropped open in surprise when Treana swaved at them. The first man in line stopped in his tracks, halting the men behind him.

"There's a child!" The large man's red eyes blazed in anger. "Those bastards, what do they want with children?"

"Or old people," another man said. He shook his head. "We know what they want with them, Bohandran. Food."

The man's voice sounded familiar. Kaieli extended her senses. "Rolstrun! Rolstrun, what are you doing here?"

"Kaieli?" Rolstrun hurried to the fence and pushed his fingers through the mesh, grasping her hand.

The other men crowded around him, astonishment on their faces. Kaieli let out a small cry at the sight of so many men from Strunland Keep.

"It is you," he sighed. "How did you get here? Is anyone else from Strunland Keep with you?"

She shook her head. "No. It's just me. I was at Posanreande Keep when the invaders attacked it."

"Why—" Rolstrun interrupted.

"No time, Rolstrun." A man with pale yellow eyes touched him on the shoulder. "The second horn will blow any milcron now. We can find out more tonight."

"But she's from my clan, Nederposan."

"And they are from mine." He motioned to the others in the cage. "I don't want them to get hurt because of us."

"He's right, Rolstrun," Calistrun said. "If the invaders know they are our kin, we won't be punished if we're late. They will."

Rolstrun's shoulders slumped. He reluctantly pulled his fingers back from the fence. "Tonight, we'll talk."

The men hurried away from the pens, and a moment later, the horn blared again.

The captives took turns using the latrine trench dug in the back corner of the cage. Greens in the group covered the mess with a thin layer of dirt to mitigate the smell. Those who still had travel bars shared them until everyone had something to eat. The few remaining elders tried to demur, but Kothera made them eat. A small water barrel provided only enough water for them to have a gulp or two. Kaieli grimaced at the dust coating her throat. The small amount of water didn't slake her thirst. Mothers used the dredges to wash their babies and children. Kaieli longed for a bath. After nearly a chedan, she— and everyone else—stank.

Three-quarters of an octar after the second horn, another one broke the silence with a series of three short bleeps. As the last bleep faded away, an invader stepped into view, a ring of keys rattling in his hand. Behind him stood Tre'nok and another of his race who had dark blue skin, dark blue hair, and pale yellow eyes.

Kothera and Kederposan faced the gate. Kaieli stood a few steps behind them.

Tre'nok smiled at Kaieli and nodded in greeting to the alphas. "Momentarily, the Scourge will officially process you as slaves and assign you work duties. Ladies, make note of the horn you just heard. When it sounds, your work shifts begin and end. Gentlemen, your duties start with the first horn. Do not be late. Punishment is swift and painful, and as you've learned on the march, it doesn't necessarily land on the guilty person. My companion, Vy'shol, and I will guide you through the process as much as possible."

Kaieli studied the dark blue person while Tre'nok talked to the invader. Like Tre'nok, nothing about her indicated her gender, but she had a delicateness Tre'nok lacked. She lightly touched Vy'shol with her senses and smiled at the definite feminine energy.

The guard unlocked the gate, stepped back from the opening, and held his weapon ready. Several other invaders lined a path leading from their cage and out another gate into the main encampment. The enclosure holding the Posairs' slave pens stood lonely at the edge of the crater. Kaieli counted twenty cages, each capable of containing three hundred people. Besides their cage, only two others appeared occupied. Ahead of them was an enormous building with several smokestacks poking into the sky. The invader's ship dominated the bustling compound. Kaieli stared as they passed a large, hairy alien carrying building supplies over its shoulder.

Tre'nok and Vy'shol led them to a beige tent. Several alien species, also dressed in orange coveralls, stood at various tables.

"These must be slave uniforms." Kaieli plucked the front of her coverall.

Tre'nok nodded.

"You're a slave too. Why are your coveralls gray?"

"To let the invaders know we are untouchable," Vy'shol said.

"Our value as translators is great," Tre'nok added. "It means none can kill us but Commander Ke-ke-tak. And even he must answer to the king if they kill one of us."

"Why?" Kaieli wondered if it might be a weakness they could exploit when the time came to fight these invaders.

"The Scourge do not speak any other language but their own. Will not? Cannot?" He shrugged.

"We can learn any language after hearing it once." Vy'shol sounded proud.

The Posanreande Keep people finished filing into the tent, and Tre'nok climbed onto the raised platform. "I must remind you that the masters do not tolerate resistance or escape attempts. Any deviation from acceptable behavior removes your value as a worker and makes you food. They will inject a tracker into your arm, which contains an explosive they can remotely activate. The Scourge have conquered many worlds. The different species you see are a small sample of the worlds that have fallen to the Scourge.

"Separate into two groups. Males to the left, females to the right." He paused, his eyes on Treana, and his voice softened. "Children stay with their mothers."

A few of the children had lost their mothers during the attack and march. Several mothers had already adopted a child to replace the ones they'd lost, or had embraced an orphaned child as their own.

Vy'shol led the women and children to a back section of the tent where they were stripped. They took away any personal possessions the Posairs still possessed, even the children's few toys. Kaieli gasped with indignation when a tall, black-skinned alien poked and prodded her in places no woman should be poked, except by her lover. When they examined her teeth, she felt like a horse being evaluated for age. After a quick spray with some sort of liquid with an antiseptic odor, a slave handed Kaieli a new set of slave-orange coveralls. At the next station, a small, delicate woman with fine blond hair and pale white skin motioned for Kaieli to put her arm in a device. The cold metal gave her goosebumps. A sharp jab followed. When she removed her arm, she detected a tiny object underneath her skin.

She moved away from the station to stand with the other women, who had completed the gauntlet. Frowning, Kaieli examined the bump on her arm with her fingers and her senses. *It must be the tracking device.* She glanced up when Vy'shol approached her.

"May I ask a question?" A puzzled expression pulled Vy'shol's thin eyebrows together.

Kaieli nodded, curious.

"Why do the women with shades of red hair have so many scars, and yet those who have other hair colors do not?"

Kaieli studied the translator, wondering if she was a spy for the invaders. She mentally shrugged, as the information was innocuous. "The Reds have fire magic and are fighters. The rest of us do not fight."

"Fighters? Women?"

"Yes, warriors. Our survival depends on them and the men battling the Malvers' monsters."

"What are these monsters?"

"You must not have seen the Malvers' monsters yet. It's only a matter of time before you do. The crater is a breeding ground for them, and this many warm-blooded people will attract them."

"The Scourge are cold-blooded," Vy'shol said thoughtfully. "Will the monsters avoid them?"

Kaieli shook her head. "The janacks are heat-seekers, but the brechas use smell to find their prey. And the invaders rival the monsters for stink."

Vy'shol snorted a laugh. "Yes, they do." She surveyed the room. The last people had received their tracking device and waited for what happened next in their conversion to slavery. "Thank you for being candid with me. I will try to protect the children. You must keep them from the Scourge's notice. They have no leniency for the weak."

"So we learned during the march. Thank you for the warning."

Vy'shol tilted her head and gave a small bow. "Follow me to where you will work and prove your usefulness to the Scourge as something more than food."

The women and children trooped from the tent and across the encampment. Gangs of aliens worked at different tasks. The young boy, Baerenposan, avidly stared at the aliens, some of them strange and frightening looking. His head whipped back and forth to take them all in. He bumped into the stout legs of one with tusks curving from its lower jaw and small eyes in its brutish face. Short, bristly hair covered its body. It snarled and swung a meaty fist at him. Baerenposan scuttled away quickly, avoiding the alien's blow. He quivered in anger, fur sprouting on his hands.

Kaieli rushed to him and grabbed his hand, hiding the fur. She sent calming energy through her hands to him. "No!" she whispered. "Don't shift, Baerenposan. They'll punish you." The brute roared and swung at them. Kaieli huddled in a ball around the boy, shaking with fear.

Kothera and Nelieh rushed between Kaieli and the creature. Flame arced from their hands to the creature, igniting the hair on its hands. It howled, waving its hands, causing the fire to creep up its arms. A circle cleared around him as he flapped his burning arms. A group of invaders swarmed the slave and surrounded him. Their thin tongues rapidly flicked in and out.

Kaieli remembered what Tre'nok had said about them feeding off emotions. The fear and pain of the creature was a banquet for them. She hurried to Kothera and touched her shoulder to get her attention. "You have to stop. His pain is feeding them."

Kothera gaped, horror streaking across her face. "Oh, sweet Goddess! You're right. Nelieh, stop. We have to stop." The fire immediately went out.

"Faliciden, help me," Kaieli called. Faliciden ran to her side, and linking hands, they smothered the creature with cool, soothing energy. Working quickly, they healed the worst of his burns to make them appear only superficial and like he'd overreacted more out of fear than pain.

"Hurry, while their attention is on the Kaigor," Vy'shol called, pointing to the building's entrance.

They didn't run. From long years fighting the Malvers' monsters, the Posairs knew running attracted predators, and the invaders were certainly predators. They walked quickly to the big building and slipped inside. Kaieli gagged on the fumes, which reeked like Malvers' monsters and malevolent magic.

"This is where we process the nucla." Vy'shol held up a chunk of black rock.

Waves of evil wafted off it, surrounding the women. Bile rose in Kaieli's throat, and she swallowed it back down.

Loshera pushed her way to the front, her white hair tangled and so covered with dust that it appeared black.

"That... that's what the invaders are after?" The white priestess pointed at the rock, her hand shaking.

Vy'shol nodded.

"May the Goddess protect us! We are doomed."

Rolstrun - 48 de Sandar, 1075

Rolstrun drove his pickax into the section of the pillar he toiled on. Chunks of rock clattered at his feet, and a cloud of black dust enveloped him. In the chedan he'd been in the crater, the men had carved another terrace into the pillar, fifty feet above ground level.

A commotion at the ladders broke his concentration. The men from Posanreande Keep were making their way down, their hair freshly shorn. They reached the bottom without any mishaps, and their overseer directed them to a nearby section of the pillar. Rolstrun turned back to his work. Their presence reminded him about seeing Kaieli. How had she managed to be captured with a Posanlair keep? The invaders had captured the entire keep, not simply the men or fighters. He remembered the glimpse he'd had of a little girl. What did the invaders want with the little ones? Why would they bring them here?

The sound of Bohandran and Nederposan's pickaxes swinging in a syncopated rhythm brought him back to the present.

"We can't try to escape now," Nederposan said. "The risk of the invaders harming the children is too great."

"We must," Bohandran disagreed. "Now more than ever because of the children. We don't want them here any longer than necessary."

"I swear if they eat a child, I'll tear them apart and no weapon of theirs will stop me."

"You won't be alone," Rolstrun said. He had become close friends with the alphas during their captivity. "I can't believe they captured a whole keep!"

"I can," Bohandran said. "They didn't have any trouble with the fortress. And we were all hardened warriors. A small keep like Posanreande would only have a small fighting force."

An older Posanreande man ambled past, pushing a cart piled high with black rocks. He paused and looked around. The guards weren't paying attention to them. "Illness decimated our fighters before they attacked us. Otherwise, we'd have killed more of them. I'm Kederposan, the keep alpha." He held out his hand, and the men clasped wrists quickly in a warrior's greeting.

Kederposan's light green eyes snapped with satisfaction. "I think they've learned their lesson. On the march, they tried eating a sick infant who died. We rioted."

"And yet, you are still captives," Bohandran observed.

Kederposan narrowed his eyes and leaned forward. "We did our best," he snarled. "Their weapons are superior. And they threatened to kill the women and children if we didn't back down."

"Then we learn from this and make sure our women and children are safe before we do anything." Rolstrun glanced sideways at a guard. "We need to stop talking."

The exhausted men shuffled toward the cages where the women, already done with their work, waited inside the Posairs' slave enclosure. Inside the central cage, crude trestle tables and benches made from a hard material with a pebbly surface served as their mess hall. Women with green Talent tended the several huge pots bubbling over an artificial fire. The watery soup held few vegetables and little meat. A nearby table held travel bars purloined from the fortress's and keep's stores. Without them, they'd be starving worse than they were. The travel bars provided their morning and midday meals.

A glad cry called Rolstrun's name, and Kaieli hurried toward him. A swish of black marred her right cheek. As he hugged her tightly, his heart lightened with hope. Laean tried to hide it, but she hadn't fully recovered from the injuries she'd received when they'd been captured. She might get well now that Kaieli was here. He squeezed his left arm above the elbow where the thick scar reminded him he still had the use of it because of her.

"Have you treated Laean yet?" Rolstrun asked as they broke apart. "I'm worried about her."

Kaieli nodded and placed her hand on his forearm. "She'll be okay. The blow to her head caused internal bleeding. It took Faelyn, Faliciden, and me to stop the bleeding and make repairs. If it weren't for this awful black sand filled with malevolent magic, Faelyn could have easily healed her. It interferes with our magic."

They joined the food line and took their bowls to the table occupied by the other Strunland fighters. Laean smiled at him as he sat. Her color was still off, but she looked better than she had in days.

"How did you end up captured, Kaieli?" Maheli asked, pushing her empty bowl aside.

"I went to Posanreande Keep to help them with a nasty plague. It affected the Reds more than the others and resisted our healing magic, almost as if someone designed it to leave the keep unprotected."

"You don't think these invaders caused it, do you?"

"No, it started before they arrived. I suspect the Malvers' monsters are the carriers. We'd just found the way to cure it when the invaders arrived." Kaieli stared into space as she told them about the fall of Posanreande Keep and the march to the crater. Horror filled her voice as she relived the atrocities inflicted by the invaders.

"The invaders have us mining the crater." Bohandran leaned forward, his elbows on the table. "Does anyone know why?"

"For some reason, the translator Tre'nok is friendly with me," Kaieli said. "I'll ask him. White Priestess Loshera was pretty shaken when she saw the mineral. She couldn't touch it. It made her ill. I didn't work the processing line much today— there were too many injured to attend—but the little I did, I found it difficult to touch. It makes my skin crawl, and my soul shudder."

An irritating buzzing alarm interrupted them.

The other joined Rolstrun in glaring at the speakers.

People pushed back from tables and walked to their sleeping pallets. Kaieli gave him a questioning glance.

"Lights out warning." Rolstrun stood and escorted Kaieli toward her cage. "In a quarter octar, the guards will come and lock the cages. Anyone caught outside will be beaten, or worse."

He slipped into his cage milcrons before the gate slammed shut. As he held Laean close, he said a prayer of thanksgiving for the three healers who had helped her.

Rizelya - 48 de Sandar, 1075

Early in the morning, Rizelya climbed back on Glork and the Gryphons leaped into the sky, and followed the clearly marked trail made by the marching Posairs. After the night's rest, Baekeek could fly, although not far or fast. Only one place existed in the Barrens for the invaders to take the people from the keep: the crater. Rizelya's team, designed for scouting and quick movement, was too small to fight the invaders and rescue the people taken. Especially since the invaders possessed weapons able to injure a Gryphon in flight. Instead, they backtracked along the trail toward the keep, hoping to find any survivors and to learn more about the intruders.

A measure from the Barrens, a body sprawled on the ground. Rizelya's stomach plummeted when they landed to check it. Blazel carefully turned the dry and desiccated corpse over. Rizelya's hand flew over her mouth at the terror frozen on the young man's face. On closer examination, they discovered a strange wound puncturing his chest, and no blood remained in the body. Using her helbraught, Rizelya burned the corpse.

Bodies littered the trail to Posanreande Keep. After checking the first few, and finding they all possessed the same wounds, they didn't disturb the bodies they came across. However, Rizelya insisted on burning each one they found to allow their souls to return to the Mother.

When they arrived at the keep, scorch marks blackened the gates, which hung lopsidedly on their hinges. Rizelya scrambled off Glork's back, with Blazel following her a moment later.

A strange quiet blanketed the keep. No children ran in the streets. No women bustled around houses or in the fields. No men guarded the gates. Blazel shifted to his warrior form, lifted his muzzle, and choked. The stink of death stung Rizelya's nostrils and made her gag. They stalked inside. Half a dozen men sprawled on the cobblestones. Multiple holes punctured their bodies, but when Blazel turned them over, they lacked the strange wounds on their chests and necks.

Blazel stooped and checked a dark splotch on the ground. He inhaled deeply and shook his head. *Something died here, but I can't tell what it was. The only thing I can smell is death.* He stood, rubbing the stench from his nose.

They continued into the keep. Behind them, Graak motioned to the Gryphons, who spread out to investigate the buildings. Clearly, no danger remained, and Blazel shifted back to his natural form.

Rizelya and Blazel jogged to the Clan-house to search for the Keep Alphas. Inside, a Red sprawled in the foyer, her helbraught still gripped in her hands. Purple stains covered a man's hands. The signs of struggle indicated the invaders had snatched people from their beds.

They checked the other houses. Broken furniture showed the Posairs had fought before succumbing to the attacker's greater force. But thankfully, they didn't find any more dead. Their luck changed when they reached the infirmary. Rizelya gagged at the discovery of the corpses of two fighters and an old man, still in their sickbeds, with similar gaping holes in their chests.

"These invaders are inhuman, to kill the sick and injured." Rizelya choked back her tears. They hadn't uncovered any murdered children—the only good thing in this catastrophe.

Shaken, she and Blazel trudged to the stables, hoping they wouldn't discover the same situation as they had at the fortresses. She sighed in relief at the lack of bodies. Blazel paced through the barn to the pasture and stopped at the gate.

"They're here. How could they do such a thing?" He covered his face in his hands, and his shoulders shook.

Rizelya didn't want to see what caused Blazel to break down, but her feet carried her to stand next to him. A horse lay dead, drained of blood, just like the Posairs they found on the trail. The lumps of more carcasses littered the pasture.

"Why would they kill the horses?" Tears streamed down her face.

Blazel shrugged and wiped at his eyes. "To keep our people from escaping?"

Rizelya and Blazel left the stables and regrouped with the Gryphons in the main courtyard.

"Did you find anything?" Blazel asked.

Only death, Graak said, his eyes bleak. *They killed all the livestock.*

"I didn't see any bodies of the invaders," Rizelya said. "Surely, our people would have killed some of them."

"I found signs in the courtyard where something died," Blazel said. "It appears they took any of their wounded or dead. Too bad they did. It'd be helpful to study our enemies."

Have you seen enough? Graak grimaced. *This place makes me feel ill. Can we return to the Sanctuary?*

Rizelya surveyed the keep. Deep sorrow welled up in her heart for those who had died. Rage burned under her skin at the invaders who had taken her people. She gestured sharply at the carnage. "This proves they aren't here for peaceful purposes. The Supreme must know what we've discovered, and so must everyone else. I swear they will pay for this."

"Yes, they will." Blazel put his hand on her shoulder. "They will pay for every death they cause."

Rizelya could perform one service for the Keep's dead by burning their bodies to allow their souls to return to the Mother's Womb. She directed Blazel and the Gryphons to gather the dead. It was late afternoon by the time she fired the pyres. Sadness gripped her. She didn't know any of the deceased, and therefore, couldn't enact the traditional ritual of reciting the names of the dead to the Goddess as they burned.

We must go. Graak laid a gentle talon on her shoulder. *Moraak and the Supreme need our information as soon as possible.*

Rizelya turned from the pyre, rubbing her face to dash away her tears. She was a warrior and had seen death before. But these people hadn't deserved to be murdered like this. And these were only the first to die because of the invaders. She shuddered at the thought.

Blazel - 48 de Sandar, 1075

Rage filled Blazel at the evidence of the alien invader's ill-intent. They'd killed the old and those too injured to travel on foot. Thankfully, they hadn't discovered any bodies of babies or children. But his heart grieved for the livestock. What kind of monster could do this?

Numbly, Blazel climbed on Graak's back and buckled into the saddle. "Fly low, would you, Graak? Maybe someone escaped."

With the amount of carnage here, I doubt it, Graak rumbled as he leaped into the air. *I'll skim over the land for a few measures. If we haven't discovered anyone, we'll need to fly with the wind to inform Prince Moraak and the Supreme.*

Graak, Glork, and the other Gryphons separated, so they could search a greater area. Blazel kept his eyes on the ground and noticed Rizelya did the same. They'd flown several measures, and Blazel was losing hope of finding anyone.

"Glork! Glork, go down," Rizelya yelled, pointing. "There's someone running. Well, stumbling."

I see them. Glork dove.

Graak turned on a wingtip, jerking Blazel against the straps. Glork landed softly in front of the runner, who moved as if they were terrified beyond their endurance. Rizelya dropped off Glork before he crouched for her. Her feet thudded, kicking puffs of dust into the air, and she grunted. The person screamed and cowered on the ground, arms over their head.

By the time Graak landed and Blazel unbuckled his harness, Rizelya crouched, holding a young girl in her arms. Rizelya's water skin lay abandoned beside her, in a small puddle of water.

"They're dead, all dead!" the little girl wailed.

"No, they're not," Rizelya assured the girl in a calm tone. "We saw the tracks of marching people, so some of your clan has survived."

"It's true." Blazel hunkered on heels to be less imposing. "Can you tell us what happened?"

"Can you save them?"

Rizelya shook her head. "We don't have enough people with us. What's your name, little one?"

"I'm Dreana de Posanreande. I woke up, wanted a drink of water, and went into the kitchens. A loud noise shook the Keep. Lights flared and beamed from the sky. It scared me, and I hid in the pantry. A big sack of flour hid me good. I heard screaming, and I stayed where I was. After a long time, the screaming stopped, and the lights flew away. I waited and waited for the pack to find me, but they never came. When I crawled out, there were bodies everywhere, and I ran and ran. And then you found me."

"How long ago was the attack?" Blazel asked.

"Four, maybe five days ago, I think. I lost track of how long I hid."

Blazel stood, staring south toward the Barrens and the crater and digging his toe into the dirt. "Her clan will be at the crater by now. We need help to rescue them."

"They aren't the only ones." Rizelya rose to her feet, still holding Dreana in her arms. "The guard-packs are missing too."

Let us fly! Graak snapped his beak.

Dreana cringed and held tighter to Rizelya.

"This is Graak," Rizelya said.

"He's big..." Dreana's eyes widened, and her mouth dropped open.

"Yes, he is. We aren't riding on him. We'll ride on my friend, Glork."

Glork stepped forward and bowed to them. *I am honored to carry one so brave.*

"But I wasn't brave. I hid."

You were brave to hide and survive, so you could tell us what happened. You are but a little girl and did the best you could do. Glork reached out and ran a gentle knuckle over

Dreana's cheek. *There is no shame in surviving, little one. Come, I will take you away from here to where you'll be safe.*

Tears slipped down the girl's face. "Will you rescue my clanpack?"

Glork nodded solemnly and placed a talon on his chest. *We will do our best to bring them home.* He crouched, and Rizelya settled Dreana on his back in front of her, then looped the straps around them both.

As they flew north, Graak angled their flight path toward the Storengher River. When the moonlight shivered off the river's silvery water, Graak descended, landing near the riverbank. Blazel hurried to help loosen the straps on Rizelya's harness and lift Dreana off Glork's back.

"How did you like your first flight, Little One?" he asked.

"It was okay, I guess. I fell asleep." Dreana stretched, then grimaced, rubbing her belly. "What's for dinner? I'm starving."

Blazel pulled a trail bar from his pack and gave it to her. "Here, this will hold you over until we fix dinner. We're having fish." He pointed to the Gryphons in the river and raised his voice. "That is, if they share."

Glork grumbled, but a few moments later, plopped a big trout at Blazel's feet.

"Do you want to help me?" Blazel hadn't spent much time around children, but he knew what it was like to be alone.

Dreana nodded. She'd already devoured the trail bar.

Together, they dug a fire pit and gathered rocks for it. Blazel discovered some wild carrots and onions by the river and added them to their dinner. Rizelya found driftwood for their fire, and soon, the scent of roasting fish and vegetables made Blazel's stomach rumble.

Graak padded to their fire and perched next to Blazel. His tail wrapped around his feet. *We shall sleep for a few hours and then fly again.*

"What about Baekeek?" Rizelya asked. "He just arrived. He won't be able to keep up with you."

No, he cannot. Only Glork and I will take you the Sanctuary. The others will follow at a pace suitable for our injured scout. Get what rest you may. He rejoined the other Gryphons.

In too short of a time, Graak prodded Blazel and Rizelya awake. Rizelya groggily put the riding harness on Glork and fastened it. Once she'd settled on Glork's back, Blazel handed her the sleeping child. The two Gryphons were larger than the other scouts, and each beat of their wings took them farther. Without the smaller Gryphons to slow them, they raced through the rest of the night.

In the morning, they stopped a few octars after passing Strunland Keep. Dreana talked Blazel into letting her ride with him. She chatted to him, telling him about Kaieli and how she'd saved not only her little sister, but the whole keep from the plague. Finally, Dreana dropped back to sleep. Blazel worried about the strange illness, especially that people became sick after fighting the Malvers' monsters. Was the Malvers woman who haunted Rizelya's dreams—and his, although he hadn't told anyone about them—responsible?

Soon, the landscape below him changed into the familiar mountains and forests of the White Mountains. In another octar, they reached Blazel's home, the Sanctuary.

He lifted Dreana from Graak's back and carried her toward the Supreme's audience chamber. Whatever the Supreme and Prince Moraak decided, Blazel was determined to fight the invaders and stop their atrocities. He knew the Supreme well enough, after having grown up around her, to know she wouldn't sit back and allow the invaders free rein. Blazel shifted Dreana in his arms and she snuggled deeper into his shoulder.

"You're safe now, little one," he told her. "The Supreme will make sure you are."

No matter what happened next, they'd protect the children— the hope of their future.

Chapter 7

Rizelya - 49 de Sandar, 1075

Two red-robed, veiled women holding helbraughts stood guard on either side of the huge black ironwood double doors leading into the Supreme's audience chamber. Painted on the door were the symbols of the seven Talents. Beginning at the top with the Whites, the symbols circled around to the Grays, Reds, Yellows, Greens, Blues, and Browns. The black background was the symbol for the eighth Talent, Black, someone who wielded all seven of the magics. Although no one held that Talent any more. The lintel above the door depicted the cycle of the three moons—Kelar, Zelar, and Chelar. Nodding in acknowledgment to Rizelya's team, the guards opened the doors.

Inside, white sheadash and marble formed the floors and walls, white curtains hung on the windows, and tall candleholders held white pillar candles. Along the sides stood numerous priestesses in their white robes, all with white hair, except a few with gray hair, indicating their Gray Talent. Someone must have seen or sensed Rizelya's team arriving and spread the word for so many people to be in the audience chamber.

The audience chamber, which could fit several hundred people, felt small with the Gryphon prince, Moraak, and his entourage in it. The sunlight glinted off Moraak's dark gold collar, which contrasted with his lighter gold feathers and tawny lion's body. He cocked his head at the newcomers, reminding Rizelya of an eagle. Sitting on his hindquarters, he towered over everyone, except his two bodyguards from the huge black-winged, black-furred Thunder Wings.

Sheekeek, a much smaller Gryphon with silver-gray feathers, a gray feline body, and a silver beak, sat next to her friend Chariel.

The walk through the audience chamber to the dais seemed to stretch before Rizelya. She stumbled, but caught her balance with a hand on Glork's shoulder. The Gryphon touched her hand with his beak. He folded his wings close to his creamy tan and brown feline body. His light brown and white feathers drooped. He looked even more exhausted than she felt from the grueling flight to the Barrens and back to the Sanctuary. He'd done all the flying, while she had only ridden on his back.

Blazel pushed his dark auburn, tangled hair behind his shoulder. The streak of gray hair framing his face was unusual for a male. The long scar across his right cheekbone stood in stark relief on his tired face. Dreana, the little girl they had found outside of Posanreande Keep, snuggled into his shoulder. She seemed to feel safe with him after her ordeal, surviving the capture of her keep.

A throne carved from one massive piece of clear crystal occupied the dais. It dwarfed the ancient woman sitting in it. The Supreme's dazzling white silk gown covered her feet. She wore a white veil over her snow-white hair. Intelligence gleamed in her white eyes. The symbol of her office, an eight-pointed star, hung on her chest. The large diamond in the star's center caught the light in the room and tossed it at Rizelya. She blinked away the dazzle and bowed in obeisance.

"Rise, rise," the Supreme said, motioning impatiently with her fingers. "What have you found out?" Then she saw the little girl and her voice softened. "Who is this child?"

Blazel stepped forward. "This is Dreana de Posanreande. She is the only one who escaped the invader's attack on her keep. They took those they didn't kill in the fight into the Barrens."

Rizelya shuddered. "The guard-packs are not in their fortresses, which means the Malvers' monsters range unchecked in the Barrens."

We discovered the invaders established a stronghold at the crater, Graak added, his mental voice reaching everyone in the room. While the Gryphons' spoken language consisted of clicks, screeches, and hisses, they could mind-speak with anyone, and in the Posarian language. *My scout only managed a quick glimpse before they attacked him. The missing guards are prisoners, or so we assume, as many Posair men worked in the crater. He couldn't tell if any of them were from the keep. I am sorry, he didn't see any women or children.*

The Supreme's face tightened in anger, and her fingers drummed a staccato on the arm of her throne. Her rings chimed against the crystal. "We can only pray they have survived. It is clear the invaders are not peaceful. We must protect our people and our land. We should drive them from our home. But," she nodded toward Leistral and Eidstrun, "word has reached me the Malvers' monsters are as bad, or worse, than when you first arrived here, Rizelya. Whom do we fight?"

Even though it seemed a rhetorical question, Rizelya answered. "We must fight both if we are to survive."

The Supreme sighed, sadness darkening her eyes. "So many will be killed."

"It will be worse if we don't fight," Blazel said.

Chariel's face paled and her eyes clouded over as visions of prophecy assailed her. "They will kill and kill until nothing is left if we don't fight."

Moraak clicked his beak. *We will join you.* His deep mind-voice reverberated in Rizelya's head. *After hearing this, it confirms the madness our mystics warned us about has arrived. But I can only lead the three hundred I brought with me into the war. My father, King Zorlaak, will not send more unless the invaders directly threaten our homes.*

"Then we must pray they are enough." The Supreme stood, the rings on her hands sending sparks of light throughout the room. Her ancient voice filled the room, augmented by magic. "Send word to every province and clan. We are at war. With the attack on Posanreande Keep and the guard-packs at Shandir's Crater, the invaders have already declared war. We must stop them and send them back to where they came from, or destroy them. All who can fight will be called to the Warrior's service."

War! The word reverberated through Rizelya's mind. The last war had nearly decimated the Posairs. What would a fight with aliens do?

Blazel - 49 de Sandar, 1075

Pandemonium rocked the audience chamber at the Supreme's declaration. War!

Blazel had mixed feelings. For over a thousand years, the Posairs fought against the Malvers' monsters, but somehow, this war seemed different. Even with the nests maturing completely out of the previously established patterns, and with the new control-janack, they knew how to fight the monsters and win. These invaders weren't mindless, hunger-incarnated beasts like the monsters. Their use of machines and weapons proved they were an intelligent species. He recalled the destruction at Posanreande Keep and the murdered people and shuddered at the terror on the people's faces, even in death.

The little girl in his arms trembled. A war council wasn't a place for her. Dreana had suffered enough. His mother stood among the group of priestesses. She could take the child to some place quieter. *Mother,* he called.

She smiled at him, lines crinkling around her gray eyes and mouth, and motioned with her head to the side of the vast chamber. She was a kind, gentle soul, and as a priestess who lived closely with the Goddess, was calm and serene. Except when she had to deal with an unruly, active son. A rueful smile lifted the corner of Blazel's mouth as he moved through the crowd. As the only male raised in the Sanctuary, his mother and the other priestesses hadn't always known know how to handle him.

Once more, he thanked the Goddess for Histrun, who had seen the needs of the young boy. After the tragic death of his bond-mate, Zehala, Histrun stayed in the Sanctuary for an entire winter and started Blazel's warrior training. For many years, Histrun would return for several chedans to teach Blazel how to be a Posair male. Blazel's only regret when he'd left the Sanctuary when he was seventeen was not being able to say goodbye to Histrun. He'd only learned in the past lunadar that he'd had a place in Histrun's pack all along.

He glanced at Rizelya. Funny how life circled around. The love of his life was the daughter of the man who had had a large part in raising him. From their discussions, Blazel was closer to Histrun than Rizelya.

"Ah, who is this little one?" his mother asked.

"This is Dreana." The little girl clung to his neck and peeked over his shoulder at his mother. Blazel shifted into mind-speech, something he'd never done with his mother before. *She shouldn't be around all this talk of war. She saw her entire keep destroyed.* He held his breath until she responded, also in mind-speech. He'd learned so many new skills since meeting Rizelya.

I'll take care of her. His mother smiled at the girl. "Bright Blessings, Dreana. I'm Priestess Blenora. You've come a long way. You were very brave to ride a Gryphon. I'm not sure I could be so brave." She gave a mock shudder.

"You don't have to be afraid. Glork and Graak are nice."

"Why don't you go with Priestess Blenora?" Blazel suggested. "She will get you some food, and I think there are other little girls here you can play with."

"I want to stay with you," Dreana wailed and clung tighter to him.

"Blenora is my mother. She'll take good care of you. She did me." He grinned at his mother. "I'll come visit you later, Dreana."

"You promise?"

Blazel nodded. "I promise." He set the girl down.

Dreana looked at Blenora's outstretched hand for a moment before she took it. "I guess it's okay, since she's a priestess and your mother."

"You couldn't be in better care." Blazel tousled her hair and kissed his mother on the cheek.

He watched the pair walk out of the audience chamber, turning away only when Rizelya touched his shoulder. Her pinched face and the dark circles under her rich brown eyes showed her exhaustion. They'd only had one brief rest since finding the devastation at Posanreande Keep. Wisps of red hair escaped her braid, and dirt smudged her red leathers. Lean muscle from years of fighting packed her petite frame.

"You were thoughtful. Dreana will be better off with your mother taking care of her than us. We'll be heading to war soon. The Supreme said we should go get some rest. We've done enough for now."

"Good. I'm about to drop. Where are Glork and Graak?" He turned, scanning the room. The Supreme, Moraak, and Sheekeek were deep in discussions. But none of the other Gryphons were in the chamber.

"They returned to the Gryphon's area to rest."

Leistral and Eidstrun approached them, and Rizelya gave them a hug. Outside the audience chamber, their pack mates, Aistrun, Wisah, and Chariel, met them.

Aistrun openly held Chariel's hand. Her charcoal-gray eyes and hair set her apart from even the White Priestesses. Her position as a Gray Priestess forbade her from taking a lover, but when she met Aistrun, she rebelled.

"Where's Jaehaas?" Blazel's forehead furrowed. "He hasn't taken a turn for the worse, has he?" A sabertiger had badly injured Jaehaas during an attack on their way back to the Sanctuary from Alkaak, the Gryphon city.

"No, no, he's fine," Wisah assured them. "He's still a bit stiff and sore. He's waiting for us at the guesthouse." During the journey, the White Priestess and Jaehaas became close, as close as a human and centaur could be.

Wisah and Chariel defied the Supreme and continued to stay with the team in the guesthouse rather than return to the priestess dormitory. The Supreme was allowing it—for now.

They took a side door out of the temple and crossed the grounds to a wall separating the temple proper from the guest areas. The group passed through the gate and walked down a cobblestone road to the first pack-house in the row. The wide porch had several tables and chairs strewn about for guests to gather outside.

Jaehaas leaned a shoulder against the door frame. His rich chestnut-brown hair matched his horse half, which had dark blue-gray stripes the same color as his eyes. He hadn't been born a centaur. As a man of the Haaslair horse clans, he had made the irrevocable choice to shift into a centaur. Only a few men went to that extreme.

"Welcome back," Jaehaas said. "I heard the reconnaissance did not go well. You both look beat."

"No, nothing good came of it." Blazel stepped onto the porch. "The Supreme just called for war against the invaders. They have machines and weapons I'm not sure we can match."

"Ah, but we have magic." Jaehaas smiled at Wisah and held out his arms.

She snuggled into his embrace. "And the Goddess is on our side. She will help us."

"We aren't helpless," Aistrun added. "Don't forget our warrior form."

"It didn't seem to help the men of Posanreande Keep." Rizelya sighed, then rubbed her face. "I need to wash this Barrens dust off me. We'll share with you what we found after we clean up. And," she patted Leistral's shoulder, "you two can tell us why you're here."

Blazel followed Rizelya into the house and down the stairs to the bathing room. He gave her a regretful smile when he saw they were alone. "If I wasn't so tired, I'd take advantage of our solitude and make love to you."

"If I wasn't exhausted, I'd let you."

They quickly washed and skipped soaking in the hot tubs. In clean clothes, they trudged up the stairs to the main room where their friends waited. Someone had thoughtfully ordered food for him and Rizelya. He dug into the hot food, sighing with pleasure at eating something besides trail bars.

"How are the new members of our squad-pack doing?" Rizelya asked. When she was in Strunven Keep, Rizelya had added women with Talents other than Red to her fighting squad. Blazel had only witnessed the revolutionary idea in action once, but the group had been spectacularly effective.

"They're making the rest of us look bad." Leistral grinned. "They're that good. Clan Alpha Beladi is impressed with the new techniques we developed with the mixed pack. She's ordered several more to be formed. Strunlair Keep's population is large enough for plenty of people to volunteer to be in a mixed pack."

"It's a good thing, too," Eidstrun broke in. "The nests are forming faster than ever. The new normal seems to be nests with eight to ten janacks and forty to fifty brechas, and all of them have a damned control-janack. Although, a couple of days after the strange comet passed over, all monster activity stopped for five days. It resumed with even larger nests, which reform within a few days of being annihilated. It's a mystery why they can regenerate so quickly."

"Histrun thought the Supreme needed to know of this strange behavior," Leistral added. "If something the invaders did stopped the monsters, we need to discover what they did. Perhaps we can replicate it and get rid of them once and for all."

Blazel recalled the dead they'd found. Suddenly no longer hungry, he put his utensils down and pushed away his plate. "I don't think it's going to be that simple. The faces on the dead people we found were locked in terror. Strange wounds marked their chests, and something drained their bodies into dry husks. The aliens shot at a Gryphon over a hundred feet in the air and hit him. They came here from the-Warrior-knows-where in flying machines! How can we fight them?" He leaned his elbows on the table and rested his chin on his fists.

"We'll find a way," Rizelya said, rubbing his back.

"The madness can be stopped," Chariel added.

Blazel lifted his head. Her eyes and voice were normal. "That wasn't a prophecy. How can you be sure?"

"Because we are fulfilling the prophecy." She leaned forward, the intensity of belief burning in her eyes. "We took the quest to the Deep Mountains and brought the Gryphons back with us to fight this new enemy—and the old. The Goddess sent us to find our ancient allies for a reason. Remember, the prophecy said, 'A menace comes. No allies, the enemy wins and all die.' The menace is here, and we have allies. We can win against the invaders. The Goddess has given us the means to win."

None of Chariel's prophecies had never been wrong before. Blazel had to believe this one wouldn't be the first.

Rizelya - 50 de Sandar, 1075

Rizelya luxuriated in sleeping in a real bed with Blazel curled up beside her. With the coming war, this comfort wouldn't last long. They had both been so tired last night they'd fallen instantly asleep as soon as their bodies were horizontal. Morning light peeked through the curtains.

Blazel's arm hooked over her waist, and she snuggled into him. His hard manhood informed her he was waking up. She turned to face him, lightly kissing his cheek, then trailed kisses across his jaw and down his chest. His rumble of pleasure rewarded her efforts. His hands caressed her back, her face, and her breasts. Ecstasy rippled through her as they joined. Their lovemaking was gentle and sweet.

They lay together in the afterglow, her head nestled under his chin. "I'll miss this," Rizelya said. "There won't be much peace, or privacy, with this coming war."

"I will too. I'll have to get over my prudishness." Blazel kissed the top of her head. "There'll be more people around than the six of us. I was becoming comfortable with our little pack. Although, I doubt the Supreme will allow Chariel and Wisah to fight with us."

Rizelya lifted her head to look at him. "Why not? White Priestesses have fought before. After all, it took a White Priestess to end the Great War. It just might take a Gray Priestess to end this one. The Supreme seems open-minded. She hasn't forced them back into the dormitories."

"Only because of this new threat. She's been too worried about the invaders to concern herself with two defiant priestesses."

A soft knock sounded on the door. Blazel quickly pulled the covers over them as Leistral poked her head in. "Oh, good, you're awake. The Supreme wants to see all of us."

"Do we have time for breakfast?" Blazel asked.

Leistral shook her head. "We knew how tired you were, so we waited as long as we could. I asked the staff to make you a breakfast roll." She scurried in and placed two packets on the desk.

Rizelya and Blazel nibbled on their breakfast while throwing on clothes. One didn't make the Supreme wait for you.

Outside the temple, Graak and Sheekeek met the six questers on the tiled plaza.

"Where's Moraak?" Rizelya asked.

Already inside with the Supreme, Graak said with a flick of his tail. *Or I should say still with her. They stayed up plotting all night.*

Rizelya lifted her eyebrow in surprise when they entered the audience chamber empty of everyone except for the Supreme and Moraak. The Supreme slumped in her throne and her haggard, wan face showed her exhaustion. She was too old for this kind of stress. Rizelya hadn't heard any news of a new supreme being born. Rizelya shivered. It would devastate her people if the Supreme couldn't pass her knowledge and wisdom to her successor.

The Supreme waved away their obeisance. "There is much work to do, as you are the only ones here besides my priestesses and people. The Clan Alphas must be informed of what is happening, and they must choose a Supreme Alpha—"

"A what?" Blazel interrupted.

"A Supreme Alpha," the Supreme snapped. "In times of war, the clans choose an alpha pair to lead everyone. Of course, Zehana and Halistrun were the last. They devised the plan to draw out all the magic in the Malveranlair Province and turn it against the Malverans."

Rizelya blinked in confusion. She'd never heard of a Malveranlair Province or Malverans. She knew about Zehana and Halistrun, but she didn't pay much attention to history when surviving the present took all of her energy.

"Who were the Malverans?" Rizelya blurted. "And where was the Malveranlair Province?"

The Supreme sighed and rubbed her face. "You've already met one of them, Rizelya."

"The Malvers," she breathed, thinking about the gaunt women from her visions.

"Yes." The Supreme took a deep breath and folded her hands together. "It is time to tell their story. Once, before the Great War, there was a ninth clan, the Malveranlair Clan. The far southern peninsula was their province. They turned to practicing death magic and created beasts with only one purpose: to devour and destroy. Partnered with death magic is blood magic—the need to spill blood. Even a small amount of blood can make the magic more powerful. How much more powerful, then, is magic fueled by violent death?

"The Malvers made themselves royalty and believed their power gave them the right to turn the rest of the Posairs slaves. But that wasn't their worst crime." The Supreme stopped, gazing toward the window, swallowing and blinking her eyes. Her hands gripped the arms of her throne until her knuckles turned white. When she resumed her story, sadness and grief filled her voice, and she continued to gaze out the window.

"Their greatest, or lowest, act was to consume the dead rather than burning them to release the souls to return to the Mother's Womb. They believed they consumed the soul when they ate the body. Because of their atrocities and their greed, we fought them, even though by then they were nearly immortal." The Supreme turned back to her audience, light glimmering in her eyes. "However, the Goddess walked on our side, and we prevailed. By the end of the war, we decimated the Malvers, as they became known. Only their strongest magicians remained alive. We exiled them with the hope they would die in their banishment. But you, Rizelya, have brought us proof they have not."

Rizelya shuddered, remembering the malicious woman in her dreams. She gripped her arms across her abdomen, trying to ease the queasiness twisting her stomach.

The Supreme leaned forward and caught each person's eye. "I share this with you, so you know we have once fought a war against those considered more powerful than ourselves. We threw off the yoke of slavery. We, the Posairs, survived. And we will continue to survive. The Goddess has stood beside us before and She does so now. I've read the accounts of the Malvers and their atrocities, and believe me when I tell you, I doubt these invaders can do any worse. We won the war against the Malvers. We will win the war against these invaders and toss them off our planet!"

Our histories also speak of the heinous acts of the Malvers. Sheekeek rustled his feathers as if he shivered at some awful memory. *We cannot allow another such to gain a foothold on our world.*

I agree. Moraak cocked his head, his head feathers rising. He quickly settled them back into place. *It is why we are here. Madam, how may the Gryphons serve you?*

"I have already sent messengers to the clans with the call to war. My calling is not to lead my people to death. I lead them in life. There must be a Supreme Alpha pair to lead the war. They will become the leaders of the entire population with the authority to send people wherever they are needed and to requisition supplies. To do that, all the Clan Alphas must gather and elect a pair. And that will take time. Time we may not have."

We can fly faster than horses can run, Moraak said. *I will send my people to the Clan Alphas and carry them to your gathering place. As Sheekeek said, we cannot allow the invaders to become comfortable on our world.*

"Thank you." The Supreme inclined her head. "I agree this is urgent. Your people have been gone from our lands for a long time. I doubt the Clan Alphas will believe I sent you. But," she turned to stare at Wisah, "they would, however, listen to a White Priestess. Wisah, are you ready for another adventure?"

Wisah stepped forward and knelt before the Supreme. "Yes, Supreme. I will add my word about the danger the invaders present."

And I shall be your ride. Sheekeek stepped to her side. He rotated his head toward Moraak. *The prince must stay with the troops. I can add the testimony of a mystic. If we do not triumph over these invaders, nothing will be left of this world.*

"I'll go with you." Rizelya held up her hand.

"So will I," Blazel added.

"No, my children," the Supreme countermanded. "You have other work ahead of you. You will be pivotal to our victory. But, you two," she pointed to Leistral and Eidstrun, "may go. You can provide protection for my priestess."

Leistral and Eidstrun stood blinking with surprised looks on their faces.

"Yes... yes, Supreme," Leistral stuttered. She stared at Graak, who towered over her, with a touch of fear.

Moraak lifted a sharp talon. *I will assign a phalanx of Gryphons to accompany you. As you travel to each keep, they will convey the clan alphas back here, thus saving time.*

"Not here, Strunlair Keep. Wisah, come back in two octars, and I will have letters for you to give to the alphas." The Supreme stood, and without waiting for them to bow to her, tottered off the dais and disappeared through the door behind it.

Summarily dismissed, Rizelya's head spun. She inwardly fumed all the way back to the guesthouse. She hadn't seen Leistral and Eidstrun for nearly four chedans, and the rest of her pack in a lunadar. And now her pack was being split up—again! At first, she hadn't wanted to be a squad-alpha, but after all they'd gone through, they were her people, her friends, her responsibility. How could she ensure their safety when they weren't even around?

She and the other women gathered to help Wisah and Leistral pack for their sudden journey.

"I don't like this at all." Rizelya said, plopping down on a bed and scowling.

Wisah pulled the tunic Rizelya had wrung into a ball from her hands, shook it out, then tossed it to the side and put another tunic in her bag. "You don't have to like it. None of us do. But with the Supreme's explicit command, there isn't much we can do about it. Before our quest, I'd only traveled to Strunlair Province and the Sanctuary. Now I'll be flying the entire continent of Lairheim!" Wisah sunk onto the bed next to Rizelya. "I'm scared, Auntie."

Rizelya pulled her niece into a hug. She looked over at Leistral, who was stuffing her saddle bag with clothes. "How long have you and Eidstrun been here?"

"We arrived the afternoon you left for the Barrens." Leistral put another pair of socks into her pack. "Do you think we'll ever see home again? Histrun made it sound like we'd only be gone for a few chedans when I volunteered to go with you to find out about the control-janack. It's already been over a lunadar since we left Strunland Keep."

"You volunteered?"

Leistral nodded.

"Naila didn't order you to be in my squad-pack?"

"No, I asked to be part of your pack. I've always thought you'd be a good alpha, if you'd stop being stubborn about it." Leistral grinned. "I was right. You are good."

"Do you regret it? After everything we've been through?"

Leistral shook her head. "Even if we never see Strunland Keep again, I wouldn't give up this adventure with you. You've shown us women with other Talents are just as needed to fight the monsters as the Reds. My little sister wants to be a fighter, but since she is a Green, Naila won't let her. Now, she'll get her chance."

Rizelya sat up straighter. She'd been unaware how many women with Talents other than Red were interested in fighting until she'd met the women at Strunven Keep. Her unusual pack now consisted of members representing every Talent. She missed her squad-pack. "How were our girls when you left? Tell me what you have been up to."

Leistral pulled the chair from the desk and sat on it. "They were doing well. Saffren especially. She has a whole cadre of warriors at her beck and call."

Rizelya leaned back against the headboard, still holding Wisah, listening to and laughing at the stories of her pack. Soon, she'd be able to see them all again herself.

Chapter 8

Rizelya - 50 de Sandar, 1075

Half a flight of Gryphons gathered in the grassy practice area. Twenty of the huge, black Thunder Wings dwarfed the fifteen fast-flying owl and falcon type scouts. A mixture of the other gryphon-types made up the remaining fifty. Sheekeek was the lone Silverbeak. His silver and gray feathers stood out in the mix of black, brown, tan, and cream. Screeches and trills filled the air as the Gryphons talked among themselves.

Rizelya's eyes widened in surprise at the huge Gryphon towering over Sheekeek. He was longer and taller than Graak, although not quite as big as a Thunder Wing or Moraak. His head feathers were black and his black wings were white at the shoulders. When he twisted his head to gaze at her, she gulped and took a step back. The tuft of short black feathers sitting between his eyes and above his prominent hooked beak gave the big Gryphon a perpetual angry mien.

"Who... who are you?" Rizelya asked.

I am Sterkek. I'm the only one large enough to carry your pack-mate, Eidstrun. The Gryphon's gentle voice belied his angry appearance.

As if conjured, Eidstrun strode to them with a bag slung over his back. He eyed the riding harness dubiously. "Are you sure it's safe?"

"I'm sure." Rizelya put a hand on Sterkek's shoulder. "I rode to the Barrens and back on Glork and made it one piece."

Leistral bounced up to the group. "So, who am I riding?" Her eyes sparkled with excitement.

Me. A smaller Gryphon glided forward. The falcon-type Gryphon had light black head feathers, white feathers on his cheeks and neck, and his wings were black and white stripes. White and black striped fur covered his feline body.

I am Morru. Sterkek shouldn't have all the fun. I am honored to carry such a brave warrior. He dipped his head in greeting.

Leistral blushed. "It is I who am honored. Until a few days ago, I believed you were just a mythical creature."

Morru let out a trill and dropped his beak in the Gryphon way of laughing. *I like that. I think I shall remain a creature of myth and legend.*

Morru, you will have a hard time with that, Graak said as he joined them along with Blazel, Aistrun, and Chariel.

Moraak, a step behind them, gave the same trilling laugh. He twisted his head from side to side as he examined the group. At seven feet tall, he towered over everyone except the Thunder Wings.

We seem to be missing someone, Moraak observed. *Ah, there she is.*

Wisah came into view, her long, white hair bound in a twist of small braids. She wore white leathers and white ankle boots. The golden pendant of her office as priestess hung between her breasts, the sun catching the diamond in the center of the eight-pointed star. Rizelya's niece looked every bit a priestess and representative of the Goddess. No one would be able to mistake her for anything else. Her hand rested lightly on Jaehaas's withers. They both wore unhappy expressions.

At her approach, the noise quieted and every Gryphon—including Moraak—lowered into a crouch and bowed their heads.

In the silence, Sheekeek strode forward and bowed. *Priestess, we are greatly honored to be your escort. We are here to serve you, and through you, the Goddess.*

Moraak straightened. *You have my people in your hands, Priestess Wisah. Use them wisely and well. Bring them back to me.*

"I will do my best." Wisah regally dipped her head, appearing confident. She turned, gave Jaehaas a kiss, then approached Rizelya.

When Rizelya hugged her, she could feel Wisah's trembling. "You'll do well, niece," she whispered before stepping away. "Be safe. We'll meet you at Strunlair Keep." She had already instructed Leistral and Eidstrun to take care of Wisah, and they'd said their goodbyes before leaving the guesthouse.

Wisah nodded, gave a brave smile, and hugged Blazel, Aistrun, and Chariel. The two women shared a few quiet words before Wisah pulled away and turned to Sheekeek. Even as the shortest Gryphon at four-and-a-half feet tall, he had to crouch on his belly to allow Wisah to climb onto his back. Rizelya buckled Wisah into the harness while Blazel helped Eidstrun and Leistral into their harnesses.

Wisah raised her fist high in the air. The Gryphon contingent crouched in readiness. Her fist dropped, and fifty-one Gryphons bolted into the air, wingtip to wingtip. They gained altitude, disappearing over the horizon.

Rizelya watched them leave, a faint jealousy squirming in her heart. They'd reach Strunlair Keep by nightfall. She missed her squad-pack, and now, three more of its members flew away. Sadness washed over her. Blazel pulled her into his side.

"It won't be long before you join the rest of your squad-pack. We'll be right behind them."

"The Supreme has given us leave to go?" Hope filled her voice.

He shook his head. "But I expect her to soon."

My people will be ready to fly at dawn. Moraak sat back on his haunches. *I did not bring them away from their homes and families to hide in the Sanctuary. You need our strengths in this war.*

"We're leaving too," Rizelya announced. "Whether or not the Supreme gives us permission."

"What about me?" Chariel asked, her hands clasped in front of her so hard her knuckles were white.

"What about you? Of course you're coming with us. You're part of my pack now." Rizelya stepped away from Blazel's warmth. "We have packing to do. At least our horses received rest. I can't say the same for me."

Her group hurried back to the guest house.

Rizelya soon lamented letting Leistral leave before she organized their supply packs. Dragging Chariel with her, Rizelya went to the quartermaster to arrange supplies. As they finished their requisition, a young girl ran up to them informing them the Supreme requested their attendance.

Chariel led the way to a small side door, opening directly into the maze of corridors behind the temple sanctuary. A temple guard told them to go to the Supreme's private quarters rather than the audience chamber.

The Supreme sat behind a big desk, braziers burning on either side of her chair and making the room stifling hot. Papers were strewn across the desk, with another stack off to one side. A pot of taevo warmed on a side table, and a cup steamed at her elbow. The scratch of her quill, and the soft hiss of the braziers, broke the silence in the room, making a peaceful scene. Trepidation rippled through Rizelya. The Supreme hadn't looked up when the guard had knocked softly on the door and let them in.

Rizelya and Chariel stopped before the desk and made obeisance. After what seemed a long time, the Supreme finally allowed them to rise. She didn't offer them a seat.

"I hear you are preparing to leave," she said, pinning them with her gaze. "I did not give you permission. And I especially did not give you, Chariel, permission to leave the Sanctuary."

"Supreme," Rizelya said, holding the Supreme's gaze, "we can't stay here. We have fulfilled our quest to find our ancient allies, the Gryphons, and have brought them back. Our duty now is to fight the invaders."

"Your duty is what I tell you it is," the Supreme shot back. "But you are correct, Rizelya. Your duty lies in the fight. But you, Chariel, your duty is to stay here."

"No, Supreme." Chariel's jaw tightened, and she threw back her shoulders. "I must go with Rizelya. We have not fulfilled the full prophecy yet, only a small part of it. All of us, including me, are needed to win against these invaders. And you know it."

The Supreme slumped in her chair. "Yes, I do. But I fear for you, my child. Even here, where there are some with Gray Talent, people view you as different, strange. I would protect you, keep you safe. Here, with me."

"I know." Chariel rushed to the Supreme's side and knelt, her hands on the arm of the Supreme's chair. "I am not a child, Supreme. I am an adult woman, and as much as I'd like to stay here safe at your side, my duty is calling me into the world."

The Supreme gently stroked Chariel's hair, then bent and kissed the top of her head. Rizelya turned her head away to allow them privacy.

"You have grown strong, my child," the Supreme said, her voice shaky. "I am so proud of you. But this isn't the only reason I called you two here. Rizelya, I fear you will again have trouble with the Malvers woman once you leave the Sanctuary's protection."

Rizelya also worried about it. She'd been driven insensate by the woman's assaults on her mind during her journey to the Sanctuary. Because of them, her memory of the trip from Strunhelos to the Sanctuary was nothing but a blur of nightmare images of the Malvers' monsters killing people. She didn't know why she dreamed about the woman or heard the damned control-janack when no one else could.

"Chariel, you too may have problems, as you are so perceptive. And Blazel. I believe the Malvers can affect anyone with Gray Talent."

"But... but..." Rizelya sputtered. "I don't have Gray Talent."

"You're developing it. Have you looked in a mirror lately?" The Supreme motioned toward the front of Rizelya's hair. "I can see a thin streak of gray in your hair and sense it will grow bigger. Chariel, you have the strength to fight the Malvers' call and maintain the block I'm going to put on both of you. Watch carefully what I do. You will need to block Blazel's mind and strengthen the blocks as needed. I'm not going to completely dampen your abilities—that is too unwise—but only place a barrier in your minds to keep her from overtaking them. Rizelya, your connection can give us valuable information about our enemies. Pay attention to what you see in your dreams. I doubt she realizes how much she shows you, and I don't want her to. Tell Chariel everything you can remember whenever you have contact with the woman. Now, come here, child." The Supreme imperiously beckoned to her.

Rizelya reluctantly took Chariel's place, kneeling in front of the Supreme. She remembered the last time the Supreme had meddled with her mind. It had knocked her out, and she'd suffered from a headache for two days.

"This is not going to hurt," the Supreme assured her. She put her hands on either side of Rizelya's face.

Rizelya felt a trickle of warm energy seep into her mind, but nothing more. After what seemed a short time, the Supreme lifted her hands.

"There, done. See, it didn't hurt at all." The Supreme looked tired.

A glance at the timepiece on her desk told Rizelya more time had passed than she'd thought. The pain in her knees as she stood also attested to how long she'd knelt in front of the Supreme. It took less time for the Supreme to block Chariel's mind. Whatever she did seemed to take a lot of energy, because when she dropped her hands, her face was wan and circles of exhaustion darkened her eyes. Worried, Rizelya refilled the cup with fresh taevo and urged the Supreme to drink it. Once she revived, the Supreme blessed them before dismissing them.

Rizelya prayed whatever the Supreme had done would work. She didn't want the Malvers woman to take over her mind again. Rizelya would only know if it worked after she passed from the Sanctuary's protections. She wanted to rejoin her pack-mates and play her part in freeing her world from the invaders. But the thought of the Malvers woman invading her thoughts and dreams again almost made her wish she could stay in the Sanctuary. But she couldn't cower in safety while her people fought a war. As she'd told the Supreme, she had a duty to her people, even if it meant her own discomfort—and sanity—to accomplish it.

Blazel - 51 de Sandar, 1075

Blazel's brow furrowed in confusion at the large herd of horses waiting in the courtyard, already saddled. A string of fifteen multas, including their own Kressy and Gemmy, also stood tied to the railing with huge packs piled on their backs. The sturdy animals could carry a load larger than three times their own weight, and these appeared to be pushing the limit.

Blazel's mare, Lighzel, whinnied a greeting when he passed through the gate. The big bay had a black mane, tail, and socks. The white blaze on her nose vaguely resembled a lightning bolt. Her fine, pale black stripes marked her as a plains horse. Blazel offered her a carrot to assuage his guilt for not visiting her since they'd returned from the Deep Mountains. Lighzel gently nibbled the offering from the palm of his hand. He spoke softly to her as she nuzzled his shoulder.

He heard other soft murmurs as his friends greeted their horses. Rizelya's mare was a striking dark blue roan. Fine blue-gray stripes marked her face and body. Her mane, tail, and ears were a deep charcoal-gray, and she had unusual teal-blue eyes.

Eidstrun and Leistral's horses also waited with saddles on for the trip back to Strunlair Keep. Their back legs cocked as they dozed. Wisah's stallion, Tejen, on the other hand, kept shaking his head and rearing onto his hindquarters. His wide black strips on a pure white hide shone in the early morning light. He had black socks up to his knees and a dark gray mane and tail.

"Stop that," the horse-master, Shaela, said, and jerked on Tejen's reins to bring him down from another rear. The large horse shook his head. "I know you miss your rider, but she isn't gone. She's on an errand. She'll meet you where we're going." Tejen snorted and pawed the ground with a forehoof. "If you keep acting so ill-behaved, Wisah won't want to keep riding you." Tejen shook his head once more before settling down.

Jaehaas hurried to the horse and took the big stallion's head between his hands. "It be all right, boy. I be missing her too." Tejen quieted while Jaehaas continued to speak softly to him.

Shaela shook her head, then turned toward the people watching the tableau. "The damn horse saw Wisah fly off, and now he feels betrayed." She'd pulled her light brown hair into a tight braid that hung down her back. She wore dark brown leather pants and a plain shirt, not her usual attire.

"Are you coming with us?" Blazel asked, puzzled. Shaela had been born in the Sanctuary the same year he had, and he doubted she had ever left.

"Someone has to keep that brute under control. Besides, you'll need support staff to effectively fight the war. I volunteered. This is my home, and I won't stand for the invaders to pollute it. They're coming with us." She nodded to a group of nearly fifty women entering the courtyard from a different gate. Brown and Green Talent dominated, with a smattering of Yellow and Blue. Blazel raised an eyebrow at a white head in the mix. It surprised him that the Supreme allowed any of the White Priestesses to go to war. The courtyard echoed with the women's chatter.

Blazel sighed. They wouldn't be able to travel as fast with so many people.

"Now the string of multas makes sense," Rizelya said, coming to stand next to him.

"They also carry meat for the Gryphons." Shaela pointed to one of the multas. "We're afraid the Gryphons will over hunt and kill off too many animals."

Blazel frowned. "They are careful hunters. It's surprising how little it takes to sustain them, but they'll appreciate the thought."

Rizelya climbed onto a mounting block and put her fingers to her mouth. Her loud whistle pierced through the noise. The chatter ceased. "Hello, everyone. I'm Rizelya, and I'm the alpha of this expedition. You will listen to me and follow my orders. Blazel and Aistrun are my seconds. Once we pass Strunhelos Keep, we will have to watch for Malvers' monsters. We are severely short of fighters, and I hope a contingent of Strunhelos fighters will join us. Stay together. Don't go wandering off. You will be responsible for the care of your horse. Horse-master Shaela will help you, but she won't do it for you. Now, mount up!" Kymaya moved to stand next to the mounting block, and Rizelya stepped off it and onto the back of her horse.

The gates opened, and she gave the order to march. Blazel rode at her side, with Aistrun, Chariel, and Jaehaas following them. Blazel turned in his saddle, grimacing at the large group meandering behind them. Trailing the group, Shaela rode Tejen. She and two other brown-haired women each led a line of multas.

"I know a shortcut through the forest," Blazel said. "It will cut our travel time to Strunhelos Keep by half."

"You sure? Can we take this many people on a trail?" Rizelya frowned.

"I believe so. What do you think, Jaehaas? You traveled with me on it."

Jaehaas paused for a moment with his fist on his chin before nodding once. "We should be fine taking the shortcut."

"What about the Gryphons?"

"With this big of a group tromping through the forest, they'll have no trouble finding us." Blazel grimaced. "Besides, we haven't gone far and are still in mind-speaking range."

"Good. We'll take your shortcut." Rizelya chewed her lower lip. "I hadn't expected to lead such a large expedition."

"Get used to it." Aistrun grinned. "You've proved yourself as the capable alpha that Histrun and Naila suspected. I wouldn't be surprised if they didn't make you a battle commander."

"What about you?" Rizelya cocked an eyebrow. "You're my co-alpha."

He shook his head. "Nope, that honor belongs to Blazel, remember? I'm just your lackey and best friend."

"Well, lackey, help me keep this gaggle of people in line and safe. You and Jaehaas ride down the column, and let me know if there are any problems."

Aistrun gave her a cocky salute. "Ride with me?" he asked Chariel.

She nodded, and the two turned their horses around to ride on one side of the marching line while Jaehaas rode on the opposite side.

Blazel communicated the change of plans to Graak. He turned off the road and rode across the wide meadow, leading the group to the hills above the Sanctuary grounds. He'd expected to feel sad leaving home again so quickly and not spending much time with his mother and grandmother. But instead, excitement thrilled through him of a new adventure unfolding before him with his love. He grinned at Rizelya and kicked Lighzel into a canter. Rizelya laughed and followed him.

Rizelya - 51 de Sandar, 1075

Various species of evergreen trees soared above them. Aspen leaves shivered and sang in the slight breeze. The accumulation of forest debris muffled the horse's hoofbeats. Squirrels scurried away from the approaching riders to scold them from a safe distance. They had ridden a few measures in the forest when Rizelya glimpsed the rushing waters of the Storengher River on their right.

Birds taking sudden flight caught her attention. Her heart raced as she searched for oncoming Malvers' monsters. It settled when she spotted the Gryphons soaring high above them. Graak angled toward a clearing ahead of the group. Rizelya kicked her horse into a trot, with Blazel falling in on her left. They reached the clearing as Graak landed. He settled his wings along his back and sat on his haunches. The horses eyed him warily and pulled against the bit to get away, even though they'd traveled with him before.

Graak snorted and said to the horses, *Silly beasts. We do not eat friends.*

Blazel leaned forward and patted Lighzel's neck. "You're safe, girl. Settle down."

She shook her head once, then with feigned nonchalance, lowered her head to snatch a mouthful of grass.

Your group has grown, Rizelya. There are quite a few more than the last time you journeyed.

"Tell me about it," she groaned, slapping the ends of the reins into her palm. "They are just traveling to Strunlair Keep with us. They are *not* part of my pack."

"You can hope." Blazel chuckled.

Blazel, do you have a spot in mind where we'll spend the night? Graak asked. *Moraak suggests we fly ahead and start making camp for you.*

"I do. Although, it will be octars before we reach it."

We'll hunt the surrounding area while we wait.

"We brought supplies," Rizelya said, "so you don't have to hunt."

While we appreciate your thoughtfulness, we prefer fresh meat. Hunting will allow us to become familiar with the area. Depending on the quality of the game, we may need to supplement our meals with your supplies.

"You should find it plentiful," Blazel said. "I've hunted here and had good success."

If you had success, then the game must be easy to catch. Graak lowered his beak and gave a sharp trill as he laughed.

"I'm a much better hunter now than when you first met me, I'll have you know." He scowled in mock anger at Graak. "Here is where I have in mind for tonight." He imagined the spot and projected it via mind-speech to Graak and Rizelya.

Rizelya approved. The space was large enough for everyone, and the river ran beside it, providing fresh water.

Got it. Graak nodded. *Gryphons will keep pace with your group. Whistle should you have any troubles. Until tonight.* Graak leaped into the air with a crack of his wings.

"Did you account for people unused to riding all day when choosing your campsite?" Rizelya slumped in her saddle as she watched the approaching group.

"I did. They'll be sore no matter where we stop. I estimate it will take us three days to reach Strunhelos Keep and then another three to Strunlair Keep. That is, if we don't run into any trouble along the way."

"Are you sure?" Rizelya crinkled her nose as she thought. "It took us four days to travel from Strunlair to Strunhelos and another four to reach the Sanctuary."

"Ah, but you were sick, from what I hear. And you didn't know the shortcuts."

The group caught up to them. Rizelya pulled Kymaya's head up and away from her grazing, then kicked her sides to urge her to move. The horse gave a big sigh before going.

The shadows lengthen into evening when the party passed out of the trees and into a meadow. For the last octar, Rizelya ignored the women's grumbled complaints of being tired and if they were ever going to stop. When they entered the clearing with several fires burning, the women gave relieved cries. Rizelya's mouth watered at the scent of deer carcasses sizzling over the fires. She rode to the one Graak, Moraak, and Glork sat beside and gratefully slid out of the saddle.

"Thank you," she said. "This is very thoughtful of you." The Gryphons preferred their meat raw and had only roasted the meat for the sake of the Posairs. "It looks like you had a successful hunt."

We did. Moraak blinked his eyes. *We thought we'd share the bounty.*

While Rizelya and Blazel pulled the saddles off their horses and rubbed them down, the women shook out their legs. A few recovered quicker than the others and began to pull the packs off the multas. They dug cauldrons from a pack, filling them with water from the river. One group built new fires, placing the pots over them. A troop of Greens added vegetables and grains to the pots, and soon savory, delicious smells filled the clearing.

Rizelya moaned in pleasure at her first bite of food. "We need to bring Green Talents with us all the time. They are much better cooks than I could ever be."

Aistrun laughed. "Hey, almost anyone is a better cook than you. But I agree. This is heaven to have good food on the trail. This is much better than trail bars." He made happy noises as he ate.

"We have some of those too," Chariel said. "Whoever packed didn't want us to go hungry."

After eating, Rizelya stood and stretched. With her hands on her hips, she surveyed the camp and sighed. Whether she had asked for it or not, these women were now her responsibility— at least until she foisted them off on Naila or Beladi at Strunlair Keep. The women sat around several fires, laughing and chatting as they ate, like the old friends they were.

Rizelya moved among the groups, meeting and speaking to each one for a few moments. Many women were sore from the long horse ride but assured her they could ride the next day.

When she returned to her fire, everyone had already curled up in their bedrolls. Blazel lifted a corner of his for her, and she slid under the covers, snuggling into his warmth. He tucked an arm around her and pulled her close. She drifted off. A moment later, she jerked awake and quickly sat up. She hadn't set a watch.

Be easy, Rizelya, Moraak said, his voice quiet in her mind. *We rested while waiting for you. We guard the night.*

Rizelya murmured a thank you, lay back down, and let herself relax into sleep.

Chapter 9

Blazel - 52 de Sandar, 1075

Blazel led the group deeper into the forest. Whenever the trees opened to reveal a wide meadow, he pushed the horses into a canter. The line of multas barely kept up, but he wasn't concerned. They'd catch up once more on the twisting paths of the forest. The Gryphons flew ahead and set up camp for them again, this time at the top of a canyon where the river cut through it. A thundering waterfall dropped a hundred feet into the churning water below. After this, their path would veer away from the river.

That night, the women didn't talk or laugh much around the fires. Exhaustion sapped their strength. Blazel estimated they'd toughen up soon—about the time they reached Strunlair Keep.

The next day, the route skirted cliffs and ravines. As they rode down the mountains, the day grew warmer. The spring flowers dotting the landscape on Blazel's trip to the Sanctuary had given way to the dry grasses of summer. Bees hummed in the meadows, birds chirped, and squirrels scolded them as they passed. Blazel sat back in his saddle, closed his eyes, and lifted his head toward the sun, enjoying the peaceful ride.

"You look content," Jaehaas said.

"I am." Blazel sighed and opened his eyes. "Even though we're heading to war, I can't help feeling my life is better than it's ever been. I've found a woman who loves me and friends who put up with me. It's more than I ever expected."

"Do you miss being a lone wolf?"

"Sometimes I miss the solitude." Blazel glanced over his shoulder at Rizelya riding behind them. "But she's worth it." He turned back around and gazed at Jaehaas. "You too. After all we've been through, you and the others have become my pack. My clan. I could never willingly be a lone wolf again. I'd be too lonely."

The muted footfalls of the horse's hooves on the forest floor changed to a loud clopping as they moved onto the sheadash stone roadway.

Jaehaas looked around him. "I recognize where we be. Strunhelos Keep be only a half-day's ride from here."

Blazel nodded. "Perhaps a bit less."

Steep cliffs, bare of any vegetation, soon replaced the tall trees. The road led into a canyon, narrowing until they had to ride single file. The horse's hooves echoed off the steep rock faces towering over them. Blazel caught movement on the top of the cliff. The Strunhelos guards followed their progress through the pass.

Blazel shuddered as they entered a tunnel. By stretching out his arms, he could touch either side with his fingertips. He focused on the dim light ahead and took deep breaths to calm his nerves. When he was a teenager, he'd been stuck in a small cave for more than a chedan while two huge sabertigers paced outside, waiting for him to leave. He'd nearly starved before the pair had left to hunt easier prey. Ever since, small, close spaces caused him problems. After a hundred breaths, they finally exited the tunnel. Blazel surreptitiously wiped the sweat from his brow as his heartbeat settled.

They reached Strunhelos' north gate. Blazel frowned at the closed gate. He thought the keeps only shut them at night or in times of peril. He glanced at Rizelya, who scowled at the guard standing in front of it.

"Why is the gate closed?" Rizelya grumbled. "I'm Rizelya de Strunlair, and we've traveled from the Sanctuary."

The guard studied them, then leaned around them to stare at the rest of their party. "We'll inform the keep alpha. Until she arrives, you'll have to wait here."

Another guard stepped from the surrounding forest. The gate opened enough for him to hurry through it, then shut again. Jaehaas, Aistrun, and Chariel joined Blazel and Rizelya.

Several milcrons passed before the gate creaked open slightly. Keep Alpha Joydan, a tall, older woman with pale red hair and brown eyes, exited.

"Sorry to keep you waiting," Joydan said. "I remember you, Rizelya. You look much better than when you came through here earlier. You were pretty sick. Jaehaas, Blazel." She nodded to them. "Welcome back. Your party seems to have grown. We can't be too careful, what with a strange comet passing over not long ago, followed by unusual flying creatures—the same kind flying ahead of your group. You wouldn't know anything about them, would you?"

Blazel mentally called to Moraak and Graak.

"Yes, we do." Rizelya rested her hands on her saddle pommel. "They are our allies, the Gryphons."

Joydan scoffed. "You're not serious, are you? They're nothing but myths."

A shadow blocked the evening sun. Joydan glanced up, then gasped. Moraak soared overhead. His tawny feline body was fourteen feet long, excluding his tail, and his head and wings were those of an eagle. His wingspan was nearly forty-foot across. He snapped into in a dive, and the thunderous blast made Joydan cringe.

We are not mythical creatures, Moraak said as he landed, folding his wings over his back. *We have come to offer aid against the invaders. Keep Alpha, will you allow us to camp below your keep for the night?*

"Keep Alpha Joydan, let me introduce you to Prince Moraak of the Gold Wings," Blazel said.

"Yes, yes, Prince Moraak, you are welcome in my territory." She frowned. "You said invaders?"

Blazel ran a soothing hand on Lighzel's neck. Moraak's abrupt entrance had startled her. "The comet wasn't a natural phenomenon but an alien ship. They've captured the fortress guards and at least one keep in Posanlair Province. May we take this discussion inside and care for our horses?"

"Oh, of course." Joydan waved to the guards at the gate, and it swung open. Moraak glided through, with Blazel and the others following after him.

At the stables, the keep's horse-master joined Shaela, and they took charge of Blazel's team's horses. Blazel and his team hurried to the practice arena, which was the only building in the keep large enough to accommodate Moraak and Graak. Members of the kitchen staff brought in chilled taevo, fresh fruit, and steamy pastries as Blazel's group told the keep alphas about the call to war.

"We must maintain a force here." Bolstrun had a short, slight build, wavy brown hair, and pale yellow eyes. "This keep has stood guard to the entrance of the White Mountains for thousands of years. It is our ancient duty to guard the mountain pass, and thus, protecting the Supreme and the Sanctuary."

Joydan rolled her eyes. "We can send three platoons with you, Rizelya. And we won't have reduced our ability to secure the Sanctuary, and you know it, Bolstrun. They will be under your direct command."

"But... but..." Rizelya stammered. "I'm only a squad-pack alpha."

"No, you were. Now you are a battalion alpha. I know your sister, Naila, quite well, and your father, too. They both speak highly of you. I trust you to lead my people well."

Rizelya appeared thunderstruck. She kept blinking her eyes and opening her mouth, although no words escaped. Blazel hid his chuckle behind his hand.

"Hey, that takes care of our problem of being understaffed," Aistrun said. "Go on, Little Red, take the people. We need them."

Rizelya shook her head. "You're right, of course, Aistrun. Joydan, we accept your offer."

Relief swelled in Blazel. They needed the extra fighters. Malvers' monster nests infested the area beyond Strunhelos.

They ate dinner with the Strunhelos platoon leaders and stayed up late getting acquainted with them.

"Sweet Mother, help me!" Rizelya lamented, when they finally fell into bed. "I'm not ready to lead a battalion. I'd hoped

Naila or Beladi would take over the women from the Sanctuary. But I doubt they're going to now that I have three platoons under me. How did that happen? I tried so hard not to lead anyone. First, under protest, Naila gave me a squad-pack of six. It grew to eleven when I added the girls. Well, more like twenty, with the girl's warrior protectors. It expanded again at the Sanctuary to include you, Chariel, Wisah, and Jaehaas. What am I going to do?"

"Be your magnificent self." Blazel leaned over and kissed her. "Don't underestimate yourself. Aistrun told me how your alphas have groomed you to lead since birth. And how you and he tried desperately not to become alphas."

"When did he tell you that?"

"When you weren't watching. We've become quite good friends. And as a good friend, I say give him command of a squad, if not a platoon."

Rizelya's smile grew to an evil grin. "Oh, what a great idea. He can share in my misery. So can you."

"I will share anything with you, my love, anything and everything." Blazel kissed her. The kiss deepened and even as tired as they were, they made love.

Rizelya - 54 de Sandar, 1075

Dawn had come and gone several octars before Rizelya's new troops were ready to leave Strunhelos Keep. Over two hundred people marched out of the keep. Thirty multas, huge packs piled on their backs, followed. Moraak and his Gryphons had left an octar previously to fly ahead to the safe house where they would stay for the night. From here on, they wouldn't—couldn't—sleep outdoors. The night-hunting narhili beasts roamed the hills. Rizelya shivered, remembering the narhili attack on her. Whenever she was tired or cold, her leg still ached where she'd been poisoned.

As they rode through the surrounding pastures and fields, Rizelya noted the teams of Red teenage girls and their wolf counterparts guarding the non-fighters as they worked. The girls saluted at their passing. A few wore envious expressions, like they wished they were heading to war. Rizelya wished she, and those she led, weren't.

They soon passed the cultivated fields and rode into the wilderness. Rizelya continually scanned either side of the road. They were far from the influence of the Sanctuary. She remembered her last ride to Strunlair Keep, when the monsters attempted to prevent her and her team from reaching the Clan Alphas. Monsters had attacked them several times a day in unexpected places.

They hadn't ridden very far when Rizelya started hearing a horrible buzzing. It was nothing like the hum of a control-janack. It made her feel anxious and jittery. She kept glancing all around her, afraid they were being attacked by Malvers' monsters. As the day wore on, the buzzing never stopped, and her head pounded.

"Hey, Rizelya!" Aistrun called. "Are we ever going to take a break for the midday meal?"

She blinked and glanced at the sun. Noon had come and gone. "Oh, sorry. Yeah. Whenever we find a spot to accommodate all of us, let's stop."

He gave her a concerned look, then nudged Jezhan forward to ride beside Blazel and Jaehaas. A few moments later, they both turned in their saddles to gaze at her. She made a face at them, and when they returned their attention to the road, she rubbed her eyes. She wished she had a hat. The sun hurt her eyes. A few times during the afternoon, women would ride next to her and try to engage her in conversation. She didn't want to talk, and sent them quickly away, sometimes not as nicely as she should have.

They arrived at the safe house without any trouble as twilight descended. Her nerves strung taunt, Rizelya snapped at everyone. In the chaos of settling so many horses, Blazel stepped in front of her, and she smacked into his back. Rubbing her nose, she cursed him soundly.

He shrunk into himself, dropping his eyes as he silently turned and walked away from her.

Shaela glared at Rizelya as she took Kymaya's reins from her and led the horse into the stable. Still swearing, Rizelya stomped into the safe house. She wanted to kick or hit something or someone. Good thing no one occupied the building. She whirled as the door slammed shut.

Aistrun leaned against the door, his arms folded across his chest, and fury burned in his eyes. "What in the Crone's Fires is wrong with you, Rizelya? You had no call to treat Blazel like you did. You've been moody and crabby all afternoon. Maybe you shouldn't lead this many people if you can't handle the pressure."

Rizelya rubbed her temples, trying to ease the headache. "That isn't the problem," she snapped. "My head hurts, and I can barely hear anything over the horrible buzzing in my ears."

Aistrun's eyes narrowed as he studied her. "Is it the humming of a control-janack?"

"No." She shook her head, instantly regretting it when it caused stabbing pain behind her eyes. Blackness started closing in on her, and dots swam in front of her. She reached out a hand for a chair back to steady her. Aistrun rushed to her side and helped her to sit, pushing her head between her knees.

"I'm going to get Chariel and a healer," he said. "You don't look so good."

Rizelya groaned, wondering if the mind-block was causing the headache. Remembered images of people being killed by the monsters, and the Malvers woman gleefully eating their death essence flooded her. She swallowed the bile rising in her throat. She decided she'd rather have a headache than experience those horrors again.

A gentle hand rested on hers and pressed a cool cloth against her forehead. Lavender and chamomile scents swirled around her. Energy flowed from the healer's hand into Rizelya's head, easing the pressure behind her eyes. After a while, the pain lifted, and her nausea eased.

She raised her head. In the background, she heard the quiet sounds of dinner preparations and people whispering. She'd been out of it long enough for the troops to care for the horses and gather inside the safe house.

"Chariel tells me the Supreme put a block on your mind," the healer said. The woman appeared to be in her mid-thirties and had chestnut-brown hair and blue-gray eyes. She was a little on the plump side, with wide hips and a generous bosom. "Your budding Gray talent is fighting the block as it tries to expand. I'll brew a potion for your headache."

"Thank you..."

"Bethlyn. I'm your head healer." She laughed. "I mean, I'm the leader of your healers."

Rizelya frowned. "How many of you are there?"

"Four. Joydan couldn't send her people to war without providing healers. I specialize in battle wounds."

"Have you ever been to a monster battle?"

Bethlyn's eyes clouded, and she nodded. She patted Rizelya's shoulder. "Hold the cloth over your eyes and let the essential oils work while I fix a headache potion."

Chariel watched her leave, then leaned close to Rizelya. "It's also the Malvers woman," she whispered. "I can sense her in the buzzing in my ears. Are your ears buzzing too?"

Rizelya nodded.

"I'll show you some exercises after dinner to ease it. But we don't want to get rid of it completely. We need to know what she's doing and planning."

Rizelya grimaced. Even though she agreed, she wished to be rid of the annoying buzz. She lifted the fragrant cloth and covered her face with it, breathing deeply. Once her headache eased, she apologized to Blazel. He hadn't deserved her anger.

Later, headache gone, ringing dimmed, and Blazel snuggling next to her, Rizelya lay in a cot staring at the ceiling, dreading going to sleep. She didn't want the terrible dreams to return. The past few chedans, nightmares of the Malvers woman hadn't plagued her. It had been bliss. Finally, Blazel's deep, steady breathing lulled her to sleep.

Kaieli - 54 de Sandar, 1075

Steam rose off the processing machinery. The small, open windows near the roof did little to let in cool air or ventilate the building. The rumble of conveyor belts carrying the mineral through the various stages made it difficult to talk. Teams stacked the finished product—cubes of purified and pressed nucla—into crates. A crew of the hairy, four-armed aliens moved the heavy crates from the processing plant to the mother ship's hold.

Kaieli swore when she inadvertently touched a cube as she wove through the narrow aisles between the machinery. She, along with the other healers and the White Priestess, avoided the mineral, which burned their skin and fogged their abilities. Kaieli finally reached the out-of-the-way corner they'd set up as an infirmary, holding out her hand for Faliciden to heal the burn.

The poor conditions of the slave camp created plenty of sick and injured Posairs for the healers to treat.

On her daily treks to and from the processing plant, Kaieli witnessed a number of the other slave species with treatable injuries. Three days ago, she'd mentioned to Tre'nok her willingness to help them, but no one had ventured into their corner to use the healer's services.

Just before the midday break, two short males with pointed ears, purple eyes, and fine blond hair carried in a diminutive woman of their species. Their orange slave coveralls had gray trim around the necklines, sleeves, and hem. The woman had one eye swollen shut, a torn ear, and a bleeding lip. She sat listlessly when they placed her gently on the crate used as an exam table. The beating looked bad, but the convulsions shaking her frail body worried Kaieli more. She frowned at the unnatural pulling on the right side of the woman's face.

Kaieli followed the trail of her Talent as it sought the problem. Her stomach clenched at the woman's swollen brain. The damaged areas appeared as dark smudges to her magical sight. One of the men said something to her. She opened her eyes. "I don't understand you."

"He asked if their mate would survive," Vy'shol said. She stood to the side of the injured woman. "They just discovered she carries their children."

"Oh! Her head injuries are bad. Brain injuries are difficult to heal in the best of circumstances, but here?" Kaieli shrugged. "I don't know if I can heal all the damage."

Sorrow darkened the two men's faces as they gently stroked the woman's face and arms. Kaieli leaned closer to Vy'shol. "Are they both her mate?"

Vy'shol nodded. "The Faeorn species has three genders: male, female, and gomale. It takes all three to procreate. Can you heal her?"

"I'll do what I can, but I need help." She called to the other two healers and Loshera, who immediately joined her. "Loshera, your task is to tether her soul to this world and her babies."

The White Priestess placed her hands on the woman's feet. Faelyn and Faliciden stood on either side of the Faeorn, each with a hand on the woman's shoulders and the other on Kaieli's. As Kaieli cradled the woman's head in her hands, the woman's fear overwhelmed her senses. "Tell her mates to hold her hands."

At the touch of her mate's hands, the woman calmed. Kaieli closed her eyes and worked on repairing the damage caused by the beating. Kaieli struggled to heal the woman, even with the support of Faelyn and Faliciden. By the time she finished, sweat drenched her, and she shook with fatigue.

"I've done all I can," Kaieli said, pulling away from the woman and rubbing the tiredness from her face. "There may be some residual paralysis, but she'll live."

The mates smiled in jubilation at the news. The taller one asked Vy'shol a question, to which she answered with slow enunciation, "Thank you."

Both men approached each of the Posair women, kissed their hands, and carefully said, "Thank you."

"Vy'shol, please tell them she needs rest to finish healing."

The taller one nodded his understanding as he gently picked up his mate, cradling her in his arms.

Kaieli watched the trio wind through the plant to the exit. "Will she be able to rest without getting her mates in trouble?"

"Yes. The Faeorn are a gentle, compassionate people and have never resisted the Scourge, and receive some leniencies. Their cunning innovations are responsible for much of the technology the Scourge uses. They developed the power drives in their space ships, making them nearly as valuable to them as we, the Volkern, are." Vy'shol grimaced. The subtle swirling pattern around her eyes darkened. She took a deep breath, and when she released it, the swirls faded back to the same color as her skin, nearly imperceptible.

"A Scourge didn't beat her. Most likely it was a Kaigor. They are stupid enough to go against the Scourge's rules. I have to report this. I will try to keep you out of my report. Not many would help those who are trying to conquer their world."

Kaieli sat on an empty crate they'd dragged into their corner. "Neither they, nor you, are the conquerors. That distinction belongs solely to the invaders. We," she motioned to the three women and herself, "are healers. The Goddess gifted us with the ability to help those in need. It is our duty and obligation to do so—even for those who don't look like us."

"Admirable. But are you not just prolonging their agony?"

"No," Kaieli said forcefully. "The invaders prey on the weak. If I can help them stay strong, perhaps they'll remain alive. I saw the terror on the faces of my people who the invaders killed during the march here. No one deserves to suffer like that. I will do whatever I can to stop it from happening to anyone."

Respect shone in Vy'shol's pale yellow eyes. "You are an unusual woman and an unusual species. It does not happen often that a people under siege will help those who are perceived as an enemy."

Loshera pushed back a stray strand of white hair. "You're not the enemy. Nor are any of the slave species brought to our world. We will help you until you prove to be a foe."

"Perhaps we can be allies," Kaieli added.

Vy'shol tilted her head to the side as she ran a long finger over the ring in her nose. "It is not for me to decide." She walked gracefully away, swaying slightly.

Awhile later, Tre'nok entered their nook, leading a tall male with a long, narrow face, bulbous lips, oblong yellow eyes, and dark brown skin. Slits on the side of his neck opened and closed as he breathed. His height rivaled the Posair men at just over six feet. He had two sets of full-sized arms and a third small rudimentary set, which Kaieli guessed weren't fully functional.

"The Gheethong hurt his hand. Vy'shol said you helped the Faeorn. Can you heal him?"

"I will try." Kaieli indicated for the injured man to sit.

The Gheethong held out his wide spatula-like hand. Unlike Posairs, the Gheethong had eight fingers with sticky pads on the ends. As she examined his hand, his rough skin texture scraped against hers, almost like tiny teeth. Blood seeped from several cuts, and three fingers were crushed. Once she deciphered the bones were mostly cartilage, healing the hand was a simple matter.

Throughout the afternoon, one or another of the five Volkern brought an injured alien to the makeshift infirmary. Most of the injuries were minor and easily treated. Kaieli and her team treated several tall, hairy creatures with four arms, called Hap'thez, for minor cuts or burns.

Flo'kik ushered in a round Coufrish with rolls of fat and smooth skin in peach and pink tones, complaining of stomach troubles. Kaieli raised her eyebrows at its three stomachs, but gently treated the indigestion. "Stomach ailments often afflict the Coufrish," Flo'kik told Kaieli after she treated the third one.

Kaieli admired the beautiful Vhelopsi with their golden skin, hair, and eyes. Most of the ones she treated came in with nasty coughs and lung conditions similar to what the Posair men suffered from working in the crater. Although their illnesses weren't as debilitating because they didn't possess magic.

The end-of-day horn blew as Kaieli's last patient scuttled from the infirmary. Kaieli slumped onto a crate with a tired sigh. She counted her exhaustion well worth it if these people became allies. She believed the Posairs needed all the help they could get to overthrow the invaders.

"Why didn't you bring in any Kaigor?" she asked Vy'shol, who hadn't left yet. "I believe we treated every other slave species I've noticed in the camp, except them."

Vy'shol visibly shuddered. "You don't want anything to do with the nasty, aggressive creatures. Safer, too. They're almost as bad as the invaders in their violence. Thank you for your work today. Those you healed will survive another day. The Scourge won't kill them because they are injured." She bowed her head, and made a swirling gesture in front of her chest with her hand, before sauntering from the infirmary.

Kaieli joined the other women as they tiredly trudged across the compound. A high-pitched whine overhead pierced the air. Everyone, including their guard, ducked and scanned the sky. A ship trailing smoke bobbled into view. Black charred its shiny surface. It weaved and bucked, finally crashing nose first into the ground and sliding to a stop, digging a deep, long furrow. The women's guard stopped to gawk, seemingly forgetting their charges.

A squad of invaders ran to help the crew from the ship. Purple blood oozed from cuts and scrapes. An invader slightly shorter than the others and wearing a red-trimmed robe stumbled from the hatch. He pushed his hood back, revealing his long face shining with moisture. His skin had a pasty gray cast to it. The officer took two steps and fell to his knees.

"He appears ill," Faliciden whispered.

Kaieli nodded. "If we can discover caused it, we might be able to make the other invaders sick." Kaieli's chest tightened at the thought. It went against her morals, but she'd do it if it'd give her people an advantage over them.

She attempted to scan him, as two lower-ranking soldiers picked him up between them and dragged him into the mother ship. She swallowed the bile in her throat. "Crone's fires! I can't get past the invader's innate noxious energy signature."

The next day, Tre'nok ushered a Vhelopsi into the healing area. Tre'nok stood back, watching Kaieli work, his arms crossed over his chest. "I have news."

She raised an eyebrow in silent question as she wrapped a bandage around the Vhelopsi's forearm.

"The scout ship crew died last night."

"Do you know what killed them?"

"Nothing for certain. They flew to the large island off your east coast and ate several of the inhabitants."

Kaieli rocked back on her heels, stunned. "Are you sure? It's supposed to be an uninhabited island."

"I'm sure. Their translator, My'shel, saw it happen. The people there aren't like you. They have pale gray skin and appear malnourished."

"I don't know who they are."

Her heart raced. Were these the last remnants of the people they had fought in the Great War? How could they have survived all these years with no one knowing about them? Or did someone know, like the Supreme? They sounded like the woman in Rizelya's visions.

Her thoughts spun, and she barely noticed Tre'nok and the slave leaving. The unknown islanders had something toxic to the invaders. Could the Posairs somehow get them to share it? And if they were who she suspected they were, would she even want their help?

Rizelya - 55 de Sandar, 1075

A thick fog swirled around Rizelya, making it difficult to see but a few feet in front of her. Distant screams filtered through it, seemingly from all directions. Strange shapes wandered the dark landscape, creaking and groaning as they reached skeletal fingers toward her. Intense cold lingered wherever they touched her. She ran to avoid them. Maniacal laughter followed her as the shapes chased her. A clear voice rang out, breaking through the fog like sunlight. Rizelya trembled as she recognized the Malvers woman's voice.

"Yes, my babies," she purred. "More. We need more. Soon, we will have the strength to escape this dismal island and return to our rightful place. Come, my friends, feed and grow strong." Long, claw-like fingers dipped into a bowl of putrid black pearls. More hands joined the first, and moans of pleasure reverberated through Rizelya's head. She covered her ears with her hands and ran. Laughter dogged her heels. She screamed when a hand latched onto her and shook her.

"It's just me," Blazel said. "You were having a nightmare."

Rizelya's body shuddered, and her teeth chattered. "Hold me. I'm cold, so cold."

Blazel drew her closer, covering her body with his. Finally, she warmed up and stopped shaking. "How long until dawn?"

"An octar or so. Try to go back to sleep."

She shook her head. "I can't. I don't want to have another nightmare."

Blazel kissed her, but the dream still clung to her, and she couldn't return his ardor.

"Well, if we aren't going to make love or go back to sleep, there's no sense in lying here. Come on. Let's go outside."

They dressed, and Blazel grabbed his old, battered pack as they left the safe house. He led her to a bench near the gate. She sat on it, leaning her back against the stone wall. Blazel sat next to her and pulled his flute from his bag. The warm tones soothed her mind and soul, and she drifted into a half trance. She opened her eyes when he stopped and found dawn had arrived, and people filled the courtyard.

"Thank you," she said, smiling at him. "I feel much better." He helped her up, pulling her into an embrace before they hurried to the house for a quick breakfast.

Throughout the morning as they rode, Rizelya jumped and twisted in her saddle at every snap of a twig and rustle of a bush. She was sure the Malvers woman would send her monsters to harangue them. But the day wore on with no attack. The road took them through a dense growth of trees, dimming the afternoon light into a false twilight. Suddenly, both Blazel and Jaehaas strung their bows and held them ready.

"What is it?" Rizelya's eyes darted from one side of the road to the other. She loosened her helbraught in its holder on her saddle. "Do you smell monsters?"

"No, paethers." Blazel nocked an arrow, pulled back the string, and aimed at a bush.

A square head with long tusks curving from the lower jaw poked out of the shadow. Its two eyes faced front and tracked the group's movement, and its nostril slits flared. Two additional eyes on the top of its head allowed it to see its prey as it slashed open the underbelly.

"Paethers!" Rizelya alerted her people both aloud and in mind-speech. Her horse caught scent of the predators. Kymaya screamed and reared as a mottled-gray, long, lean body shot from the bushes toward her. Rizelya gripped the reins in one hand while clamping her legs around Kymaya's sides. Her other hand ripped her helbraught from its holder. The blade blazed, and a streak of light followed its path as she swung. The paether's head flew across the road. Kymaya's front hooves landed on its body with a sickening *squish*.

Instead of running, Rizelya and Aistrun threw their reins at Chariel as they leaped from their saddles. Rizelya took a stand on the right side of the road as Chariel rode away from the fight. Aistrun shifted to his warrior form and guarded the other side. Blazel stayed on his horse, joining Jaehaas in letting loose fiery arrows into the swarming beasts.

Rizelya's world turned into one of swinging, thrusting, leaping, then twisting to slash at a slavering muzzle. Bodies piled around her, more than the usual ten to fifteen members of a paether pack. Sweat dripped into her eyes, and she paused long enough to swipe it away, only to realize it was blood.

A beast leaped from the shadows with its razor-sharp tusk slashing toward her throat. She stepped back, blocking the attack with her helbraught, and slid on the slick, bloody ground. A beast hit her right side. Already scrambling for balance, her arms windmilled. A third beast snapped down on her helbraught. Her eyes widened in astonishment—paether attacks weren't usually so coordinated—and she ducked as another paether snarled and leaped at her. It yipped and dropped like a stone, an arrow protruding from its eye. She found her balance and twisted her helbraught out of the other paether's mouth, then thrust the blade into its skull. She jumped when an arrow zipped by her. A paether crumbled in front of her with an arrow sticking out from its side.

Panting, Rizelya crouched, waiting for the next attack.

"It's over," Blazel called. "They're all dead."

Standing, Rizelya leaned on her helbraught and stared at the massacre. At least fifty paether bodies littered the ground, many sprouting arrows. Shaela and a few others attended the horses.

"Is anyone hurt?" she croaked. Her throat burned and felt raw. She rubbed it, and her hand came away slicked with blood. "That is, besides me. Any horses hurt?" She swallowed between words, trying to get rid of the sensation of bubbles in the back of her throat.

Jaehaas shook his head. "No. It be a strange thing. Once you be on the ground, every beastie focused on you."

She studied the bodies. Double the number piled where she had stood than anywhere else.

Bethlyn wound her way through the carnage toward the group with a kerchief held over her nose and mouth. She gingerly lowered her face covering. "Gracious Mother! What an awful sight. They wouldn't let me near until those beasts were dead. Now I know why." Her eyes narrowed, and her voice sharpened. "Rizelya, is that your blood you're covered with, or the paether's?"

Rizelya shrugged. "A bit of both." She coughed. A red haze filled her vision, and her knees buckled.

Aistrun, standing next to her, caught her before she hit the ground, putting an arm around her and propping her back up. "Easy, Little Red."

Paether blood made his fur sticky. "Is any of that blood yours?" She choked and pulled away from his side.

"Naw. It all beast's." His warrior jaws mangled the words. He looked at her and made a face. "Yours too. You hurt."

Rizelya glared at him and leaned against her helbraught. Swallowing against the pain, she croaked, "I'm fine. There's too much to do."

Sometime—she didn't notice when—Blazel replaced Aistrun at her side. He put an arm around her. "We'll take care of it. Bethlyn, why aren't you doing something to help her?"

"I'm just waiting for you to get in place. Catch her, Blazel." She nodded to him and placed a hand on Rizelya's arm.

Rizelya frowned, then swayed into Blazel's arms. Black warmth closed over her as she heard Bethlyn say, "She's stubborn, like most alphas I know. They'll keep going until their people are cared for, even though they're bleeding to death. The only way they'll stop is to put them out. That's a good girl. Go to sleep."

Blazel - 55 de Sandar, 1075

Blazel gaped, aghast at the deep, ragged wound on Rizelya's throat Bethlyn revealed when she washed away the blood. When he'd seen Rizelya after the battle, he hadn't realized she'd been injured. Although, all the blood and gore covering her made it hard to tell. Her fighting so many paether at once had been magnificent to watch, and he'd had difficulty keeping his mind on the fight. He growled under his breath. Maybe if he'd paid more attention to the fight, the last paether wouldn't have snagged her throat.

After what seemed a long time, Bethlyn finally stopped the bleeding and wound a bandage around Rizelya's neck. "I'll finish when we get to the safe house. I've healed her enough we can safely move her."

Blazel nodded and carefully stood with her still in his arms. "Aistrun," he called.

Aistrun jogged into view. He'd shifted back to his human form and had a few scrapes where the paether tusks had slid through his warrior's fur. None of them appeared serious. "Yeah, Alpha?"

"What's the status? Can we leave soon?"

"Yes. The Reds are burning the paether bodies. The next safe house is only a couple of measures away." He scowled and kicked at the blood-soaked ground. "Damn things. I haven't ever seen or heard of a pack this large. Have you?"

Blazel shook his head. "On my way to Strunhelos, paether attacked me not far from here. But it was a normal pack size of about ten. This was three or four packs."

"They rarely share territory. I don't like this." Aistrun pounded a fist against his thigh. "This wasn't natural."

"No, it wasn't." Blazel frowned and glanced around. "The Reds are finished. We need to get to the safe house. Night will fall soon. I don't want to fight any narhili after this."

He handed Rizelya to Aistrun just long enough to mount his waiting horse before he took her back. Her pale face and ragged breathing worried him. He held her close, kicked Lighzel into a gallop, and raced ahead to the safe house.

The Gryphons set up their camp in the open space surrounding the safe house. Graak lounged beside the gate, his head resting on his front talons, the tip of his tail lazily swaying back and forth. He lifted his head and cocked it to the side when Blazel rushed into view.

Rizelya, still unconscious, moaned in Blazel's arms. A bright spot of blood marred the bandage around her throat. At Graak's nonchalance, rage flared in Blazel, flushing his face with heat.

"Where in the Crone's Fires were you?" he yelled. "Where were the guards who were supposed to be watching for trouble?"

Graak squawked in surprise. *What do you mean? The scouts reported just a little while ago you were only a short distance away and nothing was amiss.*

"We weren't safe. Paethers attacked us!" Blazel trotted through the gates. Tight on his heels cantered his core group and Bethlyn. He jerked Lighzel to a stop in front of the safe house and slid from the saddle, careful not to jostle his burden. Bethlyn hurried into the house ahead of him. He gently laid Rizelya on the cot Bethlyn indicated. Unable to watch her working on Rizelya, Blazel turned on his heel and stalked outside.

Aistrun and Jaehaas were speaking in low voices to Graak. They looked up as Blazel's boots struck an angry staccato on the wooden porch. He stopped at the edge, his arms crossed in front of his chest, his left foot beating in time with his lurching heart. He glared at Graak.

I swear, Blazel, no one saw any paethers waiting to ambush you. Graak's head drooped, the feathers tight against his head. *We believed you were safe. Is she okay?*

"She was seriously hurt! If we hadn't had a healer with us, she would have died. We're not in the White Mountains anymore, Graak," Blazel ground out through clenched teeth. "There's always danger, whether from predators or Malvers' monsters. You can't assume nothing is there because you don't see anything."

"You're the bigger predator," Aistrun added. "The paether probably hid until you passed by. They'd be no match for you."

Graak made mournful chirping noises. *It doesn't excuse our mistake. Rizelya was hurt.*

Jaehaas reached out to soothe Graak. "It may not have made a difference if you be there or not. The attack not be normal. They focused on Rizelya. They didn't even try to stop me or Blazel as we shot arrows into the mass."

Aistrun blew out a breath and swore. "You're right. I hope this isn't the start of a long line of attacks. You two weren't with us when we tried to reach Strunlair Keep. It was awful. We fought monsters where there shouldn't have been any, one battle after another. One day, we fought seven battles." Aistrun swore again and kicked a rock across the courtyard.

Chariel stepped out of the house and went to Aistrun, who put his arm around her. "Rizelya will be all right. Bethlyn closed the wound. She should sleep the rest of the night and be able to ride in the morning."

Relief flooded Blazel, replacing the anger, and he sagged against the porch railing.

"The Malvers woman orchestrated the attack." Chariel hugged herself and rubbed her arms. "She didn't sense me, but I sensed her through my connection with Rizelya. She knows Rizelya is back, but she can't control Rizelya like she did before. Now she's trying to determine what she can do, and what Rizelya is capable of doing. We may be in for a rough few days."

Aistrun grumbled. "I knew it."

Graak lifted his head, his eyes glowing with determination. *She does not know we are here too. We'll stay close to you, and only a scouting flight will fly ahead. During the Great War, your ancestors designed us to block the Malvers' mind attacks. Perhaps our presence will stop her from sensing Rizelya.*

And I will teach her how to block better, Moraak added, his voice sounding distant. *I have been monitoring your conversation. The courtyard is too small for me. Rizelya can ride with me where she'll be out of danger.*

Blazel doubted Rizelya would agree. "It's up to her. We're only a day's ride from Strunlair Keep, but if we run into danger, I might strap her on you myself, protest be damned."

That night, Blazel lay on his side, his cot pulled close to Rizelya's. Besides the rip in her throat, numerous cuts crisscrossed her arms and legs, a jagged cut over her right eyebrow marred her face, and she had a cracked rib. He drew in a ragged breath, remembering the last concerted effort of the paethers to bring her down. They almost had. His heart had stopped in terror when the animal raked her with its tusk. He reached out and placed his hand over hers. He'd only known her for less than a lunadar, and already he couldn't imagine life without her.

Alone in the dark, Blazel admitted to himself that he loved her. It was the type of love Histrun had talked about with his mate, Zehala—one which had lasted even beyond her death. When Rizelya looked at him, she saw a competent, brave man. It made him want to prove her right. With her, he had purpose and respect. No one treated him as a rogue wolf. In this world where survival was uncertain, he'd do everything in his power to protect her and keep her safe.

Chapter 10

Blazel - 56 de Sandar, 1075

The next morning, Rizelya awoke grumpy. Blazel took it in stride, happy to have her alive to grumble. He'd suffered a couple of cracked ribs before and knew every movement or breath was painful. Healers could only hasten the healing process of cracked ribs. It'd still be a chedan or two before the rib fully healed.

"Moraak has offered his services," Blazel said, his arm around her as she leaned on him to shuffle out of the house.

"He did? I'm honored."

"You'd probably be more comfortable riding him than your horse."

Rizelya's laugh quickly turned into a sputter of pain. She elbowed him. "Don't make me laugh. It hurts. I've ridden Glork, remember? Moraak is even larger. My ribs can't handle being trussed up like a roast. No, I'd rather ride."

"What if we run into monsters? You can't fight."

"Can too." She plunked her hands on her hips. "Ow!" She bent over, gripping her ribs.

He raised an eyebrow at her.

"Fine, I can't. I won't fight. I'll let one of the Strunhelos alphas take the lead. Will that satisfy you?"

"I'd prefer you to be on Moraak and above any fighting. After the paether attack yesterday, I don't think we'll have a leisurely ride to Strunlair Keep."

She wrinkled her nose. "You're probably right. But don't treat me like I'm an invalid. I've had worse injuries."

"We... I... want you to be safe."

"You're sweet." She patted his chest and started to rise on her toes, but instead hissed in pain. She crooked her finger, beckoning him to bend down. He obliged and kissed her.

Shaela had saddled Kymaya and Lighzel for them. The rest of the battalion had already mounted and watched with respect, and sympathy, as he helped Rizelya into her saddle. Last night, Aistrun had regaled the host with a detailed story of the paether fight, then told other stories featuring Rizelya. By the end of the evening, the Strunhelos fighters were more than a little in awe of the reluctant alpha and her squad. It felt strange when they extended their regard to Blazel.

A Strunhelos platoon alpha, Candriel, urged her horse toward them. She had scarlet hair with pale yellow stripes and pale yellow eyes. Blazel had talked to her last night about keeping Rizelya safe while she recovered, just in case Rizelya refused Moraak's offer. She saluted Rizelya. "Ma'am, I'll take point today while you heal. If you ride in the middle of the group, we can protect you."

Rizelya muttered something about not being an invalid. Blazel held his breath, hoping she'd see the wisdom of letting the other team lead. She finally nodded and motioned for Candriel to head out. After the first platoon passed, they eased into the line along with Jaehaas, Aistrun, and Chariel. Above them flew the Gryphon flight, Moraak's huge wings shadowing the riders below.

As they rode, Blazel kept an eye on Rizelya. Prior to the paether attack, she'd been jumpy and nervous. On some level, she had known something was wrong. But today, she seemed calm and unworried. Either the Malvers woman didn't plan on attacking them, or Rizelya had blocked her mind too much.

An octar after their midday break, a Gryphon overhead shrieked, *Malvers' monsters coming!*

Blazel grabbed Kymaya's reins to ensure Rizelya stayed out of the battle. Fighters sprang into action, herding his group into the center, along with the horses and multas. A group of Reds formed a circle around them and set a fire-ring. Blazel scowled. He wanted Rizelya safe, but he wanted to be part of the action.

Aistrun cleared his throat and spat. "Warrior, take them. I don't need to be treated like a child."

"My thoughts exactly," Jaehaas grumbled, a scowl on his face. He gripped his bow in front of him, his knuckles white.

"Ha!" Rizelya wore a smug smile. "If I have to be coddled, you do, too."

"Can you tell what's happening?" Blazel strained to see beyond the fire-ring. "It has to be different with the Gryphons in the mix."

Rizelya shook her head. "They made the fire-shield opaque to keep the horses calm. Let me try to contact someone." She narrowed her eyes and stared hard at the flames. "Ah, Candriel is sharing the fight with me. The Gryphons are wreaking havoc on the monsters from above. Their flames kill them as effectively as our helbraughts do. The control-janack is still alive and giving them problems." She frowned as she listened to Candriel, then her face lit with a grin and bounced in her seat, then grimaced. "Help is here! The rest of my pack is here!"

Not long after her announcement, the fire-ring dissolved. The women racing toward them consisted of a few Reds, a Yellow, two Browns, a Green, and a beautiful woman with sapphire-blue hair. They grinned in delight, and their joyful laughs filled the air. Blazel recognized them as the original squad of mixed Talents: Rizelya's squad-pack. She jumped off her horse, ignoring her injuries, to run into their arms. Aistrun close on her heels.

Blazel looked over at Jaehaas and Chariel and shrugged. They wore bemused grins as they watched the happy reunion. The three of them were so different from most Posairs—he a lone wolf, Jaehaas a centaur, and Chariel a Gray. Would Rizelya's squad accept them as easily as she had? Now that she was reunited with her pack, would she need him? Would she want him? He glanced away. Could he stay if she didn't want him anymore? The mass of fighters and flights of Gryphons reminded him they had a war ahead of them. No matter what happened between them, he would keep her safe—or die trying. They had invaders to throw off their world, and personal problems couldn't get in the way of accomplishing it.

"Blazel!" She waved at him. "Blazel, come meet the rest of our pack."

He smiled. She'd called it "our pack." He hurried to join them.

Rizelya - 56 de Sandar, 1075

Rizelya's face hurt from all the smiling she was doing. Joy bubbled up every time she caught sight of one of her women or heard their voice. All the women from her original scout-pack rode at her side, even Dehali and the twins, Tami and Kami. She hadn't expected them since the last she knew they were going back to Strunell Keep. Fortunately, Keshanal, the Strunell keep alpha, decided to extend her stay at Strunlair Keep. Rizelya hummed, happy to have her pack nearly complete. Only Wisah, Leistral, and Eidstrun were missing. She glanced behind her and grimaced. She no longer led a pack, but more like a battalion after adding the Strunhelos fighters.

Late in the afternoon, the thick stone wall of Strunlair Keep rose above the forest, pennons snapping in the breeze. Two flags reached for the sky: one the familiar dark-blue and blood-red of Strunlair, the other the emerald-green and sunshine-yellow of Posanlair. When the other province Clan Alphas arrived, their flags would be raised, recognizing all eight provinces. If Wisah accomplished her mission, they would arrive within a chedan.

The north gate stood open, both doors flung wide to allow the large host entrance into the oldest, and largest, fortress in Lairheim. Rizelya sat straight and proud in her saddle as she led the procession through the streets toward the central plaza where the clan-house and temple were located. The Gryphon flight winging overhead cast shadows over them. Shouts from the crowd greeted them, and children waved. People stopped what they were doing to follow them.

Rizelya stopped her horse in front of the clan-house. A sweeping porch of white marble graced the beautiful gray granite house. Flecks of mica in it sparkled in the sun. Columns of black marble supported a balcony, and the dark ironwood double doors were polished to a glossy shine. Helstrim alloy bands strengthened the doors.

The Strunlair Clan Alphas, Beladi and Nestrun, stood on the porch. Beladi wore her dark red hair pulled into an elaborate braid, showing off her long, pale neck. She wore a dark red formal gown with dark blue embroidery. Her gold-ringed red eyes scanned the horde filling her courtyard. Nestrun's formal dark blue tunic over red trousers emphasized his imposing stature. He crossed his brawny arms over his wide chest. His head brushed the porch's low ceiling. Pale green streaked his close-cut red hair, and his eyes matched the green streak.

Rizelya wondered why they wore their finery. She grimaced at the road grime covering her face and hair, wishing she had time to bathe before meeting with the alphas. Nervously, she fingered the mostly healed gash on her throat. Dropping her hand, she gripped the saddle pommel to still the shaking. Blazel's horse moved closer to hers, and he clenched and unclenched his jaw. On her other side, Jaehaas and Chariel came to a halt.

Nestrun's eyes widened as he stared at Chariel. Rizelya had forgotten Chariel's unusual appearance. Before he could say anything to or about Chariel, a loud clap of thunder sounded above them.

"What was that?" Beladi demanded, craning her neck to look beyond the porch ceiling.

"Our allies," Rizelya said.

Moraak, his honor guard of two Thunder Wings, and Graak landed in the courtyard. Horses whinnied and quite a few reared and tried to bolt.

Shh... you silly beasts. Graak soothed. *We promised not to eat you.*

Nervous twitters rippled through the gathered crowd as they realized the Gryphon had mind-spoken to everyone. The riders eventually brought their horses under control. Nestrun and Beladi stepped forward, revealing two strange alphas, both dressed in green and yellow finery—the Posanlair Clan Alphas. Off to the side, her sister, Naila, and her father, Histrun, stood with the territory alphas Keshanal, Layhalya, and Saehala, along with their co-alphas. Histrun gave her a small salute in greeting.

Aistrun jumped off his horse, hurried to stand in front of Moraak, and bowed. "*Oolk keee shree neekalaaak,* Prince Moraak."

Rizelya raised an eyebrow, impressed. He'd pronounced the proper greeting to Gryphon royalty correctly, with all the little clicks and squeals that were so difficult for human throats.

Moraak regally inclined his head.

"Prince Moraak, may I make your acquaintance to Strunlair Clan Alphas Beladi and Nestrun, the leaders of Strunlair Province." Aistrun turned and bowed to the assemblage on the porch. "Honored Alphas, may I introduce to you Prince Moraak, son of King Zorlaak. The Gryphons have graciously left their mountain refuge to help us in our war against the invaders."

Nestrun bowed and stepped down one of the steps to be on the same level as Moraak. "Prince Moraak. It is my great honor to welcome you. We are grateful your people have joined ours once again to fight a great evil threatening our world. Although you have been gone long from our lands, the stories of your bravery and heroic deeds are legendary."

Rizelya put a hand up to hide her smile. The Gryphons had been nothing more than mythical beasts until a few chedans ago.

Our king knows of the trouble facing our world. Moraak dipped his head, and the tip of his tail curled around his feet. *If the invaders leave the Barrens, they will be a danger to the Gryphon as well. Our mystics have warned us of the dire consequences should this happen. We are unwilling to face extinction. The three flights I bring with me are at the disposal of your Supreme Alphas, when you choose them.*

"We appreciate the help. You have flown far, and I'm sure you are tired. There is space for your flights five measures south of the keep. It is far enough away that your presence shouldn't put needless stress on our herds, but close enough for you to participate in the war councils. It should be safe, as no monster nests have occurred in that area, and sheadash stone surrounds it. A herd of billocks runs nearby for you to hunt. We also have livestock available for you, if you desire."

That is most gracious of you, Alpha Nestrun. We saw the place you speak of and my people are heading there. I am most anxious to discuss the coming war with you. For now, we will take our ease and partake of your hospitality. Until tomorrow. Moraak crouched, and with a powerful leap, took to the air. A streak of light from the setting sun gilded his golden feathers. Like a dark shadow, his Thunder Wings followed behind him.

Graak gazed at Blazel expectantly. Blazel nodded, and Graak lowered his beak in a smile. He sat on his haunches, his wings folded tight to his back, and his tail curled around his feet.

"Rizelya," Nestrun said with a shake of his head, "you do know how to shake things up. First you change the composition of the fighting-packs, and now you bring mythical beasts back into our presence. I'm not sure I want to know what you'll do next."

"Next, sir, I fight for our world."

"Come, tell us what you've seen." He turned and entered the clan-house. The other alphas followed him in, except Naila and Histrun.

Rizelya dismissed her people and gratefully handed Shaela her horse's reins. Shaela also took her core group's horses. Rizelya climbed the steps, and Naila immediately enfolded her in her arms. When they pulled apart, Naila's gaze fell on the healing wound on her neck.

"What happened?" Naila croaked and fingered her own scar. She'd received it years ago when a janack wrapped a tentacle around her neck. It had ruined her voice and made it difficult for her to talk.

"A paether tusk caught me. My healer, Bethlyn, assures me it'll heal with barely a scar. It's so good to see you."

Naila agreed.

"Well, boy, you're back." Histrun frowned at Blazel and then looked pointedly at Rizelya's injury. "You're supposed to keep her safe, boy."

"I try, sir, I try." Blazel rolled his eyes as a grin pulled at the corners of his mouth. "It's a bit difficult when trouble seeks her out like a bee to a flower."

"In his defense, sir," Aistrun spoke up, "the paether pack was three times normal size, and they all focused on Rizelya. If it hadn't been for Blazel and Jaehaas's archery skills, she'd be dead."

Histrun raised an eyebrow. "You'll have to tell us the story. Come, we shouldn't make the other alphas wait. You can fill us in on what has happened since you left and how you found the Gryphons and brought them here." Histrun clasped Blazel and Jaehaas's wrists in a warrior's greeting, gazing into their eyes and nodding solemnly. He clapped Aistrun on the back, and together, they led the way into the clan-house.

Rizelya paused and turned to the south—the direction of Strunland Keep and home. She was so close, but so far away. One day she'd get to go home, sleep in her own bed, and visit with her friends. Her thoughts flew to her heart-sister, Kaieli. Even before meeting Blazel, their relationship had changed. Kaieli had gone to Posanlair Province, which bordered the Barrens. Was Kaieli safe? Fear squirmed in Rizelya's stomach as she followed the others inside.

Over the next few days, Clan Alphas from the other provinces arrived on the backs of Gryphons, one set per day. The Andranlair alphas arrived first, followed by Haaslair, Dehanlair, Ronanlair, and Keistanlair. Only one province was missing—Ledonlair.

Rolstrun - 56 de Sandar, 1075

Life in the slave camps took on a set routine. Get up, work in the mine, eat dinner—never enough to fill hungry bellies—go to bed, then start all over again the next day. Exhaustion tugged on Rolstrun. By the time he returned to the slave pens, he could barely eat, let alone spend time with Laean. The last few nights, he'd slept alone on the hard pallet they'd previously shared. He missed her warm presence at night, and her laughter. He hadn't heard her laugh for several days. But then, other than the children, no one laughed much in this hellhole.

If they'd been better fed, Rolstrun and the other men would be the fittest they'd ever been from the hard work mining the nucla. As it was, each evening, Kaieli and the other healers healed the injured men, trying to keep them safe from the invader's appetite.

So far, it worked. The Posairs had been careful—or lucky— to not provoke the invaders and be killed. The invaders killed enough of the alien slaves to feed themselves, even with Kaieli's efforts. Rolstrun doubted their luck would hold much longer.

He dumped his load of broken-up nucla in the large bin. The Hap'thez waiting patiently for the workers to fill the bin gave Rolstrun a small smile and nod. Since Kaieli and the other healers started healing the alien slaves, they'd treated the rest of the Posairs with respect, if not friendliness. The only species they had to watch out for were the nasty Kaigor, who were almost as bad as the invaders for hurting anyone who crossed their paths.

A breeze drifted into the stifling crater. With a sigh of relief, Rolstrun turned into it. A snarl stretched his lips, and he had the overwhelming urge to shift into his warrior form. He fisted his hands, surprised when claws sunk into his palms. The Hap'thez eyes widened, and he whined as his body trembled.

"Monsters," he grumbled. "Where?" He lifted his head, sniffing the breeze. He spotted the nest far across the crater. The control-janack's sensor stalks focused on the invader guards. It herded its brood away from them and up the crater's steep sides.

Ware! Monsters! Rolstrun mind-shouted to everyone he could reach. The alphas spread the call, and within moments, all the Posairs stopped working and faced toward the escaping monsters, quivering with the need to shift. The other slaves sensed the danger and turned in the same direction.

Whips cracked. The guards barked harsh commands Rolstrun had learned meant, "Get to work." But the Posairs ignored them, their full attention on the dangerous Malvers' monsters. The guards noticed the disturbance and stopped to stare at the monsters slithering up the sides of the crater and over the rim.

A guard on a personal mobility device zoomed toward the monsters. He lifted his weapon, readying to fire. The control-janack stopped, and a tentacle snapped out, striking the platform. The invader flew, screaming, straight toward the janack. Another tentacle wrapped around him and dropped the struggling invader into the janack's wide maw. Purple blood oozed through the janack's teeth.

Rolstrun clamped a hand over his mouth to keep his cheer from escaping.

The guards gaped in shock.

Rolstrun hurried to his friends. "The monsters avoided the invaders!"

Calistrun ran a hand over his short hair, grimacing. "Yeah, it was odd. They seemed afraid. I've never seen them act that way. I wonder why?"

Rolstrun shrugged. "It might be why they haven't attacked the camp yet. We've been here two chedans, and this is the first nest we've seen. I hope they stay afraid and stay away. I'm so tired and hungry, I'm not sure I could shift."

"Me too," Alestrun said with a long sigh. "Nothing tastes good, even with the Greens trying to use their Talent. Oh, what I wouldn't give for a juicy billocks steak, mashed tubers, and mookti berries." He sighed again.

"Don't. Just don't." Rolstrun grimaced. "It makes me too hungry." He picked up his shovel and returned to work, but stayed vigilant, expecting more monster nests to erupt.

Chapter 11

Rolstrun - 59 de Sandar, 1075

Rolstrun and the men trudged across the compound toward the crater rim when a commotion on the camp's outskirts caught their attention. The familiar clacks and hisses of janacks overrode the invaders' shouting. Rolstrun tightened his hands into fists and gritted his teeth to keep himself from shifting. A man from the Dehanlair guard-pack howled as he shifted into his warrior form. The closest overseer hissed in alarm, shooting his weapon twice in quick succession at the man. Blood blossomed in the center of his chest, and he dropped unmoving to the ground. Several invaders turned their backs on the monsters to face the Posairs, weapons held ready. Rolstrun and the others helplessly watched their ancient foes attack.

A tentacle snapped scout and struck a soldier, who rolled for several feet on the ground before stopping with his neck at an odd angle. Soldiers urged Kaigor with cracking whips to advance. Three brechas loosed their spines, striking the Kaigor in their chests and faces. They howled with pain and scuttled away. A Hap'thez rushed in, a metal rod in each of his four hands. Using his great strength, he thrust the rods like spears into the side of a brecha. One went all the way through, and the brecha collapsed.

A squad of fifteen invaders swarmed the monsters, firing into them. Bursts of light sizzled from their weapons. They were as effective in harming the monsters as the fire the Reds unleashed with their helbraughts. In less than an octar, they'd killed the monsters. Rolstrun tensed as a brecha race away. An invader with blue-edged robes dropped to one knee and carefully sighted his weapon at the escaping monster. A shot rang out. The brecha jerked, tumbled, and skidded to a halt, its feet waving in the air.

Several soldiers raced to it, looped ropes around it, and dragged it back. The brecha bucked and thrashed, shooting its spines. Two invaders cried out as the spines embedded into their chests. Purple blood gushed from their wounds.

"I hope their wounds are fatal," Rolstrun murmured.

"They are," Flo'kik said. The Volkern had joined them during the battle. "The officers will drain their blood and organs, then give the bodies to the Kaigor to eat."

Rolstrun grimaced and swallowed hard. "Ugh. That explains why there aren't any bodies lying about or any mass graves. I wondered what happened to them. I don't think I'll be able to look at a Kaigor again and not want to puke."

"Many of us have the same reaction."

Commander Ke-ke-tak strode toward the brecha, his gold-edged robes glinting in the morning sun. He examined the monster, being careful of the remaining spines. He touched it with his boot, saying something in his guttural language.

"It's an ugly creature," Flo'kik translated.

Now Rolstrun knew why the translator had joined them. The invaders wanted the Posairs to know what the commander said.

"The only emotion I detect is hunger," the commander continued through Flo'kik. "Not a useful or tasty emotion. I would have expected anger. Now, the big one," he pointed to the control-janack, "was angry. Next time, keep it alive for me." He removed a knife from his belt and jabbed it into the brecha's side. His nose wrinkled. "Gaagh, it doesn't even feel pain. Let's find out if its blood is good, at least."

He motioned to an officer in red-trimmed robes. "You may have the honors."

The captain looked dubious before reluctantly stepping forward. His feeding appendages slowly unfolded. With a grimace of distaste, he plunged them into the brecha.

And screamed.

He continued to scream as his feeding tubes turned bright red. The color spread quickly to the rest of his body, which shook with violent tremors. The jerking pulled his feeders from the brecha, revealing green ichor covering the smoking ends. His feeding tubes slowly disintegrated. The putrescence worked its way to his body, where it spread. His shrieks quieted when it reached his face.

A shot rang out. The captain's body crumpled. It continued to decay at an alarming rate until only a puddle of goo remained.

Terror filled every invader's face in the vicinity, even the commander's.

He turned and glared at the officer in a silver-edged robe, who still held his weapon.

"Mo-de-tak, the commander's brother," Flo'kik whispered.

Mo-de-tak shrugged and put his weapon back in its holster at his hip. "It needed doing. His loyalty earned him a better death."

"So it did." The commander, now composed, turned back to his troops. He pointed to the brecha and the remains of his man. "Burn it. Those creatures aren't edible. We must discover if they are good for something." He speculatively studied the gathered Posairs.

Rolstrun shivered. The commander's gaze didn't bode well for them.

The commander, his brother, and the officers left. Several soldiers jogged to the scene, carrying a machine on their backs with thick tubes connected to it. Fire belched from the tubes, engulfing the monster and the goo puddle.

"What in the twelve hells happened?" Tremors made Flo'kik's voice shake.

"The monster's ichor is acidic," Rolstrun said. "Although I've never seen it do that to anyone. It only burns us."

"Ah, it explains the burn scars on your red-haired women."

"Yes, our Reds."

"Few of your men have such burns. Why? Do you not fight?"

"Our fur protects us from it."

Flo'kik's eyebrows knitted together. "Fur?"

"We fight the monsters in our warrior form."

"Ah, Tre'nok mentioned seeing the shift during the march. There are not many shapeshifting species in the universe. Their rarity makes any found valuable specimens in the Scourge's zoos. Be wary of showing it to them. I overheard they believe you can only change when the monsters are near. Since none of you shifted during this attack or the one in the crater, it will not be long now before the commander tests this theory."

Rolstrun gave him a grim smile and chuckled. "He won't like the results. Our warrior form can tear apart the Malvers' monsters. We will have no trouble with the scrawny invaders."

"They have weapons that outmatch your strength."

"Which is the only reason they still live. They took us by surprise, otherwise we would be free. Our people have been fighting those monsters for a thousand years, and we still survive. We will survive this and toss the scum back to their own world."

"If you do, you will be the first planet to overthrow them." Flo'kik gave him and the other Posairs a measuring look.

The guards motioned with their weapons for the men to move.

"Perhaps you are the ones to do so," Flo'kik said so quietly Rolstrun almost didn't hear him.

"Goddess, grant it be so," Rolstrun prayed.

Kaieli - 59 de Sandar, 1075

The infirmary was busier than usual. The monster attack on the camp terrified the invaders, and they took out their fear on the slaves. By the end of the day, Kaieli drooped with exhaustion. Not all the slaves could make it to her improvised infirmary, and she'd heard of the invaders brutally killing several people. She hadn't treated any of the Posair men, but the invaders didn't allow them out of the crater until sunset. As she plodded from the building, she prayed none of her people had been hurt—or killed.

She snapped her head up, holding her hands over her ears from the roar as one of the two larger ships lifted into the air. The large transport ship's flight path took it northwest, followed by several of the smaller ships. She rubbed her arms, hoping the next keep the invaders attacked wouldn't fall as easily as Posanreande Keep or the guard fortresses. Illness had weakened the Posanreande people, while exhaustion had taken its toll on the guard-packs. The other keeps shouldn't be in such poor condition. Kaieli would know soon enough when the ship returned. Until then, she had her own people to worry about.

Kaieli waited anxiously with the women in the slave pens for the men to return. Finally, over an octar later than normal, the men trudged into view. Kaieli gasped as the first man entered the pens. Blood trailed down his face and dripped from his arm. The next man, and the next, and the next, also sported injuries. She ran to the injured, the other healers right behind her. Even while she tended wounds, Kaieli kept watch for Rolstrun and the other Strunland men. As she bound a cut on a man's thigh, Rolstrun and the others stumbled into the cage.

"Rolstrun," she cried, hurrying to put an arm around his waist, supporting him. "What happened?"

"The invaders decided we caused the monster attack." He grimaced, putting a hand to his face. A bruise darkened his jaw and cheek. He gingerly moved his jaw. "Damn, that hurts. I'm okay, just whip lashes and bruises. Go help Bohandran. He's bad."

Kaieli wiped the trickle of blood from Rolstrun's forehead, assuring herself of the cut's shallowness. Four men carried Bohandran between them. Blood puddled over his abdomen, with smaller splotches on his arms and leg. Deep slashes crisscrossed his face.

"Gently, gently," she urged. "Bring him over here and put him on the table."

He screamed as they laid him down. She'd learned over the past few days how tough the coveralls were. A helstrablade would easily cut the fabric, but she didn't have one—no one did. Her only tools were what the Goddess had given her. She needed to remove his clothing without doing further harm. What could she use? She eyed Rolstrun's hands.

"Can you shift enough to use your claws to cut his coverall off him?"

Rolstrun glanced around and nodded. "Hide me. I'm too tired to shift just my hand."

Several men gathered close, surrounding them with a wall of bodies. Rolstrun shifted into his warrior form, clamping his jaws shut to muffle his yowl of pain. He flexed his claws and used one to quickly and gently slice the fabric down the center and along both arms and legs. It fell away from Bohandran, revealing a large, gaping hole in his stomach and deep gashes on his arms and legs.

Kaieli set to work, vaguely aware of Rolstrun's trouble shifting back to his human form. Her stomach knotted with worry as she examined the hole. Similar wounds on other slaves were difficult to heal. Whatever the invaders used for their projectiles, it resisted anything magical in nature. She sighed, regretting the loss of her healer's bag and the tools, herbs, and potions in it. But even if she hadn't abandoned it at Posanreande Keep the night of the attack, the invaders would have taken it from her.

She called Loshera to her, needing the White's magic to enhance her own. Loshera put her hands on either side of Kaieli's head. She frowned, wondering why they weren't on her shoulders as usual. Then Alpha Maheli, blinking her eyes furiously, put her hand on Kaieli's left arm. Jaelena, a Yellow, placed her hand on her right. Faliciden's hand lightly gripped her right shoulder, and a Blue, Noriana, gently held her left. Together, they represented all of the Talents, except Black. Kaieli gave them each a small smile of gratitude. She closed her eyes and reached with her senses for Bohandran's wound.

At first, her magic hit a wall of resistance. She connected more deeply with the women supporting her, adding their magic to her own. She finally located the projectile, and with great effort, pulled it from the wound. Someone took it away. With it gone, Bohandran's body stopped resisting the magic, and she knitted the torn muscles and blood vessels back together. It would take a few days for them to heal completely.

Kaieli turned her attention to Bohandran's whip lashes. Minute flakes of black dust encrusted the cuts. His blood oozed a thick black and stunk with the beginnings of putrefaction. As she scanned it with her magical sight, the malignant magic in the black dust writhed away from her and burrowed deeper into Bohandran. It reminded her of Barrens sand and the energy in a monster nest. Drawing upon Maheli's Red Talent, Kaieli blasted the particles in the first cut with fire. Charred and burned flesh puddled in the wound. She blew on it, and the ash flew into the air, leaving behind a clean wound, bleeding a normal, bright red.

Faliciden tapped her shoulder. "I can finish healing the wounds once you purge the poison from the other cuts."

Kaieli nodded. It would go faster with both healers splitting the work. The poisonous black dust laced every whip lash. After a long time, Kaieli leaned back with a sigh and opened her eyes. She'd done all she could. The women supporting the healing dropped their hands and stepped back. She swayed with exhaustion and took a deep breath to steady herself.

Rolstrun, still in his warrior form, hunkered in a crouch, panting. A wall of bodies blocked him from the invaders' view. "What's wrong?" she asked.

"He can't shift back." Fear darkened Calistrun's eyes. "He's been trying all the time you worked on Bohandran."

She squinted at Rolstrun, allowing her magical sight to scan him. "They whipped him."

"Yes, several times." Calistrun fidgeted from foot to foot. "Most of us caught a lash or two, but he and Bohandran took the brunt of the punishment."

"Maheli, Faliciden, I need your help again. We'll do what we did for Bohandran."

It didn't take quite so long to purge the poison from Rolstrun's cuts. As soon as she sealed the last one, Rolstrun whined and shifted back to his human form. His knees buckled, and he plopped on his butt onto the ground.

"Oh, thank Goddess!" he exclaimed. "I was scared I was going to be stuck in my warrior form forever."

Kaieli sat on the bench and rubbed her eyes. "They've whipped you before. What was different this time?"

The men looked at each other and shrugged.

Calistrun's eyes widened. "The same overseer hit both Rolstrun and Bohandran. His whip appeared different. The tips glistened black, as if they'd dipped them into something. The other overseers who struck us had regular whips."

"It has the same properties as the Barrens dust. It's possible they made a solution out of it. You've seen what it does. Try not to get whipped with it."

Rolstrun rolled his eyes. "I wasn't trying the first time."

The crowd broke apart, seeking food. Kaieli, Faliciden, and Faelyn hid in the back of the pen, out of sight of the guards, while they continued to treat those with injuries. Thankfully, none of which needed to be purged of poison. By the time the healers finished, the stars shone brightly in the night sky. Kaieli only took a few bites from the small portion of a travel bar before exhaustion hit and sleep claimed her.

The next morning, instead of going to the processing plant, the guards took the women to the big tent where they'd been inducted into slavery. The translators, Tre'nok, Flo'kik, and Vy'shol, waited for them inside the entrance. It appeared the same, except most of the stations didn't have an alien slave waiting beside it. Soldiers, with their projectile sticks held ready, stood widely spaced around the edge of the tent. A tall invader in bronze-edged robes watched the group, his hand resting on the handle of his whip. There wouldn't be any friendly banter with the translators today.

"A new batch of slaves will arrive shortly," Tre'nok informed them. "Your job is to process them. If you refuse, the Scourge will punish your people. They'll kill three out of ten."

Sufficiently terrified, the women willingly separated into groups, listening carefully to the instructions on what to do. They'd just finished and stood behind their stations when the roar of the transport ship landing filled the tent. Soon, dazed Posairs, many with injuries, stumbled inside, and Kaieli reluctantly helped initiate the captives into their new life of slavery. Kaieli's assignment to the health station, whether by luck or design—Kaieli thought Tre'nok had a hand it in—allowed her to covertly heal all but the worst injuries. And those, she healed enough to hide them from the invaders. She now knew the invaders would kill anyone unable to work.

She swallowed the lump in her throat, blinking back tears. Another keep, this one not decimated by plague, had fallen to the invaders' greater weapons. Fighting for their freedom seemed a lost cause. As she and the others trudged to the slave pens, Kaieli gazed at the sky, wishing—hoping—for another glimpse of a Gryphon. Her shoulders slumped. No sign of the great creatures floated over the crater. Would help from her people ever arrive?

Blazel - 64 de Sandar, 1075

Blazel stood at his and Rizelya's bedroom window, scowling at the empty sky. Wisah, Sheekeek, and their flight hadn't returned yet. He fingered a twisted strand of hair as worry squirmed in his stomach. He still wore his hair in the tangled locs he'd obtained while in the swamps. The only way to change them was to shave his head. He held the superstitious belief he'd lose his magic if he was bald. Besides, no one had time for such niceties as hair cuts.

"They should be here by now. Something bad happened."

"You don't know that for sure." Rizelya finished braiding her hair, which he noticed now reached her waist. "Why don't you talk to the Gryphons who flew with her and have returned?"

Blazel whipped around, his locs thumping his back. "Good idea. I'll talk to them while you're in your meeting."

Outside the pack-house, they separated. Rizelya headed to the Clan-house, while he tracked down the Gryphon who'd flown from Keistanlair. The last one who had seen Wisah and the others.

"Yes, Wisah, Sheekeek, and the others flew toward Ledonlair," the Gryphon assured him. "They left Ledonlair at the same time as my group returned here."

Not reassured, Blazel jogged to the Gryphon camp to talk to Graak. Ledonlair Province neighbored Strunlair, and it shouldn't have taken Wisah and Sheekeek more than a day's flight. When Blazel found Graak, his head feathers and fur stood on end, and the tip of his tail lashed furiously.

"Any sign of them yet?" Blazel shielded his eyes with a hand and scanned the sky.

Graak shook his head, still gazing to the northeast. *A storm could have delayed them or they could be lost. None of them have been here before.*

Blazel scowled at the excuse. All the other Gryphons had found their way to the keep. "Should we search for them?"

Without knowing their path, it would be like looking for a single needle in a conifer. Besides, Moraak forbids it. He does not want anyone else to become lost. Graak pulled his gaze from the sky. *How are the meetings?*

"Long," Blazel huffed. "Between Aistrun, Rizelya, and me, we have told the same story fifteen times, at least. They pick apart all the little details. I'm surprised you haven't had to tell them your story."

There is no need. Moraak speaks for all of us.

"But he wasn't at the crater. How could he know what happened?"

We performed the molktaak ceremony. He now knows everything I, and the other scouts, saw and heard. We do not share this way often or lightly.

When Blazel lived with Graak's flight years ago, he'd briefly heard about the ceremony. Times like now, with the endless meetings and repeating the same story, he wished the Posairs could transfer information as easily. Not required to attend the meetings, Blazel stayed in the Gryphon camp, visiting Graak.

The noon sun rode high in the sky when a dark smudge appeared on the horizon. Blazel squinted. A flash of silver caught the sunlight. "Isn't that Sheekeek?"

It is. The flight returns. Graak crouched in invitation, and Blazel jumped on his back.

They flew the short distance to Strunlair Keep, landing in the courtyard moments before Sheekeek and the others. The Clan Alphas streamed out of the clan-house with Rizelya, Aistrun, Jaehaas, and Chariel in the rear.

Rizelya glowered at the press of people in front of her, preventing her from leaving the porch. She jumped over the railing and hurried to Blazel's side. A commotion on the porch turned their attention from the circling Gryphons. Jaehaas elbowed his way through the crowd. They scampered out of the way of his stamping horse hooves. Aistrun and Chariel followed in his wake.

"I should have just waited for him," Rizelya grumbled, "instead of jumping over the railing."

"Ah, but I enjoyed watching you." Blazel pulled her closer to his side.

As soon as Sheekeek landed, Jaehaas rushed to his side and helped unhook Wisah from her riding harness. She squeaked when he pulled her into a tight embrace.

With more decorum, the Ledonlair alphas climbed off their Gryphon mounts and gave them a bow of respect before walking to the clan-house.

"Now that we are all here," Nestrun said after greeting the newcomers, "we can begin the process of choosing a Supreme Alpha pair for the duration of the war." He motioned for his fellow alphas to reenter the building. When Rizelya and the keep alphas stepped forward, he stopped them. "No, we don't need you any longer. This is for the clan alphas to decide. Moraak, you may join us as an observer."

Moraak dipped his head. *It will be my honor.* He followed the Clan Alphas inside.

Graak sent the flight, except Sterkek and Sheekeek, to the Gryphon camp, leaving only Blazel's group milling in front of the clan-house.

"What took you so long?" Blazel asked.

Wisah ran a hand over her hair and rubbed her neck. She leaned against Jaehaas's shoulder. "I'm exhausted. We've flown nearly the entire length and breadth of Lairheim in twelve days. I don't think anyone's ever done it before. I need to sit on something that isn't moving."

Rizelya laughed. "Ha, I know what that's like. Come on, let's get you some food. I'm starving. I've been shut up in meetings with the alphas all morning, and we were just about to have lunch when you arrived." She took Wisah's arm and walked toward the pack-house assigned to them. The rest of the group following in their wake.

By the time they settled in the entertainment room, an older woman pushed a cart filled with covered plates into the room. She uncovered them to reveal sandwiches and fruit. Behind her, another cart trundled in, pushed by a younger woman who disdainfully lifted the covers. Neatly cut slices of raw meat oozed blood onto the plates. She eyed the Gryphons, and, with a sniff, stalked out.

"We didn't have many problems," Wisah said, putting down her utensils and pushing away her plate. "Other than figuring out where we were going." She smiled at Sterkek.

Sterkek ruffled his head feathers. *The maps we had were for someone traveling on the ground. They didn't account for how different things appear from the air. Finding Andranlair was easy, but Dehanlair? There weren't any distinctive landmarks for us to use. And Haaslair? The sea of plains grass made it a nightmare to find! Afterward, it was easier.*

Wisah patted Sterkek's shoulder. "You did well, Sterkek. A storm in the mountains surrounding Ledonlair delayed us. There was too much lightning for the Gryphons to fly through."

In unison, the Gryphons shuddered. Blazel recalled his time spent with Graak's flight, and the Gryphons' terror of lightning storms. A strike could turn a Gryphon into a fiery explosion.

"Then, just before we left Ledonlair, monsters attacked the keep."

"They what?" Rizelya exclaimed. Her hand flew to the center of her chest. "They haven't directly attacked a keep in years."

"Not since your parents developed the Zehis method of fighting," Aistrun added, a haunted look filling his eyes. "My sister was one of the last in Strunlair Province killed in an attack on a keep. Now, we take the fight to them and stop them in the nests."

The Malvers are becoming bold, Graak observed. *I doubt anything will stay the same. Why haven't they attacked us directly?*

"They can't." Chariel rolled her goblet in her hands. "The Supreme told me about them before we left. When our ancestors exiled them, we believed them too weakened to do anything. But they somehow created the janacks and brechas to attack us. The priestess esof the time erected a magical barrier around the Malvers' island, stopping them from doing any further magic on Lairheim. It's held these thousand years. But something has changed, allowing them more control of their monsters." She looked at Rizelya. "Do you know why?"

Rizelya grimaced. "No. They have a device that allows them to feed off the deaths caused by the monsters. And there's been more deaths recently."

Blazel swore. "If they're feeding more, they must be getting stronger. Hopefully, they don't become strong enough to escape their island exile."

It would not be easy for them to escape, Sheekeek said, his gaze distant. *Their malignant magic has filled the seas with monsters no longer in their control. They would have to find, or create, a way to fly off it.*

"The invaders have flying ships," Blazel said. "Could they use one of those?"

Only if they allied with the invaders. A shudder rippling over Graak's fur. *That would not be good.*

The group fell silent. Blazel contemplated the horror of an alliance between their ancient enemies and their new ones. Even with the help of the Gryphons, would the Posairs survive such an alliance?

While waiting for the clan alphas to choose a new war leader, Blazel's group and the Gryphons rested, taking advantage of the respite.

Chapter 12

Rolstrun - 1 de Drudar, 1075

Dehanrandean Keep fell to the onslaught of the invaders. Over the new few days, Dehanrandevir, Haaslorndeven, Haaslornas, and Posanlynde Keeps lost the battle for freedom, and the population of the slave camp swelled to over two thousand people. The men mined the nucla in the crater while the women and children worked in the processing plant.

As each keep fell, adding more people to the slave camp, Rolstrun worried the concentration of warm bodies would draw the Malvers' monsters. So far, luck blessed them, and the monsters hadn't attacked the compound. A camp full of people unable to run or fight would provide a buffet for the monsters.

Their luck changed the day after the people from Posanlynde Keep arrived. While the men marched to the crater, the monsters attacked. Rolstrun and the other long-term captives struggled to control the instinctive urge to shift and fight their ancient foes, letting the invaders deal with the monsters. But five younger men lost the battle with their instincts and raced into the fray, howling with rage as they shifted.

They tore into a janack, flinging hunks of it with abandon. A large chunk hit the officer leading the counter-offensive. He scowled as he flicked the debris away, then started screaming as the acid ate through his glove and into his hand. A colonel in silver-edged robes strode to him and, with a swipe of his long knife, cut off the injured hand. He dragged the other officer from the battleground. Angered, the soldiers riddled the young Posairs with projectiles.

More soldiers rushed toward the monster battle. The guards pushed and shoved the Posair men into a tight circle. Whips flicked indiscriminately and weapon butts slammed into unsuspecting heads and backs. Rolstrun and the other men who'd been in captivity for a while shouted to the others to stand down and not attack. The invaders still outnumbered and outmatched the Posairs. Finally, the invaders defeated the monsters. Rolstrun waited, head held low, knowing the punishments weren't over.

The commander exited the command ship and stalked to the group. His big, bug-like eyes were even wider in anger— or possibly fear—and the feeding appendages on his back rattled ominously. He checked on his fallen man first. When it appeared the monster toxin hadn't infiltrated the man's system, nodded to two soldiers, who carried the man away to be eaten at the commander's leisure. The invaders didn't tolerate maimed soldiers or captives. Tre'nok hurried to stand behind the commander.

"Insolence is not tolerated," Tre'nok translated. "For every one slave who is insubordinate and forgets they are slaves, five others will be punished. To encourage you to begin self-regulating and keeping each other in line, the next time punishment is due, ten will be punished, then fifteen, and so on. This includes your women and children."

The commander paused.

Pitiful cries and screaming grew louder. Rolstrun craned his neck to see what was happening. Soldiers herded a group of fifty children toward a pen in the center of the compound and shoved them inside. He winced at the loud click as the lock slammed into place.

"They will be held here for safekeeping against your good behavior," Ke-ke-tak continued. "Each punishment will result in the death of one child. They provide insignificant nourishment and are of little use to us, but you seem to cherish them." He shook his head as if baffled.

Rolstrun gasped at the invaders' willingness to so callously kill children. *The bastards will receive the justice due to them,* he vowed. *It's only a matter of time, and I'll happily deliver my fair share of it.*

"I promise you, their deaths will not be easy or painless." Ke-ke-tak let the threat hang in the air. After a long moment, he motioned to an officer, who randomly selected 25 men.

Breathing out a sigh of relief, Rolstrun felt like a coward when they passed him over. Five overseers stepped forward, each with nucla-coated whips, and thrashed the chosen men until blood flowed freely, and they slumped nearly unconscious. Ke-ke-tak pointed to two battered men, and the colonel stood over one of them. His feeding tubes extended and plunged into the man's chest. Several of the new Posairs gagged and threw up. When nothing but a husk remained, the colonel disengaged and straightened, smacking his thin lips. He bowed to the commander, who barked an order, and two soldiers dragged the other man away. Ke-ke-tak followed, his tongue flicking in and out. Rolstrun suspected the man would soon feed the commander.

The guards released the surviving men, and they shuffled to the mine. Additional guards joined them as they marched to the edge of the crater. Several men muttered angrily together, but quickly stopped when the nucla-laced whips slashed across their backs. Curses burned Rolstrun's mind as the men continued to rage, this time in mind-speech. Rolstrun clenched his fists in anger and kept his thoughts to himself. *How dare the invaders treat children like livestock? We have to find a way to get the children out of this hellhole and stop the invaders.*

Rolstrun surreptitiously studied the compound as they marched. Thousands of invaders swarmed the twenty-measure area, going about their business or training with their weapons. There were more of them than the entire population of Lairheim. The Posair's were so outnumbered, how could they defeat the Scourge? He rubbed his arms as his hope flagged, and his fingers ran over the outline of the tracker buried beneath his skin. In all the other trauma happening, no one had talked to

Kaieli about removing them. Until they found a way to remove the trackers, they'd have no chance of escaping. He wondered if the invaders had also tagged the children with explosives.

Rather than the usual small complement of guards inside the crater, the additional guards stayed with the Posair men throughout the day. The guards used their nucla laced whips liberally until everyone received a whip lash or two. Rolstrun winced as the new lash on his shoulder burned anew when he started climbing the ladder.

Blazel - 2 de Drudar, 1075

After two days of deliberation, the alphas called a public meeting. People packed the courtyard, jostling each other for a better view of this historic moment. The last Supreme Alphas chosen had led the Great War. As the only Gryphons in the courtyard, a quiet space surrounded Graak and Sheekeek and enveloped Blazel, Rizelya, and their pack. Blazel sighed in relief as his stomach, queasy from having so many people surrounding him, finally settled.

Nestrun and Beladi led the procession of Clan Alphas. They took positions along the porch. Nothing in their demeanor gave away who they'd chosen. Moraak exited the building and sat off to the side. His huge, golden presence caused a stir in the crowd. Nestrun held up his hand for quiet.

"Friends," his voice boomed, enhanced by Yellow Talent to reach the farthest corner of the courtyard, "this occasion is one of great sadness. We fight every day for our survival against the Malvers' monsters, and now, we must fight to maintain our freedom from the invaders. In times of great need, we raise two of us to the Supreme Alpha leadership position. They have the authority to command all Posairs, and by law, we must follow them wherever they lead. This is a position of great responsibility, for they have our lives in their hands. Their command will determine whether we fight or withdraw. It is on their heads if we live or die during this war. For this reason, the Supreme Alphas must be ones who will take this responsibility and hold it as a sacred duty. They must also be willing to let it go when the war ends and we no longer have need of their leadership.

"We had a long discussion about who would be the right person at this time in our history." Nestrun lifted an arm, indicating his fellow Clan Alphas.

"In the end, the decision was an easy one. There is only one who has given so much already to our survival. He has years of experience in leading a host. Only one of us has shown he can be both ruthless and compassionate." Nestrun paused and looked at the alphas on the porch. Each one lifted their chin and nodded. Nestrun turned his gaze toward the keep alphas standing in the front. His eyes sought and found someone.

"Histrun de Strunland, will you accept this calling of the Goddess to lead our people? Will you be our Supreme Alpha in our time of need?"

Blazel gasped. He'd expected them to choose one of the current, and much younger, Clan Alphas. He'd met Histrun when he was a heartbroken man helping a young boy. Then he remembered Histrun had served as Strunlair's Clan Alpha for over sixteen years. But that was a long time ago. Age now faded Histrun's hair to a dull-red and his shoulders stooped.

"I don't believe it!" Rizelya threw her hands in the air. "Histrun? Supreme Alpha?" She groaned and dropped her head in her hands. "There'll be no living with the man after this."

Histrun shook his head. "No... I..." His hand drifted to the thin, gold wire torque with a ruby that he always wore. Hope, and confidence, gleamed in Nestrun's face. Histrun sighed and limped forward.

Slowly, he climbed the steps and turned around to face the crowd. "Yes." His voice trembled. He cleared his throat, and this time when he spoke, his powerful voice rang throughout the courtyard. "Yes, I accept. But only if Keshanal agrees to be my co-supreme and Naila accepts the role of my commander-in-chief."

The two women—one an old friend, the other the daughter of Histrun's love—blinked. Keshanal held up her hands, shaking her head. Naila staggered back and pinched the bridge of her nose. Their eyes glazed as they mind-spoke. Finally, they nodded and climbed the steps.

The crowd cheered and broke into happy pandemonium. Many of them remembered Histrun as their Clan Alpha, and Keshanal had been alpha of Strunell Keep for years. They made a good pairing. Together, Histrun and Keshanal would be excellent Supreme Alphas. The Posairs had their leaders.

Now they could go to war.

Rizelya - 2 de Drudar, 1075

To celebrate the new Supreme Alphas, the Clan Alphas hosted a formal dinner party. Rizelya knew Histrun didn't want any such fuss, but this celebration was for the people, not him. Besides, this might be the last happy event for many lunadars to come.

She, Chariel, Wisah, and the other girls kicked the men out of their joint room so they could get ready for the dinner in peace. Rizelya slid into the bronze silk dress Kaieli had brought her the last time they were both in Strunlair Keep. She missed her heart-sister and wished she could be here. She'd love the party. The loose cut of the dress hid Rizelya's lack of curves. The sleeveless bodice showed off her muscular arms, and the color highlighted the brown tones in her deep auburn hair and made her brown eyes even darker. There wasn't a speck of red in her wardrobe tonight. She loved the change from the red leathers she wore every other day of her life. She smoothed her hands over her dress, luxuriating in the feel of silk rather than leather under her fingers.

Leistral, in a fitted, pale rose gown, approached her holding a thin strip of cloth. "Here." She reached around Rizelya's waist and tied a belt embroidered in turquoise and rose. "You need something in our colors."

A few moments later, Dehali, Tami, and Kami bustled into the room, wearing gowns in Strunland's colors. She expected Dehali's gown to be in Strunland's colors, but not the twins. The dorm room swirled with the other women in her pack, chatting excitedly about the festivities.

"I can't wait for the dancing," Grazeen gushed, her eyes alight.

"Oh!" Chariel's eyes widened. She placed a hand over the diamond necklace hanging around her neck, symbolizing her status as a full priestess. "I didn't realize there would be dancing. I haven't ever danced with a man before."

"What about Blazel?" Rizelya asked. "Does he know how to dance?"

Chariel cocked her head to the side. "He does. But he was just a boy the last time I danced with him, so that doesn't count."

"Don't worry about it. Aistrun is an excellent dancer." Rizelya assured her.

As they walked toward the stairs, Rizelya slowed, letting the others go ahead of her. She snagged Wisah's arm and linked their elbows. She'd noticed Wisah's crestfallen face at the mention of dancing. Jaehaas, as a centaur, couldn't swirl her around the dance floor. "Aistrun and Blazel will make sure you have fun, too."

"I know." Wisah patted Rizelya's arm. "Sometimes, it's hard loving a centaur. But I wouldn't change him. He's perfect the way he is." Her face lit with joy when Jaehaas stepped forward, holding out his hand to escort her to dinner.

Rizelya waited until the others had left to take the last step down the stairs. Blazel's eyes shone, and he wore a bemused smile. He'd tied his tangled ropes of hair back into a neat tail.

"My lady," he said, with a small bow and offering her his hand.

She placed her hand lightly on his. He smiled and pulled her close to him.

"You are gorgeous!" he whispered into her ear. "I'm the luckiest man here to have you at my side."

Rizelya blushed. She didn't consider herself pretty with all the acid burns from the monsters and now the scar across her neck. Her insides warmed, and her stomach fluttered at his compliment.

The kitchen staff outdid themselves in preparing the feast. Rizelya savored each dish. Soon, her diet would consist of trail bars, pan bread, and stew. After Chariel's earlier comment, Rizelya hadn't expected Blazel to be much of a dancer. But he surprised her with how well he danced. She sat on a bench, waiting for him to bring her a cool drink, and watched the dancers. She easily spotted her special pack.

Saffren wore a tight-fitting, low-cut, dark turquoise gown—the same color as her eyes—that showed off her curvaceous body. Raeleen and her partner swirled past her. Raeleen's rose gown's long sleeves hid the scars on her arms from working stone. The full skirt of Gehan's light turquoise gown flared as her dance partner spun her in a circle. Rizelya's toe tapped in time with the music as the tune changed. Grazeen laughed as she bowed off the floor. Her tight-fitting deep rose sheath gown wasn't suitable for the lively jig.

Blazel handed her a cup. The fruity drink held just a hint of alcohol warmth. As she sipped, her eyebrows rose. Every one of her purloined pack wore shades of rose and turquoise, her territory of Strunland's colors. The men appeared dashing in dark turquoise trousers and jackets over pale rose shirts. Jaehaas sported the same jacket and shirt. Laynar and her little sister, Laynal, wore embroidered belts in Strunland's turquoise and rose over their Strunheim fuchsia gowns. Rizelya's hand drifted to the similar belt Laynar gave her, now understanding its significance.

A lump formed in her throat.

"Oh, my. How did I luck out with such an amazing pack?"

"How so?"

"I dragged them from Strunven Keep through dangers to Strunlair Keep, only to abandon them for nearly a lunadar while I went on a quest to the Deep Mountains. And now, we're in this formal setting, and they're showing to the world their allegiance to me. Even Chariel and Wisah are wearing a sash in Strunland colors over their priestess gowns. I've never seen a priestess do that before." She gestured at him. He wore the same outfit as the other men. "You, too. Our keep colors signify our loyalty and home."

"Wherever you are is my home." Blazel's eyes burned with intensity. "I never expected to find love and acceptance. Then I met you." He lifted her hand and kissed it. "Let's find someplace we can be alone."

She and Blazel drifted from the dining hall into the cool night air and found a secluded spot where they made love. As he held her in his arms, Rizelya felt she was the luckiest woman to have a man like Blazel love her. In the early morning hours, they wandered back to the dorm room they shared with the others. Many of the beds stood empty. Other members in their pack had also taken advantage of the warm summer night.

Chapter 13

Rolstrun - 3 de Drudar, 1075

As usual, the men parted ways with the women and anxiously headed toward the crater. After the attack on the camp by monsters a few day ago, they expected another one at any time. Rolstrun whirled around at the screams of terror and pain coming from behind him. "Dear Mother, no!" he cried. Without thinking, he raced back.

A group of brechas clawed their way out of the crater. Already five janacks, one control-janack, and thirty brechas had reached the top and attacked the women. Only a token guard protected them. A janack wrapped a tentacle around a teenage girl, drawing her toward its open maw. Brecha spines impaled several women.

Rolstrun yelled in pain as he tried to shift. He'd received numerous whippings over the past few days. Even though Kaieli attempted to remove the nucla from him, enough still coursed through his body to make shifting difficult and painful. He reached for his magic again. It felt like a thick haze of malignant magic blocked it from him. Another woman screamed as a janack flung her through the air and into its waiting mouth.

Rolstrun was a warrior. His job was to protect his people, and he was failing. Rage gave him strength, and he broke through the barrier blocking his magic, pulled it to him, and shifted.

Maheli, Laean, and several other valiant Reds threw fire at the monsters. But without their helbraughts, it seemed like they were throwing a bucket of water rather than the usual focused spear. Kothera knelt with her fingers touching the ground. A tiny line of fire trickled from her fingertips. Myndera and three other Reds gathered around her, gripping her shoulder. With their added strength, a thin wall of fire separated the women and children from the monsters. Rolstrun dove over the wall and faced the monsters. With a growl, he tore into them. Calistrun, Alestrun, and several more men soon joined him.

Shots rang out as the invaders finally entered the battle.

Be careful, Rolstrun warned. *Watch what you're doing so no invaders get hurt because of our actions.* He knew the commander would punish those who shifted. He hoped the commander would be lenient with them and not kill them— or any other Posairs—if they didn't harm any soldiers during the fight. If they saved their people, Rolstrun counted any punishment he received worth it, even if the commander killed him.

Keeping track of the invaders made the battle more difficult, but the warriors were all experienced fighters. They worked together in controlled and coordinated attacks. Soon, only the control-janack survived. The Reds didn't have their helbraughts to plunge into the monster's head to explode it. Rolstrun stepped back, seeking a way to kill it. An invader tossed a canister toward the control-janack. It snapped the canister out of the air and swallowed it. The soldiers bolted from the janack.

Run! Rolstrun yelled as he sprinted away. A boom thundered, and the ground shook. He crashed to the ground and curled up, protecting his head with his arms. Surprisingly, little monster debris rained on him. He cautiously lifted his head. A small, still-smoking crater filled the space where the control-janack had been. The fire-ring dissolved, and the women huddled together, fear filling their faces. The smaller children buried their faces against their mother's shoulders, sobbing.

Did everyone get out in time? Calistrun asked.

No, one of my men died. Kolhaas, the alpha from Haaslornas Keep, said. *We'd better shift. They are looking at us strangely.*

The gathered invaders stared at them with a mix of fear and awe. Rolstrun quickly shifted, wincing at the burn from a splotch of monster ichor. He and the others stood with heads bowed and hands behind their backs, being as nonthreatening as possible, while they waited for their punishment.

The commander finally arrived, with Flo'kik as his translator. He surveyed the battle scene, his tongue flicking quickly in and out. After speaking quietly to his men, he strode menacingly toward the waiting Posairs. He stood in front of them, hands on his hips, one hand fingering his whip.

"Why should I not have all of you killed for your insolence?"

Rolstrun stepped forward. He'd been the first to shift. He was responsible for the others. "Sir, we only tried to protect our womenfolk. We could not allow them to be killed. They don't fight. We did not injure any of your men."

"Some of your women fight."

"Not all, sir. They were in danger. The monsters had killed several already when we arrived."

"I'm allowing you to live, only because your actions didn't cause harm to my men, but it does not absolve you of punishment. I will spare a child, in this instance only. But do not think me weak."

Rolstrun knelt and bowed his head. "Thank you, sir."

The men who had fought with him also knelt before the commander. The soldiers forced ten more men onto their knees. *I'm sorry, but I couldn't let the monsters kill the women,* Rolstrun said to Bohandran.

Do not worry about it, Bohandran assured him. *You showed courage to do what was right, even in the face of danger.*

The commander signaled the whip wielders. Rolstrun tensed his back, waiting for the first lash and knowing what to expect from the numerous whippings he'd received. Blinding, fiery pain slashed at his senses, continuing long after the whipping stopped.

He vaguely heard Flo'kik convey the commander's orders. "These men are not to be healed by your witches."

He groaned, suddenly terrified. This may have been his last time shifting if Kaieli couldn't remove the nucla poisoning from his system. A whimper escaped from his lips.

The commander tilted back his head and laughed. He continued to laugh as he left the slaves.

Soldiers forced Rolstrun and the other men to their feet and marched them to the crater. Rolstrun moved through the day in a daze, not fighting the despair wrapping around him. He'd admired Histrun and the other warriors' fierce courage and dignity when he was a small child. When he'd turned old enough to shift into his warrior form, he'd chosen to follow the warrior path. He only knew how to fight the monsters, and it was the only thing he wanted to do. The thoughts of herding multas or tilling the land filled him with dread. He enjoyed providing an important service to his clan by protecting those who chose to live a more peaceful life. The scars he carried from the numerous monster battles were badges of honor. If he couldn't shift into his warrior form and fight the monsters, then what did he have left to live for?

Rizelya - 3 de Drudar, 1075

When the war councils began, Rizelya and Blazel believed they weren't required, and walked toward the practice arena with their weapons. A young boy ran up to them.

"Ma'am, sir," he said, panting, "the Supreme Alphas request you to join them." Without waiting for a response to his message, he raced off again.

"Damn," Rizelya swore. "I'm so tired of sitting in meetings all day. I've been stuck inside for days. Why do they want me?"

"It could be you are now a battalion alpha."

"Hush, don't remind me—or them. I'm trying to convince Naila to take them off my hands."

"Why would you do that? Don't you like them?" Blazel's voice held disappointment in it.

Rizelya kicked at a rock, sending it flying ahead of them. "They are good people. That isn't the problem. I didn't even want to be a squad-alpha, and now look at me!"

"I've watched you. You're an excellent leader." He put an arm around her shoulder. "We're in this together, love. I certainly didn't ever expect to be an alpha of anything."

Holding hands, they entered the packed council chamber. The large room seemed tiny, with Moraak and Sheekeek sitting to one side. They'd removed the conference table and added extra chairs, placing them in rows facing the front. Histrun, Keshanal, and Naila sat on a raised platform behind a table. The Haaslair Clan Alpha, Kaidel, stood next to it with her arms crossed over her chest and scowling. When Rizelya and Blazel entered, Histrun motioned to them.

"Ah, Rizelya." Histrun clasped his fingers together and leaned forward. "The other Clan Alphas noticed your unconventional pack last night."

"Hard not to notice," Kaidel muttered. "You even absconded with one of my people."

"Jaehaas is just a friend," Rizelya huffed.

"He be wearing your colors." Kaidel glared at Rizelya.

"His choice. I didn't force him. Besides, anyone can change clan affiliation." Rizelya clenched her teeth and fisted her hands in an effort to keep from disrespecting the alpha.

"Only if it be agreed upon by the respective Clan Alphas." Kaidel shook a finger at Rizelya. "And I do not agree."

Histrun pounded the table with a wooden block. "Enough!" he roared. "This is not the time to be worried about who is in what clan. We are all Posairs. Back to business." He waited until Kaidel sat next to her co-alpha. "We can't assume we can fight the invaders the same way we've fought the Malvers' monsters. Rizelya, tell us about your new fighting methods using *all* the Talents."

Blazel squeezed her hand and stepped to the side. Her knees quivered with everyone's attention on her, some of them hostile, like Kaidel. Layhalya gave her an encouraging gesture. "Well," she croaked, then cleared her throat. She focused on the people she knew. For some reason, this group intimated her. She'd spoken before hundreds while teaching the new methods at the various keeps. She could do this.

"The other Talents aren't useless in a battle, as tradition has taught us. In fact, they have some creative, and effective, ways to kill the monsters. The only way to safely reach and kill a control-janack, for instance, is by using a cold-air shield the Yellows create."

"Wait," Posanlair Clan Alpha Teleposan held up a hand. "You're able to stop the control-janack? How?"

Rizelya nodded. "We can, by working with the other Talents. The control-janack can't sense anything behind a cold-air shield, which allows a Red to jump onto its head and plunge a helbraught into it and explode it. A fire-shield keeps the burning debris from hitting anyone on the ground."

The Clan Alphas looked at each other, confused.

"What be this fire-shield?" Kaidel asked.

"Something Naila discovered and taught me. I've been teaching it to everyone I meet."

"I can attest to that," Keshanal said. "Rizelya has freely shared whatever she's learned. I'm excited to see what else she has come up with now she's added the other Talents."

Rizelya bowed to Keshanal. She'd been a supporter and mentor since they'd met. "My team will teach you everything we've learned to better fight the monsters. Some of the techniques, I hope, will be effective in fighting the invaders. They possess weapons capable of shooting a Gryphon while it's flying. We need to find some way of shielding them, perhaps with hardened air. We don't know what else the invaders can do, so we have to be ready for anything. And to do so, we need to use every Talent available. Even the Whites and Grays can help. When we fought the baethor in the Deep Mountains, Chariel and Wisah did this amazing thing with their voices that helped us defeat them."

Keistanlair Clan Alpha Farikeistan's hand flew up to cover his open mouth. "But... but a White Priestess can't fight. It's blasphemous!"

Histrun scowled at him. "You don't remember your history much. Who stopped the Great War? Shandir, a White Priestess. The warrior is one of the Goddess's aspects—not just Her consort, but Her. Have you taken time to look at the mural in the Sanctuary temple? If you had, you'd realize the Warrior Goddess has white eyes."

Farikeistan's eyes widened.

"I will use any, and all, means available to me," Histrun continued, "including White and Gray Priestesses. Rizelya, I think a demonstration is in order. Gather your people. We'll reconvene in the practice arena." Histrun pounded his wooden block again.

"This will be interesting," Blazel said as they walked out. "I haven't seen your pack fight yet."

"You haven't?"

Blazel shook his head. "But I have seen the aftereffects of their fighting. Jaehaas and I happened upon the tail end of a battle here in Strunlair Territory. These people are in for a shock when they see what Grazeen does with a monster."

Rizelya laughed at the thought.

When everyone settled into the stands at the practice arena, Rizelya created a realistic monster illusion she and Eiden developed. She'd used it to great effect when demonstrating the new techniques on her long ride through Strunlair Province.

Grazeen stepped forward first. Green light flowed from her helbraught and surrounded the brecha running toward her. It squirmed as it rotted. Rizelya smirked in satisfaction as Kaidel gagged when snelks appeared and ate the mess. The two Browns demonstrated their techniques next. Awed murmurs washed over the crowd as Maellyn used lava to destroy her monster, and Raeleen turned hers into sheadash stone. Using her Yellow Talent, Gehan pierced the brecha illusion with a cold-air spear, immediately freezing it solid. As it tumbled to the ground and shattered, the audience clapped loudly.

The crowd stilled in quiet shock when beautiful Saffren stepped onto the field and tossed back her sapphire-blue hair. She calmly fought her brecha, making it boil with her water Talent. The crowd burst into raucous cheering.

Rizelya moved forward to end the demonstration but stopped when Jaehaas and Blazel strode into the center, each carrying a bow and a quiver of arrows. She scrambled to reset the illusions for them as they shot fiery arrow after arrow. Off to the side, Saffren deftly put out their fires. Several people excitedly announced they were archers and wanted to learn the fire-arrow spell. She smiled. She would never have known the spell if Jaehaas hadn't shared it with her. The conversation she'd had with Keshanal—what seemed ages ago—about the need to share knowledge between the clans floated to her. Sadly, it had taken a major crisis for it to happen.

"Why, we do that all the time," Kaidel said.

"But have you shared the technique with the rest of us?" Histrun asked coldly.

Kaidel gulped and shook her head. "I didn't think it would be useful outside of the plains."

Histrun still glared at her. "Precisely. You didn't think." He turned to the others. "Let's take this as a lesson. We may all have developed unique methods that work in our home provinces but haven't shared with each other. Now is not the time to keep secrets. Share. Talk among yourselves. Find out what you don't know.

"Rizelya's team will train you on the cold-air and fire-shields. Those are the most useful against the monsters. When the troops converge, her pack will train your people. I'm giving you the rest of today to learn the techniques. You'll return home tomorrow to assemble your troops. Strunlair marches in two days. Dismissed!"

Histrun walked away for several steps, then turned around and returned to Rizelya. "Good work. I knew you had it in you to be an alpha. And no, I'm not relieving you of your battalion. Joydan gave her people to you. I respect her decision." He walked off with Moraak at his side, deep in conversation.

Rizelya stood stunned. In two days, they'd march to war. And with her as the unlikely head of a battalion. She should have refused the squad-pack when Histrun gave it to her. Leistral called to her. She waved acknowledgment, continuing to survey her pack. A smile curved on her lips. Having these wonderful people as friends was worth the headaches of being an alpha.

She hurried over to Leistral, and she and her team spent the rest of the day teaching the Clan Alphas.

Kaieli - 3 de Drudar, 1075

Kaieli worked in a fog throughout the day, waiting for the men to return from the mine. Her thoughts kept returning to the monster attack. When the Malvers' monsters rolled out of the crater rim and rushed toward her, she'd been terrified. None of the women possessed weapons, and the few invader guards weren't enough to stop the monsters. When Rolstrun and a few men ran toward them, relief filled her, but dismay set in. They risked punishment, or even worse, a child's death to save the women. Her heart leaped to her throat as Rolstrun struggled to shift. The nucla in him making it difficult. No matter how often she removed the nasty stuff from his numerous whippings, traces remained in his system. She feared they'd have to escape the Barrens for her to completely purge the poison from him. Finally, Rolstrun shifted into his powerful warrior form.

By then, a thin fire-ring, formed by Maheli and the other Reds, blocked her view of the fight. Worry over Rolstrun and his safety filled her mind to the exclusion of anything else. When the fire-ring lowered and she couldn't see him, her chest tightened. She'd wanted to run to him when he'd stood, stunned by the blast and blood oozing from his ears.

Kaieli paused in applying the bandage on a woman's cut hand. When had she started caring about Rolstrun as more than a friend? She raised her eyebrows at the realization. Her tastes usually ran toward women.

As she worked, the commander's order forbidding the healers from treating the men rankled more and more. It went against everything she believed in as a healer—and she couldn't let Rolstrun suffer. By the end of the day, she decided she would heal her people, no matter what the commander decreed.

That evening, her heart dropped to her toes when several soldiers entered the slave pen with the men. The soldiers kept their attention on her and the other healers. When she moved toward the table where Rolstrun sat slumped, a guard intercepted her and pushed her away. She strode to another table filled with men injured during the day's mining. The guard again blocked her and shook his head at her. Apparently, the injunction against healing extended to all the men while the ones being punished endured their pain. Fuming, Kaieli stomped to an empty table, her back to the hurting men.

Maheli sat next to her and silently put an arm around Kaieli's slumped shoulders. A few milcrons later, Jaelena and Noriana wandered over and sat across from her, reaching across the table to hold her hands. Loshera eased onto the bench on the other side of Kaieli, touching her shoulder, followed by Faliciden sliding onto the bench next to Noriana. Kaieli's brow furrowed. Together, these women formed the team who helped her heal the nucla poisoning from the men.

"What are you all doing here?" Kaieli asked. She glanced over her shoulder at the guards. They kept watch on her, but didn't make any move to break up the gathering.

"We're safe," Loshera said. "The invaders aren't aware of what we've been doing. To them, we're just a bunch of woman gossiping."

"So what are we gossiping about?" Kaieli wasn't in the mood for chatter.

"How to heal our menfolk, of course." Jaelena smiled. "We can't stand by and do nothing."

Kaieli sat up straighter. "No, we can't."

"How good are you at distance healing?" Faliciden asked. "I'm not. I have to touch my patients, but I've heard the more powerful Browns aren't limited to physical proximity."

"And you're one of the most powerful healers in several generations." Hope filled Noriana's eyes. "Can you do it?"

Kaieli looked around at the expectant faces, stunned at how much faith and trust they placed on her. "I... I... don't know. The only distance healing I've done is for simple things, like small cuts and summer fevers. Cleansing the nucla from the men isn't simple or easy."

"But we have to try." Faliciden leaned forward on her elbows. "We can't let the poison stay in their systems. They'll never shift again if we do."

"All of them are warriors." Maheli shifted to straddle the bench to face Kaieli. "If they can't shift, what else will they do? All they've ever done in their lives is fight the monsters. They're young men. It will destroy their spirit to return to the keeps and become farmers or herders."

Kaieli hung her head. Disabled warriors usually found it nearly impossible to make a life that didn't involve fighting.

"I've been thinking," Maheli added, "about the stories of the first guard-pack who spent a lunadar in the crater trying to eradicate the monsters. When they came back, the men were unable to shift, the women had lost their magic, and children born to them were deformed. What if the nucla poisoning caused it and no one knew how to heal them, or that it existed? They all died from illness within a few years. If we know how to purge the poison, can we leave our brave heroes to suffer a similar fate?"

"No." Kaieli shook her head. "No, we can't. We have to try. Now, before the guards wonder what we're doing. Hold hands."

Maheli swung her leg over the bench. The women formed a circle with their hands, and Kaieli concentrated. She focused first on Rolstrun, as she knew him the best. She found him with her magical sight and stifled a gasp. A black mass surrounded him and dug fingers into his body and soul. The brutal beating, followed by a day in the crater, had poisoned him worse than she'd expected. Firming her resolve, she reached for the combined magic of her team and wove it into a single stream of energy. Connected with the others, the magic at her disposal appeared black. Not having time to examine the phenomenon, she directed it to Rolstrun.

In one seamless action, she burned and cleared the poison away and healed all his wounds. She sensed the tracker slowly pulsing in his arm. Feeling powerful, she attempted to disarm it. But like most of the invaders' technology, it resisted her magic, even in its augmented state. She pushed a bit harder against the tracker, and its pulsing grew faster. Remembering how the tracker of the man who had tried to escape blew him bits, she quickly broke the contact and opened her eyes.

"Sweet Mother!" Noriana exclaimed in a hushed whisper. "So much power. Is that what it's like to be a Black? What wonderful and terrible things we could do with it."

"Only the wonderful," Loshera admonished. "We must always use the Goddess's gifts for good, otherwise they, and we, become perverted."

"Did it work?" Jaelena stood, craning her neck. With a laugh, she plopped back on the bench. "It did! You should see Rolstrun's face. He can't believe what happened."

Kaieli blew out a breath.

Maheli thumped the table. "What about the guards? Are they suspicious?"

This time Faliciden stood, glanced around, then sat again. "No. Rolstrun is smart enough to continue to act like he's in horrible pain."

"Pretending isn't going to last long," Noriana grumbled. "The invaders feed off emotions, and they'll be able to tell if the men are in pain or not."

Kaieli put a hand over her mouth. She'd forgotten that detail. When the women linked, it gave her a vast pool of magic. It waited, simmering under the surface, for her to choose how to use it. A plan quickly formed, almost as if it flowed from the Goddess. Kaieli scanned each woman in her group, nodding to herself when they didn't show any signs of physical and magical stress. "Are you up to healing the rest?"

Their eager nods greeted her words. First, Kaieli used Noriana's Blue Talent to overlay an illusion of pain on Rolstrun. When the invaders leaned forward, she snickered, relieved her idea worked, and they sensed the false emotion. The women spent the next octar healing the punished men, as well as every other man with nucla poisoning or other injuries.

By the time they finished, darkness had fallen. Kaieli slumped with exhaustion. "I don't think I have the energy to go get food, but I'm so hungry." Her stomach growled to punctuate her words.

"I'm the same." Faliciden leaned her elbows on the table, resting her head on her hands, and breathing out a tired sigh.

A bowl of soup appeared on the table in front of Kaieli, startling her. Anyola, the young Red she'd healed in what seemed a lifetime ago in Posanreande Keep, handed bowls to the others.

Anyola leaned in. "We know what you've done," she whispered. "Thank you. The men are hiding how good they feel. Eat. Rest. We'll watch over you." She straightened and stood slightly behind the table, her arms crossed over her chest. Another Red guarded the other end of the table.

The soldiers looked at them and shrugged. Their forked tongues flicked rapidly as they gorged on the phantom pain.

Late in the night, movement nearby disturbed Kaieli, but she didn't sense any danger. She cracked an eye open. Rolstrun knelt beside her pallet.

"Thank you," he whispered and ran a hand lightly over her face. His eyes glittered. "I was so afraid I'd never shift again." He bent over and kissed her check, then quickly stood, disappearing in the dark.

Kaieli touched where he'd kissed her. Patients usually didn't show their gratitude by kissing her. Smiling, she drifted back to sleep.

Rolstrun - 4 de Drudar, 1075

A rock dug into Rolstrun's back, and he squirmed until he found a more comfortable position. He stared into the night sky, wondering which of the many glimmering stars the invaders came from, and wishing they'd never discovered his home world. The Posair's life was a constant battle for survival against the Malvers' monsters. But in the last fifty years, the Posairs had been winning, making love and joy possible. The invader's arrival squashed any hope for the future, at least for him and the other captives.

He let out a long breath, thinking of the beautiful Kaieli. If life were different, he'd pursue a relationship with her. But he didn't have the strength of body or will after the long days spent in the crater. It ruined his and Laean's relationship. Over a chedan ago, she stopped sleeping next to him, and he didn't know where she was. While living under the control of the invaders, he doubted any relationship would flourish.

In the darkness, where no one would see, he said a prayer of thanksgiving, allowing the tears to trickle unchecked down his cheeks. The Goddess watched over him and the other men when She sent Kaieli to Posanreande Keep. If Kaieli hadn't been there and captured, he would have lost his most precious gift—shapeshifting. He'd taken his ability for granted, using it without a second thought, until the last chedan when he'd nearly been trapped in his warrior form. Kaieli saved him then, just as she saved him tonight.

He shuddered at the remembered sensation of the nucla poisoning worming its way through his body. Somehow, it created a barrier between him and the reservoir of magic he tapped into to shift. He reached for it now, not to shift, only to reassure himself it still existed. It pulsed bright and inviting, and he grinned with relief.

The new crescent of Kelar, the largest moon, told him he'd only been a captive—he refused to think of himself as a slave— for half a lunadar. It seemed much longer. The stress and the malignant magic of the crater devastated the Posair's minds and bodies. The inadequate food made everyone lose weight. He mourned the changes in his friends, Calistrun and Alestrun. Each day, they trudged more slowly, and their shoulders slumped as they lost hope. Calistrun, who always found joy and laughter, rarely smiled or laughed anymore. The children no longer played, especially after the invaders caged their friends. Whenever an invader appeared, the children cowered in terror.

Goddess, we have to find a way to escape, or at least get the children away from here. But how?

The Barrens surrounded the crater for nearly a hundred measures. An image of a bedraggled Blazel, trying to race through the Barrens, alone and on foot, assailed him. Even with his advantage of traveling in his wolf form, he'd struggled in the desolate landscape. The children couldn't survive a sustained run in the Barrens.

Rolstrun rubbed the tracker injected under his skin. The first obstacle was discovering a way to disarm it. Kaieli had told them about her attempt while she healed him. As much as he hated it, the Posairs couldn't do it alone. They needed help to escape. Would Tre'nok or Vy'shol help them? They had helped the Posairs already, but would they take that steep of a risk?

Dawn brought light into the world. Even though Rolstrun hadn't slept, a solution for the children's escape eluded him. He stood and stretched, smiling when he didn't feel any residual pain from his beating. Then he remembered the commander's order, and let his body slump into a posture of misery. He didn't want Kaieli and the other healers punished because they'd defied orders to heal him.

As he and the other men trudged toward the crater, Rolstrun noticed activity around the perimeter of the camp. Groups of Hap'thez and Gheethong worked to place large circular metal devices, spacing them about a hundred feet apart. A Faeorn triad stood next to the commander, who watched the workers critically. He glanced down at the Faeorn, who indicated if the placement was correct or not.

The compound now covered over twenty square measures, making it larger than Strunlair Keep, the largest Posair settlement. Over 100 barracks housed the soldiers and 25 buildings sheltered the slaves brought with the invaders. They stabled the lizards used for transportation in 125 pens. Rolstrun snorted. The sheezets lived better than the Posairs, who still slept outdoors in metal cages.

Before Rolstrun could climb over the crater rim, the commander barked an order. A loud buzzing swept over the compound. Rolstrun gaped at the shimmer of light shooting from the devices. The streams of light arched high overhead, flowing down to anchor in another device on the opposite side of the compound. When they activated all the devices, a dome of energy pulsed over the complex, reminding Rolstrun of the fire-ring the Reds constructed. An overseer prodded Rolstrun in the back to descend the ladder. All day, he puzzled over the dome's function, until finally he mentally shrugged. They'd find out soon enough.

Later in the morning, a group of Malvers' monsters climbed out of the crater and attacked the camp near the processing plant where the women worked. Rolstrun and the other Posair men watched from the bottom, worried about their people, but unable to do anything to help. The monsters hit the energy field.

And exploded.

"How did they do that?" Awe filled Bohandran's voice. "If we had something like it, we'd never have to worry about our keeps being attacked by the monsters!"

"Maybe the Reds could create something similar," Rolstrun said. "It looked like a fire-ring to me."

"Only if they had their helbraughts," Alestrun commented. "If only we weren't here." His shoulders sagged, and he returned to hacking at the rock pillar.

Blazel - 4 de Drudar, 1075

The Clan Alphas spent the day sequestered in meetings to finalize plans before everyone left the following day. They asked Blazel to join the war council since his extensive travels throughout Lairheim gave him experience none of the others had. Most Posairs stayed in their home territories, except to travel to the Sanctuary for the biannual Alpha Gatherings.

A large, detailed map covered the conference table, which Blazel studied with interest. He mentally traced his three-year journey to—and through—every swamp in Lairheim while listening to the alpha's heated debate on the disposition of fighters. Each alpha argued they needed to keep more fighters to protect the crops and livestock, giving examples of unusual monster activity and marauding monsters.

After the fourth alpha, with much arm gesticulating and pointing at the map, told the same story, Blazel cocked his head, studying the map. A pile of colored markers sat to the side of it. He gathered a handful, marking the indicated places on the map, continuing to add markers as the other alphas commiserated with stories of their own.

During a lull in the complaints, Histrun noticed Blazel setting a marker on the map. He stared at the groupings, then gave Blazel a puzzled look. "What are you doing?"

Blazel gestured to the map as he explained. "The red markers are the places where you've experienced unusual monster activity, and the blue are the unmarked swamps where I believe the monsters came from. The green markers are the new small keeps built in the last few years. As you can see, the attacks aren't as isolated or random as you thought."

"But there weren't any nests or swamps here," Adriandran protested, pointing to a spot on the map, "when we built the keep."

"Did you search for ruins?"

Adriandran shook his head, confused.

"We actually used the stones from a ruin," Hadronan said, pointing to a keep in Ronanlair Province and rubbing the back of his neck. "We didn't think anything of it, other than they were easily accessed building materials."

"Haven't you ever noticed the swamps are always nearby ancient settlements?" Blazel pointed to several blue markers. "Near every one of these, I found signs of old swamps, some nearly dried up, but most were growing. As more people move into the area, it attracts the monsters. Abandon the new keeps." Blazel held up his hand at the protests and continued. "Consolidate as many keeps as possible to give the monsters fewer targets. Send any excess people to the war front. While we'll need as many fighters as possible, we could also use support staff. The fighters shouldn't have to worry about cooking or laundry, or all the other myriad daily chores necessary for survival."

Histrun narrowed his eyes, assessing Blazel, before examining the map. He stared at it, one arm over his chest and resting his chin on the other fist. He nodded to himself several times. "It could work. If there aren't people around, the nests may return to dormancy."

"But what about our crops and livestock?" Brendel, the Dehanlair Clan Alpha, asked. "We must tend them, otherwise there won't be an autumn harvest. We need those crops to avoid starving in the winter."

"It's too late to plant more crops," Evellyn added. "At least in Andranlair Province."

"Move the livestock to the major keeps," Keshanal said, leaning forward in her seat. "If yours are like Strunell Territory, we have unused land where we can turn the livestock onto. Leave only a skeleton crew to tend the crops. Less than ten people per keep shouldn't attract the monsters. I have a feeling as we move troops south we'll encounter more monsters there and fewer here. Thousands of people—" she held up one hand "—or a few..." She held up the other. "The monsters should go for the many and leave the few alone. Now that's settled, let's discuss supply lines and the routes south."

"Yes, Supreme Alpha," the others murmured and bowed their heads in acknowledgment.

Blazel smiled. Having a Supreme Alpha would make things easier—no endless debates. He listened to the new discussion on the routes south and the supplies needed, adding his observations based on his years of travel.

Might I add something, Moraak said, stepping forward much later.

Histrun nodded. "Of course. We value the wisdom of our allies."

Moraak placed a claw on the map, north of the Barrens and near the river. *This appears to be a good place for a base camp.*

Raehaas scowled, then cleared his face. "It's a good area. The plains provide game, and the river water and fish. If we move to here" —he pointed several measures north— "there is a keep to protect us against monsters and narhili beasts."

"And across the river," Melidehan said, "lies one of our keeps. The two should be able to provide protection and supplies."

Ah, but would they also not become a place to trap us? Moraak asked. *You may have forgotten the Great War, but we have not. We remember people trapped in keeps while the enemy laid siege. I will not place my people in such jeopardy. If these keeps are so close, they can indeed be beneficial in providing supplies and protection for noncombatants. If they have not already fallen to the invaders.*

"What?" Melidehan exclaimed. "Why do you say that?"

The keep...

"Posanreande," Blazel supplied.

Moraak nodded. *Posanreande Keep and the guard fortresses surely are not the only places the invaders will attack. They are here for reasons we do not yet know. But we do know they are not friendly.* His head feathers laid tight against his head, and the tip of his tail thumped an angry beat. *We need information, and quickly. I propose sending a flight of my Gryphons, along with the same number of your fighters, to erect a base camp. Now. They can begin spying on the invaders while the rest of us travel south, gathering your army.*

"It's a good plan," Histrun said. "I concur. For those of us living farther north, we will hasten to the river and use it to travel quickly through Lairheim. Dehanlair, Haaslair, and Posanlair, you will assemble troops and march to the base camp. Your people are in the most danger. Evacuate the small keeps and send your noncombatants north where we'll give them shelter." He turned to Moraak. "Can I ask for your help in the evacuations?"

Moraak dipped his beak. *Yes, of course. I'll send a half flight with each of the clan leaders to help. I'm keeping half a flight to travel south with us.*

The leaders finalized their plans, and the meeting ended. The setting sun colored the clouds a riot of reds and oranges, deepening into mauves.

Blazel hurried to find Rizelya. He found her and the others in the outside practice arena, training in the fading light. People crowded the practice floor, with more watching in the stands. Blazel estimated over a hundred women, from every Talent, were learning to fight, and not all of them had dark hair signifying strong Talent. Rizelya formed them into teams consisting of at least one woman from each Talent, except White and Gray, with just as many or more men. Blazel frowned at the fighting methods they practiced. They weren't anything like what Histrun had taught him, or he'd witnessed other fighters doing. These new fighters used whatever the various Talents could do to the greatest effect, no matter the power level of the women.

A loud screech made Blazel jump. A flaming Gryphon dove toward one group. Air fanned the Gryphon's flames hotter while a cold-air shield blocked an arrow shot at it. Rizelya was integrating the Gryphons into the new fighting techniques.

Rizelya saw him and waved. She looked around and frowned. Putting her fingers to her lips, she whistled loudly. All the fighting stopped. "You're all doing very well. We'll continue practicing as we march and modify as necessary after fighting real battles with the monsters and invaders. Remember, we leave tomorrow. Rest up. Dismissed!"

The fighters saluted Rizelya before making their way from the arena. Blazel fought the flow, going in the opposite direction, until he finally reached Rizelya. She stood on her toes and gave him a kiss.

"I missed you today," she said.

"You look like you had more fun than I did. I attended meetings all day." Blazel quickly filled her in. "Let's go talk to Histrun. I want to go with the lead team."

"Me too."

She took his hand, and together, they searched for Histrun. They finally found him in the Clan Alpha's office.

He looked up from the papers strewn across the desk and glared at them. "I figured you two would show up, eventually. You want to be on the lead team."

They nodded in unison.

"Yes, sir," Blazel said. "We've already scouted down there and have seen the invaders. We could be more valuable there than here."

"Sorry to disappoint you, boy. You're both traveling with me. Rizelya, you have a battalion to lead. And I want you to continue teaching the troops your new fighting methods. I hear you've already devised a few new ones today using Gryphons." He smiled at her, fingering the bond-mate torque at his neck. "Always knew you took after your mother. She's the one who prodded us to develop the Zehis method. Blazel, I'm assigning you to train under Naila. Learn everything you can. I want you ready to be her second as battle commander by the time we reach the base camp."

Shock coursed through Blazel. He never expected to be part of a pack, let alone become a battle commander and leader over the new army. He didn't know why Histrun thought him capable of such leadership. Being around people still troubled him. He saluted Histrun. "I'll do my best, sir."

"That's all I ask. Now, both of you leave me." He scowled at the papers on his desk. "I have a mountain of work to do before morning."

Rizelya linked her arm through Blazel's as they walked toward their room. "Battle commander, huh? You'll do well."

"You know what this makes you?"

She quirked an eyebrow at him.

"My second. We're partners, Rizelya, in everything."

She stopped and stared at him, her eyes wide, and a hand over her mouth. After a long moment, she blinked and swore. "Damn that manipulative, twisty bastard! And I thought I was going to stay just a battalion alpha. Damn that man!"

Blazel laughed. Histrun was a crafty old man. With Rizelya at his side, he wasn't worried. They'd already accomplished so much together. They would survive this too.

Chapter 14

Rolstrun - 5 de Drudar, 1075

The guards led the men on a different route through the compound to reach the crater rim. Rolstrun followed the overseer, puzzled. Worry squirmed in his stomach. Outside the energy-field, a gang of Hap'thez were building a large square cage using the metallic mesh. Their four hairy arms made quick work of the construction. When they finished, soldiers herded them—along with several Gheethong, Coufrish, and Vhelopsi—into the cage. The alien slaves huddled near the mesh fence, avoiding a dark splotch in the center. Even from a distance, their fear was noticeable, providing a feast for the platoon of invaders who stood in a loose circle around the cage.

A Gheethong laid a wide, spatula hand on the mesh, gibbering pleas to the invaders. The mesh glowed with a bluish light, and the Gheethong screamed, its body curled in a spasm. Several of the soldiers' forked tongues snaked out, savoring the Gheethong's pain. The others gripped their weapons expectantly. Ke-ke-tak stood off to the side, idly slapping his whip into his hand.

The marching men stopped without being reprimanded. Their overseers were as transfixed on the tableau as they were.

A roiling mass erupted in the center of the cage. Rolstrun gasped as the mass resolved into two janacks and six brechas. They'd built the cage on top of a nest site, and what the slaves had tried to avoid was monster larvae ready to spawn. Putting warm-blooded people in it was like ringing a dinner bell, especially in the Barrens where the nests formed faster than anywhere else on Lairheim.

A janack flung out a tentacle, wrapping it around a Coufrish and dragging it to its waiting maw. Pandemonium broke out in the cage. The Coufrish's great strength wasn't a match for the janack's tentacles. The brechas quickly killed the Gheethong. A Hap'thez still held a hammer, and in a fury, buried it in a brecha's head. The Hap'thez crumpled under a barrage of brecha spines. The Vhelopsi jumped and leaped, attempting to use their long nails to damage the janack tentacles. But they weren't the sharp claws of a warrior and couldn't penetrate the thick hides.

Once the monsters devoured the slaves, the brechas ran toward the waiting invaders, hitting the mesh in a bright flash. The stink of burning hide filled the air. They hit it again. The fence sizzled and flashed. Fires erupted on the monsters wherever they touched the fence. The soldiers fired into the cage, light bursting from their weapons, easily passing through the mesh. They methodically killed the monsters. Ke-ke-tak rocked on his heels, pleased.

The overseers prodded the men to move. Throughout the day, Rolstrun worried about the danger the corrals brought. Nest sites riddled the Barrens, especially near the crater. The invaders wouldn't have trouble finding more places nearby to build their awful cages and serve a banquet to the Malvers' monsters. When Rolstrun finally climbed over the crater rim, the Hap'thez had built four more corrals.

The next morning, as the Posairs left their cages for the day, the guards separated ten people from the group. Rolstrun's mind froze with horror when the soldiers prodded them into one of the corrals, surrounded by a platoon of soldiers. It didn't take long for a nest to form and the screams to begin.

The men inside the cage began to shift, but guards shot them in an arm or leg. The pain caused them to instantly abort their shifting. Rolstrun suspected the invaders had laced the projectiles with nucla. A Red in the cage formed fireballs and threw them at the monsters before the soldiers shot her. Injured people writhed on the ground, screaming in terror and pain. The monsters ate three people when an officer ordered the guards to kill the monsters. The survivors cowered in shock while soldiers pulled them from the cage and carried them off. Rolstrun gritted his teeth, knowing they'd never return to the slave pens.

That night, the Posairs gathered in the center slave pen to mourn their lost comrades and friends. A circle formed around White Priestess Loshera, who led the rites for the fallen. "Many times, our brave warriors fall in battle with the Malvers' monsters and we can't recover their bodies. Those who fall in this place of terror are no less brave than any warrior who has gone before them. We can't burn the bodies of our dear friends to send their souls back to the Mother, and we lack the sacred incense to guide their way. But all isn't lost. We hold their memories in our hearts.

"At this time, please recall our friends and loved ones who are no longer with us. Bring the memories into as clear of a focus as you can." Loshera paused for several milcrons.

Rolstrun glanced at his friends Alestrun, Calistrun, and Myndera, happy they were still here with him. He searched the crowd and found Laean leaning against a fighter from Haaslornde Keep, who had his arm around her waist. She turned, saw Rolstrun, and gave him a sad smile. He returned it, glad she found someone to share comfort with. A set of blue-gray eyes caught his gaze. Kaieli smiled at him shyly before ducking her head again. Rolstrun felt his heart lift, and he promised himself he'd seek her out after the ritual.

Maheli and Kothera stepped forward, and together, created a fire in an empty cooking pot sitting on the ground in front of Loshera.

"This fire represents the funeral pyres for all our fallen," Loshera explained. She closed her eyes, bowed her head, and took several deep breaths. When she opened her eyes, white light gleamed from them—the presence of the Goddess shone through her.

"Great Mother," Loshera intoned, lifting her hands toward the sky, palms upward, "accept these, your sons and daughters, into your loving embrace. Hold them close and give them comfort as they release the burdens and joys of this life. Gentle and Wise Matriarch, guide your children through the Summerlands, where they may remember and learn from the lessons gifted in this life. Gracious Crone, may your purifying fires be gentle as they burn away the dross accumulated in this life, so their next life begins in pure love and joy. Go with love and grace." Loshera lowered her arms, and the fire flared high.

Rolstrun watched the flames for several long moments. Since no one close to him had died, he moved to the outskirts of the crowd. Groups gathered to quietly reminisce about their friends and loved ones.

Kaieli came to stand next to him, slipping her hand into his. He gently squeezed it and grinned. They talked until the horn blared, announcing lights out. He escorted her to her pallet before going to his own. He fell asleep with a smile for the first time since the fireball had lit the sky.

Rizelya - 5 de Drudar, 1075

The first group to leave Strunlair Keep consisted of the Ronanlair, Keistanlair, Ledonlair, and Andranlair Clan Alphas returning to their homes. Along the way, they would stop to evacuate the small keeps and gather troops, which would immediately travel to the Storengher River, where they would join the Strunlair fighters.

As the Gryphons winged north, the next group prepared to leave. The three southern Clan Alphas each had fifty Gryphons with them to help facilitate evacuations of the keeps in danger from the invaders. Each contingent included several of the fast-flying scouts, who also doubled as messengers. Once they completed the evacuations, the Gryphons and any fighters would join the advance team at the new base camp. With the sound of thunder, the Gryphons launched. They would separate into smaller groups farther south.

Once word spread about the advance team, several groups practicing with the Gryphons approached Rizelya with a plan. A team of Blues and Yellows could boost the telepathic range of the Gryphons to reach a hundred or more measures. If they established multiple teams, they could relay communications back to the main war host. Histrun jumped at the chance of having reliable and timely intelligence.

The advance team marched onto the open field, packs on their backs. Rizelya wandered through the crowd, helping a person into their harness here, checking the straps of another, or boosting a pack up to someone else. The group included quite a few of the people she'd trained over the last few days. She prayed what they'd learned would keep them alive.

The communication teams would drop back and stay behind when they reached their assigned posts. Where possible, they would use safe houses for the communications posts, but a few would be in open land along the river, subject to monster attacks and narhili beasts. Rizelya gave extra encouragement to the people on those teams.

An octar later, she stood on the edge of the field with Blazel. She shielded her eyes with a hand as Gryphons crouched and wings swept downward, flinging dust into the air. A hundred Gryphons darkened the sky, blocking the sun, and a few moments later they disappeared over the horizon, and the sunlight beat on Rizelya's upturned face. She surveyed the once-packed area. Only fifty Gryphons remained behind with their prince, including Graak, Broogk, and the others she counted as friends. They'd be flying with her troops.

Rizelya and Blazel hurried back to the keep. Pandemonium filled the keep as people hustled to the practice-arena-turned-staging-area. Multas bawled, horses whinnied, and adults shouted. Children, both in wolf form and human, raced through and around legs.

"Come on," Blazel said, pulling her hand. "I see our group."

He led her through the crowd. Both Kymaya and Lighzel stood tied to a railing, already saddled, and their bags secured onto the back of the saddles. Wisah, on her tall stallion, waited beside Jaehaas, their hands linked. To their left, Aistrun and

Chariel sat on their horses, chatting. Beside them, her original squad-pack—Leistral, Eidstrun, and Dehali, waited. Seeing them together, a sharp pang of regret knifed through Rizelya. She hadn't thought of Keandran since he'd disappeared. What had happened to him? Was he even alive?

Her expanded squad-pack stood behind them, arrayed in a small semicircle. Her Strunhelos battalion gathered beyond them. Sitting off to the side, wearing anxious expressions, were the support women who'd followed her from the Sanctuary.

Rizelya walked over to them.

"Are we going with you?" Shaela nervously ran her horse's reins through her hands.

"Of course! Fall into your usual positions when we leave. The battalion will make room for you."

"Oh good." Shaela sighed with obvious relief. "We didn't want to be assigned to anyone else."

Rizelya smiled. "You're my people now. Stick close." A sharp whistle blew three times. "There's the signal. We'll be leaving soon."

Rizelya hurried back to her horse, jumped into the saddle, and waited.

Citizens not leaving for the war lined the streets, waving. Histrun, Keshanal, and Naila urged their horses through the gauntlet, backs straight. A young man carried the new flag for the Supreme Alphas braced on his stirrup right behind them. The Strunlair battalions followed after. When space opened up, Rizelya urged her horse forward, her people keeping pace with her. They rode proudly through the streets and out the gate. Once they were away from the keep, those ahead of them broke into a trot. The war host quickly fell into a ground-eating pace, with occasional breaks for the horses and riders.

Early the next morning, troops from Strunland Territory joined the main column. Rizelya happily greeted her friends. Throughout the day, troops from the other Strunlair territories caught up with the war host. Her friends Shaydan, Drustrun, Bren, and Maestrun from Strunell Keep hailed Rizelya during the first break. Later, Laynar joyfully reunited with her twin brother, Laenstrun, and her sister, Laynad. Their grandmother, Layhalya, had stayed behind in Strunheim Keep, claiming at 110, she was too old for such a journey. When the Strunven contingent rode into camp that evening, Rizelya's girls from Strunven met with their friends. Laughter boomed around their campfire.

Rizelya quietly led Saehala and Saehalstrun through the camp and shook the bells hanging on Histrun's tent entrance.

"What is it?" he snarled. "Can't an old man get some rest?"

Rizelya poked her head through the tent flap. Histrun hunched over a low table covered with maps and papers. A steaming pot of taevo and an untouched plate of food sat at his elbow.

"Sorry, sir. You don't look like you're resting. I think you'd like to meet with these new arrivals."

"Everyone thinks they need to see me." He put down the paper in his hand and rubbed his face. "Well, since you've interrupted me, who are these important people?"

"Your other children." Rizelya grinned and motioned Saehala and Saehalstrun into the tent. "I know Sujeen wouldn't let you visit them. They've wanted to see you for a long time."

Histrun's eyes devoured the twins, moisture gathering in the corners of them. "It's been so long." He struggled to his feet.

Rizelya noted the similarities between Histrun and the twins' golden-red hair, high cheekbones, and slightly slanted green eyes. She didn't think she looked much like him, especially compared to them. As the three embraced, she slipped away, feeling uncomfortable. Between the tradition of fighter's children raised in a crèche, and Histrun's frequent absences after her mother died, Rizelya knew him more as her mentor than as her father.

The next day, the trees thinned and gave way to low-lying grass and brush. Soon after, they entered Haaslair Province and rode through the vast expanse of grass. As they rode, the line strung out into smaller groups, partly to mitigate the dust and noise.

Because the route Blazel mapped avoided any old nests or new swamps, they hadn't battled any monsters during their journey through Strunlair Province. The afternoon breeze swayed the tall grass, brushing the horse's bellies, and Gryphons floated high above them. Sweat trickled down Rizelya's back, and she almost wished she was riding Graak and soaring with them above the summer heat.

"This seems so strange," Rizelya said as she took a sip of water from her canteen.

Blazel raised an eyebrow. "What is?"

"To travel for so many days without trouble. I could get used to this."

Aistrun groaned. "No. You did *not* just say that."

"What?" Rizelya drew her eyebrows together, perplexed.

"You jinxed it, Rizelya." Aistrun put his head in his hands and pulled at his hair. "You had to go and say out loud that we haven't had any trouble. Now we're in for it. You're a trouble magnet, and you know it!"

Rizelya glared at him. "No I'm not. Trouble likes you just as much. You're always with me when it finds me."

Blazel laughed. "She has you there, Aistrun."

They rode in silence as the heat pressed down on them. Now troubled, Rizelya warily watched the road on all sides. Not long after, a herd of wild horses raced out of the tall grass. Rizelya's heart faltered as the fifty horses thundered across the plains—straight at her group.

Jaehaas galloped toward the herd, waving his arms, and yelling, "Hai!"

The horses turned and ran parallel to them, the whites of their eyes showing. They were terrified. Rizelya stood in her stirrups to survey the plains in the direction where the herd had run from. A janack's tentacle appeared above the tall grass for a moment before it disappeared again.

"Monsters!" Rizelya yelled, both out loud and in mind-speech.

Overhead, a Gryphon screeched and dove.

"I told you. You jinxed it," Aistrun grumbled as he threw Jezhan's reins to her. He and the other men slid off their horses and shifted.

Shaela appeared out of the chaos and held out her hands. "Give me the reins. I'll watch out for them."

Rizelya nodded and tossed Kymaya's reins, as well as Jezhan's and Lighzel's, to Shaela.

This will be a good time to practice our new techniques, Rizelya said, reaching out with her mind to her people. She heard their acknowledgment. Soon, her team stood next to her and two other groups lined up on either side of them. With a loud crack of wings, Graak, Broogk, and Glork took positions ahead and above her group, like they'd practiced. The Gryphons flared, glowing as their flames surrounding them.

Graak screeched, and a spear of flames zoomed to engulf the lead brecha. Saffren formed a bubble of water around the burning creature. In moments, the brecha burned to ash. Rizelya silently applauded when Saffren released the water bubble, soaking the surrounding grass. They didn't need to fight a wildfire as well as the monsters.

Rizelya readied her fire-shield. Before she released it, the control-janack's high-pitched humming slammed against her senses. Frantically, she attempted to raise her mental shields like Saffren and Chariel had taught her. But this close to the source, she was fighting a losing battle. Black crept into her vision. "No! You can't have me!" she yelled.

Suddenly, another mind wrapped around hers, building a barrier to the Malvers woman's mental attack, block by block. Chariel's strength made Rizelya feel small. Finally, the hum melted away. Rizelya glanced back at Chariel, wincing at her pale face contorted with pain. Chariel grimaced, but gestured that she was alright. Rizelya nodded and turned to the control-janack. The new fighting methods, combined with the Gryphon's aerial attacks, quickly destroyed the monsters.

By nightfall, the host reached the riverbank and camped for the night. The sound of the flowing water lulled Rizelya into sleep. Once again, she dreamed about the pale, emaciated woman, hatred filling her black eyes. The strange collection device covered her head. Thin wires connected it to a contraption of various tubes on a table next to her. A steady flow of thick, pus-colored smoke snaked out of a tube and wound around a large glass funnel. As the smoke swirled around the bowl, droplets coalesced into thick, viscous beads. They dripped from the funnel and into a matte-black bowl.

The woman wore a pleased smile as she took off the device and dipped her needle-like claw into the bowl. She scooped several of the pearls out, popped them in her mouth, and sighed in ecstasy. "Oh, this is good," the woman said. "So filled with terror and death. Soon. Soon, my friends, we will have the strength we need to leave our long exile and exact our revenge.

Come, my friends, and eat." More hands dipped into the bowl as the woman laughed.

Rizelya thrashed, trying to escape the Malvers woman's hold on her. Strong arms gripped her and tucked her into a hard chest. Rizelya took a deep breath, letting Blazel's scent surround her.

"Shh... shh... it was only a dream," Blazel crooned as he stroked her hair and back.

"The Malvers woman." Tears crept down Rizelya's face. "I dreamed about the Malvers woman. They are getting stronger."

"I know, love, I know. There isn't anything we can do tonight. Go back to sleep. I'll watch over you." He kissed her forehead.

"You promise?"

Blazel nodded and pulled her closer to him as he cocooned her body with his. Even within the refuge of his arms, it took Rizelya a long time to go back to sleep. How could they fight both enemies?

Kaieli - 5 de Drudar, 1075

The summer heat pressed down on Kaieli, making her feel heavy and listless. The black sand and petrified wood boulders seemed to soak up the heat and intensify it as it radiated off them in waves. Kaieli longed for a cool breeze or a swim in a cold mountain lake.

Water was in short supply, and Kaieli treated as many people for heat stroke and dehydration as she did for injuries. The poor Hap'thez suffered greatly with all their hair. Many collapsed and died from their body's inability to handle the intense heat. The hairless Coufrish received deep sunburns with a few milcrons. Those burned too badly to work became food for the invaders.

The heat and sunlight also adversely affected the invaders. The soldiers developed red, runny sores, which cracked whenever they moved before sloughing off in large, bloody patches. Their eyes hurt from the light reflecting from the sands, making them twitchy and shooting at shadows. The officers stayed inside their ship during the worst octars of the sun. Only the low-ranking soldiers remained outside, and the heat made them lethargic.

While healing a woman's arm burned in the processing plant, Kaieli scanned the woman's tracking device. She whooped, quickly covering her mouth.

"I don't think your tracker contains any explosive! It doesn't react like the ones in the men or mine."

"Can you remove it?" the woman asked.

"What if I'm wrong?"

The woman laughed nervously. "Then we'll both go out with a bang. It's better than being eaten by a monster—either in a cage or in the ship."

"Let's step outside, just in case." Kaieli led the woman out the door near the infirmary space. No buildings blocked their view of the Barrens, dropping into the horizon. "Please, Mother, let this work!" Surrounding the device with her magic, and holding her breath, Kaieli eased the capsule upward and out from the woman's skin. She tossed it, watching it as it clattered to the ground several feet away, lying inert in the black sand. She counted slowly. When she reached 100, she trotted to the tracker and picked it up.

Maheli, she called in mind-speech, *would you join me outside?*

"Is that a tracker?" Maheli stared at the small device in Kaieli's palm.

Kaieli nodded. "I removed it from her." She pointed to the woman. "Can you burn it?"

Maheli raised an eyebrow and scrunched her face. "Are you sure it won't blow up?"

"Nope. But I don't think it will."

Maheli gingerly held the capsule between her index finger and thumb. Her eyes narrowed as she concentrated. Fire danced over her hand, enveloping the device. Maheli opened her fingers, dropping the bit of melted metal.

"You know what this means?" Maheli rubbed her hands together and her eyes lit up.

"We have a chance now."

Maheli studied the destroyed device. "We shouldn't destroy any more trackers. A few could be attributed to the horrendous conditions here, but more?" She shrugged.

"It may tip off the invaders." Kaieli agreed.

After dinner, Kaieli examined as many women as possible captured in the second wave. None of their implants included any explosives. However, keeping the possibility of alerting the invaders in mind, she didn't remove them. When she checked the children, none of them had an implant.

"Apparently," she mused, "the invaders don't think our women, or the children, will attempt an escape."

"Their oversight is our opportunity." Maheli grinned as she rubbed her hands together. "I've been studying the energy-field, and I think it's similar to the fire-ring we create. With this new development, we should try to neutralize a small section to give us a chance to escape."

The others agreed.

The next day, Kaieli nervously stood guard, watching the furtive movements of several women at the edge of the energy-field. She kept glancing around, making sure no guards came toward them. Maheli, Kothera, Myndera, and several other Reds faced the fence. Maheli picked up a small rock and tossed it. It hit the fence with a shower of sparks before disintegrating.

"Damn!" Kothera took a step back. "This technology would protect the keeps."

"We don't need the invaders' technology." Disdain darkened Maheli's voice. Her eyes narrowed as she studied the fence. "If we can neutralize the energy-field, we should be able to determine how it works and recreate it. Let's get to work. The guards will come this way soon."

The Reds squatted and lifted their hands, which glowed with red and orange light, and held them close to the fence, near the ground. Their energy slowly extended until it touched, then merged with the energy-field. When they pulled their hands away, the energy-field didn't distort a two-foot by four-foot section of fence. Maheli tossed another rock at the fence. It clattered against the metal and fell unharmed to the ground.

A smile lit Maheli's face. "We did it! Your turn, Sorlenda."

Sorlenda, a Brown and Yellow from Posanlynde Keep, stepped forward. Before being captured, she worked with helstrim and other metal alloys. Earlier, she'd experimented on the fence behind the latrines, made with the same metal. She'd cut through the fencing and created an illusion to cover the hole. Sorlenda wrapped her hands around the now inert metal mesh and closed her eyes. A wave of energy pulsed from her hands to the fence. A seam formed in it and a small section folded back on itself, creating an opening.

"Yes!" Myndera pumped her fist in the air. "We now have a chance to save some of our people."

Kaieli leaned down and inspected the hole, gingerly touching it, grinning when it didn't zap her. She stood. "We need to be careful. The invaders can't suspect any of us are escaping. If they do, they might put the explosives back in the trackers. Then none of us will get away from this horror."

The two alphas nodded in agreement. Sorlenda formed the illusion, and the hole disappeared. The women hurried back into the processing plant with the first stirrings of hope since the Scourge captured them.

Blazel - 7 de Drudar, 1075

In the dark, Blazel curled around Rizelya, protecting her with his body, wishing he could also protect her mind. Their ancient enemy was invading her dreams, and he could do nothing to stop it because the enemy was plundering his own dreams. Since leaving Strunlair Keep, he dreamed of the pale, gaunt women every night. He heard her cackle as she directed her pets to kill and squirmed as he watched her eat pearls of death. He should tell Rizelya and Chariel about his dreams, but they made him feel unclean. As he'd told Rizelya, they couldn't do anything yet about the Malvers woman. He'd deal with her when she finally showed her face in something other than a dream. Blazel stayed awake the rest of the night, unwilling to be subjected to the dreams again.

As they marched south, the war host followed the river, staying close to its banks. Jaehaas assured them the monsters stayed clear of the river. Blazel had experienced the same thing during his mad race across the plains.

Even so, the female fighters rode with their helbraughts loosened in their carriers and their hands hovering over them, and the men kept their eyes on the tall grass. The tension wrapping around them eased when they reached Haasperlyn Keep late in the afternoon.

The small keep sat on the riverbank. Large barges crowded the docks extending into the river. From here on, they would travel south on the river, using its speed to reach the Barrens. To accommodate so many people, the keep alphas turned the pastures into temporary campsites.

As leaders, Blazel and Rizelya bunked in the keep while their people slept outside. Blazel groaned inwardly when they walked into the room stuffed with makeshift beds. Any thoughts he entertained of making love to Rizelya fled. He'd become more used to having people around—it didn't make him as twitchy—but a place this crowded curbed his libido.

In the dark, Rizelya snaked her arm around his neck and pulled him into a passionate kiss. Her hands wandered over his body, and a groan of pleasure escaped him. Someone coughed. Blazel stilled and stopped kissing Rizelya.

"I can't," he whispered.

"Just hold me. Help me not to dream."

He turned to lie on his side with her tucked into him, his arm draped over her hip. Finally, deep into the night, they fell asleep. He awoke the next morning, blinking. He hadn't dreamed of the Malvers woman.

"Did you have any dreams?" he asked Rizelya.

She frowned, then smiled as she shook her head. "No, thank Goddess!" She stretched, her hand brushing against the stone wall. She stared at her hand on the wall. "Sheadash stone. We're surrounded by sheadash stone. I don't recall having any nightmares while sleeping in a keep. The stone stops the monsters. Its properties must also stop the Malvers woman from accessing my mind. Argh," she groaned. "Where we're going, there isn't any sheadash stone."

"Only in the fortresses."

"That's an idea." She leaned on her elbow, facing him. "Use the fortresses. They have water and fortified walls."

"But only the food we bring in. If the invaders blockaded us, we'd be dead."

Rizelya snorted. "So much for that idea. I don't look forward to dreaming about her all the time."

"Maybe she'll get bored and leave you alone." Blazel didn't actually think it would happen. "It's as if she wants you to know about her and what she's doing. She's baiting you. Your fear, our fear, feeds her. We've become more afraid of the monsters since you starting having visions about her."

"We've had more to be afraid of." Rizelya flopped onto her back and stared at the ceiling, twirling the end of her braid. "Somehow, I need to turn it around and use these dreams to our advantage." She made a face. "The Supreme told me that before I left. But so many things have happened since then, I'd forgotten. I refuse to be terrified by this woman any longer."

"Good. It's always better to be on the offensive rather than the defensive." Blazel paused. "We need to remember that with the invaders. Take the battle to them, put them on the defense. They don't know our land like we do. We use it to our advantage. We can even use the Barrens against them." His mind replayed his run through the Barrens. "A monstrous sandstorm tore through the Barrens after I left the guard fortress. It nearly killed me and Lighzel. Our forces include many powerful Yellow and Brown Talents. Perhaps it's possible for them to create and control such a storm."

"We'll explore your idea when we reach the Barrens."

The morning bell boomed, calling the keep to breakfast. Blazel and Rizelya quickly dressed, putting aside the concerns of war to fill their empty bellies. Three more battalions arrived while they ate.

The war host had grown so large, the Haaslair didn't have enough barges to carry all the horses. Histrun insisted the leaders and their packs needed their horses when they reached the edge of the plains. Blazel said a prayer of gratitude when the barge crew led his and his pack's horses onto the barge he and Rizelya sailed on. Lighzel had become an important part of his life, and he couldn't imagine traveling without her now.

The days took on a routine as they traveled south. Wake up at dawn, devour a quick breakfast, and board the barges for the day's journey. At evening, they'd anchor the barges at the river's edge to train for an octar while the support folks prepared dinner, eat, then sleep. It only varied when new troops arrived and needed to be absorbed into the war host. Their ranks swelled to over fifty thousand, with thousands more marching behind them.

One afternoon as they floated down the river, Blazel draped his arms over the railing, watching the plains flow by. This mode of travel was much faster than the wild ride he'd taken as he'd rushed to the Sanctuary from the southern swamp. This time, though, he traveled with friends. He looked over at Rizelya when she laughed at something Aistrun said. Jaehaas flicked his tail in irritation while Chariel smirked. His heart tightened when he thought about where they were heading. There was a good chance some, or all, of them wouldn't return from fighting the invaders. He'd just found them, and didn't want to lose them so soon. So why was he standing here, alone? He pushed off the railing, ambled over to them, and slid onto the deck next to Rizelya, sliding his arm around her waist. She leaned into him. He decided to enjoy what time they had together, however long the Goddess allowed them.

Chapter 15

Kaieli - 14 de Drudar, 1075

Kaieli stood by the back doorway of the processing plant, shifting from foot to foot and craning her neck to watch the corridor. Finally, a woman with two children scurried into sight.

"Hurry," Kaieli whispered, motioning to them with her hand. "There isn't much time."

When they reached her, she quickly healed any injuries they had and removed the woman's tracking device. Last night, she and the others had cleared any nucla poisoning in the escapee's systems. "You have water? Food?"

The woman nodded, pointing to the canteen and small pack slung across her back. "We'll send help, if we find anyone."

Kaieli cupped the woman's face. "Don't worry about us. You get yourself and the children far away from here." Kaieli checked outside with her senses. Nothing stirred in the heat. "Now go! Run, and don't look back."

The woman grabbed the children's hands and slipped out the door. They squirmed through the hole in the fence. Kaieli watched them race into the Barrens and disappear behind a jumble of boulders. She didn't know if any of the twenty escapees made it out of the Barrens. Even if they hadn't, their deaths would still be cleaner than being killed in the corrals by monsters or eaten by the invaders. Between the heat and corrals, enough deaths plagued the Posairs, the invaders didn't notice the women and children's escape.

"It only delays the inevitable," Tre'nok said, stepping out from the corner of the building.

Kaieli jumped, putting a hand over her racing heart. "How long have you known?"

"Not long." Tre'nok shrugged. He leaned against the building, crossing one leg over the other. "Neither I, nor the other Volkern, will say anything to the Scourge. Even if they—" he pointed to where the woman had run "—make it out of the black sand, they will not be safe. The Scourge will conquer this world, just as they have hundreds of others. Although, they did not count on the radiation from your sun. There may be hope for your world yet."

"We won't go easily into the darkness of annihilation."

"For 400 cycles, years in your lexicon, the Scourge have wandered through space, conquering wherever they go. My home world was the first. Yours is simply the latest. The nucla is very valuable to them. It powers their spaceships and machinery. They've nearly depleted the mineral on their home world. What they discovered here will supply them for many, many cycles."

"We don't want it. It's poison to us. If they take it all, will they leave us alone?"

Tre'nok shook his head. "They do not share."

"Why are you helping us?"

"Your people are strong." He gazed in the direction the woman had gone. "After all you have suffered, you continue to fight. By this time, most other people surrender to the Scourge's greater force, not organize escape attempts. There is a chance—a small one—you can drive the Scourge away. If we help you, your chances increase considerably."

Kaieli narrowed her eyes. "What do you want in return?"

Tre'nok leaned in, bending down to look her in the eye. "Your help in destroying the nucla. All of it. The pillar and what they've processed. We must ensure the Scourge do not leave here with even a gram of it. If they cannot power their spaceships, they cannot travel between worlds. Perhaps one day in the future, my world will be free of the parasites. Do we have an agreement?"

She studied him. His eyes burned with suppressed hatred. Four hundred cycles of slavery. She didn't blame him. She would do anything to rid her world of the Malvers' monsters.

"I can't speak for all of my people," she said. "The Supreme is the only one with that authority. But I and the others here will do what we can. If the rest of our people fight, I'm sure they will also agree."

"It is all I can expect." Tre'nok inclined his head. "A fighting force has established a camp at the edge of the black sands."

Excitement thrilled through Kaieli at the news. Help was coming. She gripped Tre'nok's arm. "Do you know where? It would give our people more of a chance of survival if we sent them in that direction."

"Those who just left are going in the right direction. Here, I will show you." He knelt and sketched a quick map in the sand. He pointed to a spot where the river entered the Barrens. "It is here. Why do they not enter the black sands?"

"The plains offer food and water."

"Ah." Tre'nok rubbed the sand with a hand, obliterating the map before standing.

She gazed longingly to the north. "It is a long journey through the Barrens to here."

"I doubt it will be a problem. They are riding strange flying beasts."

Kaieli's eyes widened as her jaw dropped open. Did he mean the mythical Gryphons? She remembered the day after the invader's arrival and she'd spotted what she thought was a Gryphon soaring in the night sky. Hope lit a fire in her heart.

He took a small device out of his pocket and handed it to her. "I am giving this to you as a sign of good faith. The Scourge cause enough deaths to cover the few who have escaped, but if you try to get more out, you'll need this. It will deactivate the tracking device implanted during your slave induction. My friends deactivated the ones in those who have already escaped."

Kaieli tipped her head down, hiding her smile as she put her hand into her pocket, fingering the several tracking capsules stored in it.

"Thank you." Kaieli took the offered device. "What about the explosives?"

Tre'nok laughed. "A subterfuge. The Scourge do not waste nucla on killing slaves."

She raised her head and narrowed her eyes. "That isn't true. My tracking device, and all those who arrived with me and from the crater fortresses, contain explosives."

He raised an eyebrow, but didn't comment on her knowledge. "The Scourge arm the trackers of the first captives with explosives. Usually, one person is stupid and tries to escape, and the rumor about their demise and the threat is enough to deter any further attempts. I'm sorry, we can't do anything for those who have the implanted explosives."

"How far from the compound can we travel before the explosives go off? Will we still be in danger after the invaders leave?"

"If you succeed in forcing the invaders to leave, you'll be the first to do so. But I think you might accomplish it. You won't be safe until the control beacon is destroyed." Tre'nok tilted his head and looked upward. Kaieli followed his gaze to a tall tower extending to the top of the energy dome. A blinking light adorned its apex.

"As to your first question," Tre'nok said, "you can travel about two of your measures away from the beacon before its signal triggers the explosive. It allows your men to work in the crater without blowing them up. The distance also coincides with the farthest extent of the Scourge's scanning devices. Although it could be more or less. The petrified wood in this area is interfering with the signal, as is the nucla deposit. Be careful." Tre'nok bowed slightly to her. He sauntered between the buildings and out of sight.

Kaieli studied the device he'd given her. Now she knew the explosive was a nucla derivative, perhaps she and the others could remove it.

As Kaieli tromped back to the slave pen, she glanced at the sky. A spot moved high above them. Was it a Gryphon? She lifted her hand to wave at it, but thought better of calling any of the invader's attention to it.

Hello? she called in mind-speech.

Lady? came a deep, questing voice.

Yes! I'm here! We're here!

We are here to help. I am Kaaik. Delestrun is with me.

It took all of Kaieli's control not to sob out loud with relief. She'd met Delestrun a few times while at Strunlair Keep. Her clan-pack was here.

I'm Kaieli. There's a woman and two children running through the Barrens, heading north. Find them, oh please find them.

We shall. His mental voice faded as he flew northward.

The invaders, Kaieli added quickly, **they sleep during the noon heat.**

This is good to know. Until tomorrow noon, Kaieli.

The dot disappeared. Even though she wiped the smile from her face, hope lightened her step. Help had arrived.

Kaieli - 14 de Drudar, 1075

Maheli, Kothera, Bohandran, and Nederposan quickly became the alphas of the captive Posairs—the ones to whom everyone looked for guidance. Kaieli wanted to immediately share the good news of Kaaik and Delestrun's arrival with them. But she needed to wait until after the nightly ritual of clearing the men of nucla poisoning. The men had to stay healthy if they were to survive the ordeal of working in the crater.

Since developing the method to purge the nucla poisoning, Kaieli attempted to teach more groups how to merge their Talents. However, they discovered it wouldn't work if the group didn't include someone with at least a modicum of Gray Talent—the most uncommon one. So far, nobody else captured possessed any Gray Talent. The method only worked because of Kaieli's modest Gray Talent. It left her group working all evening purging the nucla poisoning from the men.

As the invaders added more captive men to the population, it became harder for Kaieli's team to treat them all each night. Some men suffered two or three days until the healers could cleanse them. Worry niggled at Kaieli when Rolstrun, Bohandran, and the other men from the fortresses scuttled into the area. Each day, removing the malignant magic from them grew increasingly more difficult. There may come a time when it became impossible for her team to clear the nucla from their systems.

The constant contact with the nucla in the processing plant also affected the women. Although not as bad as what the men experienced. The pernicious, malignant magic wormed its way into their bodies through the black dust they breathed. Even if they all escaped with the Gryphons tomorrow, the malady would still infect them. To completely heal them required more than she could do in the primitive conditions of the slave camp.

When her team finished clearing the men for the night, Kaieli put a hand on Maheli's arm to stall her. "Stay, please. I have news I need to share with the alphas." Maheli sat back down while the rest stood, stretched, and then headed to the stew pot for dinner.

Hope lit Maheli's eyes as she sent a call via mind-speech to the other camp alphas. "Is it good news?"

Kaieli nodded. The other alphas soon joined them at the table. "Help is here," Kaieli said. "I talked to a Gryphon named Kaaik today."

"That's impossible!" Kothera objected. "They are only mythological creatures."

"We thought we saw one," Bohandran said, "right after we arrived, flying over the crater. Are you sure they're here to help?"

Kaieli smiled. "Yes, Delestrun was with him. He's from Strunlair Keep. My Clan Alphas, at least, know something is wrong."

"This is good news!" Maheli grinned, then immediately frowned. "But how can the Gryphons help?"

"Kaaik and Delestrun appeared right after our latest escapees left the compound. Kaaik was going to pick them up and take them to a camp at the edge of the Barrens. I arranged to meet with him tomorrow at noon."

"But we can't leave." Kothera protested. She covered the tracking device implanted in her arm with a hand. "It won't do any good if we're blown to bits."

"I have another piece of news to share." She removed the device from her pocket and showed it to them. "Tre'nok gave me this. It deactivates the tracking device so more people can escape." She held up a hand to forestall their excited outburst. "Unfortunately, it won't work for us and the early captives. The device can't do anything about the explosives in our trackers."

Nederposan's shoulders slumped. His fortress had been the first to fall to the invaders. "So we're stuck here until we can remove the implant. While I'd love to talk to this Gryphon, we can't leave the compound and he can't come here, especially with the dome in place."

"The explosive won't automatically trigger unless we go more than two measures from the compound. It's far enough away the invaders won't see us."

"Well, then," Nederposan said, "that helps. You ladies will have to meet with him. It's impossible for Bohandran and me to leave. The overseers watch us too closely."

The next day, Kaieli and Maheli slipped out the processing plant's back door and ran into the Barrens. About a measure and a half from the compound fence, they reached a huge outcropping of petrified wood boulders. It sheltered them from the sun and blocked the view of any invaders. They scurried to the far side and slumped to the rocky ground to rest. Kaieli's chest and legs ached from running. She hoped the ugly orange coveralls they wore provided a beacon for the Gryphon to find them. She assumed, as part bird and part feline, they possessed naturally keen sight.

Her breathing slowly returned to normal. An unexpected wind stirred the sand at her feet, and a large body dropped from the sky toward her. She squeaked and covered her head. Wind and sand battered her as the Gryphon landed.

I did not mean to startle you, a voice said into her mind. *I am Kaaik. Delestrun is with me.*

Kaieli uncovered her face. Before her stood a being that she'd only seen pictures of in the ancient ruins. He had tawny-beige head feathers and darker brown wing feathers mixed with the tawny-beige. His face reminded her of a hawk. She stood, brushed off her coveralls, and extended her hand. Glancing at his taloned forefeet, she lowered her hand.

"I'm Kaieli." She turned to introduce Maheli and found her and Delestrun hugging each other.

"It's so good to see you, my friend," Maheli said.

"And you too." Delestrun stepped back, keeping an arm around Maheli's shoulders. "Kaieli? What are you doing so far south?"

Kaieli quickly told them about her capture and life in the slave pens.

Are you ready to go? Kaaik asked. *You two are small enough I can carry both of you.* He dropped his lower beak, in what Kaieli assumed was a grin. *I might have to leave this big lug here and come back for him.*

Maheli sighed. "I wish we could go with you, but we can't." She explained the problem with the explosive trackers to them. "The invaders are holding some of our children hostage, ensuring our good behavior. We're getting out as many people as we can without attracting too much attention from the invaders. If they notice, they'll kill the children."

Kaaik's head feathers rose, making him appear even more fierce. *That is heinous! There aren't many of us, since we're only the advance scouts. The war host follows, but they won't arrive for several more days. But we must rescue the children as soon as possible. My team will get them out.*

"They have an energy dome covering the compound," Maheli warned. "We managed to neutralize only a small portion of it near the ground. The hole isn't big enough to allow someone as large as you through it."

"No problem," Delestrun said. "We have Reds with us. They'll take it down. Where are the children being kept?"

Maheli gave him a skeptical grimace. "I'm not sure you can break through the dome at the top. The children are in a cage in the center of the camp where everyone can see it. You'll need a miracle to get in and out without the invaders seeing—and killing—you."

It won't be an issue. Kaaik winked. *We have magic allowing us to become invisible. They won't even see us. We'll rescue them tonight.*

Kaieli shook her head. "No, the invaders are too active at night. Our sun troubles them. Noon would be a better time when they're somnolent. Delestrun, could you have someone go to Posanreande Keep? In the chaos of being captured, we left a little girl behind. If you could burn her body, it would give her mother some sense of peace."

"Her name didn't happen to be Dreana, did it?"

Kaieli nodded, not daring to hope.

Delestrun smiled. "She's safe in the Sanctuary. Rizelya and Blazel found her when they scouted the area right after the invaders landed."

"Oh, thank Goddess! Her mother has been so worried about her." Kaieli had wanted Treana to be one of the first children to escape, but Jaelena wouldn't let her go. Even though Treana faced death every day she stayed in the slave camp, Jaelena couldn't face losing another daughter. Now they knew Dreana was safe, Kaieli would insist Treana leave.

As Kaieli and Maheli ran back to the compound, Kaieli hoped the Gryphons could break through the energy barrier and rescue the children. The rest of the captives would suffer repercussions, but saving the children took precedence.

Rolstrun - 16 de Drudar, 1075

What had been a bad situation soon became intolerable. Every day, the soldiers took people to the monster corrals to be terrorized before being eaten by the invaders. The invaders captured more keeps to replace the captives they killed. Soon, the population swelled to over three thousand. So far, the invaders hadn't locked any of the children into the monster corrals. Rolstrun worried it was only a matter of time before they did.

As Rolstrun trudged to the crater rim, he slowed his steps as he passed the cage full of children. They huddled together in the center, having learned that touching the bars resulted in getting zapped at best, and burned at worst. A Kaigor holding a club stomped to the cage and banged on the bars, seemingly unaffected by the energy flowing through them. A girl screamed, cowering away from the Kaigor. Several soldiers stepped forward, their tongues eagerly lapping up her terror. One, with blue-edged robes, nodded at the Kaigor, and it beat on the bars again, growling at the children while saliva dripped from its tusks. More children screamed, and the officer's tongue greedily flicked in and out. Rolstrun swore. But he was powerless to stop the atrocity.

He glanced up at the dome. If all went well this afternoon, the children would be gone. Last night, Kaieli warned the prisoners the Gryphons were going to attempt rescuing the children. They needed to know to prepare for the promised punishments. Rolstrun, like everyone he talked to, considered getting the children to safety as the highest priority, and would accept any punishment the commander meted out.

"Do you think it will work?" Alestrun asked as they waited their turn to climb down the ladder.

Rolstrun shrugged. He didn't know anything about the Gryphons, other than what the legends and myths said about them. He hoped their magic was strong enough to break through the energy-field.

Summer heat baked the crater bottom. Several terraces now snaked up the side of the pillar. Rolstrun's crew climbed to the highest one. Sweat skimmed along his spine as noon approached. He craned his head, searching the skies for signs of the Gryphon. The horn announcing the noon break blared. He and the others reluctantly rappelled to the ground to receive their allotted cup of water and a quarter of a travel bar.

The guards leaned on their weapons. Their eyes drooped with lethargy. Sores oozing pale liquid marked most of their faces and hands from the sun's radiation. Their heavy black robes must be stifling hot in the heat, which was even greater at the crater's bottom than at the top.

Rolstrun took the cup of water from the Vhelopsi and stepped aside. As he nibbled on his rations, he casually glanced upward. Bright flashes of light bounced off the dome. Streams of fire assailed it. In one flash of light, he glimpsed a huge, black Gryphon, but then it disappeared.

Alarms blared in the compound above them. Angry shouts drifted down to the men. Weapons fired, and booms reverberated on the crater's walls. A loud, whistling sound followed by a long projectile screamed through the air toward the attack on the dome. It penetrated the energy-field, and a moment later, an explosion lit the sky. A Gryphon suddenly appeared with one of its wings missing, blood pouring from the wound. It spiraled down, crashing on the ground outside of the dome, and Rolstrun glimpsed someone in red leathers strapped to a harness on its back. Two huge black Gryphons swooped down and picked up the injured Gryphon and his rider.

Five of the smaller fighting ships roared into the sky. An opening formed in the dome, and the ships slipped through it. White and blue light streaked from them as they fired their weapons. The Gryphons hightailed it with the invaders after them. Rolstrun prayed the Gryphons were faster than the ships.

Rolstrun hunched as a whiplash stung his shoulders. The crack of whips filled the air as the overseers laid into the gaping men. Dejected by the Gryphon's failure to pierce the energy-field and rescue the children, Rolstrun trudged back to the pillar.

The overseers called work to a halt early, and when the men reached the top of the crater, soldiers herded them to the center of the compound. The women already stood crowded in front of the cage. Hordes of invaders filled the space, vastly outnumbering the Posairs. In an unusual show of force, dozens of soldiers towered over the captives, sitting on their tall sheezets with weapons held ready. Others lined the building's roofs, gazing down on the proceedings. The slaves brought by the Scourge stood to one side. The faces of the Faeorn and Vhelopsi were pale, as if they dreaded what would happen. Three of the nasty Kaigor rocked from foot to foot near the children's cage with their eyes riveted to it.

Rolstrun's stomach clenched into a tight knot. So far, the invaders had only terrorized the children. This didn't look good.

Commander Ke-ke-tak stood by the cage, Tre'nok by his side. Once the soldiers pushed all the Posairs into the square, Tre'nok translated for the commander.

"Resistance is not tolerated, from you or your people. The only hope for your people is to surrender. Other worlds have fought against us, and they found they could not win against our might. Your world will discover the same thing. We have destroyed the people and their beasts who tried to infiltrate our base. As will all those who pit themselves against the great Scourge!" The commander flung a fist into the air.

The assembled soldiers roared and beat their chests. The dry rustling of their feeders sounded ominous, and Rolstrun trembled. *This is it. This is when I die. Goddess, may my soul find its way to the Mother's Womb.*

Commander Ke-ke-tak dropped his fist and nodded. Soldiers opened the cage and entered. They selected five children, dragging them out kicking and screaming. They tossed three children toward the Kaigor, who caught them. The soldiers then beat the remaining two children until their cries and movements stopped. Two Kaigor fought over a child, pulling it between them. Rolstrun turned his head, unable to watch. When he looked back, one chomped on the child's head and torso while the other gnawed on its legs. Bile rose to Rolstrun's throat, and he covered his mouth with his hand as he gagged. Others in the crowd lost the battle.

The commander struck his feeders into the two children beaten by his soldiers and sucked them dry.

Tears streamed down Rolstrun's face. After this, what more terror could the invaders inflict on them?

Rizelya - 17 de Drudar, 1075

Rizelya climbed onto a stack of supplies, stopping when she stood several feet above the barge railing. She tossed her bedroll on the crates to cushion her butt and propped her back against another crate. The summer sun warmed her face while a breeze from the river kept her from becoming too hot. The plains rolled by as they sped down the river. She could get used to this mode of travel, which allowed time to relax and to catch up with her pack-mates.

Her eyes drifted closed as the warmth and exhaustion weighed down on her. The only mar to the trip downriver was the Malvers woman plaguing Rizelya's dreams almost nightly. The Supreme's blocks on Rizelya's mind helped. She now watched the dream events as if from afar, rather than experiencing them first-hand. Rizelya's brow furrowed. Over the past few nights, the Malvers woman appeared less gaunt from starvation. Rather than a few black pearls oozing from her device as in the past, the death pearls filled the bowl to overflowing. Somehow, the Malvers' monsters were killing more people, providing their masters with more strength.

Unease interrupted Rizelya's rest. She stood facing south toward the Barrens. Her gut told her something the invaders were doing with the monsters caused the influx of power to the Malvers. She couldn't imagine what. They'd discover it when they reached the base camp tomorrow and engaged with the invaders.

The afternoon passed as uneventfully as the past eight days. In the evening, the flotilla of barges pulled ashore, and Rizelya joined her people debarking. While the support staff prepared dinner, she and her people led the new teams in practicing the techniques developed with the other Talents. She smiled in approval as the newly designated illusion masters created the training illusion for their groups. The war host included too many for her and Dehali to be the only ones using the illusion monsters to train the new fighters. A large portion of their force was untested in a battle against the Malvers' monsters.

She paused in her inspection as a Gryphon dove toward a training illusion. He flared, and flames surrounded his body. The fighters held their positions before racing to join the Gryphon attacking the janack. It amazed Rizelya how quickly her people adapted to fighting with the Gryphons. Although, the first few times a Gryphon had flared, the new fighters had screamed and fled. Rizelya continued walking around the practicing fighters, stopping here and there to adjust stances or to give advice.

Rizelya finally made her way back to where her squad-pack practiced. Even as more fighters joined the war host, Rizelya's squad pack remained unique. Out of the two hundred multi-Talented squad-packs, only her team included someone with Gray and White Talents. Chariel and Wisah were the only priestesses brave enough to learn how to fight. And Chariel was the only Gray in the entire war host, which was unsurprising, considering the rarity of women with Gray Talent.

Two dozen White Priestesses accompanied the war host. Out of those, only a few claimed Gray as their secondary talent. Rizelya loved that the force included White Priestesses to usher anyone killed in the coming battles through the veil. She sighed, wishing more would follow in Shandir's—and Wisah's—footsteps and fight with them. Chariel's Gray Talent allowed her to weave the energies together into tight nets. Wisah saw the woven magic and energy streams, and could direct them into various forms and over long distances.

Rizelya's group practiced the fighting forms, and Chariel easily flowed through them, including the more advanced forms. It surprised her to discover Chariel had learned them as an adolescent from Histrun during his sojourn at the Sanctuary the year Rizelya's mother died. When they played jelehan, Chariel caught and threw the various sized sticks as quickly and accurately as anyone else. She won quite frequently, much to the dismay of the warriors.

Rizelya joined her group in the forms to warm up, then called their Gryphon teammates to practice fighting. Until they engaged with the invaders, they wouldn't know how well any of the new techniques worked, but Rizelya believed they would. Why else had the Goddess guided her to add the other Talents to her squad-pack? She pushed her teams hard, expecting the invaders to attack the vulnerable war host at any moment. The invaders weren't sticking close to the crater.

Yesterday, the relay team delivered the disturbing news that the invaders captured ten more small keeps bordering the Barrens. They took the captive Posairs to the crater to become slaves. The evacuation teams weren't able to reach the keeps in time to save them. Histrun expected a report from the advance team any day now.

A dot in the sky flew toward the camp. Rizelya cocked her head, listening for a man-made sound, but nothing reached her. She hurried to Blazel and Graak.

"Can you make out what it is?" she asked Graak. "Your long-distance vision is much better than ours."

Graak peered into the sky. *It's Kaaik and Delestrun. Something bad has happened.*

"What was it?"

Graak shrugged. *Kaaik would not say. He's very disturbed, though.*

Rizelya, Blazel, and Graak ran to the command tent. They reached it at the same time as Kaaik landed. A nasty burn oozed on Delestrun's right cheek, and a few of Kaaik's wing feathers were singed. Horror squeezed Rizelya's chest. Delestrun hunched his shoulders, his head drooping. She caught his gaze as he trudged past, and devastation filled his eyes. Had the invaders killed all their people?

She followed Blazel and Graak as they slipped into the command tent. To one side, a tall folding table held a map. Histrun, Keshanal, Naila, and several older alphas sat on camp stools, while Moraak curled up on a thick rug. Kaaik and Delestrun stopped in front of the leaders. Delestrun eased into a parade rest stance with his hands behind his back. Kaaik's sat on his haunches, swishing his tail.

"We've made contact with the captives in the crater," Delestrun said.

"Are they all right?" Keshanal asked.

"For the most part. The men work on mining the huge pillar in the crater's center. For what, we don't know. They've taken away all the women's helbraughts." Delestrun grimaced. "Some have died."

The invaders, Kaaik added, *call themselves the Scourge. They keep the Posair captives under guard and underfed. As punishment, they put fifty children in a cage—*

"We have to get them out!" Keshanal blurted.

"You tried, didn't you?" Histrun observed. "What happened?"

"We couldn't reach them, sir." Delestrun swiped at the pus running from his burned cheek.

Kaaik rustled his wings against his back and chirped in pain. *The invaders installed some sort of energy dome over their compound. It stopped us from entering, even with our magic. The Reds with us tried to deactivate it, like the Reds in the camp did. But they can't get close enough to the field while in the air. The energy field didn't stop their weapons from getting through. The invaders killed one of our team.*

Histrun's jaw set, and his brow furrowed. "If we can't get in, we'll have to draw them out from behind their protections."

"That shouldn't be hard, sir," Delestrun said. "Staying alive will be difficult. From what we saw, they have thousands more troops than we do. Probably more than the entire population of Lairheim—"

Including the Gryphons, Kaaik added. *Our quick count estimates their number to be over half a million.*

"Sweet Mother!" Keshanal swore, slumping back. "How will we ever win against so many?"

"It's our home." Histrun stood and stared at the map. "We're fighting for our very survival. The Malvers' monsters haven't eliminated us after a thousand years. These Scourge—" he made the name a swear word "—will not either. Tell me everything you saw in their camp."

As Delestrun and Kaaik related their observations, Rizelya reeled at the news. The Scourge outnumbered the Posair forces at least five to one, and it seemed like the invaders' technology outmatched their magic. Her heart stuttered at the impossible prospect of throwing the interlopers off their planet.

Chapter 16

Blazel - 18 de Drudar, 1075

Guards patrolled the perimeter of the camp with watchers focused toward Barrens. Histrun expected some sort of reprisal after the advance teams' failure to rescue the children. Blazel held Rizelya close on their shared cot. Soon, they'd engage with the invaders, and who knew what would happen when they did?

The Malvers woman disturbed his dreams. She chuckled gleefully as she gorged on her device's death pearls. Blazel's stomach roiled at the number of deaths needed to create so many pearls. He rejoiced when shouts and a loud whistling sound interrupted his dream. As he became more awake, the ground beneath him shook, and he scrambled from his bedroll.

"What's happening?" he shouted.

"The invaders!" someone running past yelled at him.

Rizelya jumped to her feet, her helbraught already glowing in her hands. "Where are they?"

The rest of their squad-pack also surged out of their cots, ready for action.

Blazel turned at the crack of the Thunder Wings taking off. In a few moments, a dozen Thunder Wings flared, turning the gray dawn bright as full day. Five ships hung in the air, with ropes dangling from open hatches on their sides. Alien soldiers slid down the ropes, landing within the camp. A light burst from one of the ships and sped toward the command tent. Blazel, Rizelya, and their team raced the few yards to it. The women worked the magic to form a net-shield while they ran. He sensed Chariel grab hold of the various magics and weave them together.

"Do you have it, Wisah?" Chariel yelled.

"Yes!" Wisah stopped and threw out her hands.

Jaehaas galloped past her. He slid to a stop, reared onto his hind legs, then whirled to gallop back to her. With an arrow already nocked on his bow, he stood at her side while she worked her magic.

A sheet of fire, laced with molten lava, formed above the command tent, then dropped over it to form a dome. The anchoring streams solidified into sheadash stone. The invaders' projectile struck the net and exploded. Blazel ducked with his hands over his head, expecting shrapnel to pelt him. When a spray of water washed over him, he peeked from under his arms. He raised his eyebrows at the lack of debris. The weapon used a type of light-energy.

Another blast from the invaders' ship streaked toward them. The new net—combining fire, stone, water, and air—easily absorbed it.

Above them, Gryphons attacked the ships. Blazel glimpsed several tall, hunched-back shapes scuttling between the tents. *Invaders!* Blazel shifted into his warrior form. When Aistrun and the other men on their team also shifted, he realized he'd yelled in mind-speech. He shrugged off the new development. He'd relish it later. The warriors positioned themselves in front of the women, who couldn't fight while concentrating on holding the net-shield.

An invader raised a stick-like weapon to its shoulder and fired. Points of red light shot from it. Blazel ducked and dodged, avoiding the lights. The grass sizzled and blackened wherever they hit. He raced forward, surprising the enemy as he jerked the weapon out of the invader's hands. He snarled, baring his teeth, nearly gagging on the invader's stench. Blazel quickly took in the long face with big, bug-like eyes, the longish nose topping a small mouth before he shredded its neck with his claws. Purple blood poured from the wound as he threw the dead invader away from him. As he attacked another soldier, his greater strength in his warrior's form gave him an advantage.

He discovered the weapons shot a mix of metal and light projectiles. A yellow light struck a warrior, who immediately gasped for breath and grabbed his throat. Foam dribbled down his chin as he convulsed, falling to the ground. A moment later, he died.

Ware the yellow lights! Blazel yelled. *They're poisonous!*

A projectile nicked his shoulder. He growled and swiped at the soldier's weapon, slicing it in half with his claws. A loud screeching above him made him glance up. The Thunder Wings angled away from the ship they'd torn to bits. The remaining four ships zoomed back toward the Barrens, leaving any invaders still on the ground to the Posairs. Blazel turned back to face another enemy. The invader's eyes bugged even wider as a helbraught tip peeked from its chest. It fell, revealing Rizelya, a streak of purple blood on her cheek. They fought as a team, tearing through the invading soldiers.

At last, no alien soldiers remained alive, although a few escaped on foot. They'd have a long run to reach the Barrens and the crater. The temporary camp sat in the plains over fifty measures from the edge of the Barrens.

The invaders had killed twenty men and women and one Gryphon during the attack. While the rest broke up camp, the White Priestesses sent their souls through the veil.

After having the healers tend their minor wounds, Blazel and Rizelya checked on Histrun and the other commanders.

Keshanal hugged Rizelya when she walked into the tent. "If it hadn't been for the new net-shield, Rizelya, they would have killed us. Thank the Goddess for your inventiveness!"

"I believe this was an exploratory attack for the invaders to learn about our capabilities." Histrun ran a hand through his mussed-up hair. "As soon as we reach the base camp tomorrow, we'll need to settle in quickly. I expect more attacks."

My Gryphons did well against the invaders' flying machines. Moraak fluffed his head feathers. *We should send more to patrol the area near the Barrens. Perhaps they can deter the invaders from capturing any more of your keeps.*

We've evacuated all we could, but a few were too large to evacuate everyone.

Histrun nodded. "Do it. It's a good plan. Blazel, Rizelya, tell me what you learned while fighting these buggers." He frowned at Rizelya. "While I appreciate your net protecting us, it kept us locked in here! I didn't get to see the fight until you released the net."

"Sorry, sir." Rizelya grinned. "We need to keep you safe."

Histrun, Keshanal, Naila, and Moraak drilled them as they made their report, pulling the littlest details from them. By the time they finished, Blazel felt drained. When they stepped away from the tent, a crew swept in and started packing it. It was the last one standing. Soon, they had it packed and loaded on the barges.

The Gryphons launched into the sky. A large team peeled off from the rest and flew southeast, while another team split off and headed southwest. They would augment the fighters in the keeps along the Barrens border to repel any incursions from the invaders. Histrun didn't want any more people captured.

Blazel and Rizelya climbed aboard their assigned barge, and he sank gratefully onto the deck, leaning against the side. Rizelya curled up next to him. Aistrun and Chariel found them and handed them a travel bar and a canteen of hot taevo to break their fast.

"We can kill the invaders," Blazel said around a mouthful of food. "Their weapons are a problem."

"Yeah, you never know if it's going to be a metal projectile or something worse," Aistrun agreed, sliding down to sit next to them. "The yellow light is nasty. Did you see what the blue light did? It paralyzed the person, allowing the invader to casually kill them. I saw one of those ugly creatures sticking some sort of tube into a warrior." Aistrun shuddered. "I don't know what it was doing, because I killed it before it could finish. But the warrior died anyway."

"What are these creatures?" Blazel asked. "And what do they want with our world?"

"Something in the crater," Rizelya answered, and gave him the last of her bar. He smiled when he noticed hers contained dried fruit. She hated dried fruit.

"Nothing good ever comes from the crater," Chariel observed. "Only great evil."

Blazel remembered his flight across the Barrens and the malignant magic pervading the place. "Evil calls to evil. Even though we prevailed against the invaders this time, they have many more people to throw at us. How can we win against such odds?"

"We have to. I refuse to let them conquer our world." Rizelya's jaw set in a determined line.

"We'll find a way. The Goddess will guide us," Chariel added. She pointed to their unusual pack. "We have all the pieces to the prophecy."

Blazel straightened his shoulders. He was part of the prophecy, and he'd play his role to the fullest. Rizelya leaned against him as she dozed. Hope filled him. With her at his side, and his companions at his back, they would triumph against the invaders.

Kaieli - 18 de Drudar, 1075

Two days after the failed rescue attempt, Kaieli awoke to the roar of engines. She hurried to the latrine pit. Overhead, five fighter ships zoomed north in the predawn light. Each one held fifty soldiers, plus a piloting crew. They normally accompanied a transport ship when the invaders attacked a keep. She frowned when no other ships left the compound. *Does this mean the Posair war host is close enough for the invaders to attack them?* Kaieli didn't dare hope their salvation was near.

She'd expected the commander to retaliate on their people for the rescue attempt before this. He'd immediately inflicted his displeasure on the captives, ordering decreased food and water. Between the summer heat and the already deficient rations, too many people were suffering from dehydration. Her make-shift infirmary held several patients. Kaieli anxiously waited for the guards to usher them to the processing plant so she could check on them.

The morning horn blared, jerking the Posairs from their uneasy sleep. A quiet despair blanketed the captives as they formed lines to march to their work assignments. As the women plodded toward the processing plant, the normally boisterous children didn't run and play, terrified the Kaigor would tear them apart. Kaieli scowled at the increased guards in and around the plant. With so may about, it would make it impossible for them to slip any more people out the back door.

Inside, the heat reached unbearable temperatures. Kaieli brushed sweat soaked hair from her face, as she rushed to the infirmary where they hid anyone ill or injured. If any guards saw her patients in their weakened condition, they'd feed on them.

Kaieli bent over her most critical patient, placing a hand on Laean's forehead. She burned with fever, and her eyes were dull. Her skin was dry and sagged on her nearly skeletal frame. Even if Laean received more food and water, Kaieli doubted she'd recover.

Vy'shol entered the infirmary, and joined Kaieli at Laean's pallet. "She does not look well."

"No, she isn't. None of us are. We can't survive this heat without water. I've noticed even the Scourge need water in these conditions. If they want us to continue working for them, they need to give us food and water. In another day or two, he won't have any workers. Killing us this way won't stop our people from fighting them."

"The tactic works on other planets. Your war host nears the camp on the border of the Barrens. The commander waits for them to gather in one place before he annihilates them."

Kaieli snorted. "I doubt he can. We have fought the Malvers' monsters for a thousand years, and they haven't managed to do eliminate us yet. The Scourge won't either. Are you spying on us for your masters?"

Vy'shol frowned. "No. I'm trying to gauge your people's resolve. Already you have shown you are different from most species. I wonder what it is. Is it your shapeshifting abilities or your magic?"

"Probably both. Or it could be our faith in the Goddess, knowing she protects us."

"But she has not. The Scourge has enslaved your people."

"Only a few of us. The rest are free." Kaieli leaned forward, her voice determined. "We will throw the Scourge off our planet."

"If you do, you'll be the first in hundreds of planets."

"Someone has to be the first." Kaieli shrugged as she sat back. "Can you get us water?"

Vy'shol nodded. "I will talk to the masters, but do not expect any mercy from them."

Kaieli laughed. "No, we've learned they are incapable of mercy. Remind them that we need food and water to work and produce more of the nucla for them."

Vy'shol strolled out. Kaieli whirled around at Laean's low moan. She'd somehow rolled off the crate used for a cot and laid on the floor, gasping for breath. Kaieli slid down and gently placed Laean's head on her lap. "I'm here." She ran a soothing hand over Laean's face.

Laean's eyes popped open for a moment, then she sighed deeply. "I'm free." She didn't inhale again. A slight smile played on her lips.

Kaieli bent her head, letting the tears slide down her cheeks as she watched Laean's soul cross the veil and into the waiting arms of the Mother. *Maheli,* she called. *Laean has passed.*

Maheli pushed back the cloth doorway. Behind her stood several other women from the Strunland guard-pack. Tears pooled in Maheli's eyes and she bent her head. "Thank Goddess. She is free now. We'll take care of her body."

A loud disturbance near the entry doors punctuated the normal sounds in the plant. The guards hustled toward the diversion created by the other women.

"Quickly," Maheli ordered. The women with her gently lifted Laean, carried her to one of the blast furnaces, and dropped her body in. Now, the Scourge or Kaigor couldn't eat her.

Later in the afternoon, a Hap'thez lugged in a large barrel of water. It held only enough water for everyone to have one cup, but it was enough for them to continue living. After dinner, the captives mourned Laean and the ten men who died during the day from the heat and poor rations.

Rolstrun slumped on a bench after the ceremony, crying. Kaieli sat next to him, holding him in her arms while he wept.

"I should have tried harder," he said, wiping away the tears. "But she wanted more than I could give her in this place. I'm not willing to risk a child being born in this hellhole."

"The Goddess must be protecting us, because even without our herbs, I haven't treated one case of pregnancy yet."

"Or else no one is having physical relationships."

Kaieli laughed. "You must sleep deeply to think that! I hear lovemaking all the time. When we live in these conditions, it's natural to turn to something like sex to remind us of the joys of life." Rizelya had been the last person she'd had intimate relations with. Her forehead crinkled as she did the mental calculations. Their last rendezvous occurred nearly a year ago. She admired Rolstrun's determination to keep going. Kaieli smiled shyly at him.

"I like you, Kaieli. I really do." Rolstrun turned his face away from her. "I don't want to disappoint you, like I did Laean."

She gently took his chin and turned his face back to her. "I understand how you feel. Let's just hold each other and give each other what comfort we can find in this place of horror."

He nodded and wrapped his arms around her. Later, they laid on her pallet in each other's arms. It didn't bother her that he didn't make love to her. Truthfully, she was too tired and worn out. Perhaps someday, when they escaped, they'd pursue a deeper relationship. But for now, this was all she wanted.

Rolstrun - 19 de Drudar, 1075

Rolstrun fell into line with the other men for their morning march to the crater. His heart plummeted and a wave of dizziness swept over him when the guards counted off every twentieth man and dragged them toward the monster corrals. The guards also separated a dozen women. As if the withholding of water and food wasn't enough, the commander was enacting more punishments for the rescue attempt. Rolstrun's hands fisted as he searched for Kaieli in the group standing frozen in horror at the gate. A long sigh escaped him when he noticed her plodding toward the processing plant.

He joined the quiet cheer when the soldiers prodded ten of the nasty Kaigor to the gate leading to the monster corrals. The damned Kaigor deserved whatever vileness the invaders heaped on them after the events with the children. His guts lurched at the large group of Hap'thez, Coufrish, and Gheethong herded toward the fence. None of them deserved to die such a horrible death. Although, it might be a merciful end to their suffering from the dry, hot summer heat. Instead of waiting for the elements to kill them, the invaders systematically sent them to the monster pens, where they fed off the alien's fear and pain. The Vhelopsi, however, thrived in the heat, and the sun burnished their skin into deeper shades of gold or bronze.

Rolstrun jerked at the hard slap on his shoulder. The overseer pointed toward the stables. The Coufrish had cared for the invaders' lizard-mounts, but with their number significantly reduced, they needed help to feed the lizards. Rolstrun stepped smartly out of the line, looking forward to doing something besides digging and shoveling rock. He stifled a grin when his friends Calistrun and Alestrun joined the group of thirty men jogging to the sheezet pens.

Outside the pens, Flo'kik instructed them about their new duties. Rolstrun wrinkled his nose at the stench. They hadn't even entered the pens yet!

He grabbed a pitchfork and swung it over his shoulder with a rueful shake of his head. He'd been mistaken when he expected his new job would include something besides swinging a shovel. The sheezet stalls needed mucking. Based on the towering piles behind the building, the lizards dumped way more manure than the Posairs' horses.

Rolstrun, along with Calistrun, and Alestrun, entered a large stall, chattering and relishing a day without the constant threat of an overseer whipping them. They stopped in their tracks. Ten of the massive beasts still milled inside. They sniffed the air, and the eyes of the largest one darkened to an angry red. It dipped its head and raced toward the men. Calistrun and

Alestrun yipped, leaping to the side. Rolstrun leaped the other way—at least that was his intention. Instead, his foot slipped on the manure, and he flailed his arms to keep his balance.

The beast barreled down on him. Rolstrun regained his feet and lunged for the door. Before he reached safety, the sheezet hit him, bowling him over. As he rolled, one of the beast's sharp horns stabbed him in the lower back. He tumbled into the wall and flung up an arm to ward off the beast's jaws. He screamed as it chomped on his left hand. Calistrun and Alestrun pushed the sheezet away from Rolstrun. A Coufrish ran in and brought the beasts under control, jabbering at the Posairs as if they had caused the problem.

"We have to get you to the infirmary, fast!" Calistrun grabbed a somewhat clean rag from the wall, used to polish the lizard's hides, and wrapped it around Rolstrun's bleeding hand. Another rag bound his back. "If any invaders see your injuries, you'll be their next meal."

Darkness edged Rolstrun's vision.

"Hang on, Rolstrun! I'm getting out of this mess, and so are you. Do you hear me, Rolstrun? Come on, Alestrun, help me!"

Together, his friends half-carried, half-dragged him across the compound, hiding behind buildings or equipment to evade any wandering invaders. Rolstrun gritted his teeth, attempting to suppress his pain. Fire burned his back where the sheezet gored him, and he nearly passed out every time they jostled his hand. Finally, they reached the infirmary.

"Sweet Goddess!" Kaieli cried. "What happened?"

While Calistrun and Alestrun explained, Kaieli unwrapped the makeshift bandage from his hand. The color drained from her face.

"How bad? Did it take my hand?" He panted as fear iced his blood. If he lost a hand, he couldn't fight the Malvers' monsters. The prospect terrified him nearly as badly as never shapeshifting again.

"No, only the fourth and little finger."

He moaned when she prodded his back.

"Thank Goddess the horn missed your kidneys. Faelyn, come help me!"

Rolstrun blacked out as the two healers bent over him. When he blinked back to consciousness, a soothing warmth enveloped his hand and lower back. He took his first deep breath since the incident as the pain receded.

Sweat bathed Kaieli's face. "We've done all we can. We finally stopped the internal bleeding," Kaieli gently wrapped his hand with the roll of cloth Faelyn handed her. As part of the escape runs, the Posair army brought them supplies. "You're lucky the horn missed anything vital. You should be up and moving in a day or two. We saved your hand. I'm sorry about your fingers."

"That's okay," he slurred. "Hard to save them when the damned lizard ate them."

A smile tugged at Kaieli's lips at his humor attempt. She took his face in her hands and tilted it so she could look him in the eye. "You're still a warrior. You'll be okay. We'll hide you here until you're healed. The invaders aren't going to eat you if I can help it."

They moved him to a pallet behind a stack of containers and threw a covering over it. Even in the stifling heat of the processing plant, Rolstrun soon drifted to sleep. He awoke later when Kaieli gently shook him.

"We have to go back to our pens. I'm leaving you some water and a couple of trail bars. Eat, sleep, get well. I'll see you in the morning."

Quiet descended in the processing plant. Rolstrun nibbled on a travel bar, eating slowly. In the darkness, he carefully prodded his injured hand. Two fingers gone. *Thank Goddess Kaieli saved my hand.* While difficult, he could still fight the Malvers' monsters—that is, when he finally escaped this place— and remain a valued member of society.

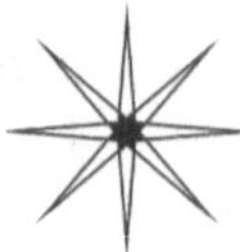

Rizelya - 19 de Drudar, 1075

On the afternoon of the tenth day after leaving Haasperlyn Keep, Rizelya spotted a tent village on the horizon. The flotilla arrived at the prepared base camp well before dark. As soon as they disembarked, Histrun called a meeting with the division leaders, even though the support staff still worked on setting up the command tent.

"Settle your people quickly, and set watches." Histrun paced with his hands behind his back. "I believe the invaders used their blitz attack to probe our strength. I expect them to throw more at us. In fact, I'm surprised they didn't harass us again today." He turned toward Rizelya. "Rizelya and Blazel, I want your team to guard the southern perimeter facing the Barrens. The way you weave your people's Talents together will be useful for stopping an encroaching army. And it will be an army."

Rizelya nodded in acknowledgment. She expected her battalion to be in the front lines. Even though only her squad-pack could weave their magic together, the other teams in her battalion discovered ways to join their Talents to create some pretty impressive magic. Their shields were like nothing anyone had ever experienced before. Her teams would provide the first barrier against the invaders.

"I intend to test our limits on how far we can extend our net-shield, sir. They'll attack us from both the air and from the ground."

Histrun narrowed his eyes at her. "Make sure our fighters can get out so they can fight."

She dipped her head. Apparently, he hadn't forgiven her yet for locking him and the other leaders in their command tent during the invaders' first attack.

My Gryphons will take out any ships, Moraak said. *The Thunder Wings have fun tearing the machines apart.* He chuckled darkly.

Histrun turned to the division alpha of the Andranlair contingent. "Nadandran, your group will be here," he pointed to a spot on the map. "We need to guard our access to the river. Voledon, Telekhaas, your divisions will defend our rear. We don't want Malvers' monsters to attack from the plains. Belistril, your centaurs will be runners between the various divisions. Send them to Naila so she can get to know them and mind-speak with them. Her mind-speaking skills are highly developed after all these years of speaking mostly that way." He gave Naila a sad smile, who unconsciously touched the scar on her neck.

I'll assign a Gryphon to you, Naila, Moraak said. **We are capable of mind-speaking with anyone. But it is easier and more efficient if we've met the person first.**

"Thank you, Moraak," Naila said in her gravelly voice. "I'll take any help I can."

Histrun gave the rest of the division leaders their assignments for the upcoming battle. He held back the Ronanlair and Keistanlair divisions as emergency fighters to keep some troops fresh, and available for monster attacks.

Released from the meeting, Rizelya and Blazel rejoined their team members, and they fell into the routine they'd established while traveling to find the Gryphons. They raised their tents, lit a fire, and put a pot of taevo over it in a short time. As they relaxed after eating, Rizelya stared into the flames, wondering what the new battle would bring. Would she lose some of her pack-mates? She glanced around the fire, memorizing the faces of her loved ones, just in case this was the last time they shared a fire together. Soon, they'd fight the invaders.

Rizelya - 20 de Drudar, 1075

Dawn glimmered, washing the sky a pale orange. Rizelya leaned her head against Blazel's shoulder, dozing. They'd opted to spend the night outside the tent. Her helbraught lay at her side within easy reach. She felt a thrumming at the same time Blazel sat up straight. He and the other men looked about expectantly.

"Do you hear that?" Blazel stood and scanned the southern sky.

"I do." Aistrun gently moved Chariel from where she leaned against him and stood, his hands clenching and unclenching.

They're coming! Graak announced, his mental voice waking anyone still asleep.

Light bloomed above their heads as the Gryphons flared. Their glow revealed three smallish ships, with a larger one trailing behind them. It paused, hovering, allowing the smaller ships to advance.

Streamers of light zoomed from the ships, targeting the Gryphons, followed quickly by staccato bursts of sound. The nimbus of fire surrounding the Gryphons incinerated most of the projectiles. A Gryphon's scream of pain shattered the calm. The ships fired again, and the Gryphons dipped and soared, weaving through the barrage. Another Gryphon cried out as a projectile hit him.

The metal and light type projectiles the Gryphons missed fell on the watchers in a deadly rain. One buried into the ground next to Rizelya's foot.

"Net-shield," she yelled, grabbing her helbraught and feeding power into it. Leistral, Dehali, Eiden, and Gehan, standing on her right, also activated their helbraughts. On her left, Grazeen, Maellyn, Saffren, and Raeleen did the same. In the center, Chariel and Wisah waited to gather and direct the merged Talents. Streams of different-colored light zipped from the team's helbraughts. Chariel gathered them together and wove them into a tight net of rainbow light. Rizelya sensed Wisah's power grab hold of the energies, expanding the net above them, and the rain of projectiles stopped falling around them.

"Push!" Rizelya ordered, as she added more of her power to the net. "More!" Her team increased their efforts, creating their largest net yet. Soon, an impenetrable shield hovered above the Posair fighters, although it didn't quite reach the rearguard. Rizelya trembled with the effort needed to hold it in place.

Blazel and Jaehaas joined the archers and raised their bows, letting loose a shower of fiery arrows. They flew impossibly far, carried on currents of air formed by Yellows. With a *thunk*, the arrows smashed into the ships' hard surfaces. As the arrow's fire died, a collective groan swept through the fighters. They hadn't damaged the ships.

Five huge Thunder Wings converged on a ship, dwarfing it. They sank their talons into the metal and heaved. The metal screeched as they ripped off the weapons attached to the top and sides of the ship, leaving gaping holes. A hawk-type Gryphon zipped into an opening, and a moment later, flew out with a struggling invader—his black robes flapping—in its talons. The hump on the invader's back started growing. The Gryphon noticed the movement and flared. In milcrons, the invader erupted into a ball of fire, his screams joining the clamor. The two remaining ships swerved and accelerated quickly back into the Barrens.

The larger ship flew forward a few feet above the ground. Rizelya gaped at the massive number of dark shapes jumping from it before it climbed and flew away. She estimated more than four hundred alien soldiers ran toward them.

Blazel tossed his bow to Jaehaas and shifted into his warrior form. Blazel and Aistrun led a contingent of warriors in a counterattack, slipping through the women's protective net. Their claws extended, dripping venom, and they raced toward the invaders. Snarls and cries filled the air.

"Drop the net," Rizelya ordered. They didn't need the net now the barrage of projectiles flying from the invaders' ship had ended. "Form the fire-shield. Don't let any of those buggers past us." The Reds stepped forward and the familiar fire-shield they used against the monsters flared in front of Rizelya and her team. She sagged, leaning on her helbraught and taking deep breaths.

An invader broke through the skirmish line, running toward the women. He bounced off the shields. His robe caught on fire. He dropped and rolled, putting it out, then jumped back up, snarling as he lifted his weapon and fired. She threw an arm up and ducked. A small projectile slammed into the shield in front of Rizelya's face.

The fire-shield held.

The invader fired again, a sneer of contempt on his face. Rage gave Rizelya a jolt of renewed energy. She dropped to the ground and crawled along the shield's edge. *Cover me!*

Leistral stepped into her spot, yelling, "Come and get me," at the invader while beckoning to him. She laughed when his weapon had no effect.

Meanwhile, Rizelya scurried a few feet down the edge of the shield before she formed an opening in it and slipped out. Orange flames licked her helbraught's blade. She ran, lifting the blade high as she aimed at the invader's head. His thin neck was nothing compared to the girth of a janack's tentacle. At the last milcron, he turned and blocked with his weapon. It sizzled with heat as it connected with her fire. A whimper escaped him, but he held on and squeezed the trigger.

Pain lanced through Rizelya as the projectile ripped across her left biceps and buried into her shoulder. She pulled back, and this time, directed her blow at the weapon. Her blade sliced through it, melting the end of the barrel. The invader gaped. With an upward motion, she thrust her blade through his belly, wrinkling her nose at the smell of charred flesh. The light went out in the invader's big, bug-like eyes as he burned to ash.

She didn't have time to celebrate, as more soldiers swarmed around her. The women had dropped the fire-shield and fought the invaders as savagely as they did the Malvers' monsters. Saffren and Maellyn teamed up and killed an invader with ice and lava. Grazeen's magic didn't have any effect on live invaders, but any dead ones were quickly rotting. As expected, some of their new techniques worked against the aliens and some didn't. She turned to face the next invader.

The day warmed as the sun climbed higher. Heat waves shimmered. Sweat slid down Rizelya's nose and made her grip on her helbraught slippery. Still, the invaders came at them like a never-ending tidal wave. Suddenly, a loud horn blared, and the remaining soldiers immediately retreated into the Barrens, purple blood marking their passage.

Rizelya leaned on her helbraught, breathing deeply. The pain in her shoulder intensified with each breath. She surveyed the battlefield. Dead and wounded scattered across more than a two-measure swath in the grass.

Nearby, three Strunhelos women lay in awkward positions, holes in their chests, their eyes open, staring unseeing at the sky. Rizelya turned her gaze from the dead, searching for her squad-pack. She hurried to help Saffren, who had a cut over one eyebrow, marring her perfect beauty, as she struggled to tie a bandage around the gash in Leistral's leg. Jaehaas limped toward them, not putting any weight on his left hind leg. They moved through the field, finding and helping the others in their squad-pack. No one had escaped the fight without minor injuries.

Together, her squad-pack shuffled back to their tent where Chariel and Wisah waited for them. Too necessary for the shield-net, the two priestesses had retreated to the rear once the fighting broke out. They used their magic for defensive measures, not offensive.

On the fire, a pot of taevo brewed and a pot of stew bubbled. Rizelya's stomach grumbled. The smell reminding her she hadn't eaten breakfast and lunch had long passed.

As her pack filled bowls, Rizelya's brow creased. She was missing two of her pack—the two men she cared for most in the world.

"Have you seen Blazel or Aistrun?"

Wisah shook her head. "The last I saw him, he was leading the counterattack. I haven't seen him cross the veil, and we're close enough that I would."

Relieved by the news, Rizelya spun around to return to the battlefield.

"Wait!" Chariel said, putting out an arm. "You can't go anywhere. You need to visit a healer. Your arm is dripping blood."

Rizelya glanced down and shrugged. "I'll get it looked after when I know everyone is safe." She fed fire into her helbraught and touched the glowing blade to her arm, hissing at the pain and the smell of burned flesh. "There. The bleeding has stopped." She pulled away from Chariel and hurried back to the battlefield. Worry nipped her heels that her lover and best friend lay somewhere, alone and mortally wounded.

Chapter 17

Blazel - 20 de Drudar, 1075

Blazel snarled and ripped into another invader. Their weapons made them deadly, but once disarmed, they were no match for his warrior form's strength. Blazel and Aistrun tag-teamed their opponents with one attacking the weapon, while the other attacked the invader. The purple blood soaking their fur attested to the effectiveness of their alliance.

A horn blared, and suddenly the invading army turned tail and ran into the Barrens. Although exhausted from fighting in their warrior form for who-knows-how-long, Blazel and Aistrun shifted into their wolf forms and chased the retreating soldiers. They estimated about seventy-five invaders escaped the battle. The two of them couldn't fight so many on their own, but they could track them. He reached out to Naila and informed her what he and Aistrun were doing.

Memories of racing through the Barrens rushed to flood him as Blazel stepped on the black sand-glass. *Slow down,* he advised Aistrun. *We don't want the glass to shred our paws.*

Aistrun paused, picked up his front paw and shook glass from it. *Good plan. We can't fight any lone invaders we discover with injured paws.*

A few measures inside the Barrens, a shadow darkened the sky above them.

Ho, Blazel! Graak called out.

Graak and Broogk flew overhead and swooped toward them. Blazel crouched, burying his head under his stomach, protecting his eyes and nose from the sand-glass. After the Gryphons landed, Blazel stood and shook out his fur before shifting back into his natural form. Purple blood covered his clothes. The aliens stank about as bad as the Malvers' monsters did.

Aistrun shifted, revealing a bloody furrow sweeping across his right cheek, narrowly missing his eye.

"Are you okay?" Blazel asked. He had a few cuts, and his thigh pulsed with a bruise, but his fur had mostly protected him.

Aistrun wiped at the wound and shrugged. "It's nothing."

"I'm glad to see you, my friend," Blazel said to Graak. "We're tracking the fleeing invaders to discover where they're going. How about a ride?"

It's also our mission, Graak said. *We can follow their trail from above. They seem to be heading to a definite place. They're all taking the same path. Get on, let's find out what they are up to.*

Graak and Broogk crouched for Blazel and Aistrun to climb onto their respective backs. Blazel grimaced at Graak's lack of wearing a saddle. Riding a Gryphon wasn't like riding a horse, especially without a harness.

Blazel clamped his legs around Graak's middle and dug his fingers into the fur on Graak's shoulders. Graak's leap into the sky threw him forward and back. Finally, Graak's flight evened out, and Blazel sat up. The air whipping past them removed some of the invaders' stench from his clothes. A ripple of magic flowed over Blazel as Graak became invisible.

Twenty-five measures inside the Barrens, they located the invaders beside a sheltering jumble of huge petrified wood boulders. A herd of large, lizard-like creatures waited with their reins tied to the rocks. The beasts stood nearly erect, with powerful hind legs and much smaller forefeet. Their three toes explained the tracks Blazel found at Posanreande Keep. Sharp horns curved to the side of their smallish heads. The invaders strapped a saddle at the juncture where the neck met the body.

A bridle hooked over their long snouts, with reins for guiding them.

Two of the soldiers laid crumpled on the ground. Their wounds gushed blood and dying the reddish-brown rocks a dull purple.

It will be interesting to watch what they do with their wounded, Broogk observed, keeping his mind-voice quiet. They didn't know yet if the aliens could hear it. *Death rituals reveal much about a society.*

An invader, wearing black robes edged in bronze, barked orders in a harsh language at the other men. They quickly mounted the lizards. The officer approached the more badly wounded of the two soldiers and kicked him. He moaned weakly. The hump on the officer's back enlarged, and two long tubes with sharp ends extended. The officer plunged them into his man, who jerked and thrashed. When he stopped, the officer withdrew the tubes and did the same thing to the other man. Without a backwards glance, he climbed on a waiting lizard, and the group thundered off, leading about thirty riderless lizards.

When the invaders rode over the horizon, the Gryphons landed. Blazel warily approached the dead aliens. The same wounds punctured their chests as the people they'd found from Posanreande Keep. Like those Posairs, their blood was drained and their bodies were empty husks.

I doubt that was a ritual mourning their dead. Broogk's head feathers drooped.

"No, it wasn't," Blazel agreed, trying not to gag. "We know now what causes those strange wounds."

Graak shuddered from tail to beak. *Kaaik told me they ate blood and emotions. I didn't believe him. What manner of creature are these invaders?*

"Evil," Aistrun said with conviction.

Blazel concurred. He and Aistrun climbed onto their Gryphon friend's back and flew back toward camp.

Blazel's stomach growled loudly as the late afternoon heat beat on his shoulders, reminding him he'd missed both breakfast and lunch. He glanced down to gauge how much further they had to fly before reaching camp. A figure, leaning on a helbraught, stood on a small outcropping of petrified rocks. Blazel tapped Graak. "Can you tell who it is?"

Graak dipped his head. *It's Rizelya!*

Blazel clamped his legs tighter around Graak's middle as the Gryphon dove. "Rizelya!" he shouted. He jumped off Graak and ran to her, frowning at the blood running down her arm. "What in the Crone's Fires are you doing?"

"Looking for you." Her eyes widened when Broogk landed with Aistrun astride him. Her lips tightened in anger. "Although it appears you were out for a jaunt."

Graak pointed a talon at her bleeding arm. *Rizelya, why are you out here, alone and wounded? It isn't safe.*

Rizelya rolled her eyes and huffed. "Fine, I was worried about you fools. You should inform someone if you go haring off."

But we did. Moraak knows we followed the invader's retreat. He sent us.

"And I told Naila."

"Oh," Rizelya's shoulders drooped. "I didn't ask them."

"Does anyone know where you are?" Aistrun asked, his arms folded across his chest.

Rizelya hunched and shook her head sheepishly.

Climb on. Graak crouched by her. *I'll take you back so a healer can tend your wound.*

She steadied herself with her helbraught as she threw her left leg over Graak's back. When she reached out to wrap her arms around Graak's neck, she cried out. Blazel straddled Graak behind her and snuggled her close to his chest. "Easy, love, I have you."

Rizelya moaned when Graak leaped into the air, then went limp in Blazel's arm. "Hurry, Graak. She needs a healer."

As they sped toward the camp, Blazel vacillated between being infuriated with her for searching for them while injured and elated she cared enough to search for him. His stomach fluttered. Did she love him? He loved her, and this cinched it for him.

Blazel - 20 de Drudar, 1075

Pillars of oily, black smoke spiraled into the air as Blazel's group approached camp. Blazel wrinkled his nose, gagging on the stink of death. Normally, the smoke from funeral pyres wasn't so dark. "What is causing the foul stench?" he asked, knowing Graak could tell with his better distance vision.

It's coming from the burning invaders. They are just as nasty and stinky in death as they are in life. Graak angled away from the pyres and toward the healer's tents. Rizelya moaned with each stroke of his wings. *I've informed Bethlyn we're on the way in, and Rizelya is injured.*

Bethlyn met them as soon as Graak landed and examined Rizelya's shoulder. "She has a projectile lodged against the bone. We've dealt with a number of these little beasties."

"Will she be okay?" Blazel wrung his hands.

Bethlyn nodded, then scowled. "The projectile's metal resists our magic, so we must dig them out. Once they're removed, we can heal the patient using our normal methods. Carry her into the tent for me, will you?"

After leaving Rizelya in Bethlyn's capable care, Blazel headed to the center of the camp. Aistrun walked beside him, with the two Gryphons keeping pace behind them.

The white silk of the command pavilion shone in the harsh sunlight. The black-and-white Supreme Alpha's pennon hung limply on its pole. A second pole held a gold flag, representing the royal Gryphon house. One of Moraak's Thunder Wings guarded the tent opening simply by crouching in front of it. He rested his head on his fore-talons, and the tip of his tail lazily twitched, thumping the ground. As Blazel and his party approached, the guard sat up, scooting aside enough to allow them entrance.

Maps and markers lay scattered over the surface of a conference table, dominating the center. A desk piled high with papers hunched on one side, while a collection of camp chairs and stools occupied the other side. Several thick rugs covered the dirt floor. A curtain divided the living quarters from the work space. Histrun and Moraak stood by the table, studying the map.

Histrun glanced up. "Ah, what did you discover? Since you didn't raise an alarm, I assume there isn't another attack imminent."

"Not that we could tell, sir." Blazel stepped to the table. He scanned the map, picked up a marker, and placed it on a spot. "Here's where their mounts waited."

"Mounts?" Histrun frowned.

"Hey, nothing we'd ride," Aistrun said, standing across from Blazel. "They rode some sort of lizard. After they ate their wounded—"

Ate? Moraak's head feathers stood straight out. *They're cannibals?*

They only consumed the blood and organs, Graak said, the tip of his tail swishing in agitation. *When the officer finished, only an empty husk remained, which they left behind.*

Broogk curled his tail around his feet. *Fewer than seventy-five invaders returned to the crater. They expected more to make it to the rendezvous because they led thirty-odd extra mounts.*

"So, this was another exploratory attack." Histrun smoothed his short beard he'd grown during the journey south. "They wanted to test what kind of resistance we'd offer. I'm pleased we did better than they expected. Before we counterattack, we need more information."

Kaaik has a contact within the captive compound, Moraak said. *If you know what you want to ask, I'm sure Kaieli—*

"Kaieli's here? Where?" Aistrun interrupted. Excitement lit his face.

"She's a captive." Histrun put a supportive arm around Aistrun's shoulder when he sagged. "She was at Posanreande Keep when it fell. She, Rolstrun, and Maheli are our spies in the invaders' compound."

"Rizelya is going to be devastated when she finds out," Aistrun said.

"Why?" Blazel thought the name sounded familiar, but he didn't think he'd met her.

Aistrun gulped. "Rizelya and Kaieli are heart-sisters."

Heat suffused Blazel's face, and his stomach dropped to the soles of his feet. *I was a fool to believe Rizelya loved me. Heart-sisters are a step below bonded mates. I'm nothing more than a convenience to Rizelya.* He lowered his eyes, unable to look Aistrun in the face.

"But, hey," Aistrun said quickly, "that was before she met you."

Histrun cleared his throat and went back to business. "We need to know why the invaders are here. What do they want? They're digging in the crater for something, but I can't imagine what it is. Do they have any weaknesses we can exploit?"

Kaaik told me they don't do well in the noon sun, Moraak said. *That's the time he meets with Kaieli and we help people to escape.*

"I'll go," Blazel volunteered, "and find out what we need to know." He wanted to meet this woman who held Rizelya's heart.

Graak cocked his head, and the feathers around his beak wrinkled. *Fine. I'll take you.*

"Tomorrow," Histrun said with authority.

"But—" Blazel argued.

"We can't risk the captive's lives," Histrun continued. "They already suffer enough. Meet with Kaaik and Delestrun and accompany them on their rescue run. We'll also use the opportunity to deliver food and other necessities to our people. The damned invaders work them too hard on too little food. Go get cleaned up and eat, both of you. You look awful."

Outside, they parted company with the Gryphons. Blazel stalked toward his tent.

"I want to go with you," Aistrun said.

Blazel scowled at him.

"The captured guard-pack in the northern fortress were… are from my keep. They're my friends. I want to find out how they're doing and help them if I can."

"I met them," Blazel said quietly. "They caught me when I tried to cross the Barrens unnoticed. Instead of killing me, Maheli took me in. They befriended me, especially Rolstrun. It was the first time someone besides Histrun treated me like a man, not something to be despised. Maheli invited me to join your clan."

"And now you have." Aistrun thumped him on the back. "Rizelya's made you part of our pack. I notice she has a knack for bringing in strays and making them pack."

Blazel turned his head away and swallowed hard, several times. *I don't want to leave the pack, but if Rizelya's heart belongs to someone else, I can't stay. I lost my heart to her chedans ago.*

They walked past the healers' tent.

"Hey, aren't you going to check on Rizelya?"

"No, it's late. She'll be sleeping."

Aistrun cocked an eyebrow at him, shrugged, shaking his head. "Not my ass on the line."

Soft snores greeted them when they entered their shared tent. On a chest by the door flap sat two large bowls of stew, along with several rounds of pan bread. Blazel's stomach rumbled at the smell. He hadn't eaten all day. He wolfed down his food and crawled into his empty bedroll. The strangeness of sleeping alone kept him awake.

The next day, Blazel helped ready the packets of food, water, and other necessities the captives needed. He used the preparations for the excursion to the invaders' camp as an excuse not to visit Rizelya.

Bethlyn found him and handed him a bulging pouch. "Please give this to Kaieli. It's medical supplies." She narrowed her eyes at him and pursed her lips. "I haven't seen you in the infirmary all day. What's wrong?"

"Nothing." He took the bag and slung the strap crosswise over his chest. "I'll make sure the healer gets this."

He ignored her scowl and strode away to find Graak. The pouch gave him the excuse to meet Kaieli. But he wasn't so sure he wanted to, even though he used it as the reason to volunteer for this mission. He didn't want to let go of the one amazing thing in his life—Rizelya.

Graak tried to talk to him during the flight to the crater, but Blazel didn't—couldn't—engage. His heart constricted into a tight ball, making it hurt to breathe. Bile kept rising to burn the back of his throat. He blamed the wind off Graak's wings for the moisture collecting on his cheeks.

In too short of a time, Graak circled high over the invader's compound. Below them, a small figure in garish orange coveralls darted from a large building, sprinting toward the Barrens. Over a dozen people, half of them children, raced behind the first person. Now he understood why so many Gryphons accompanied them.

It's time. Kaaik dropped into a fast descent.

Blazel clutched Graak's harness as he dove to land. Blazel took a deep breath, willed his heart to keep beating, and climbed off to meet Rizelya's heart-sister.

Kaieli - 21 de Drudar, 1075

Kaieli, Rolstrun, and the other escapees barreled behind the rocks. Sweat dripped off her nose. She bent over, hands on her knees, panting. The Gryphons landed, and a familiar man scrambled out of his harness. He leaped toward her.

"Kaieli!" He pulled her into a tight hug.

"Aistrun?" Kaieli wriggled out of his arms, tears making muddy tracks on her cheeks. "Oh, sweet Mother, I didn't think I'd see any of you again. Is anyone else with you?"

"Oh, about fifty thousand or so fighters. Is that enough?"

"It might be. Is Rizelya here?"

Aistrun nodded. "She is, and so is all of our pack. She was shot in the skirmish with the invaders yesterday, otherwise she'd be here now."

The other people reached the boulders. Rolstrun gaped at the man with the wild, tangled hair, then a smile lit his face.

"Blazel!" Rolstrun clapped him on the back. "You made it north. Did you reach the Sanctuary?"

"I did."

"How is it you two are here together?" Rolstrun pointed at Blazel and Aistrun.

Aistrun laughed. "Who else? Rizelya. Hey, do I have a story for you—"

"Too bad we don't have time for it," Kaieli said, slipping an arm through Rolstrun's. "We must hurry back before we're missed. Are you ready to make a trade? Your packs for my people?"

Of course we are, Kaieli, Kaaik said with a dip of his head.

While the rest talked, Delestrun untied the packs from the Gryphons and helped the escapees climb onto the extra Gryphon's backs. The Gryphons took off with their new burdens, zooming toward freedom. Soon, only Blazel, Aistrun, and Delestrun and their companion Gryphons remained.

Kaieli grimaced at the full packs waiting for her and Rolstrun. Hopefully, they weren't too heavy for their run back to the compound.

Blazel pulled the pouch from around his chest and held it out to her. "Here, this is for you. Bethlyn sent it."

Kaieli clapped her hands. She'd hoped someone would think of this. "Ooh—medical supplies. Thank you, Blazel."

"We're here for more than exchanging supplies for people." He smiled. "Histrun needs information so we can plan our counterattacks."

"We'll help in whatever way we can," Kaieli said. "What do you want to know?"

Blazel and Graak grilled her and Rolstrun about the slave camp and the invaders.

"They have—or had until the recent battles—over half a million soldiers," Rolstrun said. "They only have two objects: conquer our world, and strip it of all the nucla they can find."

Blazel frowned. "What is nucla?"

"It's what they call the malignant magic solidified in the crater," Kaieli said. "It's from Shandir's last magic that ended the Great War."

"They force us to hack chunks of rock from the big, black pillar in the crater's center." Rolstrun pointed back toward the now diminished pillar and shuddered. "You remember the story we told you, Blazel, about the people who stayed in the crater fighting the Malvers' monsters?"

The color drained from Blazel's face. "You've been in there a long time! Are you able to shift? How sick are you?"

"We're fine, because of Kaieli." Rolstrun put his arm around her shoulder and pulled her close.

Kaieli blushed. Hopefully, the Posair army's arrival meant they'd escape the hellscape of the slave pens. Rolstrun coughed. No matter how much she worked on him, she couldn't completely remove the damned nucla from his lungs. Her eyes widened, and she threw a hand over her gaping mouth. The nucla poisoning could decimate the Posair army! She needed to tell them how to heal it. Surely, the fighting force included some Whites and Grays.

"How close to the Barrens is the army camped?" Kaieli asked.

"We're on the plains, less than a measure from where the black sand-glass begins." Blazel dug a toe in the sand and grimaced. "Why? Is there a problem?"

"If this war lasts for any length of time, you'll risk falling ill from the nucla in the black sand-glass. We're calling it the unimaginative name of nucla poisoning. The malignant magic worms itself into the body, and it doesn't like to let go. The only way we've found to purge it is through merging Talents."

Surprisingly, Blazel and Aistrun nodded in understanding.

"Our squad-pack does something similar," Aistrun said. "You won't believe the changes Rizelya has made. Are you sure you don't want me to tell you about it?"

Kaieli grinned at him and shook her head. If Aistrun started telling stories, they'd be here for octars, and the invaders would miss her and Rolstrun, putting everyone in jeopardy. "We discovered we need someone with each Talent, including White and Gray, to merge together. When we do, it forms a magic very akin to what I've heard Black Talent is like."

Blazel and Aistrun looked at each other and frowned.

"The girls haven't mentioned anything like that happening," Blazel said. "Rizelya would tell us if they did. And two of the strongest White and Gray Talents in Lairheim, Wisah and Chariel, work with them."

"We only have one of each Talent. How many are on their team?"

"Hey, there's more than that!" Aistrun grinned. "You know Rizelya, overachiever and all."

"Maybe that's the difference." Kaieli glanced at the sun, grimacing at how low it hung in the sky. "We must go! The invaders can't discover our escape route. We need to continue getting the women and children out."

We could take you, Graak offered. *It is our fault you will be late.*

"Sorry, but we can't risk the invaders seeing you and wondering why you're so close to the compound." Kaieli wished she could take him up on the offer and save her tired feet the run back. "After losing the two battles with you, the commander has made our life even more miserable. We want to get our people out alive, not dead."

Our magic allows us to become invisible, Graak added.

Kaieli gazed at the packs, but shook her head. "The risk is too high and our people are too vulnerable."

"We understand." Blazel touched her shoulder in sympathy.

After quick farewells, she and Rolstrun slung the packs over their backs. With an aching heart, Kaieli ran back toward the slave camp rather than leap into the sky to freedom.

Rolstrun - 21 de Drudar, 1075

The run back to the slave camp proved more difficult than Rolstrun expected. The heavy packs he carried bumped against his still healing wound. He glanced at the sky, where the Gryphons had disappeared over the horizon. Talking to Blazel and Aistrun again stirred the longing in his heart to fly away with them—away from the horror and pain. Rolstrun tongued the sore in his mouth from biting down to keep from accepting their offer. He didn't know Kaieli kept her sanity, meeting Kaaik and Delestrun, time after time, and returning to the compound.

Rolstrun shifted the bag to his other shoulder, and the strap brushed over the tracking device in his arm. No matter how much he—or Kaieli—wanted to leave, they couldn't until they found a way to disarm it.

The supplies would help more people survive this ordeal. Besides the culling by the invaders for the cages and for feeding, they lost too many people from starvation and dehydration. They didn't dare make supply and escape runs every day. Since making contact with Kaaik, they'd made two, but it was too little and too late for some.

He and Kaieli passed a monster cage. Rolstrun wrinkled his nose and threw an arm across his face, inhaling shallowly to keep from breathing in the stink of death and malignant magic. Dried blood dyed the black sand rust. A dark mist floated just above the ground, swirling into motion as they passed, almost as if it sensed their presence. Fingers of malevolence reached for him, and he ran faster, chanting a prayer of protection under his breath.

We're coming, Kaieli called out in mind-speech. *Is it safe?*

Wait, Maheli said. *You're late. We need to make a distraction.*

Kaieli slowed to a stop.

Rolstrun kept running several more feet until the pernicious energy lost its grasp on him. He stood, gasping for breath, with his hand pressed against his chest. The running hadn't been good for his battered lungs. He coughed, deep and rattling.

"Your cough is getting worse," Kaieli admonished as she caught up with him. "You shouldn't have come with me, or come to me to heal you more often."

She rubbed his back, and tendrils of warm, healing energy seeped into his skin.

Rolstrun turned around, embraced her, and kissed the top of her head. "You have more than enough to do. I'll be fine." A coughing fit hit him. When the spasm eased, he wiped away the black phlegm with the back of his hand.

Mining the nucla and breathing the Barrens dust for so long damaged his lungs—and everyone's in the slave camp. The constant healing of injuries and removing enough of the nucla poisoning to keep the men functioning drained the healers. They relieved the worst of the problems, but they couldn't heal everything and everyone until they had more energy. He glanced over his shoulder toward the meeting place. Now they had help, they could get more people out and more resources in.

A boom shook the ground. A spout of fire shot into the air, and shouts erupted from the encampment.

"There's our distraction." Kaieli resettled the pack onto her back and sped off.

Rolstrun kept pace with her.

Flames licked a building that previously housed Gheethong, but now stood empty. Noxious black fumes boiled from it. A squad of soldiers rushed toward it, carrying heavy canisters. Foam spit from them, smothering the fire.

Maheli waved at them from the processing facility's open back door. Rolstrun and Kaieli bolted inside, and Maheli slammed the door behind them. Several women took the packs from them and retreated deeper into the plant while Rolstrun, Kaieli, and Maheli crept to the infirmary.

Kaieli slid the curtain closed, hiding them from prying eyes. "I didn't think the substance they use for their buildings would burn."

Maheli rocked back on her heels and smirked. "It does if you freeze it first, then apply intense heat. We've been experimenting. Although, we didn't expect the fumes."

Rolstrun wrinkled his nose at the nasty odor. A breeze wafted over him as several Yellows funneled the tainted air from the building, while another group brought in fresher air.

"I have good news." Rolstrun tucked an arm around Kaieli.

Maheli snorted. "I know about you two."

"Not that. I talked to Blazel today."

"You did? How's the boyo?"

"Alive and well. He's here with an army." Rolstrun grinned. "We have help!"

"Histrun wants us to do what we can," Kaieli said, rubbing her cheek, "without putting ourselves in more danger. We should assist Tre'nok in destroying the nucla."

"How?" Maheli gestured toward the machines. "They guard every speck of dust from the time it's unloaded from the mine until it's carted off to their ship."

Kaieli scratched her head. "That is a problem."

Rolstrun laid on his hidden pallet, more exhausted from the run than he wanted to admit. Soon, quiet filled the plant as the women left for the day. He waited until darkness fell, before sneaking to the slave pens. When he slipped inside, the alphas of the various groups clustered together at a table in the cage they used for a mess hall.

"The Posair army has arrived," Kaieli said. "We now have help to get more people out."

"But only the women and children can leave," Aradehan, the alpha from Dehanrandean Keep, complained. "The men can't escape. We're always in the crater."

Maheli rested her chin on her fist. "The Gryphons can't penetrate the energy dome."

"There isn't a dome over the crater," Aradehan observed. "They could fly down and retrieve us."

"And get shot to bits," Nederposan sneered. "The invaders possess long-range weapons. You weren't here when an invader shot a Gryphon when it flew over us."

"What about the pass by the northern fortress?" Rolstrun said, feeling a bit presumptuous. He wasn't an alpha. "Could the men without the explosive trackers use it to escape?"

Bohandran's eyes widened in surprise. "I'd forgotten about it. The formation of the monster nests inside the crater has slowed considerably since the invaders started using the monster corrals. We'll need to distract the guards." He glanced over at Kaieli. "Do you think the Gryphons would help us with creating a distraction?"

She shrugged. "I'm sure they will. I'll ask. It's time we stopped acting like slaves and remember we're prisoners of war. We can find ways to sabotage the processing plant. Sorlenda is mechanically inclined and has learned much about the plant's machines."

"Agreed." A malicious glint gleamed in Maheli's eyes. "We discovered today we can burn their building material. We can cause more fires, maybe this time, in one of the barracks. Traditionally, we've relied on our helbraughts to focus our magic, but I remember once, when I was a teenager, the women in Dehanlair Keep had their helbraughts taken away. Zehala and Histrun were at the keep, teaching them the Zehis method, and I was part of their pack. Zehala trained us to use our magic without our helbraughts. It's more difficult, but it's possible. I think I remember some of the exercises. We can start training again."

"Excellent!" Bohandran said, rubbing his hands together. "Now, what else can we do to sabotage the invaders' plans?"

They continued to plan until the lights-out horn blared.

"Good work," Maheli said, standing and stretching. "Share this with your people, and explore any potential ideas. The more we upset things here, the faster our army out there can throw these damned invaders off our planet!"

For the first time since his capture, Rolstrun went to bed with the hope he'd return home again one day.

Chapter 18

Rizelya - 23 de Drudar, 1075

An annoying *drip-drip* broke through Rizelya's dreams. She struggled to make sense of the sound as she blinked away the last vestiges of sleep. She frowned at the pale green silk above her head. Rizelya winced in pain when she lifted her hands to rub her face, and she gingerly felt her left arm and shoulder. It brought her to full wakefulness, and with it, the realization she lay in a healer's tent.

Her mouth tasted awful, and she swallowed several times to get her saliva working again. Her shoulder twinged as she sat up, but she'd suffered worse injuries. A cup of water sat by her cot. She gulped it down and searched for more. A pitcher with water condensation beading its sides perched on a table by the tent door. Her wobbly legs told her she'd been out for longer than a day. As she poured more water into her cup, she finally figured out where the *drip-drip* came from. A sheet of thin ice lined the tent roof above the door, and a constant breeze blowing over it cooled the room and caused the ice to slowly melt. She raised her eyebrows at the ingenious use of Blue and Yellow Talent. She whirled around at the movement behind her.

Bethlyn peeked over a tall stack of toweling and bandages. "Ah, you're awake." She tucked the linen in a basket before joining Rizelya. "Let me examine your wound. How does it feel?"

"Fine, it doesn't hurt too bad." Rizelya watched curiously as Bethlyn cut off the bandages over her shoulder and biceps. A thin scar marred her biceps where the projectile had slid across it. A round, puckered scar, still red and swollen, marked where it had slammed into her shoulder. "How long have I been out?"

"Three days. The metal the invaders use for their projectiles resists our magic." Bethlyn pressed on the tissue surrounding the scar on her shoulder.

"Ow!"

"Serves you right." Bethlyn scowled at her, her tone brusque. "You should have come to the infirmary after the battle instead of traipsing into the Barrens. The wound became infected."

"Oh."

"We've discovered the Barren's dust and dirt causes wounds to fester when they wouldn't otherwise. It's challenging for the Reds and warriors to remember to get their wounds treated quickly rather than wait." She frowned, her hands on her hips. "You fighters seem to think you're indestructible and don't need healers."

"It isn't that. Most of us have learned to shrug off injuries during a battle. Until Kaieli started coming to monster battles with me last year, there usually wasn't a healer at the battleground. Even now, not every platoon has a healer with them. We have to wait, sometimes several octars, before we can see one. When can I get back to fighting?"

"I'd rather you wait another few days—"

"Days!"

"—but I know you're anxious." Bethlyn huffed. "Tomorrow. You can join the battle tomorrow. Aistrun's been bugging me about when you'll be back."

"Aistrun and not Blazel?" Rizelya's chest constricted. "He isn't hurt, is he, or—"

"No, no, he's fine." Bethlyn patted her uninjured shoulder. "Histrun has kept him busy." She turned to the basket.

Rizelya's brow furrowed. Something in Bethlyn's tone made her wonder if more was going on with Blazel.

Bethlyn wrapped clean bandages around her shoulder. "Keep it covered a few more days, and come back to have a fresh one put on after you fight. I don't want it to become infected again. Your clothes are in the basket at the foot of your cot."

Someone cried out, and Bethlyn gave her a last pat before hurrying to the patient.

Heat smacked Rizelya's face and coated her skin when she stepped from the healer's tent. She appreciated how much cooler it had been inside as beads of sweat lined her top lip. She jogged toward her tent, but after a few steps, she slowed to a walk, gasping. Maybe waiting a day or two to finish recovering would be a good idea. Rizelya squinted in the sun's glare. She passed several women in wide-brimmed straw hats and envied their shade. Sweat dampened the back of her shirt and the top of her pants by the time she reached her tent.

Aistrun's voice seeped from it. She paused outside.

"...you should have seen it," Aistrun said. "She stood with one foot stuck in a basket, mookti berry juice dripping off her chin, staring at the rustling bushes, sure she'd disturbed a bear. A snout poked out of the bushes, and she scrambled back and fell on her butt, her hands up in the air, shouting, 'Please don't eat me!' A long tongue flicked out... and a multa licked the juice from her face."

Laughter blossomed from inside the tent. Rizelya grimaced. She'd been ten, and Rolstrun still told the stupid story.

"You know she's just outside, don't you, Aistrun?" Wisah said softly.

"She is?"

A stool banged, and Aistrun tore the door flap from her hands.

"You're here!" Aistrun engulfed Rizelya in a hug, squeezing her tight. "Don't scare me like that, Little Red."

She returned the hug before pushing him away. "Our life is dangerous, Wolf. I can't promise I won't be hurt again." She stepped into the tent, and Wisah, Chariel, and even Jaehaas smothered her with hugs. Blazel waited off to the side, his arms akimbo. Rizelya bit the inside of her lower lip. Had she done something wrong? Maybe she shouldn't have followed him out into the Barrens. Did he think it meant she thought him incapable of taking care of himself? Or could it be he tended to be a private person and didn't like to display his affection in front of people? He'd greet her more properly when they were alone—she hoped. She rubbed her sore arm, suddenly cold in the stifling heat.

Aistrun escorted her to a stool, then righted the one he'd tipped over. "When can you return to duty? We've missed your helbraught."

"Oh, my weapon, but not me?" She raised an eyebrow while trying to ignore Blazel's continued silence. He hadn't moved to sit closer to her. "Bethlyn told me I could fight tomorrow."

Aistrun clapped his hands together. "Good. Our, well, your, battalion is going to attack the crater tomorrow." He leaned forward, his elbows on his knees. "It's time we counterattacked those aliens. Taught them a lesson. The way they treat our people, it just... just makes me so angry!" He thumped his thigh with his fist. "Kaieli has lost a stone of weight she didn't have to lose—"

"Kaieli? Where is she? Why isn't she in here with us? Is she in the healer's tent?" Rizelya rose off her stool.

"She can't leave the prison camp." Aistrun clenched his teeth.

"Crone's Fires!" Rizelya plopped back on her seat.

"The invaders implanted her," Aistrun continued, "and the first group of captives with explosive tracking devices. They can't remove them without detonating them. She says she can do more good there than here, anyway. She's heading the escape runs, so you'll probably see her soon."

"Histrun plans on a two-prong attack tomorrow," Blazel broke in. He sat hunched over and wouldn't look at her. "One from the air and one on land. Our battalion will take the land, except for you and me. We'll be leading from the air, where we can oversee the battle."

"Where will Histrun be?"

"He's too old to fight."

"Or to be trussed up like a bird on a spit," Aistrun added with a grin. "His words. Moraak has yet to get him to fly with him."

They continued to discuss the battle plans until dinner. Rizelya didn't know which would be better for her shoulder, to fly on Glork or fight on the ground. As she followed the others to the mess tent, she took a few tentative swings, wincing as the movement pulled on her injury. Dinner consisted of fire-roasted ducorn and pan bread laced with chopped vegetables, surprisingly good for travel fare. She grinned around another flavorful bite. Having support personnel accompanying the fighters made life so much more bearable.

Blazel's utensils clattered onto his empty plate, and he abruptly stood. "Histrun needs to go over any last instructions with me. Don't stay up late, we leave at dawn." He wound his way through the close-set tables.

"What is going on with him?" Rizelya asked, setting down her cup. "What did I do?"

Aistrun shrugged. "He's been like that since after the first battle."

Jaehaas rolled his eyes and crossed his arms across his chest, his tail swatting Aistrun's face. "Aistrun, you be a daft idiot." He turned his glare to Rizelya. "He be worried sick because of you."

She blinked and leaned back. "What did I do?"

"Are you, or are you not, heart-sisters with Kaieli?"

"I... I am, but what does it have to do with anything? We decided several lunadars ago we weren't going to become bond-mates. We're simply friends."

"He thinks you be playing him." Jaehaas dropped his hands to his side. "Rizelya, he be in love with you. Your heart belonging to another be breaking his heart."

Rizelya's hand flew up to cover her mouth. "Oh! It isn't like that at all." She frowned at Aistrun. "I could beat you."

"Me?"

"You. You're probably the one who let Blazel believe Kaieli and I were still lovers."

"No, I—Oh! I did." Aistrun tugged at his hair. "I didn't mean to, Rizelya, honest. You and Kaieli have been heart-sisters for so long, that's how I think of you."

Rizelya snorted and threw up her hands. She hurried outside, striding to their shared tent, and slumped when she saw its dark outline. She wandered all over camp without finding him, stopping at last at the picket line.

Kymaya whickered a greeting. "Hi, old friend," Rizelya crooned, sliding a hand along her horse's jaw and rubbing her nose. She found comfort in the warm horse breath blowing across her hair and over her back. "How could things get so messed up? I never expected to fall in love. My life is too unpredictable, too dangerous to consider letting anyone into my heart. Kaieli wriggled herself in, damn her. Our separation over these past chedans has showed me she will always hold a part of my heart, but our love has mellowed into friendship.

"And then I met Blazel." She heaved a sigh. "Kymaya, girl, he is so unlike anyone I've ever met. He's sweet and gentle, even a bit shy and naive, and so strong. I doubt I'd have the fortitude to face alone what he has. Sweet Goddess, help me, but I love him. Oh, girl, I don't know what I'll do if he doesn't want to be with me anymore."

Kymaya stamped a hoof and shook her head. An image floated to Rizelya's mind of Kymaya and their small herd surrounding Rizelya and her friends. Feelings of love accompanied the image. Kymaya rarely communicated so clearly. Whatever happened, Rizelya would be loved. She leaned her head on her horse's neck.

She lifted her head at a rustle in the grass.

"Did you mean it?" Blazel stepped around the front of her horse.

The dim light made it difficult to make out his expression.

"Is it me you love and not Kaieli?" His soft, earnest voice tugged at her heart.

Heat suffused her face. She nodded.

He let out a long breath of air, as if he'd been holding it. "Oh good. Rizelya, I love you." He closed the gap between them and gathered her in his arms.

His strength and love enveloped her like a warm blanket. Arm in arm, they moved away from the horses and found a private spot in the tall grass. Their lovemaking was sweet and tender.

Kaieli - 25 de Drudar, 1075

The summer sun pummeled Kaieli as she ran. Sweat dripped down her back and nose. She'd only run a short way from the camp when wing-beats sounded over her head.

Reach up! a familiar voice commanded.

Rizelya! Is that you? She threw her hands into the air, following the command, but not knowing why.

Talons gently gripped her arms and torso, lifting her off the ground. She stared at the Gryphon's light brown feathers mixed with white melding into a creamy tan and brown feline body. Dark brown wings with white stripes swept the air.

"Hang on," Rizelya said. Apparently, they were now far enough away from the invaders' camp to risk speaking out loud. "We'll be there in a few milcrons. Glork, be careful. She's my heart-sister."

I shall, Rizelya. She hardly weighs anything at all. Glork chuckled.

The jumble of petrified rocks serving as their meeting place came into view, and Glork hovered low to the ground before releasing Kaieli. Even so, her legs buckled from the short drop. Strong arms caught her before she fell. Blazel made sure she had her balance before stepping away.

Kaieli, honored healer, I did not mean to drop you, Glork sounded contrite. *Are you okay?*

"I'm fine." She brushed at her coveralls even though it didn't do any good. "I'm not as strong as I used to be. Poor food will do that to a girl."

To anyone, Glork agreed. *I will be more careful next time.*

Rizelya grabbed Kaieli and pulled her into a tight hug. "I've been so worried about you. I hate you can't leave. Any luck on getting rid of the explosive device?"

Kaieli shook her head. She surveyed the group of escapees as they arrived. She grinned when Treana waved at her. The little girl gawked at the large Gryphons.

"I understand you saved her sister," she nodded toward Treana. "Thank you. Her mother is relieved she is safe. It broke our hearts to leave Dreana behind, but we had no choice."

"We saw the aftermath of the attack. It was a miracle we found her, or that she survived. We're moving all the escaped children to one of the Haaslair Keeps, then we'll ferry them farther north where they'll be out of the war zone. Any adults who don't wish to fight, or are too sick, are also being taken north. I wish you could leave."

"So do I, Rizelya. So do I. You can't believe the evil I've seen."

"But you're doing great good there. Blazel told me what you're doing to cure the nucla poisoning. Combining your Talents to form Black Talent is amazing! My team merges their Talents, but we haven't come close to forming anything like Black Talent. How do you do it? How did you figure it out?"

Kaieli smiled at Rizelya's inquisitiveness. She found a rock in the shade and sat, leaning against it. Rizelya settled next to her and put an arm around her. She quickly told Rizelya about the plague and how she and Faliciden had discovered the cure.

"There are cases of something similar in camp." Rizelya grimaced. "The ones who've fallen ill have all fought Malvers' monsters. You'd think we'd get a break from them, but they are hitting us as hard as ever. I'll tell Bethlyn—she's our head healer—what you did to cure it. I'm excited to try merging our Talents like you have to form a Black Talent. Hmm... you said you used your Gray Talent to weave them together? I'm sure it'd be easy for Chariel to do."

"Who is Chariel?"

"She's Blazel's friend. You've heard of the Gray Oracle, haven't you?"

Kaieli nodded. The Gray Oracle had frightening prophecies.

"That's Chariel. She's the reason Aistrun, Blazel, Wisah, and I journeyed to the Deep Mountains on a quest to find the Gryphons. We wouldn't have their help now if not for her prophecy."

"Wisah went with you? Is she here, too?"

Rizelya nodded. "Oh, yes. She and Chariel are integral parts of my squad-pack."

"Who would have thought quiet, sweet Wisah would become a warrior?"

"She only fights defensively. Wisah reminded us all, including the Supreme, our greatest warrior, Shandir, was also a White Priestess. Afterward, the Supreme had to allow other white priestesses to join the fighting force."

Kaieli dropped her head to her knees, wishing she could do more to fight the Scourge. But she was. She lifted her head. "We're doing our part in the compound." She told Rizelya about the sabotage plans. "Oh, one last thing. It may be possible for some men to escape through the crater's northern pass. They'd need help to leave the Barrens. They'll all suffering from nucla poisoning."

"I'll tell Histrun and Moraak. They'll come up a plan. We want our people out of there. I wish there was some way to help you and the others with the explosive trackers."

"Me too. Maybe if we discover how to neutralize the nucla, it will give us a way to deactivate the devices."

Kaieli glanced around and noted the most recent batch of escapees were mounted on the Gryphons. As much as she wanted to stay and catch up more with Rizelya, she had to return to the invaders' camp, or compromise the escape route. After hugging Rizelya, Kaieli ran back toward the crater. She allowed the quietness to soothe her mind as she contemplated ways to destroy the malignant magic in the black rock. Over the years, the various Supremes had tried to eliminate the malignant magic in the swamps but had failed. How could she succeed when they hadn't?

Blazel - 26 de Drudar, 1075

The Posair forces gathered to launch a counterattack. Early in the morning, the plains beyond the camp steadily filled with Gryphons and fighters. Blazel walked with his squad-pack surrounding him to where Graak and the other Gryphons assigned to their squadron waited.

Of the 150 Gryphons waiting, the majority carried a double load of passengers. Only those directing the battle from above rode alone. Blazel greeted Graak, then strapped himself into Graak's harness. Rizelya checked the straps holding her helbraught to Glork's harness one last time before buckling herself in. To his left, Aistrun struggled with a buckle. He finally finished and gave the signal he was ready.

This would be Blazel's first time as a battle commander. His stomach clenched in a tight knot and apprehension zipped along his spine. He worried no one would listen to his orders, or worse, that he'd give the wrong ones and end up killing his people. He mentally shook his head. Two lunadars ago, he had lived in the swamps not far from here, alone. Never having been in a pack, he hadn't known what he had been missing.

Aistrun gave him a crooked grin. Laynar and Leistral nodded. Eidstrun thumped his chest. They had become good friends over the course of the journey south. He didn't want to lose any of them after having just found them, and sent a prayer to the Warrior to protect them.

He turned his head toward Rizelya. She smiled and blew him a kiss. Chuckling, he mimed catching it, feeling a bit silly, but love would do strange things to a man. He grinned, thinking about her confession last night and their make-up sex.

We're ready, Laynar, leading one of the platoons, announced. The other platoon alphas chimed in with their readiness.

Graak crouched, and immediately the other Gryphons followed. *The flight is ready whenever you are, Blazel.*

Let's go! Blazel ordered, still smiling.

Thunder rippled across the plains as the Gryphons leaped into the air and gave the first powerful down-sweep of their wings. Graak led the flight high into the atmosphere, where no one, even the invaders, could see them from below. Glork and Broogk flew on either flank.

The cold air stinging Blazel's face felt good after the summer heat. Wind-forced tears streaked his cheeks. The ends of his ropes of hair whipped his eyes. If they were going to continue flying with the Gryphons, the Posairs needed to find some sort of eye protection.

The black sand glittered below them, broken only by the jumble of petrified wood boulders. Blazel remembered his nightmarish run through that barrenness. He patted Graak on his shoulder, grateful he didn't have to do it now.

The crater came into view on the horizon. Teams of ten spiraled away from the main force to surround the enemy's compound and drop off the extra riders.

The first teams have landed, Graak informed them. *So far, the invaders haven't noticed them.*

His keen eyesight allowed him to see the details of what looked like ants to Blazel. Graak, Glork, and Broogk flew in lazy, wide circles high above the compound. Blazel's stomach lurched as he gazed down. He grinned at the lack of shadows flitting on the ground.

They are in position, Graak said.

Blazel searched for any sign the invaders knew they were there. The activity in the camp remained sedate.

Now! he commanded.

The dozen Gryphons hovering over the dome dropped their invisibility spell, and a blast of fire burst from them, striking the dome. They concentrated their fire on a single spot, hoping to break through the energy field. Blazel flung up an arm to shield his eyes from the resulting conflagration. When it died down, a collective groan went through the assembled fighters. The dome remained in place.

On the ground, several teams of Reds and Browns worked on the fence, creating holes in it using the technique developed by Maheli and Sorlenda. Laynar's team, closest to the Posairs' cages, broke through and streamed inside. Ambrelya's team tore a hole near the mother ship.

An alarm clanged, and black-clad invaders rushed from the barracks. Blazel drew in his breath at the multitude. Hearing about many invaders there were wasn't the same as seeing what they were up against for himself. A large contingent ran to protect the mother ship, while other teams sprinted toward the fighter ships. Fighting broke out between the infiltrators and the soldiers.

A phalanx of aliens knelt with their weapons pointed at the sky and fired pulsating red light at the Gryphons. They dodged, but one didn't move fast enough, and the light punctured his wingtip. He screamed in agony, then flared to seal the wound. Graak ordered him to get back to camp.

One hundred Gryphons dropped their invisibility spell and appeared over the crater. Booms sounded as the invader's enormous weapons squatting on the crater rim fired. Explosions lit the sky. Gryphons dived and swooped, attacking the weapons. The fighters riding them fired their helbraughts, and red, yellow, and brown streams of light slammed into the guards. The enemy burned, froze, or turned into stone.

Thirty men flung down their tools and raced northward, covered by the Gryphon fighting teams. "What in the Crone's Fires?" Blazel swore when several men with golden hair and skin joined the throng speeding from the pillar. "Who in the seven hells are they?"

Other slaves? Graak guessed. *But are they friend or foe?*

"We'll find out soon enough."

Two Thunder Wings attacked the huge weapons, tearing into them with their talons. Kaaik and Delestrun sped toward the rim, flying low, Kaaik's wingtips only inches above the ground. Blazel held his breath, hoping their gamble paid off. He pumped his fist in the air when they sailed into the compound. The dome didn't cover the crater rim!

Go! Go! Go! he ordered, and five other teams zoomed after Kaaik toward the cage holding the children.

The fighter ships roared as they took off, and twenty-five Thunder Wings and other Gryphons broke off from the attack on the crater to meet them. The staccato sound of metal projectiles being fired at them filled the air.

Graak circled lower. Blazel carefully watched the action, his attention darting from one pocket of fighting to the next. He searched the compound and found the children's cage. A small team had reached it, including Eidstrun, Leistral, and Grazeen. Eidstrun banged on it, struggling to open it. A blue light sizzled along the metal, striking him and flinging him away. He staggered back to his feet and, with a roar, attacked it again. This time, the energy threw him farther from the cage. Behind him, four squat, brutish creatures with tusks curving from their lower jaws stalked him, carrying heavy clubs. These were definitely foes.

Eidstrun, watch out! Blazel called.

Eidstrun turned, ducking as a club whizzed by his head, but a second creature slammed his weapon into Eidstrun's ribs. He snarled and tore the club from its hands. The creature punched Eidstrun, and they exchanged several more blows, until Eidstrun broke its neck.

Leistral fought with another of the creatures, her helbraught giving her the reach to remain out of its club's range. The fourth creature lifted his weapon to bash Grazeen's head. Kaaik dove, screeching as his target dropped and rolled. The beast howled as talons gouged its back and staggered to its feet. Delestrun leaned over Kaaik's back and slid his helstrablade across the creature's throat.

A squad of soldiers raced toward the cage, firing their weapons. The children cowered together in the center. Eidstrun sped back to it, fists raised.

Get out of there. Now! Blazel ordered. *Before you're captured. We'll come back for the children later.*

But, sir! Eidstrun complained. *It's children, little ones too.*

You won't do them any good by joining them. There are two contingents heading your way. If you don't leave now, you'll be cornered.

Eidstrun, Rizelya said, her mind-voice laced with Alpha power, *move your ass. Now!*

Yes, Alpha. He sounded like a petulant child, but he obeyed and led the others away from the cage. They raced toward the crater rim, where they leaped off the edge to land on the backs of waiting Thunder Wings.

Invaders hurriedly saddled their lizard-mounts.

Time to go! Blazel called.

Men and women finished their individual battles and scrambled through the fence openings. Blazel groaned at the lack of time to seal the holes. Several fighters supported wounded comrades as they ran, and a few warriors carried injured slung over their shoulders. The Yellows and Reds threw up shields of air and fire to protect their retreat. As the fighters exited, Gryphons swooped down, scooping them up in their talons.

Soon, only those fighters killed remained in the camp. The twenty dead were more than Blazel had hoped, but less than he'd expected. Small groups of invaders, all with plain black robes, converged on the corpses. Blazel's gorge rose.

Rizelya swore. "They can't have our dead." She unhooked her helbraught and fed fire into the blade. Once orange flames licked it, she directed it toward the bodies. A beam shot from her helbraught.

Blazel didn't think her magic would penetrate the energy field, but then he sensed other power being added to hers.

We will help, Graak said.

Invaders bent over the dead Posairs with their appendages extended. So engrossed with their feeding, they didn't notice the magic streaking toward them. Suddenly, the bodies burst into flames and consumed the feeding invaders.

Shots rang out from below. Graak tilted quickly, avoiding the barrage, and beat his wings to regain height. He and Glork circled, making sure their people made it out. Once away from the compound, the teams landed to allow the Posairs picked up by the Gryphons' talons to mount properly. They administered emergency first aid to anyone injured, hoping to mitigate the infection caused by the nucla.

The teams returned to the air and flew out of firing range before the mounted invaders raced into the Barrens.

"Did the men get out of the crater?" Blazel asked as they returned to camp.

Yes, Graak answered. *They're almost to the pass.*

"We should reopen the northern guard fortress," Rizelya said. "It would make a good base for operations near the crater."

"Excellent idea! Especially now we know we can enter the compound and do some damage."

Satisfaction filled Blazel. His first mission had accomplished its goal! During the flight, he puzzled over how to breach the cage holding the children. He'd talk to Eidstrun when he returned to find out what he'd learned while trying to open it.

Plumes of smoke rose a few measures beyond the camp. Without Blazel asking, Graak winged toward it. Reds walked through monster debris, burning it. The aftermath of a monster battle. Blazel clenched his jaw at the reminder they fought a two-front war: one with the invaders and one with their old foes, the Malvers' monsters.

Rolstrun - 26 de Drudar, 1075

Chaos reigned. Even though Rolstrun expected the attack, seeing the huge Gryphons in action above his head was disconcerting. He'd returned to work that morning. His hand healed enough he couldn't remain hiding in the infirmary any longer. Bohandran sent him to the highest terrace, away from the guards' watchful gaze. The vantage point gave him a good view of the fighting, both inside the crater and in the compound.

The workers on the northern face of the pillar waited until the Gryphons attacked the crater, then they ran. Rolstrun moved to the edge, wishing he was running with them.

"Who are they?" Calistrun asked, pointing at several tall, golden figures joining the escaping men.

Rolstrun squinted. "Vhelopsi!" he said with surprise. "It's the team of Vhelopsi who were loading the carts. I thought they were as cowed by the Scourge as the Volkern and the rest of the slave species."

"Apparently we were wrong. We might have more allies."

Rolstrun hoped so. He silently cheered as the group sped away, the guards too busy defending themselves from the attacking Gryphons and the Posairs riding them to notice them.

The men must cross over ten measures before they reached the crater's northern face and the only way into or out of the crater. At the northern fortress, Rolstrun had been on several rotations guarding the narrow pass. Every few lunadars, stupid kids dared each other to climb down into the crater's depths. Before Shandir created the crater, the Storengher river had flowed through the area, and the fissure was the old, dry riverbed. The men had a difficult climb ahead of them.

Rolstrun turned his attention back to the fighting. He made a gesture of hope, willing the successful release of the children from the cage. When the Gryphons zipped out of the compound without any small passengers, he slumped to the ground and wept. The crack of a whip below him snapped him back to his surroundings. He climbed to his feet and awkwardly gripped his ax, his injured hand protesting the hard usage. He chanced looking northward. Only fast-moving dots appeared in the distance.

Throughout the afternoon, he waited for the guards to spot the escaping men and chase after them. But after a couple of octars, with no alarm sounding, his hopes raised. The distractions had worked! The men without the explosive trackers could escape this hellhole. He brushed his hand over the device buried in his arm. He swore at the unfairness. The cursed thing trapped him, Kaieli, and the rest of his friends here.

Rolstrun gingerly climbed the ladder out of the crater. His injured hand made it difficult to grip the rungs, and he slipped several times. Only Calistrun, climbing close behind him, kept him from falling. As he crawled over the edge, he paused. "Thanks, Calistrun," he panted. "I thought I was going to die."

"Not if I can help it," Calistrun said, helping Rolstrun to his feet.

Rolstrun gazed at the ladder. Death hovered over the camp daily, and it had almost taken him. He said a prayer of thanks that he was still alive.

As they marched to their quarters, Rolstrun's eyebrows rose in surprise. Confused disarray swamped the compound. Commander Ke-ke-tak rode a large sheezet, inspecting the various points of entry. He stopped at a pile of ashes, climbed off his mount, and crouched, fingering the ash. His faced darkened in anger, and he stomped on the mound, shouting. His soldiers cringed away from him, shaking their heads. He reached out, grabbed one by the robes, and dragged the hapless soldier to him. He lifted the man off his feet, yelling at him. The soldier gibbered in fright. The commander's feeding tubes slammed into him, draining him dry.

"Hurry!" Nederposan said. "Get to the pens quickly."

The Posair men walked faster, knowing running would draw the commander's attention to them. A whine filled the air, and a battered fighter ship limped into view, black smoke trailing from it. It wobbled as it angled in to land. While the incoming ship held the commander's attention, the Posairs sprinted to their cages, sliding into them as the ship crashed. A moment later, it burst into flames. Soldiers raced to the landing area, shouting as the fire encroached on two nearby ships.

"What happened?" Nederposan asked when they reached the safety of their pens.

Maheli grinned. "Our people attacked. They tried to rescue the children." Her smile faded. "But they couldn't pry open the cage. It had some sort of magic on it."

Nederposan paced, then whirled around to face Kaieli. "Kaieli, do you think we can talk Tre'nok into helping us disable it? He's helped us before."

Kaieli shrugged. "I don't know. I can ask."

Late in the night, the slave pen's gates clanged open. Rolstrun jerked awake. Frightened shouts punctuated the dark. Terrified, he held onto Kaieli. The invaders had never entered the pens at night before. Lights carried by the soldiers flashed, and Rolstrun threw up an arm, blinking in the bright light. Soldiers roughly pulled three men, including Nederposan, and one woman from their pallets. They dragged the kicking and screaming Posairs from the cage. Rolstrun sat on his pallet, trembling and holding Kaieli, slightly ashamed to be glad neither one of them had been taken.

The next morning, guards surrounded the cages and drove the Posairs to the central area of the compound. A stage loomed adjacent to the children's cage. Several men and women hung chained spread-eagle to frames forming an "X". Blood dripped from wounds covering their bodies, and their faces were so misshapen from the beatings they'd suffered that they were unrecognizable. On the stage, Commander Ke-ke-tak held a nucla whip, slapping it into his hand. Tre'nok stood off to the side.

"These slaves refused to answer my questions," Tre'nok translated for the commander. "Resistance is not tolerated. They claim they knew nothing of the attack on my compound!"

The man in the center raised his head. "How could we know?" Nederposan rasped. "We were locked in here."

The commander's whip snaked out, striking Nederposan across the face. He cried out. "We will throw you off our planet, you misbegotten monsters!"

Ke-ke-tak roared in rage, and whipped Nederposan into unconsciousness. As the commander's feeders pierced his chest, Nederposan jerked into awareness, screaming. His fists clenched, Rolstrun chanted a prayer to the Goddess under his breath to calm his mind and emotions. He refused to feed the enemy with his terror or his anger.

The invaders beat and fed upon the other people on the stage, including ten children. After which, soldiers marched the Posairs back to work. The heavy guard remained watchful throughout the day.

Rolstrun vowed he'd avenge their dead, somehow, someday.

Chapter 19

Rizelya - 27 de Drudar, 1075

Following their attack on the invader's compound, sentries guarded the boundaries of the base camp, warriors on the ground and Gryphons in the air. Everyone, including support staff, carried weapons and traveled in groups. Rizelya and her team set traps, both magical and mundane, around the perimeter.

Histrun and his commanders analyzed the battle in detail, ferreting out which tactics worked, and which ones failed. They discussed what to do against the possibility the invaders closed the crater's weak points.

Early the next morning, a Gryphon sentry shouted the warning, *They're coming!*

Rizelya raced to her assigned spot. The Reds raised their fire shields, and she sensed Eiden and other Yellows add hardened air in front of it. Heat wafted from the shield, letting everyone know where the invisible boundary lay. Rizelya's squad-pack waited, readying their helbraughts to form the net-shield to protect the army from air attacks. They hadn't experimented yet with refining their merging using the new information from Kaieli.

Dust rose from the Barrens. Invaders on reptilian mounts charged toward the base camp. Sunlight glinted on the array of weapons. The enemy's line stretched a measure in either direction and appeared to be two or three deep. Rizelya wondered how so many had traveled through space on their ship. Even as massive as it was, it didn't look large enough to accommodate that many men and their mounts, plus the slaves she'd heard the escaped captives talk about.

Rizelya kept watching the sky for any glint of metal. She cocked her head, listening for the telltale noise of the invader's flying ships. The Gryphons patrolling the skyline confirmed this attack lacked any air support.

"Chariel, Wisah, move to the rear," Rizelya ordered. "We won't need you for this battle."

"But we can fight," Chariel argued, putting her hands on her hips. "We're here to fight, Rizelya, not cower behind the lines."

"This is simply the beginning of a long war. We need you for its entirety. I need to know you're both safe so I can kill these bastards!"

"Come on, Chariel." Wisah tugged on Chariel's sleeve. "She's right."

"But why do we practice so hard, if not to fight?"

Rizelya glanced at the advancing horde. "So in case we're overrun, which is a definite possibility, you can survive. Now go!"

Chariel glowered at Rizelya, but turned and ran with Wisah toward the rear. Rizelya heaved a sigh of relief.

Gryphons dove at the approaching army, pulsing flames at the lead invaders. The lizard-beasts tossed their heads and reared. But their riders tightened their reins and pushed them forward through the flames. Several caught on fire, and their high-pitched screams hurt Rizelya's ears. Gryphons plucked soldiers from the back of their mounts, soaring high before releasing them to smash into their fellows or splat on the ground.

A few riders pulled ahead. A contingent of Yellows hurled brecha spines, harvested from the last monster attack, with their air magic. They slammed into the advance riders. Their skin smoked and turned a bright red as the acid inside the spines ate into them. Rizelya gagged as the affected invaders disintegrated. Their mounts bolted away from the barrage.

The Haaslair archers loosed a volley of arrows. The missiles struck their targets, taking them down. To Rizelya's left, a soldier screamed, all color drained from his face. He'd tripped one of the Blue's traps, which fed fear into his mind. Rizelya smirked at his distress. The emotion bombs worked! He fell into a comatose state, dropping like a rock from his mount. The beast behind him ran over him, crunching his skull.

Then the wave of riders crashed into their shields. The sheer numbers pushed through and broke sections. Rizelya kept a personal shield locked tight against her body, trusting—hoping—it would stop the enemy's projectiles. She threw fireballs at the beast barreling toward her. Its rider shot at her. Dodging, she ran under the lizard, slashing its legs, and thrust her helbraught blade deep into its body. It shuddered as it screamed. She hated attacking animals, but the towering beasts gave the invaders too much of an advantage.

The soldier jumped off his dying mount as it collapsed. Using the reach of her helbraught, she knocked the weapon from his hands. With a lunge, she closed the gap, and her blade slid into him and out his back. Fire erupted inside of him. She turned away from the corpse, blocking the next attack.

Her muscles quivered, and she breathed heavily. Blood dripped into her eye. Her shoulder burned. Even after octars of fighting, invaders still advanced into the melee. She ducked a blow and slipped on the slick ground, landing on her back. Her eyes widened as an invader aimed his weapon at her chest. A red-brown streak of fur leaped over her, toppling the enemy. With a snarl, Blazel ripped out the invader's throat. Blood and gore matted his fur.

A horn bleated. The invaders retreated into the Barrens, ending the battle. Rizelya slumped, leaning against her helbraught. Bodies littered the battlefield—Posair, Gryphon, invader, and beast. The injured cried and moaned. Already noncombatant women walked the ground, giving aid to the wounded, while fighters stalked the field, killing any surviving invaders. Teams picked up any weapons left by the retreating enemy. Histrun wanted to determine if the Posairs could use them.

Blazel shifted and wiped away a smear of blood from his cheek.

"You better get that looked at." She pointed to his calf, where blood oozed from a gash.

He glanced at it and shrugged. "Later. How are you?"

Rizelya tilted her head side-to-side and rolled her shoulders, then rubbed away the annoying trickle of blood from her eyebrow. "Fine. Nothing serious." She stepped closer to him, put her arms around his waist, and laid her head on his chest. Rizelya didn't care about the smell or the mess. She wanted to feel him, to affirm they were both alive. After a long moment, she sighed. "Let's go find our people. I lost track of them in the battle's furor."

She sent out a mental call. Everyone responded, except one. *Aistrun? Aistrun? Where are you? Answer me, Wolf!*

She stumbled as fast as her exhausted legs could take her to the infirmary. Women rushed around, pressing bandages on wounds. The healers moved from patient to patient, working on them. A few lay still, beyond even the most powerful healer's skills. She stopped a woman. "Have you seen Aistrun?"

The woman shook her head and hurried on her way.

Frenzied fire built under Rizelya's skin, and her heart hammered as she searched cot after cot to no avail. Tears streamed unchecked down her face. Aistrun had been her best friend since they were little. He'd protected her when the older boys bullied her. They'd caused mischief together and fought monsters as a team. He couldn't be gone. He just couldn't.

A familiar figure caught her attention. "Bethlyn!" She grabbed the healer's arm. "Bethlyn, have you seen Aistrun?"

Bethlyn frowned, then shook her head. "No, but wounded are still out in the field." She glanced down the row of cots. "I'm sorry. Are you hurt?"

Rizelya lifted her hand to her forehead. Her wound had stopped bleeding. "No."

"Then I have to go."

Rizelya sat on the ground outside the tent door, checking every person who was brought in. Her heart sank deeper and deeper into despair as evening descended.

I found him! Blazel's mind-shout broke through her hopelessness like a ray of sunshine. *He's hurt, but still alive.**

"Thank you, Great Mother!" Rizelya stood, waiting anxiously for them to arrive. And waited. Finally, Blazel and Eidstrun approached the healer's tent, carrying an unconscious Aistrun between them.

"Where was he?" She plucked at Aistrun's blood-soaked shirt.

"Damned near to the Barrens," Blazel huffed. "I nearly missed him. One of those lizard beasts partially buried him."

"Bethlyn!" Rizelya called. "Bethlyn, we need you."

The men carried Aistrun into the tent. A middle-aged woman met them, her eyes widening at Aistrun's injuries. She directed them to an empty cot. A few moments later, Bethlyn arrived, slightly breathless. She did a quick scan.

"Three broken ribs, a crushed forearm, a projectile in his leg, and one in his abdomen." She cataloged his injuries. "He's lucky to be alive. Ah, his nose is broken too."

"Is he going to be okay?" Rizelya bit her lip.

Bethlyn nodded distractedly, already working on healing Aistrun.

Blazel took Rizelya's arm and gently pulled her away. "Come on, he's in good hands. She'll let us know when he's awake. In the meantime, we need to clean up and have something to eat. I'm starving. It's been a long time, and a long battle, since breakfast."

Her stomach growled, and she walked with him to the bathing tent.

Blazel - 30 de Drudar, 1075

The wind blew in Blazel's face, and he squinted against its force. "Ugh!" he cried, wincing and rubbing the bug out of his eye.

Graak chuckled beneath him. *You seem to be a bug magnet, Blazel. This isn't something we have troubles with.*

"Maybe if you extended your nimbus a little farther up, they'd burn before they reach me."

Now, what fun would that be?

Even as Graak continued to laugh, the air in front of Blazel hazed, and the bombardment of insects stopped. Blazel glanced down at the black sand-glass flowing beneath them. Unlike the last time when they'd flown to the guard fortresses, no Malvers' monsters streamed from the crater. After the invaders started using their horrid monster corrals, the number of monsters inside the Barrens dropped off to more normal levels. Teams placed along the Barren's borders protected against any encroaching monsters. It split their fighting force, but they couldn't allow the monsters to molest the nearby provinces.

Blazel led a small force to the northern guard fortress to pick up the escaped prisoners and determine the possibility of reopening the fortress as an additional base. He grimaced, remembering Rizelya's fury at not being included. Histrun needed her team to erect a net-shield in case of an attack on the base camp. Since the Posairs' raid on the invaders compound four days ago, the invaders had hit the camp every day. Only Rizelya's net-shield protected the fighters from the deadly barrage of weapons from the enemy's ships.

Graak angled into a dive, and Blazel gripped the harness straps tighter. Graak landed in the center courtyard, with their team coming in right behind them. He folded his wings along his back and carefully surveyed the area. *I don't smell any invaders,* he said as he crouched to let Blazel off. *But where are the escapees?*

Blazel took a deep breath. None of the enemy's stench pervaded the air. He threw his leg over Graak's back and stepped off. "Perhaps they're hiding. They've been prisoners for a long time. Eidstrun, Drustrun, come with me to check the keep-house. The rest of you spread out and remain alert. Remember, other captives escaped too. We don't know anything about them."

Blazel held his helstrablade in front of him while gathering his magic to him, ready to shift to his warrior form in an instant. He sensed Eidstrun and Drustrun on either side of him do the same. It seemed strange not to have the keep alphas meet him at the porch. The quiet in the fortress made the hair on the back of his neck stand up. He warily approached the keep-house.

"Ho, the house!" he called when he reached the steps.

The door slowly opened, and a man peeked out. "Oh, thank Goddess!" he cried and threw open the door. "Help has arrived." He called over his shoulder. "We can finally leave here." He led a ragtag group of men from the house and down the stairs.

The men wore ugly orange coveralls. They'd been to the bathing room, as no grime clung to their hair and faces, but a layer of black seemed to be ingrained into their skin. They were gaunt from malnutrition and fatigue.

Blazel stepped forward and held out his hand. "I'm Blazel de Strunland. This is Drustrun and Eidstrun. That over there is Graak, Broogk, and Glork." He indicated the Gryphons.

The leaders gripped Blazel's wrist. "I'm Aradehan, former keep alpha of Dehanrandean Keep."

"How many of you made it?" The group in front of him didn't look like the thirty-odd he'd seen run from the pillar.

"Only twenty. The rest weren't strong enough." Aradehan's gaze shifted back to the keep-house. "We weren't the only ones who escaped. Seven Vhelopsi, our fellow captives, joined us."

"I noticed them. Are they friends?" It felt like a stupid question, but he had to ask it.

"Yes. The Scourge conquered their world fifty cycles ago, which we understand to be Scourge years. They want to fight with us. Will you vouch for them? Will the Supreme Alphas listen to you?"

Blazel tilted his head. "Let me meet them first." He turned to his men waiting behind him. "Drustrun, you and the rest check the fortress and determine how much damage it took. Eidstrun, you're with me. Graak, you too." He wanted people he trusted with him in case these aliens weren't as friendly as Aradehan thought they were. He wished Aistrun were with him, but he was still recovering from his injuries. Blazel strode up the stairs and into the keep-house. Aradehan led him to the recreation room.

Seven men of varying heights stood at his entrance. Their skin tones ranged from gold to bronze, and they had golden hair and eyes. They had the look of defeated warriors, who now were being offered a chance to strike at their enemies.

A gold-skinned man stepped forward, put his right hand over his chest, and dipped his head. He didn't extend his hand in greeting. "I Hairan Aziru, alpha of Vhelopsi. Please excuse not knowing your language more."

Blazel narrowed his eyes. "How did you learn our language?" Even though the grammar wasn't proper, and the Vhelopsi mispronounced many words, Blazel understood him.

"Tre'nok teach me—" he gestured to the men with him "—us. We think there be a time it needed. Also the healer, Kaieli teach me. Heal me, too." He held out his left arm and pushed back his sleeve to reveal a scar circling his forearm.

Blazel noticed Hairan's fingers were longer than normal and had long, sharp nails, almost like claws. The tip of a fang peeked from the Vhelopsi's lips as he talked. These people were predators and had fallen to the Scourge. "Why did you escape? What do you want from us?"

"Saw chance to escape. Took it." Hairan smiled, showing more of his fangs. "We not the meek slaves the Scourge believe. See you fight good. We wish fight with you. The creator not make us slaves, but apex predators of Vhel, like you here. We not able to free Vhel, but may help keep here free."

Blazel studied the men. *What do you think, Eidstrun, Graak? Is he telling the truth?*

That they are predators, yes, Graak said. *A predator knows its kind, and these people are fighters. It will be interesting to learn how their world fell, so we can stop ours from suffering the same fate. I say let them stay, but here, in the fortress, until we know if they are truly here to help us or are spying for the Scourge.*

I concur, Eidstrun said, with a slight nod. *Let them prove themselves.* He folded his arms over his chest and glared menacingly at the Vhelopsi. "If you want to help us, tell us how to get our children out of that miserable cage. You do this, we won't kill you."

"It a despicable practice. The Scourge use on us, too. I will tell. But," he lifted a long finger, "if it works, you help rescue more my people."

"Deal!" Blazel said. It would be a small price to pay to remove those children from the enemy's clutches. He held out his hand. Hairan studied it and him for a moment, then grasped it.

Drustrun strode in. "The fortress is good. There's only minimal damage, which we can easily fix. All the food is gone. We'll have to bring some in, but the water source is still flowing." He glanced at Blazel and the Vhelopsi's clasped hands. "Looks like they're friends."

"Allies, for now." Blazel answered, as he released his grip. He indicated the table. "Let's sit. Tell us how to deactivate the cage."

The men passed around travel bars and canteens of taevo. Blazel's optimism plummeted as he listened to the Vhelopsi's instructions. The Scourge's technology was beyond him. He'd have to include a Vhelopsi on the raid. If the Posairs hoped to defeat the invaders, they needed to learn the technology.

Ten days later, Blazel, Rizelya, their squad-pack, and Hairan flew to the enemy compound. Kaaik and Delestrun's team created a diversion, attacking the crater and dome, while Blazel's team raided the compound. True to Hairan's word, the Scourge hadn't closed off the crater rim. They couldn't, and still bring the nucla up to be processed. Glork led the charge, with Rizelya and the others using their helbraughts to attack the invaders manning the enormous weapons guarding the rim. They destroyed two, creating a narrow path for the attackers. Graak zoomed in, flying as fast as he could, the wind of his passage causing Blazel's eyes to tear up. They quickly reached the cage with the children.

Twenty small bodies huddled together in the center, their eyes hollow from constant fear. Saffren sent a blast of frigid water at the cage, freezing the metal. The low buzzing from it stopped. Blazel dropped from Graak, shifted into his warrior form, and guarded Hairan as he worked on the lock.

"Hurry!" Blazel growled. "They come."

"I work fast," Hairan grunted.

Blazel snarled at the approaching invaders. A streak of red and orange flames ran along the ground between him and the invaders, quickly blazing into a fire-shield. He felt a blast of cold as Dehali added a layer of hardened air. The soldiers fired their weapons. Blazel sneered at the enemy while the projectiles hit the shield, sizzling as they vaporized. A soldier stumbled back, and Blazel growled and lunged menacingly at him. He dropped his weapon and fled.

Chuckling under his breath, Blazel glanced behind him. The cage door hung open, and fighters lifted the children onto the Gryphons. After a last glare at the remaining soldiers, he released his warrior form. He jumped into Graak's harness, folding over the two small children huddled there, protecting them with his body. Graak leaped into the air, and the girl shrieked. The invaders fired at the retreating Gryphons, but Rizelya kept the shield up until they zipped out of the compound. Graak led the rescue team in a steep climb, getting their precious cargo out of danger.

They stopped several measures from the crater where a flock of Gryphons and fighters waited. They'd carry the children to Haaslorn Keep, where they'd join the rest of the children. Over the last ten days, Kaieli and the others had spirited away all the remaining children in the camp. The invaders wouldn't be able to use them as leverage anymore. Once they recovered, a detail of Gryphons and warriors would take them to the Sanctuary, where they'd be safe from any harm. In addition, the White Priestesses, like Blazel's mother, Blenora, could heal their minds of the trauma they'd suffered.

Blazel watched the Gryphons with the children disappear over the horizon. It would take a miracle for the small Posair army to lock the enemy in the Barrens, keeping the rest of Lairheim safe from their terror and deprivations.

Rolstrun - 50 de Drudar, 1075

The captive's celebration of the children's successful rescue broke off as the Scourge tromped into the slave pens. They dragged twenty Posairs to the stage. Forced to watch, Rolstrun locked away his emotions, as the commander took out his rage on the prisoners. The torture, and subsequent feeding, didn't assuage Commander Ke-ke-tak's fury at losing his hostages. Rolstrun silently cheered as three times as many invaders lost their lives.

The Posairs continued to fight the Scourge nearly daily. Sometimes, the battles raged close enough to the crater for Rolstrun and the other men to witness it. More often, they only knew a skirmish occurred because the commander took out his frustration on the captives, or when Posair fighters joined the ranks of prisoners. Pride of his people filled Rolstrun. The Scourge didn't capture many fighters.

One night, Rolstrun and Kaieli cuddled on his pallet, too exhausted to do much more. "We must be having an effect." Rolstrun idly traced patterns on Kaieli's arm. "The commander is always in a tizzy anymore. Although we suffer for it, our people are making his life miserable."

"Tre'nok mentioned today that the Scourge don't usually encounter so much resistance. It frustrates him to lose battles against 'an inferior race' with so little technology." She chuckled. "He discounts our magic as useless, even as we win skirmishes with it."

The Gryphons continued to raid the crater, allowing more men to escape in the chaos. Rolstrun wished he could flee and to actively fight his tormentors. But a few days ago, he'd been reminded why he couldn't leave.

A Keistanlair man, captured while guarding the western fortress, tried to make the run to the northern pass. The resulting explosion nearly jeopardized the secrecy of the entire escape route. There hadn't been enough of him left for the guards to bother retrieving his body.

As much as possible, the Posair prisoners of war worked to sabotage the enemy's equipment and the mining operation. Sometimes, it rankled Rolstrun that while he was trapped in the crater, hacking at the pillar of nucla, the women's plots succeeded in halting production.

Late one afternoon, four chedans since his accident, Rolstrun stopped to rest, rubbing his sore hand. After losing his fingers, his grip on the pickax was awkward. Blisters continually formed on the base of his hand. He thanked the

Mother he hadn't had to muck out the lizard stalls again. The damned things seemed to like the taste of him, and he'd rather not lose more of him to them.

He stood on a terraced ledge of the pillar—much smaller now—when suddenly the noisome odor of malignant magic filled his nostrils. He sniffed deeply, twisting his head around to locate the source. The strongest scent came from the northwest. He squinted and put up a hand to shield his eyes. Half a measure away, black dust swirled in the still air. The stink grew stronger. Repugnant energy nibbled at his senses. The twisting sand expanded into a small cyclone as shapes appeared in the center. Familiar shapes.

"Monsters!" Rolstrun yelled and pointed to the spot. The Malvers' monsters appearing in the crater no longer ignored the miners. They only had their pickaxes and shovels for weapons. The guards killed any man who shifted into his warrior shape.

The dust settled, revealing a large nest of four janacks and thirty brechas. Rolstrun clenched his hands, the pain reminding him he couldn't shift. The men below him and on the ground held their tools like weapons. The guards in the crater rushed to surround the monsters, shooting into the mob. Several on mobility devices flew toward the nest. The invaders had learned their lesson by now, and they'd attached flame throwers to the front of the machines. They aimed at the brechas breaking away from the main group. Fire gusted from the nozzles, igniting the monsters.

A janack, missing three tentacles, trundled lopsidedly toward the pillar and Rolstrun, who stood higher than the rest and making him an easy target. He held his pick ax ready. A tentacle whipped up, questing for him. He drove the sharp point into it and tugged. He met resistance, then the ax penetrated the tissue before it stuck again. The whine of a projectile whizzed by his head. The janack jerked, lifting the injured tentacle—and Rolstrun with it. His legs swung in the air. He let go of his ax, smashing into the ground and rolling.

Hands stopped him from plummeting over the edge.

"Stay here, boy." Bohandran helped him to his feet. "It's almost over. You were brave."

"Or stupid." Rolstrun brushed off his coveralls, wincing at the new bruise on his shoulder. "I know now why we bargained with the Goddess for the ability to shapeshift. It's much easier to fight the damned monsters."

A few milcrons later, the sounds of shooting died away.

He dashed down the pillar. Calistrun and Alestrun had been in the line of attack. "Thank the Mother! You're still alive!" he said, clapping them on the back.

"Us?" Calistrun looked at him askance. "You were the one dangling over the edge. Don't you know once you stick the monster, you need to let go of the ax?"

"Apparently not. I wanted something to slam into it again."

"I'm surprised you managed to penetrate its hide." Alestrun lifted his own pickax to examine the blade on it. "These aren't very long."

"But they are sharp, and I was desperate."

The guards shooed them back to work.

Rolstrun had lost his pickax. It had burned with the janack it had been stuck in. As he plodded to the tool shed for another one, he pondered about the incident. In his life beyond the Barrens— it seemed so long ago—he hadn't ever noticed an increase in the malignant magic when a nest matured. Malignant magic saturated the swamps where the nests formed enough to mask any upsurge of it. Did the malignant magic increase there, too? Was there a connection between the magic and the monsters?

He trudged toward his ledge, black dust puffing with each step. Rolstrun stopped and stared at it. He crouched and grabbed a handful, lifting it to his nose. It reeked of malignant magic. He glanced around, making sure an invader didn't see him, and tucked a small rock in his pocket. *Kaieli needs to examine this with her Gray Talent.*

A guard snapped his whip, striking Rolstrun's back. He flinched, stood, and returned to work, feeling lighter than he had in chedans. If he was correct, and his idea worked, they might have a way to rid his world of monsters.

Kaieli - 50 de Drudar, 1075

The whir and bang of the processing equipment screeched to a halt. Kaieli kept her head down but allowed herself to smile. Maheli and Sorlenda had found another way to sabotage the machines. Since the people in the slave camp decided to be prisoners of war rather than slaves, the production machinery had developed problems: belts broke, pins snapped, and scoops jammed. Holes in the conveyor belts dropped hidden quantities of the mineral onto the floor to be swept up and incinerated. They did all their sabotage using their Talents, leaving no physical trace for the invaders to find.

"What is it this time?" Vy'shol asked, exasperated. With all the problems, a Volkern now stayed in the processing plant during working hours to translate for the guards.

"It just stopped," Sorlenda said, holding up her hands and stepping back. "I don't know what's wrong with this stupid machine. I didn't do anything."

Pei Yoon, a Faeorn, hurried to the machine and took off the cover. Pei Yoon's delicate, supple fingers examined the insides.

After some banging, the gomale held up a bolt in its fingers.

"Not good," it said with a sigh and shake of its head, making its fine, blond hair swing. Several of the Faeorn had learned some of the Posarian language. "Can fix." It moved to a parts cabinet and stuck its head in, rummaging around, muttering as it worked.

"It says this machinery is suffering from unusual bad luck," Vy'shol translated. She strolled to the machine and picked up the errant bolt. "The machines work properly everywhere else. Commander Ke-ke-tak is quite vexed at all these delays and production losses."

"Then he should go home." Maheli folded her arms and glared.

"Oh, he will. But not until he has mined and processed every last bit of the nucla." Vy'shol leaned in. "How are you doing it? They've examined the machinery and can't find any fingerprints or anything else to indicate someone touched it."

Maheli chuckled and wiggled her fingers. "Magic."

Vy'shol pulled back, her eyes wide. "You're joking."

"Am I?"

Pei Yoon slapped the cover back onto the machine and flipped a switch. The machine chugged as the mechanism turned over, then ran smoothly. The conveyor belt moved again. Sorlenda and Maheli returned to their jobs.

Kaieli turned her attention to the woman in front of her. She concentrated on the gash on the woman's forearm, knitting the muscles back together and closing the skin. A red mark showed where she'd been cut, but it would fade in a day or two. She could do this type of healing easily. However, purging the nucla poisoning from everyone took nearly everything she and the others had. The woman thanked her and returned to work. Kaieli glanced up. Vy'shol stared at her with a strange expression on her face.

"You and the others really do magic, don't you?"

"We do."

Vy'shol tilted her head and clasped her hands together. "I saw how you healed that woman, and I was there when you healed Mei-Ying, Pei Yoon's mate. You work under the surface. Can your magic do anything to make the nucla stop working? I know Tre'nok talked to you about our desire to destroy it."

Kaieli tugged on her bottom lip. "Our magic might work, but we'll have to experiment. Our people are fighting—"

"We have seen the battles."

"We'd have more success if we knew more about the invaders. What is their physiology? What are their motivations? The Volkern have served the Scourge for a long time. Surely you know something about them. Anything you share could help us defeat them."

Vy'shol gazed in the distance quietly for several milcrons. Kaieli wondered if she'd gone too far in her attempt to turn the Volkern into allies.

Finally, Vy'shol gave a huge sigh. "I cannot make the decision on my own to help you more than we have by looking the other way during your escape runs. I will talk to Tre'nok and my people. One of us will inform you about what we decide."

"Fair enough."

After Vy'shol moved away, Kaieli stared at the nucla moving through the processing plant. She didn't spend much time around the stuff. It made her too ill. Not busy at the moment, she wandered to the line and studied the mineral, from raw chunks to the finished, compressed bars. Malignant magic radiated from it in all of its forms. Her thoughts whirled as she meandered back to the healing station.

Maheli, she said, connecting with her and speaking only to her with mind-speech, *can you get me one of the bars?*

I'll try. What do you want with the nasty thing, anyway?

Experimenting.

Then you'll have one.

A commotion sprung up near where the bars exited the machine, drawing the guard's attention. A few moments later, a bar landed on Kaieli's lap. She squirmed at its touch and gingerly put it on the table. She spent the rest of the afternoon attempting to affect the bar's properties without success. The malignant magic resisted her efforts and pushed her away. Faliciden, Faelyn, Maheli, Sorlenda, and Loshera all tried, with the same result. By the time the horn sounded at the end of the day, Kaieli nearly cried with frustration. Before leaving, she hid the bar, using her Talent to create a concealment shield around it. Even doing that made her cringe from the malignant magic.

After a meager dinner of watery soup, Rolstrun pulled Kaieli into a private corner. Over the last few chedans, they'd become close. Although he still hadn't made love to her, they slept together every night. He gave her a quick hug and kiss.

"Kaieli, I heard you were experimenting on the nucla. I saw something strange today when the Malvers' monsters attacked us in the crater."

"You're not hurt, are you?" She quickly examined him for injuries.

He shook his head. "No, I'm fine, and so is everyone else. Before the monsters broke out of their nest, I sensed an increase in the malignant magic. It made me wonder." He dug into his pocket and pulled out a nucla nugget. "Have you noticed it's condensed and solidified malignant magic?"

Kaieli blinked. "No, I haven't." Making a face in disgust, she gingerly took the rock. This time, she examined the mineral more deeply with her magical sight, peering under the surface into its molecular structure.

Whatever terrible evil had occurred in this area during the Great War, it had manifested into physical form. Another, more powerful magic—most likely the blast from Shandir's magic creating the crater—had locked it into that configuration. The rock contained the evil to prevent it from infecting everyone. Unless they were getting it whipped into them or breathing it on a daily basis.

The baneful energy within the nucla in her hand spread slimy fingers toward her, almost as if it possessed a consciousness. She dropped the rock, shaking her hands and rubbing them against her thighs to rid them of the awful energy. She dry-heaved, imagining the evil invading her body and soul.

"It's that bad, huh?" Rolstrun rubbed her back. "I didn't like having it in my pocket." When she recovered, he continued. "Could you purge the malignant magic from the nucla, you know, like you do for us?"

For the second time that evening, she blinked in surprise and stared at him. She slapped a palm to her face. "Now, why didn't I think of that? We attempted to do something, anything, to the damned stuff all afternoon."

"You just needed a genius like me to point it out." Rolstrun grinned.

"Yes, I did." She put her hand on his face, rose on her toes, and kissed him. He deepened the kiss and pulled her tight against his chest. His hard muscles were a nice contrast to her soft bosom. His hand cupped her butt, causing tingles of desire to dance in her pelvis. Loving a man had certain advantages over a loving a woman. All thoughts of ridding the nucla of the malignant magic fled when his fingers caressed her breast. Rolstrun didn't stop when she expected him to, and she bit into his shoulder to dampen her cries of pleasure as he thrust into her. After their lovemaking, before he could berate himself for his loss of control, she assured him she wasn't in her fertile time, and they hadn't created a child. None of the women had become pregnant so far, even though she knew they didn't abstain from sex. She believed the Mother watched over them, and not allowing any children to be born into this terror.

The next day, Maheli, Noriana, and Jaelena slipped into the infirmary. They waited while Kaieli, Faliciden, and Loshera healed an injured worker. As soon as they finished, the women gathered in a circle and stood over a small pile of nucla rocks. After combining their Talents into something akin to Black Talent, they blasted the rock. Nothing happened. The evil remained locked in the molecular structure of the mineral.

When they attempted other ways, the magic resisted. It pushed back, attempting to wrap around one or another of the women. It burrowed into an innocent bystander, and they wasted energy they didn't have to purge it from the person. By the time the horn blared, signaling the end of the work day, Kaieli and the others sagged with exhaustion.

She hated working with the stuff, but if they wanted the Volkern's help, she needed to find a way to make it inert. After the day's failures, she had no idea how they would accomplish the task.

Chapter 20

Blazel - 4 de Godar, 1075

In between battles, Blazel met with Histrun, Naila, and Moraak to plan their next assaults. Their fighting force wasn't large enough to field many direct offensives against such a superior opponent. They lost too many people in those types of confrontations. Small, lightning-fast raids, with the Gryphons flying their fighters in and out quickly, succeeded better.

The commanders assigned fast-flying scouts near the Scourge compound to watch for transport ship activity. Whenever one left, it meant the invaders were ambushing a keep for more slaves. The scouts followed the ships at a distance, then informed Histrun and Moraak which keep was in danger. The Gryphons and a force of fighters would race to stop the Scourge infiltration. Mostly, they'd arrived on time, but they lost a few more keeps to the enemy. Although the Gryphons attacked the transport ships, they couldn't do much damage.

As the days passed, the Posairs quietly evacuated any keeps not already emptied within a hundred measures of the Barren. They kept a few on the border garrisoned with fighters as bait for the invaders.

After the first few battles, the Posairs gathered any of the enemy's weapons left on the battlefields to use against them. The idea worked as long as they possessed ammunition for them. But the weapons became useless when they emptied the cartridges in a fight. Histrun sent several weapons, along with samples of the various types of ammunition, to the helstramiester, Maendy, asking her to develop ammunition the Posairs could use.

Blazel stood at the command tent door, gazing toward the north. Histrun approached him and put his hand on Blazel's shoulder.

"What are you looking at, boy?" Histrun asked. "Are you homesick?"

"No, not homesick, sir. I'm wondering when Maendy's going to send us word about the ammunition for the invader's weapons. We could use something to help us. We're getting killed out there. She's been working on it for several chedans now."

"She'll find a solution. I've known Maendy for a long time. She's as inventive as my Zehala was, but she won't give us anything until she's sure it works. It would be even worse for us if the weapons backfired on us."

"True, sir. I'm just anxious for this to be over."

"That, my boy, won't happen anytime soon." Histrun sighed and rubbed the back of his neck. "The Scourge have too many people they can throw at us. We need to discover a way to cut their numbers."

"It would help if we knew more about them. The healers aren't learning much from the autopsies they've attempted. The invader's insides start putrefying as soon as they're dead."

"Everything about those creatures is an abomination. It would be easier if they didn't have captives to hold against us. And we could attack their compound."

Blazel agreed. Earlier in the day, he'd been on the team attempting to knock out the control beacon. "After this latest failure, I'm worried about Kaieli, Rolstrun, Maheli, and Bohandran, especially Kaieli. They're trapped there because of those damned explosive devices. Every time she goes to the meeting place with the recent escapees, I'm so afraid it will be her last run. We never know if the invaders will expand the beacon's range without us knowing about it."

He gulped, remembering the last time when she tripped, and his heart constricted. He had long since stopped thinking of her as competition for Rizelya's affections. Now, he considered Kaieli a friend.

Histrun patted his shoulder. "I have the same worries, son. At least now she's too consumed by her experimentation with the nucla to make the escape runs. When you talk to the Vhelopsi tomorrow, ask if they know how to disable the beacon. Their information has helped us tremendously."

"Yes, sir. They are becoming valuable allies."

The next day, Blazel traveled to the northern fortress as part of his job as liaison with the Vhelopsi. Vhelopsi continued to flee with the Posair men from the crater, and after the alliance, their women joined in the escapes through the fence. Fifty Vhelopsi now lived in the fortress. When Hairan's wife, Zebba, arrived via Gryphon over a chedan ago, he'd become even more willing to help the Posairs fight the invaders.

Blazel smiled at the beautiful golden Zebba cuddling next to Hairan.

After they exchanged pleasantries, Blazel leaned forward, his elbow on his knee. "The control beacon is a stumbling block. The dome prevents us from attacking the compound directly. Plus, we have many people still in the slave camp that we can't get out because of the explosive tracking device. We've learned if we destroy the control beacon, they won't be in danger."

"The beacon is well protected," Hairan said, rubbing his chin. His language skills had grown over the chedans he'd stayed with the Posairs. "The housing at the base is thick, and the Scourge set several kinds of traps around it. In addition, they make the tower from extremely strong metal. Even on our planet, we were unable to breach its defenses."

Blazel slumped in his seat, dejected. He'd hoped the Vhelopsi held the solution to the beacon problem.

Hairan lifted a long finger. "But we will assist in any way possible. The healer, Kaieli, is one who has a device implanted, and I am in her debt."

On the flight back to camp, Blazel glared at the pillar and the enemy compound. He rubbed his arms. "Every time we fly by that thing, its slimy, malevolent energy gives me the creeps."

Me, too. A shudder passed over Graak from beak to tail, and Blazel gripped the harness tighter. *If the Vhelopsi can't help us with the control beacon, perhaps one of the other slave species has the means and motivation to do so.*

"From what I understand, it all depends on whether Kaieli's success in her experiments with the nucla."

I don't envy her working with the nasty stuff.

"Neither do I. I wish she'd find something that worked soon. We're losing too many people, Posair and Gryphon, against the invader's larger force."

I have faith the Goddess will show Kaieli the way.

Blazel bent his head, hoping, praying, for this nightmare of a war to end before he lost close friends.

Rizelya - 6 de Godar, 1075

Haze filled Rizelya's vision. Familiar dark shapes milled in a small space barely large enough for them to move. Around her, pulses of heat signatures lit her senses. A tentacle snaked out, and she heard a scream as it brought a struggling man closer to her maw. He dangled momentarily in the air before the grip loosened and he fell.

Blood squirted, filling her mouth with its sweet flavor.

But it didn't satisfy her. Her hunger drove her to reach for another morsel even before she'd fully masticated and swallowed the first. Pain intruded on her feeding. One of her tentacles no longer worked. Fire burned in its place. She thrashed to rid herself of the pesky nuisance and called to her nest mates to protect her. She must eat. The force within her demanded more, and she must give it what it wanted. Something pierced her belly. Still, she reached for another blob of pulsing heat. Success! More food to chew. The fire intensified until it fought for her attention with the compulsion to feed. Even as the fire consumed her, she reached for the last small heat pulse.

Rizelya woke up screaming, slapping her arms to stop the fire racing over her skin.

"Hey, what's happening?" Aistrun's sleepy voice mumbled.

His voice broke the last of the dream's grip on Rizelya. Sense slowly returned. Over the chedans, her dreams had steadily grown worse. Exhausted from all the fighting, her mental blocks lost their effectiveness. She felt like she was battling a three-front war, and was losing on all fronts.

"Nothing, Aistrun," she said. "Go back to sleep."

She sat up, throwing her legs over the edge of the cot, and braced her elbows on her knees, her head in her hands, shaking. Blazel rubbed the small of her back.

"Rizelya? What's wrong, baby?" He kept his voice low.

"Just a dream. An awful dream."

He moved closer, curling around her and propping his head on an elbow. He raised an eyebrow. "Just a dream? Was it the Malvers woman again?"

She shook her head. "No, much worse. This time, I was in a control-janack as it attacked people in one of those damned cages. All it wanted was to feed. All it *could* do was feed. It didn't even feel pain." She swallowed several times, gagging at the taste of blood in her mouth.

"No wonder they continue to fight until they're dead when any other creature would flee. But why would she show you this? Why give us this advantage?"

"Advantage?" She turned to look at him, incredulous. "The monsters don't experience pain and only want to eat us. They're forced to eat us. How is that going to help? I'm pretty freaked about it."

He tapped her leg. "Knowing your enemy is always an advantage. In all the time our people have fought the monsters, we've never known what drove them to attack us, to specifically seek out Posairs as their prey."

Rizelya frowned. "What do you mean? They eat anything."

"Oh, for the love of the Mother!" Aistrun complained as he sat up. "I can't sleep listening to you talk about Malvers' monsters. Blazel, what do you mean they target Posairs?"

Several more people on their team sat on their cots, abandoning sleep.

Blazel sat up and put an arm around her. "Haven't you ever noticed that once a Posair is in feeding range, they ignore all other prey?"

Rizelya started to shake her head, then stopped. "You're right, Blazel!"

"This is an opportunity to get an upper hand. Tell us what you saw."

She gulped, not wanting to relive the terrifying experience. She leaned into his strong shoulder, glad no one had lit a lantern.

"Rizelya, I know it was horrible. But anything you can remember could help us. We won't be fighting the invaders forever. What we learn may give us the advantage we need to destroy the Malvers—and their monsters—for good this time." His eyes burned with intensity. "So tell me."

She nodded and closed her eyes, recalling the dream, and shuddered. She opened her eyes to find Aistrun sat on her other side, his hand on her thigh. Chariel, on the floor in front of her, placed her hands on Rizelya's feet. Jaehaas stood to the side of the cot, Wisah cradled against his chest. Leistral, Laynar, Gehan, Maellyn, Grazeen, Raeleen, Saffren, with their warriors holding them, sat behind Chariel. People shifted as Dehali and her twin lovers, Kami and Tami, joined the circle.

Her pack.

Although fear haunted their eyes, anger tightened their mouths. Love flowed to her, supporting her.

"Whatever you need," Chariel said, "we will give you."

Wisah put a hand on Rizelya's shoulder. "The Goddess brought us together for a reason. She has allowed the Malvers woman to reach into your mind to help us, not to hurt you. Together, we are stronger than we are when alone. This is our strength, and the Malvers' weakness. Tell us what you have seen and let us share the burden with you."

Clasping her hands between her knees, Rizelya relayed her vision in a trance-like voice. When she reached the end, Blazel took a deep breath and started asking probing questions. The others joined him, and together they pushed her to remember every encounter she'd had with the Malvers woman, every dream she'd endured. Dawn came, and the day lengthened before they drained her dry.

As they finally walked to the mess tent, Rizelya stretched and released the dream. She didn't know how this would help, but she'd go through this suffering, and more, if it did. She wanted her people to do more than just survive. It was time they thrived.

Rizelya - 7 de Godar, 1075

The next day, Rizelya waited at the meeting site, pacing. She peered at Glork. "Are they coming yet?"

He shook his head. *The scouts will inform us when they leave.*

The escape runs were becoming more dangerous as the invaders patrolled a wider area around their compound. They'd had to move their meeting site three times in the past chedan to avoid detection. The increased patrols required the women to close the original hole in the fence and create a new one.

Rizelya nibbled on her lower lip. "How much longer can we continue doing this? The Scourge almost caught the last escapees."

Blazel shrugged. "It's dangerous, but we can't do anything else." He turned and glared in the direction of the compound. "We need to convert the Faeorn into allies. Hairan told me they are the true power behind the Scourge. All of their technology, all of their advancements, the Faeorn made possible. They even designed the machines powering their spaceships. But getting the Faeorn to turn on their masters is difficult, if not impossible. The Vhelopsi tried, and failed, when the Scourge attacked their home world, Vhel."

"But they didn't have Kaieli." Rizelya smirked. "She can charm anyone. I have faith she'll captivate the Faeorn, too.

They come, Glork informed her. *Kaieli is with them.*

"What is she doing with them?" Blazel thrust his hands on his hips and scowled. "We're right on the edge of the safety zone for those damned devices. She could get killed!"

Rizelya's eyebrows raised at his vehemence. She cared for Kaieli, but when had he'd started caring for her?

We are within the specified two measures, Graak assured Blazel. *She and the others will be fine.*

A few milcrons later, the ragged group of escapees staggered around the outcropping of petrified logs. Overhead, a phalanx of Gryphons appeared as they released their invisibility spell and dropped to the ground. Rizelya and Blazel helped the escapees onto the Gryphons, waving to them as they left the Barrens.

Rizelya gaped at the gauntness of her friend's face and how scrawny she appeared. Recovering, Rizelya hugged Kaieli, grimacing at the bones digging into her chest.

"How are your experiments?" Rizelya asked. "It's all anyone who escapes talks about."

She waved toward the people being fitted into harnesses on the waiting Gryphons. The space seemed tiny, with twenty huge Gryphons packed into it.

"Frustrating!" Kaieli kicked a rock. "We've learned a thousand ways that don't work. We're not making any progress. Maybe you can help. Loshera thinks we need a fresh perspective because we're all out of ideas." She told them about the experiments and the lack of results. "We can purge the poison from our people, but not from the damned rocks. The malignant magic in them resists and fights us. If it was only in them, we'd have more success. But the stones *are* malignant magic."

"It reminds me of something I read a long time ago." Blazel rested his chin on his fist, scowling. "I remember now! I read an account about the crater's creation in a book I found in a hidden stash at the Sanctuary's library." He shrugged. "Shandir intended to gather all the malevolent magic in the area, concentrate it, and destroy it. She only succeeded in the first two. The swamps are nothing but nasty, maligned magic."

Kaieli frowned. "They are?"

Blazel nodded. "I've spent enough time in them to notice."

Kaieli tapped her chin. "Rolstrun observed the Malvers' monsters need the malignant magic to form. Or the malevolent magic pools create the monsters. We're not quite sure which."

Hope surged through Rizelya. "So if we discover a way to eliminate the malignant magic, we destroy the monsters?"

"It appears likely." Kaieli said.

Blazel crossed his arms, harrumphing. "The Supreme's have tried removing it ever since the Great War, and can't destroy it. Why do you think you can accomplish what they haven't done in a thousand years?"

"Because we're using Black Talent, or as close to it as possible." Kaieli shoulders slumped. "However, we're lacking something. We just don't know what it is."

It seems to me, Kaieli, Graak said, his tone thoughtful, *if you are attempting to create Black energy, you are missing a key Talent. Gray.*

"But I have Gray Talent."

It isn't your primary one.

"True. None of the keeps captured had any Grays." Kaieli scowled and thumped her fist against her thigh. She looked speculatively at Rizelya. "How are your experiments coming? Have you and your team created Black Talent together?"

Rizelya grimaced. "No. We've been too busy fighting. The few times we've tried, we can't get our magic to meld as thoroughly as you do. Whatever you do, we're missing it. I think we'll have to observe what you do it to figure out what we're doing wrong."

Kaieli rubbed her face. "Crone's Fires! My team is the only ones able to work on the awful stuff. And everyone comes from either Posanreande Keep or the Strunland guard-pack. We all have the devices implanted. You wouldn't happen to have an extra Gray stupid enough—I mean willing—to come to the compound?"

Blazel and Rizelya looked at each other.

"She would," Rizelya said. "You know she would."

Blazel sighed. "Yes, she would. But in there? Don't you need her out here to form the net-shield?"

"We do, but this is more important." Excitement coursed through Rizelya. "If we rid the nucla of malignant magic, perhaps we can extend the process and clear it from the swamps. No more monsters! We can manage without her."

"But she reacts so violently when she comes into contact with the invaders. She'll go insane around all the death permeating the compound."

"I don't want her in that hellhole any more than I want Kaieli and the others to stay in it. But sometimes we do what we must for the good of all. This is one of those times."

She is much stronger than you give her credit for. Graak scratched his chest feathers with a talon.

"We aren't talking about the Gray Oracle, are we?" Kaieli's eyebrows raised, and her mouth dropped open.

"Yes. Chariel. She's my friend." Blazel pinched the bridge of his nose. "If you need Gray Talent, she has plenty of it."

"Would she come?" Kaieli's voice held hope.

I'm sure of it, Graak said. The tip of his tail flicked.

Rizelya whirled and faced Graak. "What did you do?"

I asked her. His tone was smug, and he lowered his beak into what passed for a Gryphon grin. *She and Sheekeek are flying here now.*

Rizelya dropped her head into her hands and groaned. "Histrun is going to kill me if she gets hurt."

"No, that will be my honor." Blazel patted her shoulder.

Graak eased onto the sand and wiggled a bit, curling his tail around his body. *They won't arrive for a while. You might as well get comfortable.*

"But I have to return soon," Kaieli protested.

Do not worry, honored healer, Glork said, as he settled next to Graak, laying his beak across the bigger Gryphon's back. *I will carry you to the compound.*

Rizelya studied Kaieli critically. "Kaieli, dear heart, let him take you. You look ready to drop." Rizelya sat on a boulder in the shade of Glork's body and patted it. "Come, sit with me."

Kaieli hesitated, then sank down next to Rizelya.

Rizelya put an arm around Kaieli, who rested her head on Rizelya's shoulder.

"It feels so nice to be gone from the invader's evil, if only for a little while." She told Rizelya about Posanreande Keep falling, life as a slave, and finding love with Rolstrun. As she talked, tears coursed down her cheeks.

When she finally finished, Rizelya brushed away her tears. "You're an amazing woman, Kaieli. I'm glad you've found Rolstrun. I hope he makes you as happy, and as frustrated, as Blazel does me."

They come, Graak said, his voice rumbly as he woke up. She'd discovered the Gryphons could drift instantaneously into a doze, like the felines they resembled. He stood, knocking Glork's head off his back. Glork jerked to his feet and shook his head, glaring at Graak.

Sheekeek landed. Chariel, already dressed in the orange coveralls of a captive, jumped off Sheekeek with practiced ease. "What do you need me to do?" She ran a hand over her gray braids.

Rizelya quickly explained.

"Well, then," Chariel said, "of course, I'll help." She gave Rizelya a wry smile. "You did tell me once the Goddess also expects her priestesses to be warriors. This is an important battle."

Rizelya smiled at her sadly. "Yes, I did. But I didn't suspect you'd be entering a viper's nest." She helped Kaieli onto Glork. "Be safe, my friends."

As they flew, she wondered if she'd made a mistake or if she'd saved the Posairs.

"I'm so dead. Histrun is going to be furious when he discovers where we sent Chariel."

"He's going to kill us both," Blazel agreed. "Why don't we avoid him as long as possible? There's just you, me—"

And me! Graak chimed in, laughter in his voice.

The comment shot down whatever amorous intentions Blazel had in mind. He pulled Rizelya into his embrace. They settled on the warm stones, leaning against Graak's soft back while they waited for Glork and Sheekeek to return.

Chapter 21

Kaieli - 7 de Godar, 1075

As Glork approached the compound, Kaieli frowned at the invaders scurrying below. Soldiers streamed into the fighting ships as they readied for another attack on the Posairs' base. She wondered when they'd learn the ships were no match for the Thunder Wings. Each time they went out, at least one didn't return. The Thunder Wings had destroyed seven of the original twenty-four ships.

The Gryphons used their invisibility spell to land next to the current hole in the fence. As Kaieli and Chariel slipped off and thanked their rides, a commotion rose near the sheezet pens. The diversion allowed them to ease through the fence and sprint into the processing plant.

While she bent over, catching her breath, Kaieli examined Chariel, hoping she hadn't made a mistake bringing her into the compound. Chariel panted, and her wide eyes darted around the plant. Her hands scrunched the fabric of her coverall. Finally, she closed her eyes for a few moments, and took long, deep breaths.

"Are you okay?" Kaieli asked, lightly touching Chariel's shoulder.

"There's been so much death here. So many frightened souls." Chariel took several more deep breaths, then stood straight, her shoulders thrown back. "We have to stop the invaders, and this work will help us."

Kaieli marveled at the change in Chariel. Perhaps she would survive this after all. Kaieli peeked around the corner. The machines clanked and hissed, but she didn't see any guards. "Let's go try zapping the malignant magic out of the rocks. And hope it doesn't take another thousand tries."

She hustled Chariel to her makeshift infirmary, where they had a modicum of privacy from the guard's prying eyes. She nodded at Loshera. Faliciden bowed her head over a woman's bleeding leg, and didn't look up at their entry. A few moments later, Maheli, Jaelena, and Noriana slipped behind the infirmary's curtain. Kaieli introduced her team to Chariel.

Maheli studied Chariel for a moment before extending her hand. "You must be Blazel's friend. He told us about you."

Chariel took the proffered hand and smiled. "Yes, he mentioned meeting you, too." She rubbed her arms. She picked up a rock, quickly dropping it and scrubbed her hands on her thighs. "Ugh, that's nasty energy. I'm excited to try this blending of Talents you've been doing. We've attempted to replicate what you're doing, but it never works for us. It keeps sliding away. Our team can combine our Talents to make a strong shield, but nothing more. Until you told Rizelya about it, I'd never heard of anyone combining their magic before, and I grew up in the Sanctuary. If anyone would attempt it, the Supreme would."

"She hasn't had to deal with that stuff." Kaieli pointed at the rocks and wrinkled her nose.

"I doubt she has."

Kaieli sat on a crate. "We first chanced upon the method while treating the plague in Posanreande Keep. We refined it when we attempted healing a man after an overseer beat him with a nucla laced whip."

"With you here, Chariel," Loshera said, "we now have all seven Talents. When we merge, the power feels like what I believe Black would be. It should be even more powerful when you join us." She rubbed her hands together. "Shall we try?"

The horn blared, announcing the end of the day.

Maheli glared at the ceiling. "No time now. We have to return to the slave pens," she explained to Chariel.

"But don't worry," Noriana added, grimacing. "We'll get plenty of practice in a little while when we heal the men."

As the others filed out, Faliciden stopped Chariel. "Here, let me fix your hair before you leave. The invaders aren't color blind and will know you're new here." She placed her hands on Chariel's head and closed her eyes. After a few moments, the strands in Chariel's braid appeared to be the same lackluster, dirty brown as Kaieli's.

Later, after the meager food somewhat dulled Kaieli's hunger, the group of women sat at their usual table and held hands. Kaieli slipped her hand in Chariel's, including her in their circle.

"Access your magic and gently add it to mine," Kaieli whispered to Chariel. She already held the other women's magic in her mental grasp. Power surged toward her, and she gasped. It immediately toned down, and Kaieli gathered the Gray strands, weaving them with the others. Silvery light pulsed along the threads, merging them, until they formed one thick, black band of power. Kaieli briefly wondered how much more powerful it would be if all the women in the circle possessed the same level of Talent as she and Chariel.

She turned her attention to the business at hand and directed the energy first to Rolstrun, then Bohandran. They moved progressively outward until they purged every man in the pens of the nucla.

Power continued to pulse in her mind. She touched her group, surprised when no one showed signs of fatigue. Taking advantage, she aimed the magic toward the other women captives. They also suffered with the nucla poisoning from their constant exposure in the processing plant, where it seeped into their bodies. Before, her team hadn't had the energy before to treat the women. When they finished, she opened her eyes and broke contact with her team. They blinked and shook their hands.

"That... was... amazing." Noriana's eyes were bright, and her face was flushed.

"With you, Chariel," Jaelena said, "we'll surely be able to destroy the malignant magic."

"I can only hope so." Chariel dipped her head. When she lifted it, her eyes danced with excitement. "I understand now what we were doing wrong. You weave each strand of magic together into a cohesive thread before you direct it. I've just been gathering it in a bunch. I'll have to tell Rizelya." Her shoulders slumped. "But because I'm here, she doesn't have a Gray to help her."

Over the next few days, Kaieli's team worked to find a way to purge the nucla. But they had as little success with removing or destroying the malignant magic from the rocks as before Chariel arrived. Outside, the battles between the invaders and the Posair and Gryphon armies continued to rage. At night, Rolstrun, and the other men, regaled the women with stories about the fighting over the crater. The Scourge added a few Posair fighters they captured to the slave pens. The invaders never apprehended a Gryphon. At least if they did, they didn't toss them into the slave pens with the Posairs.

Five days after Chariel's arrival, the women were marching to the processing plant when a bright light flashed overhead. A humongous golden Gryphon bombarded the protective barricade with four black Thunder Wings accompanying him. Pulses of energy crackled along the fence and dome. Kaieli held her breath, hoping they had at last discovered how to destroy the energy dome. The invader's massive weapons boomed, and the Gryphons dipped and dived, evading the projectiles. Her feet stumbled in dejection when the crackling stopped and the dome still stood, undamaged. Kaieli followed the others into the plant with renewed determination to find a way to purge the nucla. They needed the Volkern and Faeorn assistance to take down the control beacon and energy dome, and they would only help if the Posairs cleared the nucla.

That afternoon, Tre'nok replaced Vy'shol as the interpreter for the processing plant. When he entered the infirmary, his blue skin was paler than normal, and tense lines formed around his nose and mouth.

"Have you made any progress on the nucla?" Tre'nok's gaze paused on Chariel, and his blue-green eyes widened.

"Not as much as we'd hoped. But we have more help now." Kaieli placed a hand on his thin forearm. She sensed pain radiating from him. "Are you okay?"

"I'm fine." His grimaced belied his words.

Kaieli folded her arms across her chest and raised an eyebrow.

Tre'nok huffed. "The commander is furious with your rebellion. He lashes out at whoever is closest. Sometimes, a Volkern or a Faeorn catches the brunt of his anger, which has never happened before."

"Here, let me heal you." She placed her hand on his shoulder, allowing her healing energy to flow into him. Perhaps if she showed them their usefulness, the Volkern would help even if her team couldn't nullify the nucla.

Kaieli and the other women slumped back to the slave pens after an especially frustrating day. Even after a chedan of adding Chariel's impressive power to theirs, the malignant magic still fought them. That evening, after healing the Posairs and eating, they continued to sit at their table instead of heading to their beds. Kaieli glared at the uncooperative, unresponsive rock squatting in the center of the table. It resisted everything they threw at it. Frustration welled in Kaieli, and she brushed away the moisture in her eyes. She considered releasing the weaved magic and end the latest fiasco when she felt a hand on her shoulder.

The magic shifted.

The black braid of their combined Talents pulsed in the rhythm of a heartbeat. It surrounded the malignant magic and squeezed. The evil magic squirmed and wriggled, attempting to escape the crushing grip. Flashes of light, in all the Talent's colors, raced up and down the braided magic. With each flare, some of the evil disintegrated, until at last, a bright, pure white light blazed. Kaieli blinked away the momentary blindness and examined the stone with her magical senses. *Oh, Sweet Goddess! Finally!* None of the malignant magic remained. When she opened her eyes, the rock hadn't changed, looking like the same, glossy black.

"What happened?" Loshera blinked rapidly as she shook her head.

Kaieli gazed behind her and into Rolstrun's shocked eyes. His hand still rested on her shoulder, trembling.

"What... what was that?" he said in a shaky voice.

Chariel stared at him before whooping and laughing. "That's what we were missing! Masculine magic."

Everyone looked at her, confused.

"But... but... I don't have any magic." Rolstrun's eyes were wide as he slumped to the bench.

"Yes, you do." Chariel smiled. "Every male does. It's what allows you to shift into your wolf and warrior forms. You didn't surrender your magic, only exchanged it for a different type. Some, like Blazel, have access to more of their original magic than most. But it's still there."

Chariel steepled her hands. "The Goddess's main tenet is balance. She does not rule alone, but rules with her consort, just like the alphas rule the keeps as a pair. Our magic lacked balance without the addition of a male's magic." She leaned over the table and patted Rolstrun's hand.

Kaieli picked up the rock, grinning when her stomach didn't clench with queasiness. They'd done it! They'd discovered how to destroy the malignant magic in it.

Rolstrun - 15 de Godar, 1075

Rolstrun stared at his hand resting on Kaieli's shoulder, still stunned by what he'd just experienced. He slumped to the bench while the women excitedly talked about what happened. The magic that the women wove seemed completely different from what he accessed to shift into his wolf or warrior forms. Yet, both types also flowed from the same source. His thoughts flew back to the day before his capture when he created a small spark with his Red Talent. He hadn't dreamed then he'd ever do something like purging the nucla.

As they walked to the pallet they now shared, Kaieli chattered excitedly. "I can't believe we did it! After all those thousands of tries, all it took was you. I don't know why we didn't think of it sooner. It makes perfect sense. You know what this means, don't you?"

His eyebrows knitted together, and he shook his head.

"You won't have to work in the dreadful crater. We'll need you with us so we can purge the nucla. It'll be much easier for you to join us in the processing plant with us than for us to go into the crater." She laughed, something he'd never heard her do in this wretched place.

Rolstrun's hope rose, and the cloud of despair lifted a little. He'd much rather spend his days lost in the amazing magic he'd recently experienced than chopping at the pillar. His shoulders drooped. As nice as it sounded, the Scourge wouldn't allow him, a man, into the processing plant.

"I'd love to do that, but how?"

They reached their pallet. Kaieli examined him for a long moment, tapping her chin with her finger. "Maybe we can dress you up as a woman? Faliciden can do minor illusions. She made Chariel's hair appear dirty and brown, instead of clean and gray." Her eyes lit up, and she caressed his face. "We have hope now, Rolstrun. After I show this to Tre'nok, he's sure to help us. This breakthrough means we can strike back at the Scourge. This will hurt the commander as much as killing him would do, perhaps even more. He'll take the inert nucla back to his home world and lose status, if not his life, for bringing back a stockpile of useless rock. Just think about it." A malicious glint entered her eyes as she grinned and rubbed her hands together.

Rolstrun smiled slowly at the image of Commander Ke-ke-tak's punishment and death. He'd fantasized about tearing out the sick bastard's throat, but this revenge would work. Rolstrun bent his head and kissed Kaieli. She responded to him, pressing against his body. His hands found her soft breast through the rough slave coverall, but it wasn't enough. He needed to run his hands over her entire body and sink himself into her depths. He'd been in a fog of despair for so long, he wanted to reaffirm he was alive—that she was alive. Hope for the future blossomed as he made love to Kaieli.

Kaieli - 16 de Godar, 1075

Kaieli paced in front of the infirmary while watching the main door. Her heart thundered in her chest. She glanced at the rock they'd cleared last night. To her ordinary senses, it didn't appear any different. Would it fool the invaders? She scowled and glared at an untreated specimen. She scanned the two with her magical senses. One crawled with malignant magic, and one didn't. Did the invader's machines register the malignant magic?

Finally, Tre'nok and Vy'shol casually sauntered through the plant. A few milcrons later, the Faeorn triad she'd treated—what seemed a lifetime ago—entered as well. The female, Mei-Ying Yoon, led the three. Her belly protruded slightly, and her pale, white skin glowed. Jei-Yan Yoon, the male, and Pei Yoon, the gomale, walked protectively on either side of her. They stopped at several stations and examined the machinery.

First Vy'shol, then Mei-Ying slipped into the infirmary.

Mei-Ying ran a delicate hand over her belly. Her eyes crinkled at the corners as she smiled. "Thank you. Now have babies because you help."

"Do you need any prenatal care? I'd be glad to give it to you."

Vy'shol translated.

Mei-Ying held up her palm. "No, we fine."

Tre'nok slipped through the infirmary's curtain, followed shortly by the other two Faeorn.

Tre'nok stared at the two rocks. "Did you find a way to destroy the nucla?"

"We think so. You tell me." Kaieli gestured to the waiting stones.

Pei stepped forward and peered intently at them, picking one up and examining it before putting it down to do the same to the other one. Pei handed them one at a time to Jei-Yan, who held a small machine. He ran it over them. The device buzzed and blipped, and the same green lights lit up on it for both rocks.

Jei-Yan frowned. "Which you fix?"

Kaieli grinned and bounced on her toes. Perhaps this would work after all if the Faeorn couldn't tell the difference. She pointed to the rock still in his hand. "That one."

He ran the machine over both the rocks again. His frown deepened as he talked to Tre'nok.

"He says," Tre'nok translated, "the meter reads the same for both specimens. The scans still read both as nucla. Are you sure you did something to it?"

"The... meter? ...must not be able to detect malignant magic. This one," Kaieli tapped the rock, "is no longer saturated with it. To me, it is simply an ordinary rock."

Tre'nok translated. The Faeorn talked among themselves, until finally, Jei-Yan pulled another device from his pocket. Meanwhile, Pei used another tool to chop the rock into small chunks and placed a piece into the machine Jei-Yan held. Green lights blinked, and it hummed for several milcrons, before a yellow light flashed furiously and the hum slowed. A red light flared, and the noise ceased. In a moment, the red light faded.

The two Faeorn grinned, talking excitedly, hands waving in the air, hugging each other and their mate.

Tre'nok translated. His eyes lost their haggardness, and he stood straighter. "You did it! Sufficient nucla remains in the rock to run the invader's machinery for a short time, a very short time, enough to make them believe nothing is amiss. The residual mineral is quickly used, leaving nothing but, as you say, an ordinary rock behind. How fast can you treat the rest?"

Kaieli's eyes widened. "All of it? Have you noticed how big the pillar is?"

"I have. It is necessary if you want to protect your world from the Scourge." He sat on a crate, his elbows on his knees, as he leaned forward. "Right now, Commander Ke-ke-tak hasn't told anyone else the location of this mother lode of nucla. His greed is keeping it a secret. But if he leaves here without mining the entire vein, he will return. And next time, he won't bring a small mining operation with him."

"Small! He brought over half a million soldiers," Kaieli protested, sinking onto another crate.

"Next time, his fleet will contain five conquest ships, all three times bigger than the mining ship he brought here. The fighting force will be large enough to conquer this planet within days. When they are done, your people will be slaves—or dead—and nothing will remain of the planet but an empty husk.

"As it is, they are unused to such concentrated resistance as your people are giving them. The commander's arrogance is keeping him from contacting his house for more soldiers. He can't believe so small a population, and with so little technology, is holding him at bay."

Tre'nok tilted his head thoughtfully while gazing at the Faeorn triad. He seemed to come to a decision and talked with the Faeorn for a long time. Finally, Mei-Ying rubbed her belly, nodding. Tre'nok turned back to Kaieli. "The triads agree to help you deactivate the control beacon and the energy dome, but only when the cargo hold is filled with non-active nucla. If they assist you, and the commander finds out, it will be not only their lives, but the lives of every other Faeorn."

Kaieli gripped the sides of the crate to stop herself from jumping up in excitement. The Posairs needed more from the Faeorn to defeat the Scourge. She folded her arms over her chest and frowned. "To do this means I and all of my team must stay in the slave camp, and so must others to keep our efforts hidden. We'll be in peril of additional poisoning and death. It is as much a danger to us as it is to them. If the Faeorn want us to take the risk, they must help us in the meantime. Share with us everything you know about the Scourge, so we can throw them off our planet and ensure Ke-ke-tak never returns. The Vhelopsi are already helping. Why not the Volkern and Faeorn, too?" She leaned forward, staring into Tre'nok's eyes. "None—let me repeat—none of our people are going back with them as slaves."

"Are you not now slaves?" Tre'nok's eyebrows crinkled in confusion.

"No, we're not. We are captives. Prisoners of war. Our people are fighting for our freedom, for our planet's freedom. The battles won't stop until we're free and the Scourge gone. You've helped our children escape, which makes it easier for us to do."

Tre'nok stared at her for a long time. "If you succeed in defeating the Scourge, and we help you, we may end up abandoned on your planet with no way home. The Vhelopsi have enough people for a viable genetic pool, and this world is very similar to their home. It makes sense for them to help you. But there aren't many Faeorn and Volkern. When we die, our race disappears from this part of the galaxy." He studied her for a long time. "Will the Posair people welcome us as refugees?"

"Yes, we would welcome you. You are our allies."

"We are unlike your people. How can you be so certain?"

Kaieli laughed and gestured toward the sky. "Have you seen our other allies, the Gryphons? They are more different from us than your races. Besides, you may be getting the worst end of the deal. Life here isn't without its struggles and challenges. We'll still be in a war with the Malvers' monsters when the invaders leave, like we have been for a thousand years. Who knows how much longer it will be?"

Tre'nok talked with the Faeorn and Vy'shol quietly again. A tiny smile played at the corner of his mouth. "We are in agreement. We'll take our chances. What do you want to know?"

"Anything you can tell me about their physiology would help. We can't figure out how they feed. What is their home world like? Is there anything poisonous to them? You mentioned our sun gives off radiation they can't handle. Is there some way we could use it against them?" Excitement made her toss out the questions she'd held inside for so long.

"Sunscreen," Jei-Yan said.

Tre'nok listened to him, a smile growing on his lips. "The Faeorn will adjust the Scourge's sunscreen to make it less effective."

Mei-Ying pulled a tablet of paper from her pocket and quickly drew several detailed sketches of the invader's anatomy, while Pei and Jei-Yan made drawings of the ships.

"This ship," Tre'nok pointed to the drawing of the scout ship, "can travel interstellar. We could return home in it." His voice sounded wistful.

Kaieli wouldn't want to be stranded on a strange planet with no hope of returning home. "We'll try to retrieve it for you. It might need to be repaired, though."

"We can make any repairs, if it means we can go home."

After the Volkern and Faeorn left, Kaieli sat shuffling through the drawings and notes she'd made. She groaned at the daunting task before her of destroying the malignant magic in the nucla—the literal mountain of nucla. Her excitement drained.

Kaieli straightened her shoulders. Somewhere, in all the information, lay the answer of how to defeat the invaders. But she didn't need to find it. She'd send it to Bethlyn and Rizelya to sort through. She found a clean sheet of paper and wrote her observations. Chariel wandered in and picked up the drawings of the invader's anatomy, studying them. A silvery glaze covered her eyes momentarily, and she blinked. "Are you sending these to Rizelya?"

Kaieli nodded. "To her and Bethlyn."

"Give this one to Blazel." She tilted the paper so Kaieli could note which one to send. "Remind him he spent three years in the swamps for a reason."

"Anything else I should tell him?"

"No, that's it." Chariel put the drawing down. "I take it our procedure worked."

"It did. Better than we expected. There's enough residual magic left to make it appear and act like nucla. But it's quickly used up."

Kaieli finished with her notes, rolled all the sheets together, and stuffed it in a pouch. She tucked it in a hiding spot until she could catch a Gryphon's attention in their next raid, which shouldn't be more than a day or two.

Later in the afternoon, Kaieli took a break, and evading any guards, she strolled to the crater rim, studying the huge pillar. Terraces cut into it, making the monolith no longer symmetrical. Even though the men had removed significant chunks from the pillar already, so much more remained. As she watched, the uppermost layer tumbled down. The specks—the men—rushed to escape the falling debris. How could her small group clear the malignant magic from such a large amount of rock? The task ahead of her and her team seemed impossible.

Rolstrun - 16 de Godar, 1075

Rolstrun shaved his face for the first time since being captured. Noriana found a scarf from somewhere, which she tied over his head, covering his close-cut hair. Maheli used an extra coverall to stuff the top of his suit. Jaelena artfully smeared dirt on his face, hiding the sharp, masculine contours and making them seem more rounded, more feminine. Faliciden added a few illusion touches to finish off the facade. They stepped back from their work, eying him critically.

Kaieli studied him with a hand covering her mouth. "If they don't pay attention to him too closely, he should pass as a woman."

Rolstrun glowered at her. Alestrun and Calistrun had no trouble in dashing his sensibilities, and burst into laughter.

"You need to swing your hips more." Alestrun walked a few steps, swinging his hips far to one side and then to the other. He stopped and turned, posing with one hand on his chin and the other on his hip in an exaggerated feminine stance.

"And you have to bat your eyelashes." Calistrun fluttered his eyes and pursed his lips.

"Keep it up," Rolstrun growled, trying not to laugh with them. "It could be you next." He doubted his magic was anything special, and possibly any man could add their masculine energy. He hoped Kaieli was insisting he join them because she knew and cared for him.

The work horn blared, and Alestrun and Calistrun, still chortling, left the pen with the other men as they marched to the crater. Rolstrun watched them go, grinning. It was the first time he'd heard Calistrun laugh in chedans. A few milcrons later, the second horn blasted, and Rolstrun slid into the line, surrounded by Kaieli's team of women.

He slouched to minimize his height, and dropped his head, watching his feet to hide his face. During the entire walk from the slave pens to the processing plant, he kept expecting a guard to notice their subterfuge. He let out a whoosh of relief when they reached the plant. Rolstrun scurried into the infirmary area.

He and the other women on the team crowded into the small space, waiting anxiously while Kaieli talked to Tre'nok. Rolstrun chewed a fingernail while listening to their exchange, hoping Kaieli's demonstration convinced the Volkerns and Faeorns to become their allies. When Tre'nok agreed, Rolstrun whooped and pumped his fist in the air. Maheli slugged his arm for his outburst, then pulled him into a hug.

A while later, after the discussions with the Volkern and Faeorn, Kaieli entered the enclosed area.

"So how do we do this?" Rolstrun asked, a little unsure of himself now they'd proved their method worked.

"We hold hands," Kaieli answered. "It's easier to meld our Talents if we're touching. We'll form a circle around whatever we're clearing. I'll weave our Talents together and blast it with our combined magic. Simple." She shrugged, but her wide eyes belied her statement.

He'd hacked at the pillar and knew how many tons of rock they must purge. His earlier jubilation diminished.

Kothera brought in a crate of the processed and cubed nucla. "Did you persuade them to become our allies?"

Kaieli nodded. "But only if we cleanse *all* the nucla."

Kothera's eyes widened, then her jaw set in determination. "We can do this. Let us know what you need, and we'll bring it to you. The faster you get it done, the sooner we leave this miserable place."

After an octar without success, Kaieli finally threw her hands into the air. "Ugh, why isn't this working? It worked last night."

Chariel picked up a cube, glaring at it. "This form has compacted the malignant magic too much."

"Last night, we worked on a piece of raw ore," Rolstrun pointed out.

Maheli patted his back. "True. We're still new to doing this, so let's treat this like anything else we learn to do. We start with simple tasks, like the raw ore. Once we're accomplished in that skill, and stronger melding our Talents, we clear the condensed nucla."

The other women nodded in agreement, and Kothera brought in a small bin of ore. This time, it only took a few milcrons for their magic to drive the malignant magic from the rocks. When the end-of-day horn blared, Rolstrun surveyed the treated rock, pleased with their progress, even though they'd only cleansed half of a cartload of ore.

Chapter 22

Rizelya - 19 de Godar, 1075

Rizelya ducked another onslaught of projectiles, grimacing as they sailed past her head. She quickly gripped the harness as Glork made a sudden dive and spun away. As he leveled out, she realigned her helbraught and directed a burst of flames toward the soldiers firing on them. One screeched as he batted frantically at the fire burning his face. Glork flared, his own flames engulfing the injured invader, plus two more.

Rizelya glanced around, getting her bearings. During the fight, she and Glork had drifted toward the processing plant and the compound's fence. She wondered about Kaieli and Chariel's experiments. Had they found a way yet to purge the nucla? The day Chariel infiltrated the invaders' camp was the last time any captives had escaped.

"Let's get closer, Glork," Rizelya urged. "I want to try contacting Kaieli or Chariel."

Gladly! I too worry about Chariel. Glork angled his flight directly at the processing plant, and cloaked them with his invisibility. *I hope she is all right in that monster's den.*

Kaieli! Chariel! Rizelya called, hoping her mind-speech would pass through the energy dome's barrier. After listening closely, she called again.

Look! Glork pointed to the fence with a talon. *Someone's leaving. It appears to be Kaieli.*

The woman lugged a bulging pouch secured over her shoulder and chest, and she staggered as she ran. Glork dived, snatching Kaieli in his talons and extending his invisibility to her. He flew until they passed beyond the fighting, but still within the control beacon's confines. When he lowered Kaieli to the ground, she crumbled. Blazel and Graak, who had followed them, landed beside Glork.

Rizelya scrambled out of her harness and gathered Kaieli in her arms.

"Are you hurt?" Rizelya brushed the tangled, matted locks from Kaieli's forehead.

"Fine. Just tired." Kaieli struggled to sit up. She sipped from the water skin Blazel gave her. "We figured out how to destroy the malignant magic in the nucla. You wouldn't believe the missing piece. It was Rolstrun!"

"Rolstrun?" Rizelya's eyebrows crinkled in confusion.

"Well, it could have been any man. We needed masculine magic to balance all the feminine we were using."

Rizelya scratched her head, still confused, but Blazel's eyes brightened.

"Oh," Blazel said, "that makes perfect sense. The Goddess always works in harmony with Her Consort."

Kaieli pulled the strap over her head, opened the pouch, and took out a roll of papers. She spread them out on the ground in front of her. "We also have good intelligence about the invaders—lots of it. The Volkern and Faeorn are finally allying with us in exchange for our help."

"Oh, wow!" Rizelya knelt beside Kaieli. Finely drawn images of the invader's anatomy and ships covered many of them, along with notes written in Kaieli's handwriting. Rizelya longed to snatch the papers and rifle through them. But as Blazel crouched opposite Kaieli, and the Gryphons crowded around them, she stifled the yearning. The others also needed to see the papers.

Kaieli held out the drawings of the ships and pointed to the mid-sized ship. "They want this one so they can return to their homes. Do you think between you and the Gryphons you can take it for them? I've seen some huge Gryphons during the raids."

Graak craned his neck to peer closer at the drawings. *Three or four Thunder Wings could carry that.*

Kaieli shuffled through the papers and extracted a sheet, handing it to Blazel. "Here, this is for you. Chariel told me to give it to you specifically and to remind you that you spent time in the swamps for a reason."

Frowning, Blazel took the sheet. "Yeah, she sent me there to save our people," he said, distracted as he studied the drawing. "I don't know what this has to do with the swamps, but if Chariel said it does, then I just have to figure out what it is. Thanks." He stood and wandered off, staring at the paper and muttering to himself.

Kaieli stood, brushing off the seat of her coveralls. "I need to get back."

After letting Kaieli off near the fence opening, Rizelya and Blazel returned to the fighting. She itched with curiosity to open the pouch from Kaieli. Did it contain the key to defeating the Scourge? So far, the Posair war host hadn't won a decisive battle, but then, neither had their enemy. The Posairs were barely holding their own against the invader's superior numbers and weapons. Finally, the skirmish ended, and their team flew back to the base camp.

Rizelya glanced at Graak, walking beside her. Had it only been two lunadars since they'd met? It seemed much longer. The memory of the first prophecy she'd heard Chariel deliver floated through her mind. Chariel had said, *"A menace comes. No allies, the enemy wins and all die."* Her vision had sent them into the Deep Mountains to find the Gryphons. Rizelya thanked the Goddess for sending them the message. She grimly acknowledged the Gryphons were a huge reason the Scourge hadn't overrun them yet.

Inside the command tent, Histrun, Naila, and Moraak pored over the latest battle reports. They paused in their discussion when Rizelya cleared her throat.

"Do you have news?" Histrun put down the paper he held.

Naila rubbed the back of her neck. *Have Kaieli and Chariel found a way to destroy the nucla yet?*

"Yes!" Rizelya grinned, placing the pouch on the table. "Kaieli also succeeded in turning the Faeorn and Volkern into allies. They've given her valuable intelligence. We'll toss those damned invaders off our world soon."

They gave her schematics of the invader's flying ships, Graak added, his head feathers lifting in excitement. *We've had some success knocking them from the sky already, but now our teams can take them out more efficiently.*

That is good news. Moraak shook, resettling his feathers and fur. *Let's see what Kaieli has sent us.*

"Where's Blazel?" Naila's voice cracked, and she sipped on her cup of taevo.

Rizelya removed the roll of papers from the satchel, spreading them over the table. "Chariel gave him one of the drawings. He's with Bethlyn now. Perhaps we can use a biological agent against the invaders."

Graak pointed a talon at the drawing of the mid-sized ship. *Our allies say this one can travel through space. If we capture it, they could use it to return to their home.*

Moraak picked up the drawing in his talon and studied it. *The Thunder Wings can carry this. I will have Tuueek work with his flight. But there will undoubtedly be some damage to it from their talons, no matter how careful they are.*

"They know the risks," Rizelya added. "They say they can fix any damage, but try not to do too much. If I were them, I wouldn't want to be stranded on a strange planet with only a handful of my people."

Moraak dipped his head in acknowledgment, replacing the drawing on the table. He rifled through the other papers, cocking his head from side to side and clicking his beak. Finally, he choose a sketch of the various ships. *I'll have the Thunder Wings practice lifting the fighter and transport ships with minimal damage. We'll leave the one our allies want intact.* He dropped his beak in a grin. *Once they learn how, they can tear them into pieces. The Thunder Wings love doing that. This information will help them inflict more damage, faster and with less risk to themselves. If the invaders do not have ships, they cannot leave the Barrens.*

Naila smirked. "Easier to hunt if in one place."

Histrun rubbed his hands together, grinning. "True, true. Now, what else is here?" He picked up a document, examined it, then handed it to Naila before picking up the next one. When she'd finished her survey of it, she passed it to Moraak, who passed it to Graak and Rizelya. After everyone had a chance to review the information, they discussed the implications of what they'd learned.

Naila spread an image showing the invader's anatomies on the table. She tapped on the places indicating a weak point. *Knowing the enemy's weaknesses is invaluable. We've discovered some through trial and error. Rizelya, tell your fighters.*

"Yes, Alpha. This information will make it easier to kill them and save more of our people's lives."

"Maendy is still working on converting the enemy's weapons for our use," Histrun added, scrubbing at his beard. "Once we add those, the tide of the war should turn in our favor."

They continued to study the information the Faeorn sent. Rizelya glanced at the tent opening—again. *Did you catch a glimpse of the picture Chariel gave Blazel?* she asked Graak, whispering to him in mind-speech.

He shook his head, rubbing a talon on his beak. *It must be important. He's been with Bethlyn a long time.*

I'm curious what it was.

He gazed at their leaders. *Do you think they'll let us go soon so we can ask him?*

Rizelya eyed the stack of papers and sighed, shaking her head. She'd have to wait to solve the mystery.

Blazel - 19 de Godar, 1075

The drawing inside Blazel's shirt crinkled with every movement, reminding him of its presence. What about it made Chariel think of his time in the swamps? He didn't know anything about healing. During his time there, he had only learned about poisons.

After they'd landed, Blazel parted ways with Rizelya and Graak. They took Kaieli's pouch to the command tent while Blazel talked to Bethlyn. Between the battles with the invaders and the continual cropping up of monster nests over the past six chedans, the healers' section now consisted of over twenty tents. After searching through several of them, Blazel finally located Bethlyn.

She glanced up from her patient at his approach. "Are you injured?"

"No, I need to show you something Kaieli gave me."

"Let me finish here." Bethlyn turned back to her patient, and bronze light filtered from her hands, surrounding the wound on the woman's calf. The light seeped inside, pushing out green pus and black blood. A pan placed on the bed below the injury caught the fluids. It risked overflowing before the stream of light faded. Bethlyn wiped down the wound with fresh water, then wrapped it in a clean bandage. She stood, cleansing her own hands to the elbows with a blast of light.

"Damn stuff," she grumbled. "Normal wounds we can easily heal. But the blasted infection caused by the Barrens dust just doesn't stay purged. Kaieli's method requires all the Talents. My Gray is too little, and we don't have any strong enough Grays here, except Chariel. I've sent word to the Supreme, asking her to send us a few, but until then" — Bethlyn shrugged — "we do what we can, but it isn't much."

Blazel wrinkled his nose at the stench as he followed Bethlyn to her desk, situated by the tent opening.

"What did you want to talk to me about, Blazel?"

He pulled the drawing from his shirt and handed it to her. She took it, hitched her hip onto the desk's edge, and studied it.

"Where did Kaieli get this?" Bethlyn glanced briefly at him before turning her attention back to the paper.

"Two more of the slave species the invaders brought with them are now our allies. I understand the Volkern have been their slaves for a very long time. Chariel had Kaieli give me this."

"Chariel, huh?" Bethlyn rubbed her chin. "Did she say anything else?"

"Only to remind me I spent all those years in the swamps for a reason. Does that," he indicated the drawing, "give you any clue why she'd mention it?"

"Maybe." She put the paper on the desk, folded her arms across her chest, and turned her full attention on him. "What exactly did you find while in the swamps?"

"Besides creatures twisted by malignant magic? Lots of poisonous plants." He paused, remembering the time a carnivorous vine had wrapped around his ankle and tried to eat him, and he'd healed the wound with lengo root. "A few beneficial ones, too. I wonder if lengo would help with your infection problem."

She raised her eyebrow. "Lengo? I haven't heard of it before."

"It's an herb found in the swamps which stops bleeding. The boiled roots fight infection, especially wounds caused by swamp creatures."

"It sounds interesting. I'd like to try it."

"I think I still have a sample of it." Even after all his time with Rizelya, plant specimens half-filled his bag.

"Perhaps there's a poisonous plant or something found in the swamps that will effectively kill the invaders while not harming us." Bethlyn picked up the drawing and studied it again. "This indicates it's a possibility. For all the invader's seeming superiority, they actually have a sensitive system."

"Let me get what I have, and you can look at my samples."

At her nod, Blazel slipped out of the healers' tent and jogged across the camp to his tent. He dragged his ancient, beat-up leather pack from under his cot and pulled out his few extra clothes. At the bottom, he retrieved an old shirt fashioned into a pouch for his specimens. As he picked it up, the herbal scent wafted to his nose. Memories of his time in the swamps flooded him. The danger hadn't bothered him, but the remembrance of the utter loneliness he'd suffered nearly drove him to his knees. Shaking off the ghosts of his past, he took the pouch of dried herbs back to Bethlyn.

When he arrived, a pot of clean water bubbled over a fire. Blazel showed her the root before cutting it into chunks and tossing it into the water. "Boil it until it softens, then make a poultice to put on the wounds. It doesn't take long."

She nodded as she examined the other samples, lifting several to her nose and inhaling deeply. Soon, she'd sorted the plants into different piles. Bethlyn pointed to one pile. "These have potential. We'd need quite a bit more, and fresh ones, too."

"All those grow in the swamp on the other side of the crater." Blazel stifled a shudder. He didn't want to spend more time alone in the swamps. He'd become used to having company around. Then he remembered Graak had been interested in the swamp creatures. "I'll ask Graak if he will fly me there. What should we gather?"

"Anything poisonous." Bethlyn wrinkled her nose. "And if there are any plants useful for healing, we could use those, too. We didn't expect this many wounded and have used most of our supplies."

"Show me what you need, and I'll search for it, or something similar." He stirred the pot. "The root is ready."

Bethlyn quickly made a poultice and returned to the woman with the infected calf. In the short time they'd been talking, pus had refilled the wound. Bethlyn placed the poultice on it. "How long do I keep it on?"

"Only until it cools." Blazel waited with her, curious if the lengo root would work on this infection as well as it had on the few he'd received.

When Bethlyn lifted off the cooled poultice, healthy pink flesh surrounded the wound. She prodded the woman's calf, and pus oozed from her injury. However, nothing like before the treatments.

"Another treatment or two," Blazel observed, "and the infection will be gone."

"Remarkable! This is much better than anything I've managed to accomplish. Bring me as much of this root as possible, without depleting the rootstock. The Goddess gives us healing plants for our use, not our abuse."

"I know where to find several patches."

Bethlyn examined the partially healed wound again. She gave him a hopeful smile. "If you can obtain some lengo root before your excursion, it would be extremely helpful and appreciated." She waved a hand to indicate the filled cots. "All these patients are suffering from the infection."

Blazel gulped at the nearly one-hundred cots. "I'll get you what I can."

He hurried across the camp to the command tent.

"What did Chariel give you, Blazel?" Rizelya asked when he slipped inside.

"A drawing of the invaders, with some notes for Bethlyn." Blazel approached the table, scanned the papers, and tapped one. "Similar to this. Alphas, Bethlyn and I think there are plants in the swamp poisonous to the invaders. It's hard to believe, but there are some beneficial herbs growing there, too. There's one she needs immediately. It stops the strange Barrens' dust infection."

It also affects my people. Moraak tilted his head to the side, his head feathers laid flat. *We have not found anything to heal it. What do you require to gather this herb?*

"Just Graak."

Histrun frowned. "We need more than what the two of you can carry. Take a team of..."

"Twenty should do it, sir," Blazel said. "We don't want to strip the field bare."

"No, we don't. Twenty then."

Blazel studied the drawing of the invader again and took a deep breath. "Sir, I'd like to go with Graak deeper into the swamp and search for possible poisonous herbs. We're losing too many people. We have to find an advantage."

"I agree. Graak?"

Graak glanced at Moraak, who nodded. *I will take Blazel. He has often mentioned this swamp and its creatures. I'm interested in visiting it.*

Histrun scowled, shaking a finger at Graak. "Don't forget your mission. This isn't a sightseeing trip. Gather what you think has potential and return as quickly as possible." He held up a hand when Rizelya turned to follow Blazel out. "No, Rizelya. I want you to stay. I need you to lead your battalion."

Rizelya's shoulders slumped. "Yes, sir."

"Share this new information with your core team," Histrun continued. He handed her the drawing of the invaders with the weaknesses noted on it. "Your people are quite innovative.

Maybe they can develop new, and better, methods to use on these damned invaders."

"Good luck, Blazel." Histrun turned his attention back to the documents.

Dismissed, Blazel and Graak left the tent. Blazel's heart lifted as Graak chatted excitedly about the trip. This time, Blazel wouldn't be alone in the swamps.

Rizelya - 19 de Godar, 1075

Rizelya watched Blazel and Graak go, yearning to spend time with him before he left. Since meeting, they hadn't spent much time apart.

After her third sigh, Naila rolled her eyes and made a shooing motion with her hand. "Go. Say goodbye."

Rizelya quickly bowed to her leaders and rushed from the tent, jogging to catch up to Graak and Blazel. When she did, she slipped her arm through his.

Blazel's eyebrows rose, then he scowled at her.

"Don't worry," she said, "I'm not going with you. But I can't let you go for the Crone knows how long without saying goodbye."

Blazel smiled and tucked his hand over hers. "Graak, I'll meet you and the team at the staging area."

Graak dropped his beak and trilled with Gryphon laughter. *Do not be too long, my friend. The day is growing short.*

Blazel grinned. "Half an octar."

Rizelya squeezed his arm.

"Make it an octar." He waved at Graak, who continued trilling in laughter as he flew off.

Blazel mind-called to Aistrun and told him to gather a team. They strolled to their tent, giving the others time to quickly pack. Rizelya breathed a sigh of relief when they entered and found it blessedly empty. She sat on her cot while he tossed clothes and other necessities into his old pack. On the top, he placed two packets of herbs.

She recognized them as the herbs he used for the warding spell. She smiled, remembering when he'd taught her the spell while on their journey to find the Gryphons.

"I'll need these as soon as we land," he said. "Otherwise, the twisted creatures will tear our people apart. I'll show Leistral how to set the ward before Graak and I leave the team gathering the lengo."

"She's a good choice. You've taken to leading much better than I have."

"Thanks." He tied his pack closed and gave her a sexy smile before pulling her into his arms and kissing her.

Rizelya deepened the kiss, running her hands under his shirt. His skin raised in delighted gooseflesh at her touch. He moved his lips from hers, kissing her throat and neck. She groaned and jerked his shirt over his head. Hers followed, along with both of their pants. They fell onto the cot, which squeaked in protest at the sudden weight and threatened to collapse. They made fierce love.

"I'll be back, soon." He held her in his arms. Both of their hearts still raced. "I promise."

"Make sure you do." Her eyes searched his. "I don't want anyone but you."

"I feel the same. You stay safe, too."

They kissed again, long and sweet. Finally, she pulled away. "Graak is going to be angry if you're late."

"More likely, Aistrun will make fun of me," Blazel chuckled. "He hasn't forgiven me that Chariel left with no notice, and he didn't get this type of goodbye with her."

"If it makes you feel better, he's mad at me, too." Rizelya gave him a quick kiss before pushing off his chest. She glanced around the tent for her clothes and scowled. "Where are my small clothes?"

Blazel looked up and laughed. He pulled them from the ridgepole and handed them to her.

She stared at the pole and back at her underthings, then shook her head. She didn't have a clue how they ended up there. Finally dressed, they kissed one last time before ducking through the tent flap.

Aistrun stood outside with his arms crossed, scowling and tapping his foot. "Glad somebody got to say goodbye. Come on. While you were dallying, I gathered the team and packed food."

Blazel's face flushed. "Thank you," he mumbled. He strode toward the staging area, and Rizelya hurried to keep up. Aistrun followed behind, grumbling the entire way.

Grazeen led the team to gather the lengo root, which consisted mostly of Browns and Greens. Leistral, Eidstrun, and Laynal, along with Aistrun, would protect them from the swamp's dangers. Between them and the Gryphons, the others should be safe enough while they gathered the herb. The group stood by the waiting Gryphons, chatting excitedly. No one but Blazel had visited the great swamp in recent history.

Blazel hugged Rizelya one last time before buckling himself into Graak's harness. She watched them fly into the Barrens until they disappeared over the horizon. As she tromped back to camp, she squashed the loneliness threatening to swamp her. He'd return soon, and they'd continue fighting the good fight together. She didn't want to imagine life without him.

Blazel - 19 de Godar, 1075

Blazel's team crossed the Barrens and entered the swamps within a few octars, rather than the days it had taken Blazel to traverse the same distance on foot. Instead of a direct flight, they flew to the east coast first to avoid alerting the Scourge. Blazel squinted, trying to make out what he was glimpsing on the horizon's edge.

"Graak, your far vision is better than mine. Can you tell what that is?" Blazel pointed to the smudge. "Whatever it is, I don't like it."

After a few moments, Graak shuddered, making Blazel appreciate the harness strapping him to Graak's back.

I think it's an island. It appears to be desolate, almost as much as the Barrens. Although, something must be on it, because I'm sensing intense anger and hatred radiating from it.

"I feel the same thing. Could it be where our ancestors exiled the Malvers?"

Possibly. Goddess, may they stay there!

Blazel wholeheartedly agreed. He sighed in relief when they turned landward again.

He gaped in astonishment as the great swamp came into view. The aerial perspective showed its enormity. The swamp's muddy green trees stretched as far as the eye could see, with only an occasional break. He directed Graak to the first gap. Twilight deepened the sky to mauve.

As soon as they landed, Blazel retrieved the packet of herbs from his pack. "Leistral, join me as I cast a warding circle," he beckoned. She hurried over to him.

"Rizelya told me about your invention. I'm excited to learn it."

"Good. You'll need to create one every night you're in the swamp. Dangerous creatures live here."

Leistral nodded in understanding. He handed a separate, smaller packet of herbs to her and taught her the spell. Together, they walked around the group in a large circle, strewing the herbs and chanting the spell to form the ward.

"Stay in the circle," Blazel warned the team. "It will protect us from any twisted beasts who wander by during the night."

While they worked, Laynal lit a fire. Grazeen took charge of dinner and made a stew and savory pan bread. The group sat around the fire, eating and talking.

Grazeen's mouth formed a small "o". She pointed. "What... what is that?"

A beast crouched at the protective circle's edge. At first it looked like a large squirrel, with a bottle-brush tail curling over its back. Except a rack of sharp horns extended over its head, and fangs peeked from its upper jaw. Its eyes glowed red in the firelight.

Aistrun leaped to his feet, reaching for his helstrablade.

"No!" Blazel held up a hand to stop him. "Don't shed any blood. It will only attract more beasts, more than we can fight.

It can't cross the boundary I set, so we're not in any danger from a single beast."

"What's wrong with it?" Aistrun slowly sat back down without taking his eyes off the squirrel.

Blazel shrugged. "All the animals in the swamps are twisted, especially in this one. I suspect the malignant magic saturating the place is responsible."

The sight subdued their conversation. The twisted squirrel scampered off, and everyone breathed a collective sigh of relief, which lasted only a brief time. A rabbit hopped by and sniffed at the herbs, sneezing and rubbing its nose with a paw. Its long, sharp claws glinted in the firelight. Other animals, twisted by the malignant magic, wandered by the camp. Blazel's magical barrier rebuffed them all.

Later, as they lay curled up in their bedrolls, a dracur flew overhead. It dove, spewing fire from its jaws at a twisted rabbit. Everyone's eyes watered from the sulfuric stench. The rabbit screamed in agony as it burned. The dracur stooped, its hard knuckles striking the rabbit's head and breaking its neck. It scooped up its prey and disappeared into the darkness.

The next morning, Blazel guided the team to a clearing filled with lengo plants. "Bethlyn needs the roots, as many as you can gather without depleting the field. Depending on how long this war lasts, we may need to return for more, which we can't do if we take too many now."

Grazeen rolled her eyes. "Yes, we know. We harvest wild plants frequently."

The gathering team scattered across the field, carefully digging up the roots with the tools they'd brought. The guard team followed, keeping everyone in sight, while also checking the perimeter for danger. Blazel watched them for a few milcrons and nodded in satisfaction before turning to Graak and Aistrun.

"Are you sure you don't want more company?" Aistrun leaned against Broogk's broad body. "We're both ready and willing to go with you."

"I'll be fine with just Graak, but thank you for the offer." Blazel clapped Aistrun on the back. He swung a leg over Graak's back and buckled in. "Where we're going, it's better if there aren't too many people. The twisted beasts we saw last night are harmless compared to what else hides in the swamps. They're all attracted by body heat and blood."

"How long will you be gone?"

"Not long, I hope. Even with Graak's help, I estimate it will take at least a chedan to locate and harvest all the plants we need to test." Blazel adjusted the last strap. "Watch over Rizelya for me, will you? I know she's a capable fighter, but I'd feel better with someone keeping an eye on her."

Aistrun looped his thumbs through his belt. "I've always looked after Little Red, and don't plan on stopping just because you've joined us."

Graak leaped into the air, cutting off Blazel's reply. They flew over the swamp. In less than an octar, they reached the humongous tree Blazel had taken refuge in.

Graak landed in the clearing. *This is where you stayed?* He gazed around at it, twisting his head to see the new sights. *I do not sense anything.*

Blazel unstrapped and swung out of the harness. He carefully poked his head through the opening at the base of the tree and sniffed. It smelled musty, like everything in the swamp did, but it didn't reek of any animals. He went the rest of the way in. His fire cairn still blackened the ground in the center. It didn't appear as if anything had wandered into it since he left. He returned to where Graak waited.

"The tree cave is safe." Blazel frowned at Graak's mass, then turned to peer at the hole and shook his head. "I don't know if you'll fit, friend. It seemed bigger when I lived here."

Graak dropped his beak and trilled a laugh. *The last time you were here, you spent most of your time as a wolf. Is the space inside large enough for me?*

Blazel poked his head back into the tree, glancing around critically, then leaned back. "Yep."

Show me in your mind how it looks.

Blazel did so. A few moments later, Graak ambled to the tree and didn't stop. With a small pop, he disappeared. Blazel blinked, then remembered them flying through the window at the Gryphons' fortress and it not breaking. He ducked into the tree to find the packs they'd brought in a heap on the ground and Graak making contented cooing noises.

Ooh, this place would make a nice nest. Walls of living wood. The slow dripping of sap. The sigh of the leaves. It's nearly perfect.

You forgot about the twisted beasts rummaging a few feet away and the malignant magic under the surface."

Details, details. Graak settled on a pile of dry leaves with a contented coo and lowered his head onto his paws, closing his eyes.

Blazel smiled at his friend. Many of the swamp's pathways wouldn't support Blazel's human weight, let alone Graak's larger bulk. He'd let him nap while he gathered some baneful herbs. He took some of the protective herbs from his pack, put on gloves, grabbed an empty bag, and strode outside.

After setting a magical boundary around the tree and its clearing, he walked carefully along the path, watching for twisted beasts. He stopped and stripped the large, oval leaves from a helbore. He harvested a few clusters of the yellowish-green flowers and put them in his bag. Glancing around to assure himself no creatures lurked nearby, he knelt, pulling out his helstrablade. He dug up the root—the most toxic part of the plant. Next, he found a patch of solanar and picked the bright pink, poisonous berries. The sunny-yellow flowers of a marsh marigold caught his attention. Both the heart-shaped leaves and the blossoms caused skin blisters and irritated the eyes and nose. Blazel gathered several more poisonous plants, filling his bag. His stomach rumbled. Twilight deepened the shadows.

On his way back to the tree cave, he picked some mint, cattail, and sweet flag to add to his dinner. A quick toss of his knife killed a large, fat swamp rat. He'd discovered the ugly creatures were one of the few edible beasts in the swamp. When he arrived, Graak was awake and hungry.

"I brought dinner," Blazel said, holding aloft the swamp rat. "Do you think you can roast it for me?"

Graak glared at him. *My flames are not for cooking your dinner. And that is certainly not enough for both of us.*

Blazel laughed. "Of course not. I'll light my fire the old-fashioned way."

A rustle in the trees caught their attention. *Perhaps there is my dinner.* Graak whipped his head around and peered intently at the spot.

A large, dark-green triangular head appeared within the leaves. And a sinuous body wrapped around a tree limb.

Is it one of those flying serpents?

"An angulete, yes. I think they taste awful. But go ahead," he waved at it, "try it for yourself. You'll have to leave the ward boundary, but don't disturb the herbs when you cross it."

Graak lifted his head feathers, indicating he understood, as he carefully stepped over the line. He strolled around the glade and under the tree, seemingly without watching the snake. It leaped from its perch, spreading its wings to glide toward him, its mouth opened wide, exposing its glistening fangs. The angulete's length exceeded ten feet, and its body was eighteen inches in diameter—a worthy opponent for Graak.

Before it reached him, Graak whirled, striking with his sharp talons. Score marks on its scales showed where he raked the angulete. It hissed and twisted to strike again. Graak leaped out of the way, straight up, and used his own wings to hover above the snake. His rear claws tore into the body, while his front talons gripped the head and neatly broke the angulete's neck.

That was too easy, Graak complained. He dipped his head and tore off a chunk of flesh. *Not the best tasting meat, but it's tolerable.*

After dinner, Blazel lay curled up on his bedroll next to the dying fire, listening to Graak's soft snores in the background. This sojourn wouldn't be like his last. This time, he had a friend to share the experience with him.

Chapter 23

Rizelya - 28 de Godar, 1075

Rizelya stepped from the command tent after another tactical meeting with Histrun, Naila, and Moraak. She stretched and twisted, relieving the cramps in her back from leaning over the map table. A scout zoomed into camp.

They've taken the bait! he called. He landed in front of the command tent and bobbed to Moraak. *The Scourge are headed to Posanrehamde Keep.*

The keep was one they'd left a fighting force in, hoping to lure the invaders into attacking it. At only thirty measures from the base camp, it was an easy distance for the Gryphons to reach quickly.

Rizelya raced to her tent, grabbed her helbraught, and then sped to the landing area. She reached it at the same time as Aistrun, Leistral, and Shaydan. Rizelya paused a moment before climbing onto Glork's back, searching for Blazel. As she buckled herself into the harness, she snorted in frustration, remembering he was still in the swamps.

Her battalion, along with fifteen Thunder Wings, launched into the sky. A half octar later, they approached Posanrehamde Keep. On the ground, Posair fighters fought with enemy forces.

The transport ship sat outside the keep walls, with only a few soldiers guarding it. The Thunder Wings dove, converging on it and lifting the ship into the air. Startled shouts rose from the invaders, and several broke off from their fights to race helplessly after their ship.

"Yes!" A laugh erupted from Rizelya, and she whooped.

Glork trilled. *Let's destroy these vermin.*

He took a deep breath, readying his flame, and Rizelya primed her helbraught. He dove, gliding above the fleeing Scourge. Together, they laid intense fire on the running soldiers. Rizelya didn't even feel pity, as they screamed when the flames engulfed them.

Glork twisted away from the burning hulks. *Gah! They stink.*

Rizelya agreed, covering her mouth and nose with her elbow until they flew clear of the stench.

She and Glork added their efforts to those of Leistral on Morru, and Shaydan on Dukaaik in attacking the remaining invaders from the air. Broogk dropped Aistrun off near the gates, where he quickly shifted into his warrior form. He joined several other warriors fighting the enemy already inside the keep walls.

For the first time, the Posairs outnumbered the Scourge. An octar later, they'd killed all the invaders, but it wasn't a total victory. The death of fifty Posairs and two Gryphons dampened their jubilation. Tears streamed down Rizelya's face as Glork flew back to the base camp. Comrades had died, but without the Gryphons, the invaders would have captured and enslaved more Posairs.

During the night, Rizelya dreamed a swarm of monsters was attacking Strunland Keep. Her home. People she knew cried in terror as janacks flung them into their maw. She woke up screaming and trembling with fear, even while knowing this was simply another dream from the Malvers woman. Aistrun tried to comfort her, but he wasn't Blazel. She missed his strong arms protecting her. He seemed to understand how real the visions were. As soon as her shaking stopped, she raced to Histrun's tent.

"They've attacked Strunland Keep!" Rizelya cried as she shook him awake.

"What? Who?" Histrun sat up and rubbed the sleep from his eyes. "How did the invaders reach that far north?"

"No, no, not the invaders, the Malvers' monsters. I have to go home. I have to help them." She paced in the tent.

"Calm down, Rizelya. It doesn't make any sense. The monsters can't crawl past the Sheadash stone."

"But I saw it. The damned Malvers woman showed it to me just now."

"Have you considered it isn't true, and she's messing with your mind?"

Rizelya paused, blinking. "Why would she do that? She's shown me the truth before."

Histrun shrugged. "Who knows what motivates that woman? I need you here, Rizelya. We've been fighting the Malvers' monsters for a thousand years. It's doubtful they're gaining the upper hand. Even if they are, our people at home can deal with them. Our priority right now is to toss these damned invaders off our world. You've seen the escaped captives' condition. You've heard their stories. We have to fight this scourge on our land. Afterward, we'll finish off the Malvers' monsters once and for all."

Rizelya's shoulders drooped. Histrun spoke the truth. The invaders were the more immediate threat.

Blazel - 30 de Godar, 1075

Blazel and Graak spent their days filling the bags they'd brought with poisonous plants—in between fighting various twisted beasts and carnivorous plants. Graak flying above the marshy ground made traversing the swamp much easier. They wandered far and wide throughout the swamp, each area yielding different varieties of plants.

Every once in a while, they'd glimpse an invader's ship soaring over them, followed closely by a phalanx of Thunder

Wings. One day, while gathering dojee, a particularly nasty vine with large spines that dripped caustic fluid, Blazel jumped at the screech of tearing metal. Above them, a Thunder Wing ripped off the large weapon sitting on the ship's roof and tossed it aside. The debris plunged toward them. Blazel jerked his hand and leaped away from the plant as the ruined weapon crashed on the spot he'd been standing on.

They are making headway on destroying those ships, Graak observed. *That's the third one we've seen them destroy.* He frowned at Blazel. His beak clicked in agitation. *Wrap your hand! Hurry, grab your bag, and let's get out of here before we're inundated with twisted beasts.*

Blazel's forehead crinkled as he glanced down. When he'd jerked away from the vine, he'd sliced his hand open. The grass rustled, and a twisted rabbit hopped out. Its nose twitched. Blazel snatched his sack, thrusting the cut vines into it, then jumped onto Graak's back. His cut made tying the bag to the harness awkward. While Graak flew back to their tree cave, Blazel tied a bandage over the wound. By the time they landed, his hand had become swollen and numb. Graak helped him boil some lengo root and make a poultice. The root relieved the swelling, and by morning, Blazel's hand was stiff and sore, but didn't seem to be infected.

How much more are you going to gather? Graak surveyed the piled-up bags. *I don't know if I can carry much more back.*

"I want to ensure we collect a sample of everything. What if we left without collecting the one thing that would make a difference?"

We've been here ten days now. I'll give you one more day, Blazel, then we go back. If we need to, we can return. We won't know if we've found the right thing until you and Bethlyn test it.

Blazel scowled. Graak was correct. They needed to return and test what they'd already gathered.

"There's one more place I want to check," Blazel said. He directed Graak even deeper into the swamp, to a place Blazel had only glimpsed and had avoided when he'd been alone.

The vegetation changed, and like the animals they'd encountered, it became twisted into a sinister parody of life. They followed it to a black castle with crumbling turrets. Sludge filled the moat. An oblong obsidian block dominated the center courtyard, with rust stains dripping down its sides. Twisted beasts milled around its foundations and gave them baleful glares.

I think this is an old Malvers' stronghold, Blazel said in mind-speech, not wanting to disturb anything or draw more attention to them. *It gives me the creeps.*

Evil magic still fills this place. A shudder went through Graak, nearly dislodging Blazel.

What happened?

Something has my back paw! Graak flapped his wings, but they didn't rise any higher. Graak snapped his head to look behind him, and jerked his leg, trying to shake free from whatever trapped him.

Blazel withdrew his helstrablade from its sheath and leaned over Graak's side. Below them, a massive beast towered over the others. It stood ten feet tall, not including the sharp antlers spreading above its head. Orange eyes glowed in its human-like face, and long brown fur covered its muscular body. The lower half appeared like a multa's hindquarters and ended with wide, cloven, platter-like hooves. It gripped a black rope in its clawed hands, and its muscles bunched as it pulled the rope.

Graak squawked as the creature dragged him backwards. He frantically beat his wings against the pressure. *Get ready. I'm going to flare.*

Magic rippled over Blazel, and he gritted his teeth against the heat, even though Graak's magic protected him from the worst of it. He peered over Graak's side. The rope still ensnared Graak's paw. The creature tossed back its head and brayed. It pulled on the rope again.

Get it off me! Panic filled Graak's voice.

Blazel unbuckled his harness, carefully turned around, and crawled along Graak's back until he laid over Graak's hindquarters. He wrapped an arm around the Gryphon's belly, tightly gripping his fur. He leaned over. "Pull up your paw."

Graak's muscles bunched, and slowly the paw came within Blazel's reach. He swiped at the rope with his helstrablade. As the blade connected, sparks flew, and the sizzle of electricity burned his hand. He grimaced, hanging onto his knife through the pain.

"This isn't a normal rope! It's made from malignant magic." In desperation, Blazel reached into his core of magic and pulled it to him as if he were going to shift. Instead, he directed it to his knife. To his surprise, the blade glowed red, and he again slashed at the rope. After a moment's resistance, the blade sliced through, releasing Graak. He zoomed high into the sky, out of the creature's reach.

The creature roared in frustration and shook a claw at them. Blazel shuddered at the mouthful of needle-sharp teeth. If the beast had captured them, they'd be dead.

Graak flew to the edge of the twisted forest and landed. Blazel dropped to the ground, holding his burned hand to his chest as the pain crashed over him. His stomach heaved, and vomit covered the leaves. He pushed away and tried to drop the knife, but it felt like the helstrablade had fused to his hand.

You're hurt! Graak gently touched a talon to Blazel's hurt hand.

Blazel nearly wept as a cooling sensation eased the pain.

Try to open your hand now. I've treated the burn.

Blazel focused on his hand, willing his muscles to relax. The helstrablade fell to the ground. He lifted his hand and gaped at his burned palm, which clearly showed the pattern of the leather wrapping the knife's hilt. He flexed it, surprised he could move it. Finally, he slowly rolled over and sat up.

"I'm fine now. Thanks."

That creature wasn't like the others. It possessed enough intelligence to use tools.

"I had a good look at it." Blazel shuddered. "It had human parts twisted and blended with various animals."

Graak sat on his haunches, curling his tail around his feet. He situated himself where he could keep watch on the forest. *The Malvers had their stronghold in this area. You Posairs may have forgotten what happened during the Great War, but we Gryphons have not. Those beasts back there are the stuff of our nightmares from the stories our ancestors passed down to us. If the Malvers ever escape, we'll have to fight such things again.*

"Let's pray they don't." Blazel draped his wrists on his bent knees and gazed around the small glade they rested in. An unfamiliar tree with gray-green elongated leaves caught his attention. Clusters of dull-green nuts hung from it. Something about it made his skin crawl. He forced himself to stand and cautiously approached it. He picked a nut and opened it, gagging at the stench. A drop of juice dripped onto his hand, burning through his gloves. "Damn stuff is acidic!" He tossed the nut on the ground and rubbed his hand on the grass. Now, both hands were burned.

"Bring me the sack. I'm sure these are poisonous. They smell exactly like brecha ichor."

Graak ambled over. *Gagh, those are nasty. Surely, they will be effective against the invaders.*

Together, they filled the bag with the nuts and leaves. As they flew back to their haven, Graak stopped to gather some lengo root for Blazel's burns.

Even after applying the poultice, Blazel's hands still hurt. He held them carefully against his chest. "I'm ready to go home."

Graak bobbed his head. *I'm ready, too. It's too late to leave tonight. Besides, if we wait until morning, hopefully your hands will feel better. Although I like this tree cave, I'm tired of my skin itching from the malignant magic. This has been fun.*

Blazel agreed. The thought of Rizelya waiting for him made him anxious to return.

The next morning, even though the burns on his hands still hurt, he could function. Blazel loaded the filled bags onto Graak's back, strapped himself on, and they flew back toward the base camp.

He glanced at the packs, hoping they contained the answer they needed to stop the invaders.

Rizelya - 30 de Godar, 1075

Rizelya tried ignoring the dreams. But several days later, while she groomed Kymaya, the Malvers woman reached into her mind.

Rizelya's gut tightened as the familiar territory of home and the fields surrounding it appeared. She could almost smell the crispness of the early autumn air. Workers filled the fields, harvesting crops. Children played between the fields and pastures, unaware of the danger lurking nearby. Brechas burst from the forest, already spitting their spines. Several children fell from the onslaught. While adults rushed to the children's rescue, two janacks trundled into view, snatching adults and children into their great maws.

Rizelya's screams joined those in Strunland Keep. She collapsed, sobbing. Kymaya nosed her hair, sending comforting images. Aistrun and Wisah raced to her side.

"What happened? What hurt you?" Aistrun's gaze searched the surrounding area for whatever danger made Rizelya tremble in terror.

Wisah gathered Rizelya in her arms. Waves of comfort enfolded Rizelya, and her sobs subsided.

"I'm okay, now." Rizelya pressed the palms of her hands to her eyes, trying to block the residual images playing in her mind. "It... it was the Malvers woman. She directed her monsters to attack Strunland Keep. It felt so real, like I was there, not only witnessing the atrocity, but part of it." She shivered and spat, wishing she had water to cleanse her mouth. "I can still taste the blood, as if it were me eating those people, not the janack."

"Enough!" Wisah's mouth compressed into a thin line, and her eyes narrowed. "This has gone on long enough. You've woken up every night for at least the past two chedans. You're exhausted. Come with me. Since Chariel isn't here, we need Saffren's help." She grabbed Rizelya's arm and dragged her back to camp.

They found Saffren in a healer's tent, helping ease the emotional trauma of an escapee. As soon as she finished, Wisah explained the problem.

"Oh, my," Saffren said, placing a hand over her heart. "I agree this is becoming ridiculous, especially now that it's occurring when you're awake. It would be terrible, and dangerous, for something like this to happen while you're battling an invader."

Rizelya's mouth dropped open. She hadn't considered the possibility. Thankfully, she'd been grooming Kymaya and wasn't in any danger from the vision.

Saffren placed a stool in front of her and pointed at it. "Sit."

Rizelya sank onto the stool, and the two women stood over her. Saffren's powerful Blue Talent made her a gifted empath, sensing clearly the emotions around her. Wisah's training as a White Priestess taught her soul magic, as well as mind magic. Together, they could help Rizelya resolve her problem with the Malvers woman attacking her mind.

Within a few milcrons, Wisah dropped her hands with a sigh. "We discovered the cause. The block the Supreme had placed on your mind has eroded by the constant bombardment."

"And from fighting the Scourge," Saffren added. "You've unconsciously used it to protect yourself against their evil." She gazed at Rizelya, absently tapping her chin with a finger. "Are you sure you don't have any Gray or Blue Talent?"

"What?" Rizelya shook her head and lifted her braid. Although Barrens dust dulled her hair color, the auburn shone through. "No, I'm a Red. Blue and Red Talent doesn't mix."

Saffren shrugged. "Something is going on with you, because this isn't normal for a Red to be susceptible to other people's emotions."

"She's just special," Wisah joked, playfully bumping Rizelya's shoulder.

For the next few octars, Saffren and Wisah worked with Rizelya. As a White Priestess, Wisah helped her on the spirit level. Saffren's empathic abilities required her to have a strong barrier in her own mind to keep out other people's unwanted emotions. She taught Rizelya how to build her own barrier rather than rely only on the Supreme's. When they finished, Rizelya could create a strong mental block. She breathed deeply, feeling sane for the first time in chedans.

Later, while cleaning her helbraught, loneliness swamped Rizelya. She wanted to share the experience with Blazel—and she missed his solid presence holding her at night. She mentally counted the days, frowning. Blazel and Graak had left on their mission to the swamp over ten days ago. She'd only expected them to be gone for a chedan at most. Hopefully, nothing had happened to them. Perhaps Glork would take her to search for them. Rizelya snorted at the impossibility of finding them in the enormous swamp.

During the night, warmth enveloped Rizelya. Sighing, she turned over and snuggled into the crook of Blazel's arm. She groaned as soft kisses trailed along her neck while a calloused thumb stroked her breast. This was a much better dream than those sent by the Malvers woman. Blazel's hardness pressing against her back, and she drowsily squirmed closer to him. Her eyes flew open, and she stared into Blazel's dark gray eyes.

"You're back!" She kissed him. Their tongues entwined. Her hands explored his back, his chest, his buttocks. Blazel's thumbs found her nipples, stroking them to hardness. She ached for him and gasped when he entered her. She rode the ever-increasing waves of pleasure until they both climaxed. Afterward, they lay together, still wrapped in each other's arms and legs, panting, sweat coating their bodies.

She drifted back to sleep, a smile on her lips.

Blazel - 33 de Godar, 1075

After breakfast, Blazel sauntered to the main healers' tent, whistling. The glow of making love with Rizelya still filled him with pleasure. After his experience of falling in love with her, he would never begrudge the love his mother had found with his father. Blazel didn't know who fathered him. He'd always been too angry—and ashamed—to ask his mother. The next time he visited her, he'd find out.

At his entry, Bethlyn looked up from the basket of salves on her lap. "Did you have a successful trip?"

"If you're asking whether we brought back a lot of specimens, then yes. But if any of them will work on the invaders..." He shrugged.

She set aside the basket and surveyed him up and down. "Let me see your hands. I can tell they're hurting you."

Blazel held out his hands, wincing when Bethlyn gently took his right hand. She *tsked* at his helstrablade's hilt imprint burned into his palm. She surrounded his hand with a bronze light, easing the pain. A few moments later, the redness and swelling were gone.

"This looks like a monster's ichor acid burn." Bethlyn examined his left hand. "How on earth did you get this? Your fur should have protected you."

"I didn't have fur. This is from one of the nuts we found. It ate through my gloves."

"Hmm... sounds promising for our invader poison." She continued to scrutinize his hand. "I don't detect any necrosis, which is a good sign."

Blazel frowned when she carefully rubbed an ointment on the acid burn. He'd expected her to heal it the same way she had his other one. "Why aren't you healing it?"

"I want to find out how it affects you." She finished and wiped her hands, then grinned at him. "You're an excellent test subject since it has already burned you. Whatever potion we develop, we want it to be deadly to the invaders, but not to us. Come with me."

"Where are we going?"

"I had a tent set up for our experiments on the outskirts of the camp. While we're researching, it'll be better, and safer, if we're not in the center of camp. It wouldn't do to poison our own people."

"No, that wouldn't be good."

Bethlyn meandered through the sea of green tents.

"Did the lengo root help with the Barren's infection?" Blazel asked.

"Oh, yes!" She beamed. "And the Supreme sent us two Grays, so now we're able to heal it with both the herbal potion and using Kaieli's method. Her technique is also helpful for other wounds and illnesses. It's a blessing from the Goddess Kaieli discovered it."

They stopped at a large tent, as far away from the Barrens as possible. Inside, Blazel found two long tables, along with numerous braziers, bottles, and mixing utensils. Off to the side, the bags he and Graak had filled laid in a heap.

He located the one with the acidic nuts and gingerly held out a specimen. "This is what burned me."

Bethlyn scrunched her nose at the noxious odor. "Those are truly awful."

They sorted through the bags, grouping similar plants together. When they emptied all the sacks, Bethlyn scrutinized the multitude of piles. "You found some pretty nasty stuff."

"Which should we try first?"

"Let's start with these." She pointed to a pile on the nearest table. "I know we have an antidote for them."

She handed him a length of cloth to tie around his mouth and nose. They cut and mashed various plants, dumping them in a pot to boil. Fumes rose from the concoction. Coughing, Blazel and Bethlyn quickly stepped back. Blazel grabbed a cloth to wipe his watery eyes and runny nose. After a few moments, the fumes cleared, and they bent over the pot.

"This won't work," Blazel grimaced at the dark sludge covering the bottom of the pot.

"I didn't expect us to find the solution on our first try." Bethlyn opened a journal and jotted down notes. After she put it down, she rubbed her hands together. "Now, what should we try next?"

From then on, Blazel spent every waking moment experimenting instead of fighting the invaders. This could save their people more than an extra fighter on the front lines. For every promising mixture, they tossed aside ten failures.

Bethlyn, as the chief healer, couldn't devote all her time to the project. She assigned a young healer, Margandy, to help Blazel. She had medium-green hair and brown eyes, and took the research seriously. Blazel appreciated her quick mind, and her excellent grasp on the plants' various properties.

After their first noxious concoction threatened the camp, Histrun moved their tent even farther away. He also assigned Laynal to assist them.

The young woman leaned against the tent frame, scowling. "I don't know what I did to deserve this punishment. I'm a good fighter, and my shields are nearly as strong as Rizelya's."

"That's why you're here." Blazel stirred the most recent mixture, wishing Rizelya could help him, but Histrun needed her to fight the invaders. "We need someone who can create both fire and air shields. We're making poisons. Your job is to ensure they stay here and not affect the camp. You'll also burn any we can't use. Don't worry, it will be quite dangerous."

"Oh!" She stood straighter and peered inside the tent. "So, what do you want me to do?"

Margandy handed Laynal a long-handled wooden spoon and pointed to a pot. "Stir this mixture."

Laynal frowned and warily approached the pot. "Gagh! That's awful!" She made a motion with her hand, creating a shield of thickened air surrounding the pot, before stirring. "Ah, much better."

Blazel lifted an eyebrow. "That's exactly what we need you to do."

The days sped by as they endeavored to discover a mixture to kill the invaders while not harming the Posairs or Gryphons.

Rolstrun - 36 de Godar, 1075

As the days passed, Rolstrun fell into a routine with the rest of the nucla cleansing team. Either the Goddess blessed him, or the invaders ignored him. Whatever the cause, his disguise continued to fool the guards at the processing plant.

After joining Kaieli's team, Rolstrun allowed his hair to grow, and its length now rivaled Calistrun's locks. His longer hair helped his charade, since most of the men cut their hair short, making it easier to manage and minimized the dust from mining the pillar. Especially since the invaders provided them with limited water to bathe in. After their first day, the Scourge never bothered with cutting their hair. Rolstrun and the other men decided the buzz they'd received had been an effort to humiliate them.

Rolstrun dropped Kaieli's hand, breaking the circle. Groaning, he stepped away from the table holding the processed bars of nucla they were working on clearing. He leaned against the wall and slumped to the ground, pressing his palms to his eyes.

"What's wrong?" Kaieli asked.

"I have a raging headache." He dropped his hands and opened his eyes, promptly squeezing them shut again. "Ugh! The light hurts my eyes."

"Here, let me fix it for you." Kaieli rubbed her hands together and placed one on the top of Rolstrun's head and the other over his eyes.

Warmth seeped into him from her hands, and the headache started to ease. However, as soon as she removed her hands, the headache returned even worse than before. "Ooh, I'm going to be sick." His stomach lurched. Luckily, someone held a bucket for him, so he didn't spew vomit all over the floor.

"You shouldn't react like that." Kaieli's voice sounded worried. "Faliciden, help me, please."

Faliciden's presence joined Kaieli's hovering over him. His stomach quieted and his headache eased from the warmth of their healing. He breathed deeply in relief until they pulled back their healing energy. "Bucket!" He heaved until only bile was left in his stomach.

"Let's not do that again," he groaned when he finally stopped throwing up.

Kaieli agreed. The women helped him onto a crate used for a cot, letting him rest. Whenever Rolstrun opened his eyes, even for a peek, the blinding headache resurged. Finally, after several octars, the headache and nausea abated.

At first, the group surmised Rolstrun's illness resulted from him overusing his Talent when he wasn't used to accessing it for anything other than shapeshifting. However, over the next few days, the same blinding headache and nausea hit first Jaelena, then Maheli, followed by Loshera and Chariel.

"Sweet Mother! This is awful," Kaieli groaned, when the illness struck her. "I know now what's causing it. We've been pushing ourselves too hard and depleting our magic supply. The Black Talent we create makes us believe we're invincible. But, we're not. We need to pace ourselves better. Rest more often between cleansing batches."

Chariel's eyebrows rose, and her mouth dropped open. "Oh, this also happens when we work on the processed nucla, but not the raw ore. Let's focus on the raw ore. We haven't built up our combined strength to treat the processed stuff yet. As much as we want to, we need to consider our health. We can't finish the job if we're no longer capable of accessing our magic."

The thought sobered everyone in the group, and they returned to cleansing the nucla from the raw ore.

The work exhausted Rolstrun more than swinging a pickax had done. After working on cleansing the ore all day, they still had more work to do. Rolstrun was now an integral part of the healing team, and he helped them purge the nucla poisoning from the men. He and Kaieli collapsed each night onto their pallet, neither having the energy to do more than lay in each other's arms.

Each day, Rolstrun would awake from a fitful sleep, never feeling like he'd rested. After a meager breakfast, he and the others would purge the nucla of malignant magic. As long as the invaders kept mining the nucla, they would keep making it impotent.

Chapter 24

Kaieli - 61 de Godar, 1075

Kaieli and her team worked feverishly to cleanse the nucla ore of the malignant magic. Even so, they barely kept up with the new loads brought in from the crater. After five chedans of intense work, Kaieli hoped the team had gained enough strength to treat the processed bars. At her request, Rolstrun carried a crate of processed bars into their area and set it down.

Kaieli gazed at her crew gathered around it. Lines of exhaustion etched their faces, especially the elderly White Priestess Loshera. They'd all lost weight over the lunadars of captivity. Rolstrun coughed. His lungs still suffered from the nucla poisoning, even after several chedans out of the constant dust from mining it.

Maheli absently tugged on her braid as she rubbed her chin. "Are you sure we're strong enough now to attempt cleansing those?"

Kaieli nodded. "Yes, I believe so. We won't know until we try."

The group held hands, and she initiated the blending, concentrating on the malignant magic contained in the processed bars. At first, their magic met resistance, but nothing like when they had tried this so long ago. Kaieli drew in a bit more energy from her crew, adding it to the black braid. This time, their magic easily crushed the slimy, dark magic. Kaieli's eyes widened when she studied the crate. They hadn't purged just one bar, but all of them.

"We did it!" Kaieli cried with delight. She kissed and hugged Rolstrun. Then Maheli wrapped her in a hug. Faliciden and Loshera were hugging and laughing, while Jaelena and Noriana patted each other on the back. Rolstrun turned and, to Chariel's obvious surprise, hugged her and placed a quick kiss on her cheek.

"Now, we just have a thousand more crates to clear," Maheli snorted.

Jaelena dropped her face into the palms of her hands. "Oh no! All those bars stored in the mother ship's hold have to be cleansed." She raised her head. "How are we going to work on those when we can't get close to them?"

"We practice on clearing the bars long distance." Loshera's matter-of-fact tone brooked no argument. "We already work at a distance on the ore."

"But that's only a few feet," Maheli said. "The mother ship is over three measures away!"

"I believe we can do it." Loshera folded her arms over her chest.

Faliciden groaned. "I'm so tired. Can't we put another team together to help us?"

"Have you seen another Gray, besides Chariel?" Kaieli cocked an eyebrow. "Because I haven't. We have enough people for the other Talents, but not Gray. And I'm the only one with Gray as a secondary Talent."

"What about asking Rizelya to sneak in a second Gray?" Rolstrun asked.

Chariel shook her head. "Unfortunately, I was the only Gray in the war host. We're it." She gestured to the group. "All we can do is our best and hope it's enough. Let's get back to work."

Maheli mind-spoke to Myndera, letting her know the team needed another bin. While she waited, Kaieli squirmed on her crate, trying to find a more comfortable position, without success. She'd lost any cushioning fat on her butt in the dreadful conditions. Her stomach tensed, and Myndera pushed an ore cart into their small hideout. Once Myndera left with the crate of processed bars, Kaieli sighed and shook out her hands. When she held them out, the others completed the circle.

"Only a thousand more," Kaieli said. "We can do this, one bin at a time."

"One bin at a time," Jaelena repeated, squaring her shoulders.

Blazel - 61 de Godar, 1075

Blazel leaned over the table, examining his latest mixture. After three chedans of experimenting with various poisons, he may have found one that would do the job, but he needed to test it on live subjects. He poured the black goo into a pot, securing a lid on it, then strode from the tent. Blazel blinked in the bright sunlight. He rarely left his experiment tent during daylight hours. Sometimes, when a potion brewed, he slept in it.

Graak, he called. *Are you around?*

Blazel! You're not dead. Graak's teasing voice held a bit of censure in it.

I live. Guilt assailed Blazel. His mission with the poisons consumed him so much, he hadn't seen his friend since returning from the swamp. *I have a potion I need to test. Will you take me with you on your next skirmish with the invaders?*

We're fighting now. I'll pick you up.

As Blazel and Graak soared above the invaders, the thrill of battle washed over him. *I've missed this.*

I doubt it will end before you find a solution. The work you do is important, Graak assured him. *We are barely holding our own against the Scourge. At least, they aren't overrunning us. We need an advantage. I believe your poison is key to turning the tide.*

Blazel's heart swelled. When batch after batch of potions failed, it became difficult for him to stay motivated. "Hopefully, this one works."

There. Graak pointed a talon below them. *There's a big knot of them. Will it suffice for your test?*

"It's perfect." Blazel readied the pot of black goo.

When Graak flew over their targets, Blazel dumped it out on the enemy's heads. He held his breath, waiting for the chemical reaction. The invaders wiped the goo from their eyes, then pointed their pulsers at them. Graak put on a burst of speed and zoomed away.

"Fly over them again, Graak. I want to see if there's just a delayed reaction."

They hovered over the group of soldiers marked by the black goo, watching them intently as Laynar and her squad-pack fought them. Blazel expected the poison to slow the invader's breathing, thus slowing their responses. But nothing happened. Finally, Laynar's squad-pack killed the soldiers. Blazel's shoulders slumped. The goo hadn't affected the invaders at all. Dejected, he asked Graak to pick up a body of a marked invader and fly it back to his testing facility.

Bethlyn, Margandy, and Laynal met him in front of the tent.

"Well? Did it work?" Bethlyn wrung her hands.

Blazel shook his head. "It didn't even slow them down. I brought one back for us to autopsy and find out why."

Margandy wrinkled her nose. "Oh, gee thanks, Blazel. Those damned things putrefy as soon as they're opened up."

"Well, see if you can discover anything, anyway."

As usual, the moment Margandy cut into the body, the insides began to rot, and Blazel turned his head away, gagging. He turned back, holding open the chest for Margandy as she quickly removed the organs. From what he could tell, they appeared the same as all the others. He carted the invader's corpse well away from the tent for Laynal to burn it.

When he returned, Blazel stared at the empty pot, rubbing his face in frustration. "I was so sure the concoction would work."

"This is the way of medicine," Bethlyn said, patting him on the back. "We'll find something that works, eventually. All of you go get some sleep. You look awful." Scowling, she shooed them toward the tent door.

Finally, Blazel nodded, and for the first time in days, he stumbled to the tent he shared with Rizelya. He gazed at her face, relaxed in sleep, and kissed her forehead, reminding himself why he needed to press on. After undressing, he curled around her and dropped into a fitful sleep, dreaming of explosions and the invaders dragging him into their big mother ship.

Early the next morning, he returned to his testing facility. With renewed determination, he selected a different group of herbs. By the time Margandy and Laynal arrived, he had them in the mortar and was vigorously crushing them. They resolutely nodded to him and went to work.

Kaieli - 35 de Rokdar, 1075

The days grew shorter and colder, signaling winter arriving in the Barrens, and the first rainstorm hit. Kaieli grimaced as the cold rain soaked her thin pallet. By morning, the open slave pens turned into a miserable mud pit. Black muck covered everything, including the Posairs' scant food supplies. Kaieli swore as she slid in the slick mud, grabbing Rolstrun's elbow to keep from landing on her backside.

"This is only going to get worse," Bohandran growled. "I spent a winter at the guard fortress many years ago. It isn't the rain we have to worry about. It's the blighted sandstorms. They can rage for days." He glanced around the pen. "We won't survive if we're in here when one hits."

Bile rose in Kaieli's throat. She couldn't imagine a worse fate than to go through all the suffering, only to die because of inadequate shelter. The work horn blared, cutting off any further discussion. The women ducked their heads in the pouring rain and slogged through the mud to the processing plant. At least there, they'd be dry—and warmer.

Vy'shol entered the plant, shivering from the cold. The Volkern's dark-blue hair hung in limp strands, and water dripped from her coverall.

Kaieli hurried to meet her. "Vy'shol, the weather is only going to become worse as winter comes and not simply rain. The experienced guard-packs warned me sandstorms will tear through the Barrens, often for days. If the Scourge want us to continue to be productive, we need more protection from the elements than those open pens we're housed in. Can you help?"

Vy'shol wrung the water from her hair as she considered Kaieli. "All the Coufrish and Gheethong are gone, killed for food by the invaders. Their barracks are unused. There is plenty of space in them for your people. Perhaps the commander will allow you to be moved into them." She lifted an eyebrow, and a sly smile spread across her lips. She lowered her voice. "Yes, this would be a good thing. You would also be closer to us. We're impressed by how much nucla you've made inert. Have you noticed the Scourge are falling ill from your sunlight?"

Kaieli shook her head. She'd focused her attention fully on cleansing the nucla. She hadn't helped with any escape runs for a long time and wasn't even sure if they were still being made.

"The Faeorn adjusted the sunscreen formula. The Scourge's skin still doesn't develop sores. However, for unknown reasons," Vy'shol winked, "many experience bloody diarrhea, spontaneous bleeding, and severe fatigue. Although it's mostly affecting the common soldiers and lower officers. The higher officers, like the commander, stay inside too much. We will have to find another subtle way to weaken them."

The rain stopped during the day, and when Kaieli tramped back to the slave pen, she gaped at the dry ground. Only a few puddles marked the mud she'd trekked through that morning. She hadn't quite believed it when Bohandran said the Barrens could suffer from both rain and sandstorms. But after seeing how quickly the sand dried, she now did.

A few days later, the wind whipped the sand into a frenzy. Kaieli grimaced as the cold bit through the tough coveralls, and sand glass cut into her exposed hands and face as she walked to the processing plant. The wind blew all day, rattling the high windows. Finally, as evening fell, it dropped.

Kaieli's eyes widened when she stepped outside. Drifts of sand piled in pockets against the sides of the buildings. Hope shimmered through her when their guards took a different route from their usual one to the slave pens. The guards led the women to a long building deeper inside the compound. When she entered it, Kaieli wrinkled her nose at the residual musky scent of Gheethong. But she'd become accustomed to it if it meant she'd sleep warm and dry.

"Oh Sweet Goddess!" she crowed in delight, grinning at the raised platforms used for beds. "No more sleeping on the hard, rocky ground, breathing in Barrens dust." Kaieli took in the other changes. In addition to long tables for eating, the building contained chairs and other furniture for relaxing. Never mind that they were a bit oddly shaped.

"We have baths!" Myndera cried.

Kaieli ran to join Myndera, who smiled happily and gestured to the room. While it lacked the big soaking tubs, spouts hung from the walls, which spewed water. Kaieli immediately tossed off the nasty coverall and claimed a water spout. She scrubbed and scrubbed, attempting to remove the accumulated grime from her skin after several lunadars of not being able to bathe. The Scourge had provided them with barely enough water for drinking and a quick wipe down.

Joy filled her when she and Rolstrun made love in the dark. For once, they were both clean, and they slept in a real bed with bedding. After the harsh conditions of the slave pen, it seemed like an unusual luxury.

During the night, the wind picked up again. Kaieli snuggled against Rolstrun's warm side, grateful the invaders had moved them into an enclosed structure. As the high windows rattled, she pulled the blanket tighter over their shoulders. In the morning, the wind still howled around them, and sand blasted the sides of the building. For the first time since their capture, the Scourge soldiers didn't march the Posairs to work in either the plant or out in the crater. It seemed like a holiday. After a meager breakfast, Kaieli and Rolstrun returned to their bed, promptly falling asleep.

Later in the afternoon, Kaieli awoke with the strange sensation of feeling refreshed and energized. Her fingers trailed over Rolstrun's arm, and she frowned at the bump from his tracking device. "I might be strong enough now to remove it," she mused. "Especially if Chariel helps me. Would you be willing to allow us to try?"

Rolstrun laid his hand over the tracking device and nodded. "I want this out of me, and out of you."

Kaieli, Chariel, and Rolstrun wandered to a quiet corner where three wide chairs sat. "Oh, these are comfortable!" she said.

"I know." Chariel settled deeper into her seat. "I'm amazed, because to me, they have an odd proportions and styling."

"I forgot what sitting in comfort was like," Rolstrun sighed. He leaned his head against the back of the chair, closing his eyes. After a few milcrons, he shook himself awake. "Okay, ladies, if we're going to try this, let's do it." He rested his arm on the chair's padded arm.

Kaieli and Chariel scooted forward and concentrated on the alien device under Rolstrun's skin. As their magic touched the device, it pulsed a red warning, slowly at first, then gaining speed. Rolstrun writhed in agony.

"We have to stop, or it will kill him!" Kaieli broke their connection to the device as Rolstrun jerked his arm away from them. He hugged it against his chest, moaning.

She held her breath, hoping they hadn't activated the explosive. Cautiously, she reached out with her senses again and sighed in relief when the device's energy signature returned to normal.

"The energy feels similar to the nucla," Chariel observed. "Maybe we need to treat it like we do the nucla."

Myndera volunteered for them to attempt to remove her device. Even with the Black-type magic, the explosive resisted their attempts to neutralize it. Kaieli withdrew their energy before they accidentally detonated it.

Later, Kaieli sprawled on her platform, crying. They had to destroy the control beacon. None of the first group of Posairs captured would be safe until they did. They all risked the device blowing them apart—herself included.

When would the Faeorn ever decide Kaieli and the others had purged enough nucla to help them? Without them, she and Rolstrun could never leave this hellscape.

Chapter 25

Rizelya - 10 de Eyedar, 1075

The last chedans of Rokdar brought frequent rain to the plains, but only sporadic rainstorms in the Barrens. Instead, massive sandstorms blew for days at a time, obliterating the sunlight and making travel impossible, even by Gryphon.

Rizelya hated the howling wind and the grit in the air. But the sandstorms gave the Posairs a much needed respite from the fighting against both the invaders and the Malvers' monsters. However, even these storms couldn't drag Blazel from his obsession with finding a poison to use against the Scourge. Rizelya missed him. She understood the importance of his work in the effort to defeat the invaders. But it didn't stop her longing to hear his laughter and feel his warm presence wrapped around her at night.

At the beginning of Eyedar, a particularly bad storm crashed down on them. Finally, after nine days, the winds died, and the dust settled. In the morning, Rizelya flew with Glork to survey the damage. Surprisingly, all the tents survived. When they'd realized the storm's severity, the Haaslair fighters and centaurs had driven the horses deeper into the plains. The sunlight sparkled on the horse's hides as the Haaslair people herded them back to camp.

"Let's check the slave compound," Rizelya suggested. "Goddess, can you imagine how much worse those winds were in the Barrens?" She shuddered at the thought of her friends exposed to the storm. The petrified wood boulders provided the only shelter from the scouring sandstorms, and there weren't any such protections at the crater rim.

Glork adjusted his flight toward the Barrens. *I hope the Scourge want their nucla badly enough to move our people into a safer place than those open pens.*

The landscape sliding under Glork's wings had changed from when they'd flown in this direction before the sandstorm. Light glinted from a tower they'd never seen before. As Glork flew closer, the shifting sands revealed an ancient temple. Ages ago, the central dome had collapsed, and Rizelya glimpsed the inside of the sanctuary.

The Barrens seem an odd place for a temple, Glork said. *Our histories don't say anything about one here.*

"Well, our histories have hidden many things. This may be another example. The sand has buried it for a long time. I have a strange feeling, like we were supposed to find it. Let's investigate." Rizelya loved to explore the ruins around Strunland Territory, finding items that gave insight into how her ancestors had lived before the Great War and the Malvers' monsters.

Graak landed, and together, they entered the temple. A thick layer of sand covered the main sanctuary. Age faded the murals on the walls until only a suggestion of their beauty remained. Surprisingly, the corridor leading to the inner sanctum lacked any debris. They wandered down it. Here, protected from the scouring sands, the paint on the murals showed more brightly. In some places, rust-colored splotches marred the elegant lines.

Rizelya stopped and inspected them, drawing back in shock. "Those are bloodstains! How could anyone kill priestesses?"

Our stories warn about many atrocities committed during the Great War. Glork's ears laid flat against his head. *Even killing innocents. By the end of the war, my ancestors had had enough of killing. It is why our people escaped to the top of the world, where we could live in peace.*

"Do you think this is the temple Shandir served in?"

Perhaps. We know she came from a southern one.

They turned and walked down a corridor where the murals depicted aged women—the high priestess's quarters. The door had long since disintegrated, and Rizelya peered into the room, feeling both curious and a bit blasphemous. A stone altar sat on the opposite wall under a mural of the Goddess in her Crone form. The old woman gazed at them with wise, kind eyes, with her hand outstretched in blessing. She seemed to be pointing at something at her feet. Without realizing it, Rizelya stepped inside, drawn to what the Goddess pointed at.

Rizelya's hand, of its own accord, pressed on a carved symbol. Stone grated on stone as a section, a foot and a half wide by two feet long, extended from the wall. Inside the hollow case lay a perfectly preserved book. Rizelya couldn't read the language of the cover's gold lettering, still bright after the centuries of being buried. In a daze, she reached in and removed it. As soon as she did, the stone drawer closed.

What is that, Rizelya? Glork stood on the threshold.

"A book." She looked at it again. Her breath stilled, and her heart expanded. "An ancient holy book. I think I'm supposed to give it to Wisah." She glanced around, searching for something to put the heavy book in. Nothing but stone remained in the room. She unfastened her jacket and tucked it against her chest. A tremble under her feet startled her. A crack in the floor appeared. Her eyes flew open wide. "We need to get out of here, fast."

She ran across the room while Glork backed out of the doorway and galloped through the corridor ahead of her. She glanced over her shoulder at a loud popping. A fissure zigzagged toward them, the stone screeching and groaning as it splitting apart. "Run!"

Glork reached the sanctuary. He turned around, his feathers and fur standing on end, his tail puffed up. *Hurry, Rizelya, hurry!*

She looked behind her at the fear in his voice. The fissure's leading edge was less than a foot away. She raced to Glork, vaulting onto his back. He leaped straight up through the broken roof, flapping wildly to gain altitude. Rizelya wrapped her arms around his neck. She hadn't had time to strap into the harness. His height gave her a good view of the temple crumbling into dust. Soon, nothing remained to show any structure had ever been there.

Glork gazed down, and his wing beats temporarily lost their rhythm. *Did you do that?*

"I... I don't know." Rizelya gulped. A tingling sensation warmed her chest where the book rested. "I don't think so. The Goddess wanted us to find this book. Well, maybe not us, specifically, but someone."

Then it must be important. Glork zoomed back to camp.

Wisah stood at the edge of the Barrens, with her hand shielding her eyes as she gazed at the sky. Glork landed in front of her. As soon as his feet touched the ground, Rizelya unlocked her fingers from their death grip and slid off. They hadn't stopped for her to properly harness herself in, and she'd spent the entire flight terrified she'd fall. Glork rubbed his throat with the back of a talon and coughed several times.

"I received a message you had something for me." Wisah's eyes were wide, and her voice sounded strained. "I've never experienced such clear communication from the Goddess before. Do you know what it's about?"

Rizelya unfastened her jacket and pulled out the book. "This. We found it in an ancient temple."

Wisah reached for the tome, gasping when her fingers made contact. "Oh, sweet Mother!" She clamped her mouth shut.

"Ouch! What is it?" Rizelya rubbed her palms on her pants. When Wisah had touched the book, a zing of energy had pulsed from it. Rizelya's hands still buzzed.

Wisah shook her head. "The Supreme needs to see this, immediately."

Wings sounded overhead, and Sheekeek and two other Gryphons flew into view. Sheekeek wore his harness, and the Reds mounted on the other two waved. Supply packs hung down the Gryphon's sides.

We're here to take you, Sheekeek said. *We have your possessions.*

"How did you know?" Wisah shook her head. "Never mind. The Goddess." She gave Rizelya a wry grin. "I'm off for another wild ride. Please tell Jaehaas I've returned to the Sanctuary." She kissed Rizelya on the cheek, pulled her cloak tighter around her, and climbed onto Sheekeek's back. With practiced ease, she buckled herself in and signaled her readiness. The small group leaped into the air.

Rizelya watched them disappear over the horizon, wondering when she'd see her niece again. Over the past lunadars, she'd enjoyed her daily presence.

Rolstrun - 10 de Eyedar, 1075

Winter arrived, not with a snowstorm like Rolstrun usually experienced at home in the mountains, but with a monstrous sandstorm. He lounged on his sleeping platform with Kaieli curled next to him, and a blanket around their shoulders. Calistrun, Alestrun, and Myndera huddled on the end of the bed. Outside, the wind howled, and the sand grated on the building's walls.

Myndera shivered, staring at the windows high above them. "Are you sure they're going to hold?" She jumped when the wind rattled them.

Calistrun pulled her closer to him. "I'm positive. We're safe in here."

"Thank the Mother, Kaieli talked the Volkern into helping us," Alestrun said, gently squeezing her thigh.

A jolt of jealousy stabbing Rolstrun surprised him. The three lovers had remained close throughout their terrifying ordeal. *Why didn't he and Laean?* Kaieli snuggled into his shoulder, and the jealousy disappeared. He'd found someone he loved deeper than anything he'd felt for Laean. The magic he and Kaieli worked together to cleanse the nucla gave him glimpses deep inside his partner's souls. Kaieli's depth of compassion and love for her people made him adore her even more. He didn't want to experience life without her. He fervently wished this nightmare would end soon.

"Can you imagine being outside in this sandstorm?" Calistrun shuddered. "It would tear the flesh from our bones."

"What do you think it's doing to the lizards?" Alestrun asked. "There aren't enough enclosed pens for them all."

Rolstrun glared at his missing fingers. "Those damned things are too tough for a sandstorm to get the better of them. I'm sure they'll be just fine."

Finally, nine days later, the wind died. Bohandran and Kederposan tried to push open the door. It wouldn't budge. Anyola, a young Red from Posanreande Keep, climbed on Metherposan's shoulders to peer out the high window above them.

"We're not leaving anytime soon," she groaned as she hopped down. "The door is covered in sand. They're going to have to dig us out."

A few octars later, scraping sounds filtered through the door. At last, soldiers pulled it open.

As he stepped outside, Rolstrun blinked in the hazy afternoon sunlight. Dust swirled like fog over the compound. Sand dunes marked where several barracks stood. A fighter ship lay in a tangled mess. Sheezets wandered aimlessly, bleating in distress. Their hides bled from numerous cuts caused by the sand-glass.

"Sweet Mother! Would you look at that?" Bohandran pointed toward the slave pens.

Rolstrun's knees buckled, and he nearly fainted. Only the tips of the fence peeked from the sand, marking where they were. If the Posairs had still been living in them, they would all be dead.

The invaders, busy digging out their comrades, ignored the Posairs. Taking advantage, Rolstrun, Calistrun, and Alestrun wandered to the crater rim.

"Wow!" Rolstrun hadn't seen inside the crater since he'd joined Kaieli's nucla clearing team. The mining operation had reduced the pillar by half of its original size. Sand covered the ore carts, and it would take days to clear the cart rails leading to the lifts. The ladders, normally firmly attached to the crater's slick sides, hung tattered. They swung loose from the wind tearing them from the bolt rings.

"Good!" Alestrun said, kicking the remnants of a ladder. "Now we can't climb down. Maybe the invaders will give up on mining the stupid rock."

Rolstrun glared at him. "Haven't you been paying attention? The nucla inside the pillar's rock is precious to them. They won't stop. They won't leave until they've scavenged every last nugget. And if they don't take it all, Commander Ke-ke-tak will return with even more invaders to destroy our world. Do you want everyone on this planet enslaved, like the Hap'thez and Coufrish?"

Alestrun held up his hands, shaking his head. "No, no, I don't want that." His shoulders slumped. "But I'm so tired of hacking that awful rock. You have it easy standing around all day in a nice, warm, dry building."

"Cleansing the nucla with magic isn't easy. It takes more out of me than swinging a pickax ever did." Rolstrun paced along the edge of the rim. "We're trying to purge as much nucla as possible so the invaders don't come back. That—" he flung a hand toward the pillar "—is way too large for us to handle. But we can cleanse the rock bits you mine. You aren't cutting up the pillar for the Scourge. You're doing it for us and for our people."

Alestrun straightened his shoulders. "In that case, I'll hack at the rock until it's gone, and I'll tell the others."

It took three days for the invaders to convert one of the ore cart lines to carry the men up and down the crater walls. When the men returned to work, they did so with a new sense of purpose. They no longer walked with shuffling steps and slumped shoulders. They now knew they had a critical part in defeating their enemy. On his way to the processing plant, Rolstrun grimaced at the pillar. His team still had tons of rock to cleanse.

Blazel - 10 de Eyedar, 1075

The morning after the massive sandstorm ended, Blazel jogged across the camp, anxious to ascertain how much damage his tent had sustained. And if the storm had ruined his latest potion. The storm had come up so suddenly, he'd only been able to cover the mixture. He had high hopes for this batch. He'd mixed the acidic juice from the pods collected near the black castle, along with the liquid from boiling helbore leaves, solanar berries, marsh marigold flowers, and dojee. Margandy and Laynal had arrived before him, and they stood staring at the container.

"Is the potion ruined?" He hurried to the table.

"No, I don't believe so," Margandy said. "What did you add to it?"

Blazel screwed up his face, trying to remember. He glanced down at his hand, and his eyes widened. "At the last minute, I decided to add some of my warrior's venom to the mixture. In my hurry, I also nicked my hand. I think a few drops of my blood mixed with the venom."

Blazel scrutinized the mixture. Instead of the usual thick and gooey mess, this one appeared thin and watery. His heart pounded in his chest as his excitement grew.

Margandy nudged him aside. Her eyebrows scrunched as she stirred, lifting the wooden spoon to allow the liquid to fall back into the pot. "It looks thin enough to spray. I have an idea." She hurried out of the tent, and in a few milcrons, returned with a perfume atomizer. After pouring a small amount into the bottle, Margandy squeezed the bulb, releasing a fine mist.

She sprayed some Scourge tissue they'd collected from the battlefield. Laynal had wrapped a protective shield around it before it putrefied. When the mist hit the tissue sample, it began to liquefy, and the cells seized into a clump.

"This looks promising." Margandy examined the sample closer. "We just may have found the right solution! But let's make sure it's safe for us and our friends." She pulled out two other tissue samples, one from a Posair and the other a Gryphon, and squirted them with the mixture. They waited, but even after five milcrons, nothing happened. Several octars later, the samples still hadn't reacted.

"Let's test the mixture on a live Posair to be sure it's safe," Margandy said.

Laynal sighed and held out her arm. "I'll do it."

Margandy handed the bottle to Blazel, then rubbed her hands together. A bronze light formed between them. "Okay, I'm ready."

Blazel squeezed the bulb at Laynal, and the fine spray covered her face and arms.

"Hey!" Laynal waved her hand in front of her face, coughing. Immediately, her eyes watered, turning red. She blinked, wiping at her runny eyes, and blew her nose.

"Well, anything?" Blazel peered intently at her.

"No. Just my eyes sting like crazy."

While Blazel mixed another small batch of the concoction, Margandy watched Laynal closely. When she showed no other symptoms, she washed Laynal's eyes out with an herbal solution, which instantly stopped the stinging.

Blazel called Graak to test the solution on him. He didn't have any adverse reactions to the potion.

"Now, we need to test it on a live invader." Hope hummed within Blazel as he filled the bottle to the brim.

The next day, Blazel carried the latest mixture into battle. His huge warrior paw dwarfed the woman's perfume atomizer. Rizelya fought at his side, protecting him. Finally, he had his chance when an invader fell at his feet. He sprayed the soldier's face with the potion.

The invader gasped in surprise at the seemingly innocuous mist. A moment later, he gagged, yellow mucus spewing from his throat. His eyes leaked trails of purple blood. His hands spasmed, losing control of his weapon as he collapsed into convulsions, finally stilling. The time from spritz to death only lasted a few milcrons.

The small bottle held enough potion to kill ten invaders. Blazel grinned as he gave the empty container to Rizelya, who stuffed it in her jacket. Then, as a team, they laid waste to their enemy with tooth, claw, fire, and blade. Soon after, the remaining soldiers retreated into the Barrens.

Blazel stood panting, covered in purple blood and gore. He glanced at Rizelya. She was just as filthy.

"It worked!" Blazel howled, thrusting a fist into the air. He shifted into his natural form, grabbed Rizelya, and swung her in a circle. "It worked! It worked!"

"Yes, it did," she said when he finally set her back on the ground. "It looked agonizing, but effective. Although my eyes really sting and hurt."

"Margandy has an herbal solution that counteracts the stinging. We need a different delivery method, and find some way to protect our eyes. This darned perfume atomizer doesn't hold enough."

While Rizelya went to have her eyes treated by Margandy, Blazel jogged to the command tent.

"It works!" he crowed in delight as he entered. "We finally found a potion that kills the invaders."

Histrun put down the papers he was reading. "That is good news. How effective is it?"

"Every single invader we sprayed died. We need a better delivery device than this." He held up the atomizer.

"I'm sure Maendy can devise something. She'll be here tomorrow. She finally produced some ammunition that works in the invader's weapons."

For the first time since his quest to find the right poison, Blazel sat around the fire eating and joking with his packmates. With his invention, they were sure to start gaining the upper hand in this long war with the invaders.

Rizelya - 11 de Eyedar, 1075

Rizelya rubbed her stinging, watery eyes, wishing Blazel had warned her about the side effect of his potion. If she'd known, she'd have turned her face away from the mist. Instead of tromping all the way to his testing tent, she found Bethlyn, who washed Rizelya's eyes with an herbal solution.

"How are your eyes, Rizelya?" Bethlyn bent over and examined them closely.

"The stinging is gone, but they're itchy."

Bethlyn patted her shoulder. "You'll be fine in about an octar. Margandy told me about the side effect, so we already mixed an antidote. Although it doesn't seem like a good idea for our people to fight with running, burning eyes." She stood with her hands on her hips, chewing her bottom lip and staring at the table strewn with equipment. "How to protect your eyes?" she muttered to herself over and over. She suddenly whirled around. "Have you seen the new glass Maellyn has developed?"

Rizelya raised her eyebrows and shook her head. "No, what new glass?"

"A few measures west of here is a pit with fine, white sand. In her metalwork training, Maellyn learned how to blow glass. She's been experimenting with it. Look." Bethlyn held a piece of thin, clear glass on her palm. The rough edges would need smoothing.

Rizelya raised it up to her eye. "I can see perfectly through it! If we inserted it into a leather mask, it'd protect our eyes from the blowback of Blazel's potion. Oh! We could also use them while riding on the Gryphons. My eyes always hurt afterward from the wind and my hair whipping into them."

"Maellyn had that in mind when she started working on the glass. She'd come in here with a bug stuck in her eye."

Rizelya chuckled at the image, then grimaced. Bugs hit her in the face all the time while riding Glork. It hurt.

"Let's go talk to Maellyn about her project," Rizelya said. "I want to see how she makes it."

Bethlyn guided Rizelya to a tent set apart from the rest, even further than Blazel's.

"How come you're all the way out here?" Rizelya asked.

Maellyn made a face. "Histrun didn't want a fire to sweep through the tents, so I'm banished out here. Are you here about my prototypes?"

"Yes, I showed her your glass," Bethlyn said.

Rizelya grinned. "We need something to protect our eyes from Blazel's potion."

"He found one that works?"

Rizelya nodded.

"That's wonderful news!" She whooped, spinning in a circle. "You'll love what I've developed."

Curious, Rizelya followed her into a tent with a table covered with various projects.

"Here's the mask prototype." Maellyn held out a leather strip, big enough to cover one's eyes with glass inset in the eyeholes. A strap buckled behind the head allowed one to adjust the fit.

"Do they work?" Rizelya asked.

"Actually, very well." Maellyn smiled. "I haven't had a bug in my eye in days. You wear it like this." She put it on.

Rizelya laughed at Maellyn's now wide and bulging eyes. "You look like a goggle-eyed bass. They're goggles!"

The name stuck.

Blazel - 12 de Eyedar, 1075

Blazel ducked from the testing tent to grab some fresh air. He'd spent all morning mixing several batches of the new potion. His supply of plants used in the concoction was running low. Now that he had the right formula, he and Graak needed to take a team to the swamp to gather more. They could easily obtain most of what he required. However, they'd discovered the acidic pod in only one place. He shuddered, remembering his and Graak's experience at the black castle. Luckily, they didn't need to travel too close to it to harvest the pod.

As he stretched, he glimpsed a small flight of Gryphons winging from the north toward the camp. Curious, he trotted to the command tent, arriving at the same time as Maendy stepped from the lead Gryphon's back. Each of the accompanying ten Gryphons landed and deposited four large, bulging bags before taking off again.

Histrun and Naila fondly greeted Maendy. Blazel and Rizelya stood at the front of the crowd, where they had a good view.

"What did you create for us?" Histrun asked.

Maendy wore a pleased smile and pulled out a long, slender cylinder. "These. They're made from the helstrim alloy we use for the helbraughts and helstrablades. Because it's the same material, it allows the user to focus their Talent. For example, a Red can extend her fire magic to the projectile, and when it strikes an invader, it will ignite."

"But what about the men? Can they use it too?"

"Sure. The projectiles by themselves are deadly. They'll tear a hole through even a Gryphon, so people will need to aim carefully." She waved a hand at the bags. "My fellow helstramiesters and I have been working like fiends to make a large enough quantity to do some good." She dug into a bag and pulled out a long strip with projectiles attached to it. "Each strip holds fifty rounds, and there are twenty-five thousand strips in there."

Histrun whistled. "We've collected nearly three thousand weapons. This should help us fight better."

"We have the molds and the process down now, and we'll work on making more." She showed Histrun, Naila, Blazel, and the others how to load the cylinders into the weapons, select the right setting for metal projectiles, and shoot. As Blazel took his turn to load and shoot the new weapon, he wondered if the cylinder could hold his potion.

While others took their turns, Maendy and Blazel stepped aside. "Histrun says you need a way to dispense your poison in. What do you require?"

"We need something light people can carry on their backs, and some method to spray the poison." Blazel held up a cylinder. "Would these work?"

Maendy shrugged. "Possibly. Let me see what we can come up with. We can definitely produce containers for it. Will you be using it while flying on the Gryphons?"

"Yes. The greatest dispersal would be from the air, rather than spraying it on individual invaders."

"Do you have some of the potion I can take back with me? And the recipe?" She winked. "Just in case I'm successful in making the poison ammunition work."

"Sure, come with me." Blazel led her to the test tent and supplied her with the requested items. He also explained the process, including the secret ingredient: warrior venom and blood.

Chapter 26

Rizelya - 23 de Eyedar, 1075

Rizelya and Glork dove at a Scourge riding a lizard. While Glork flared, Rizelya aimed the new weapon, concentrating on feeding her fire into the projectiles. The process wasn't much different from what she did with her helbraught. She squeezed her finger on the trigger. A projectile zipped from the cylinder and slammed into an invader. Purple blood bloomed on its chest, and its already big eyes widened more. She released another projectile. This one tore through her target's head.

"This new weapon of Maendy's works!" Rizelya laughed.

Let's finish off this group, Glork said as he sailed higher.

You heard him, Rizelya sent to her platoon, all of whom carried the new weapon. *Let's end this skirmish!*

An octar later, Rizelya killed the last soldier. *Time to go home,* Rizelya said. *Leave the lizards alone.*

The riderless lizards galloped deeper into the Barrens and toward the Scourge compound. Rizelya didn't have the heart to wantonly kill the animals. When they died during a battle, it was regrettable, but necessary. But to seek them out to simply to kill them, carried one over the edge into committing a blasphemous atrocity.

Good, I'm tired. Glork swung wide, turning north to return to the base camp.

Rizelya patted Glork's shoulder. "Me, too, buddy."

Hey, Rizelya!

Rizelya grimaced at Maellyn's mind-shout.

I have something to show you. Come to the sandpit.

Glork sighed deeply. *While a nap sounds good, I'm interested in what Maellyn is so excited about.*

Rizelya sent her platoon to the base camp, while she and Glork flew to meet Maellyn. Rizelya raised her eyebrows in surprise. A small tent city had popped up near the sandpit, and dozens of metalworkers worked on creating the glass they needed for the new goggles.

Rizelya tiredly climbed from Glork's back, wiping the dirt from her goggles. She no longer had to squint, or even worse, close her eyes when Glork dove at their enemies.

"Thanks, Maellyn, for giving me these." She held up her goggles by the strap. "They've been a real eye saver."

"Oh, good!" Maellyn bounced on her toes and grinned. "Come. Let me show you what we've accomplished so far." She led Rizelya to a tent and pulled open the flap.

Rizelya whistled at the stacks and stacks of goggles. "You've done all this in just the past twelve days? How many have you finished?"

"Two hundred pairs. We made enough for everyone who rides a Gryphon along with a few spares."

"They'll be extremely happy to receive these. I've been the envy of all the Gryphon mounted fighters."

The Gryphons will be pleased, too, Glork added. *We won't have to listen to your complaints any more. Pfft... so much complaining about a few bugs.* He trilled a chuckle.

"A few bugs!" Maellyn huffed. "Getting a bug stuck in your eye is painful."

Rizelya agreed. "Are these ready to distribute?"

Maellyn nodded. "We need transportation and helpers to take them to camp."

I'll make the arrangements. A contingent will pick them up tomorrow.

"Thanks, Glork." Maellyn beamed. "I don't know what we'd do without you and your people."

The next morning, Rizelya and Blazel jogged to the command tent to meet with Maendy, who had returned.

"This device will dispense your poison, Blazel." Maendy showed them a metal canister. It appeared small enough to fit comfortably on a person's back and not interfere with their ability to fight. "You pour the poison into this chamber, then pump this lever a few times. When you're ready, you depress this trigger." Maendy demonstrated as she spoke. When she pushed the trigger, a thin nozzle spewed mist several feet away.

"These will work great!" Blazel said, his eyes alight. Since finding a mixture that worked, the tight lines around his mouth and eyes had relaxed. "How many did you make?"

"Two hundred."

Rizelya smiled. "That works out well. Maellyn's team made us the same quantity of goggles."

Maendy's eyes crinkled as she grinned. "I know. We coordinated our efforts. I'm very proud of her. I also made these." She grabbed a small tube, the same size and shape as the helstrim projectiles. "They're hollow for you to fill with the potion. Seal them with a wax plug, and they're ready to use just like the other ones. I'm sorry," Maendy said, giving a large bag of the hollow ammunition to Histrun. "We could only make two thousand in such a short time frame. If they work as well as we hope, we'll produce more."

Histrun took them with a nod. "We'll take whatever you give us. We have new troops arriving within a few days. The weapons and ammunition will come in handy."

With the arrival of winter, Histrun ordered the northern provinces of Strunlair, Ledonlair, and Keistanlair to send more fighters to the war effort. The snow and cold weather froze the swamps, making it impossible for the Malvers' monsters to become active.

The camp worked furiously over the next few days. Those fighters not actively engaged in the constant battles with the invaders worked on filling the canisters and hollow cylinders with Blazel's potion. Rizelya led training the fighting-packs to use the new weapons and equipment. It took practice to aim correctly, so the projectiles hit the intended target.

Rizelya - 29 de Eyedar, 1075

Rizelya strapped a canister on her back and checked to ensure the ammunition pouch for her new pulser was full. The new weapons banged against her helbraught, but she refused to abandon using it. Her helbraught worked as long as she had the energy to feed her magic into it, unlike the canister or pulser which eventually ran out of ammunition. The other women in her fighting-pack also carried their helbraughts along with the new weapons. For the first time in their lives, Blazel, Aistrun, and the men would fight using more than their teeth and claws.

At Graak's command, the flight of Gryphons rose into the air. In a short time, they encountered hundreds of invaders riding their lizard mounts across the Barrens. Clouds of black sand-glass puffed at their heavy gait. The Thunder Wings had accomplished destroying enough of the ships that the commander rarely sent the remaining few into battle any longer.

Dive! Blazel ordered, glee in his voice.

Glork snapped his wings back and zoomed toward the ground, and the passing wind burned Rizelya's cheeks. Silently thanking Maellyn for the goggles, Rizelya aimed the nozzle at an enemy and depressed the trigger. The fine mist covered the invader, who instantly began coughing and vomiting yellow mucus. He dropped the reins to his mount as he toppled over. The lizard bleated in surprise, then whirled, and like a horse free to return home, it galloped toward its pen. Glork targeted another soldier, and Rizelya sprayed it with the poison. They continued to attack the soldiers until she heard a click and no more liquid spewed from the nozzle. Rizelya switched to the pulser, firing the projectiles into any invaders they encountered while Glork flared. A few octars later, the fighting ended as the last invader on the battlefield died.

The Posairs had won the battle!

Rizelya and Blazel waited in the command tent for Histrun. While elated at their recent victories, including this one, all Rizelya wanted at the moment was to bathe, eat dinner, and collapse on her cot.

"Over the past three days," Histrun said, while pacing with his hands behind his back, "we've won every battle we've fought with the enemy. I believe it's time to attempt freeing our people from the slave camp."

"But the Faeorn haven't agreed to dismantle the control beacon," Blazel objected.

"We can't wait for them. Our people are suffering now. The new weapons should give us the advantage we didn't have before. Our past experience proves the invader's projectiles can penetrate the energy dome. I'm confident these—" he picked up a cylinder of poison "—or the poison mist, perhaps both, will also pierce their shield. If they do, we can protect a team on the ground to cut through the fence, infiltrate the compound, and free our people."

I suggest a test run, Moraak grumbled, thumping his tail, *before we send people into the compound. It can easily become a death trap, even for my Gryphons. We don't want to provide more slaves for the Scourge.*

Histrun agreed. They spent several octars planning the mission.

The next day, Rizelya and Blazel, riding Glork and Graak, led the raid on the Scourge compound. They wore poison canisters strapped onto their backs and carried a pulser slung over their shoulders. Similarly armed, Leistral and Eidstrun waited on the ground by the fence with their team.

Graak hovered invisibly over the top of the energy dome while Blazel sprayed a thick layer of the mist.

"Is it working, Graak?" Blazel asked.

Graak bent his head, peering at the thin barrier. *No, not that I can see.*

Rizelya aimed and fired a cylinder. Below, a soldier jerked from the impact, then his body convulsed. A few milcrons later, he lay dead. "Yes!" Rizelya cried. "The projectiles will go through."

Blazel and the others on the team lifted their projectile weapons and started shooting.

"Stop!" Blazel ordered after they'd fired only a few rounds. "The energy field is distorting the trajectory of the cylinders. We're hitting the ground or buildings more often than an invader. We don't have the ammunition to waste like this."

The soldiers returned fire with their much bigger weapon, and the Gryphons ducked and dived out of the way. A troop thundered from the compound on their lizard-beasts, barreling toward Leistral and Eidstrun's squad-pack. With a shriek, Graak and the other Gryphons dove to attack them. Rizelya and the other Posairs quickly changed weapons. Rizelya gripped the nozzle of her canister as Glork leveled out above the lizard's heads. She pressed the trigger, and poison streamed out. The invaders screamed as it killed them. A few escaped the poisonous spray, but not the Gryphons, who tore them to shreds with their talons or lit them on fire. By the time Glork pulled up and away from the troop, Leistral's squad-pack had raced to safety.

"How did it go?" Rizelya asked Leistral as they rested behind a jumble of petrified rocks.

"No luck with the mist," Leistral grimaced. "It didn't penetrate the energy field, but the cylinders went through just fine, except the damned field played havoc with our aim."

"Same here." Rizelya felt like stomping her feet at the failure. Now, they'd have to wait for the Faeorn to help them destroy the control beacon and take out the energy dome. Until that happened, their people were stuck in the compound.

"I'll free you, Kaieli," Rizelya swore. "Somehow, we'll get you all out."

Kaieli - 33 de Eyedar, 1075

"Come see!" Vy'shol cried, running into the infirmary area where Kaieli and her team worked. She grabbed Kaieli by the hand and tugged. "You have to see what's happening!"

Kaieli wondered what could discompose the serene Volkern so much. Standing outside the door, the Yoon triad pointed at the sky, jabbering excitedly.

"It is good." Pei Yoon grinned.

"More than good. Best." Mei-Ying Yoon held her burgeoning belly. "We have hope."

Kaieli glanced at Vy'shol, confused.

"Your people discovered something to damage the Scourge," Vy'shol explained. "Look!"

Kaieli, with Rolstrun, Maheli, and the rest of her team, slipped from the building. Kaieli's mouth dropped open in a silent "oh!"

Graak and Glork hovered above them, and Rizelya and Blazel were shooting weapons, which appeared remarkably like the invaders. The projectiles they used zipped through the energy dome's barrier as if it didn't exist, many of them striking the soldiers rushing around in a frenzy. Any invader they struck quickly choked and vomited a thick, yellow mucus. Their eyes poured purple blood, and soon after, their bodies spasmed with violent convulsions. Within milcrons, they died.

"Yes!" Maheli cried, pumping her fist in the air.

A popping sound came from the fence near the processing plant. Kaieli and Chariel ran around the corner. Leistral and Eidstrun, leading a team on the ground, all held the same weapons, along with a canister that sprayed a mist. Whatever it was, it didn't seem to penetrate the energy dome, but the projectiles did. Kaieli jumped, ducking behind the building as one zipped toward her.

All too soon, the attacking Posairs stopped shooting and quickly retreated.

A troop of invaders exited the compound, barreling after Leistral's squad-pack racing into the Barrens. Ten Gryphons appeared in the air over the mounted soldiers, and their riders sprayed a fine mist over them, with the same results as the projectiles.

"Blazel found a poison that works," Chariel said. She grinned as she gazed at the invader corpses littering the ground. "I knew the Goddess had sent him to the swamps for a reason."

"It looks painful. Good!" Kaieli smirked. She felt a bit guilty at the strength of her sentiment. It went against her calling as a healer. But after all the pain and suffering the invaders had inflicted on her people, it seemed like justice for them to suffer in return.

Hope fluttered in her heart as she tromped back into the processing plant. Tre'nok slipped in behind them.

Kaieli stalked to the Faeorn triad, staring at them with her hands on her hips. "Now, are you going to help us? We've met all your conditions. We're making the nucla inert, and our people have a weapon as deadly as anything the Scourge possess. My people will shove these damned invaders off our planet with or without your help. Which would you prefer?"

"We help," Mei-Ying said.

"It take time," Jei-Yan added.

"Why? How long?" Maheli demanded. "We need to get our people out of here."

Jei-Yan held up three fingers.

"Three days?"

He shook his head and turned to Vy'shol. "You translate, please."

Vy'shol nodded. "About three of your chedans. The Faeorn can deactivate the control beacon and take down the energy dome, but they need your people's help to do so. It is an easy matter to deactivate it, but the Scourge will simply turn it back on. To ensure they can't, we must destroy it. After watching what your people can do with your magic, they think it's possible—"

"That's all well and good," Maheli scowled. "But it doesn't explain why we have to wait so long."

"If you will be patient," Vy'shol said, holding up a hand, "I will explain."

Maheli snapped her mouth closed and crossed her arms over her chest.

"The Faeorn have an idea about how to stop the commander, but it will take them time to reprogram the navigation system without the Scourge knowing about it. In the meantime, the mining of the nucla must continue."

Maheli continued to glare at Vy'shol. Tre'nok touched his companion on the shoulder and spoke softly for a moment with her.

"As long as the commander believes his hold is being filled with nucla," Tre'nok said, "his greed will keep him here. And his arrogance will force him to fight your people. In the face of your continued rebellion, and with these new weapons of yours, he has two choices. He can leave here now with what nucla he has, and without a cargo hold filled with slaves, then return with a greater force. But if he does this, he will lose status by allowing such an inferior race to overcome him, and perhaps even lose his life.

"His second choice, which we believe he will do, is to stay and crush your world. He can't comprehend the possibility of a world of backward savages defeating him. He will throw all he has at you. But we hope your people will prevail against him."

Vy'shol gestured toward Mei-Ying. "If the Faeorn were not sure you triumph against the Scourge, they would not do this. If they reprogram the mother ship's navigation system and you do not win, they will die on the ship, and with them, their children. This is anathema to them. Also, when your people rescue us, they must destroy the second scout ship, leaving the commander only the mother ship to return home in. It also removes his ability to send someone to gather reinforcements. Lairheim is too far away from the nearest communications beacon or Scourge controlled planet for him to send a message."

Kaieli looked at the others, who all nodded. "All right, what do you want us to do?"

While they wanted to escape this nightmare, they could endure it for another three chedans.

Rolstrun - 39 de Eyedar, 1075

Life in the slave camp went from bad to worse as the Posairs won more battles. After every lost battle, the commander returned furious. Each time, he randomly selected a captive and systematically beat the person nearly to death before sucking them dry. Rolstrun lived in constant fear that the commander would choose him.

The slave population continued to dwindle. By now, the Scourge had killed all the Gheethong and Coufrish for food. Only about 275 Hap'thez and fewer than 75 Kaigor still lived. Over 300 Vhelopsi had escaped with the Posairs. The remaining 250 hoped to leave and join the Posairs when they finally destroyed the control beacon. The invader's atrocities had killed half of the nearly 3,500 Posair prisoners, but over 1,000 people had escaped. Only those Posairs captured first and had the explosive tracking implants remained in the slave camp.

Rolstrun secretly cheered when the commander abandoned the monster corrals. There were far too few remaining captives for the Scourge to waste them on the monsters.

A chedan after the meeting with the Faeorn, Tre'nok entered the infirmary area.

"The Faeorn need you to clear the nucla bars in the cargo hold," he informed them. "Can you do it from here?"

Kaieli shook her head. "No. We've tried. Something about the ship's hull blocks our magic."

"It is made from a nucla alloy."

"Ah, that explains it. You'll have to sneak us onto the ship."

He nodded tersely, scowling. "I was afraid you'd say that. If not for your skin and hair coloring, you look like Vhelopsi—"

"Except we don't have fangs." Kaieli grinned wide, showing her fangless teeth.

Tre'nok snorted a short laugh. "Any chance you can change your coloring?"

"Faliciden?" Kaieli asked.

"Perhaps." Faliciden shrugged. "I can make our hair color appear different, like I've done with Chariel. But I'm not sure about our skin coloring." She closed her eyes. Nothing seemed to happen for several milcrons, but then slowly a golden hue crept over her skin, and her evergreen hair lightened, turning dark-gold. Her eyes popped open. "Did I do it?"

Rolstrun stared at her and nodded.

Tre'nok smiled in satisfaction. "Yes, it will do very well. Get ready. A group of Vhelopsi will come to the processing plant shortly to take the load of processed nucla to the ship. They'll switch places with you. Keep your heads down—" he grinned at Kaieli "—and your mouths closed. A Vhelopsi, Sangasu Musa, has learned your language. He will guide you to the hold and ensure the Scourge don't discover you." Tre'nok left.

"Well, I better change all your appearances." Faliciden rubbed her hands together, causing a green light to glow around them. "I can only do one at a time."

When it was Rolstrun's turn, he squirmed as the magic tickled him.

"Hold still," Faliciden admonished.

A few milcrons later, he held up his now pale gold hand. He frowned, not liking how strange they looked with the same hair color.

Tre'nok stuck his head into the infirmary. "Looks good. You'll pass. Just don't smile. And for the love of your Goddess, don't look any Scourge in the eye. The Vhelopsi are here."

One at a time, over several milcrons, eight Vhelopsi slipped through the curtain and the Posairs took their places. Finally, Rolstrun joined the others, where five large crates of processed nucla bars waited. Workers helped them load the crates onto machines similar to the guards' personal mobility devices.

Tre'nok introduced them to a tall Vhelopsi with bronze skin, dark bronze hair, and pale gold eyes. "This is Sangasu Musa."

The Vhelopsi appraised the Posairs. "You will do. If any Scourge stops us, let me do the talking." He showed them how to work the machines.

Apprehension nipped at Rolstrun's neck as they crossed the open area separating the processing plant from the ship's rear opening. He scrunched his shoulders even more. They entered the large door, and the overwhelming stench made him gag. Sangasu glared at him, and Rolstrun swallowed hard to keep from vomiting. He took a moment to gaze in wonder at the cavernous space. Long blue tubes, evenly placed along the walls, provided enough light to see and not trip.

Sangasu led them deeper into the hold. The farther in they traversed, Kaieli and Chariel panted heavily, and Loshera moaned softly, like she was in excruciating pain.

What's wrong? Rolstrun asked Kaieli.

It's the nucla. Her mind-voice held the same agony. *There's so much of it.*

They finally stopped in front of piles and piles of nucla bars. Rolstrun hadn't realized how much his people had mined and processed. His stomach clench at the menace wafting from it. How could they clear the vast quantity in two chedans?

Vhelopsi emerged from the shadows, and Sangasu guided the Posairs to a hiding spot.

His eyes softened as he took in the pained expressions of the three women. "I can tell it causes you pain to be here. How long can you stay?"

"Not long," Kaieli gasped. "Two, maybe three of our octars is all."

He nodded. "I, or one of my people, will stand guard outside. Let us know when you must leave, and we'll get you out."

When they merged their Talents, the pain eased for the three women with Gray and White Talents, allowing them to do the work they must accomplish. Three octars later, Rolstrun felt like a wet rag. Exhaustion dragged on his limbs, and he dreaded the half measure walk back to the processing plant.

That night, anticipating a hot shower, Rolstrun twisted the knob to turn on the water, staring numbly when nothing happened.

Alestrun entered with a sigh. "There isn't going to be any more water for washing. The Faeorn informed us earlier they've sabotaged the water processing machinery on the ship." He sighed again. "I like being clean."

Rolstrun agreed. "Washing off the dust helps with the poisoning. It's easier to purge it from you when it isn't coating every pore."

Every day for the next two chedans, Rolstrun and the nucla clearing team returned to the ship. They worked feverishly to clear as much of the malignant magic from the mineral as possible. When they received word of the planned rescue, they had cleared eighty percent of the processed bars in the hold.

It had to be enough. They were out of time—and out of strength.

Chapter 27

Kaieli - 55 de Eyedar, 1075

After making fierce love to Rolstrun, Kaieli laid curled up with him on the platform. She listened to his breathing change as he fell asleep. Exhaustion from the past two chedans made her body ache too much for sleep. The concentrated malignant magic contained in the processed nucla caused her excruciating pain. She, Loshera, and Chariel gritted their teeth against the blinding headaches and the fire raging under their skin. But no matter what they tried, they couldn't shield themselves from its effects and still work their magic on it. Otherwise, they could have purged more bars. Although the malignant magic didn't seem to affect the others, especially not Rolstrun.

Kaieli moaned and placed a hand over her chest. Her heart hurt, and it had started beating erratically in the past few days. The pain rumbled from her heart and extended throughout her body in painful waves. Even if the plan worked, and she escaped this horror tomorrow, she worried she'd overtaxed herself.

She gently stroked Rolstrun's hand, lying across her waist. He'd grown during the lunadars of captivity. Where others, like Calistrun, had allowed it to take them down, Rolstrun seemed to rise above it. If he'd been older, he probably would have become the camp alpha. She didn't think he realized how much Bohandran, Maheli, and the other alphas relied on him, and asked him for his opinions and observations. One day, Rolstrun might become a keep alpha, maybe even a clan alpha, after this experience. Before, he'd been too self-centered and liked his pleasures too much for anyone to consider him in an alpha role.

Another wave of pain swept through Kaieli, and she hoped she lived long enough to see him become a capable leader. She knew he loved her, even though he hadn't told her. But he had a greater destiny than being bond-mated to a healer. He would need someone strong to help him lead a keep, although some keep alphas weren't mates with their co-alphas. But to her, they all seemed less effective and their leadership was prone to having problems. Bond-mates always led the strongest keeps.

Kaieli shifted slightly to gaze into his face, smiling at his handsomeness. She sighed again, admitting to herself she loved him, even more than she had her heart-sister, Rizelya. Kaieli wanted nothing more than to spend the rest of her life with him. Could she hold him back just to fulfill her desires? Or did she have the inner strength to step aside to give him the opportunity to reach the potential she saw in him? She mentally shrugged. Thankfully, she didn't need to make that choice for some time. First, they needed to succeed in their attempt to escape this awful place. Second, they must throw the invaders off their world. She wouldn't have to make the decision until then. For now, she'd love him, and let him love her.

Rolstrun - 56 de Eyedar, 1075

Rolstrun woke up early to a dawn sky painted in pale pinks and oranges and listened to the people breathing deeply in sleep around him. If the plan worked, today would be his last day of captivity. Rolstrun didn't know if he remembered what freedom tasted like. It'd been so long since the Scourge had captured him. Last night, he and Kaieli had made fierce love, scared they'd never see each other again if things went wrong.

Kaieli stirred beside him, and he turned onto his side, facing her. She blinked her beautiful blue-gray eyes open and smiled. He kissed her, realizing as he did how much he loved her. Once they were free, and the invaders were gone, he'd ask her about becoming bond-mates.

Trepidation filled Rolstrun as he waited for Faliciden to work her magic on him, making him look like a Vhelopsi. When he'd heard the plan, he insisted on going with one of the Vhelopsi teams to take out the energy dome. He needed to do something active after spending so many chedans helping to purge the nucla with his mind. Rolstrun smirked. It gave him a chance to payback the invaders for all the torment he'd experienced for so long.

Before they left the slave barracks, he took Kaieli's face in his hands. "I love you. The next time we're together, we'll be free."

"To freedom." Kaieli kissed him. A sadness he didn't understand filled her eyes as she turned to leave with the other women.

Heaviness weighed on Rolstrun's heart as he watched her go. She hadn't told him she'd loved him. Perhaps he couldn't find love in such a place as the horrific slave pens.

He marched with the other men toward the crater, but before they reached it, he slipped away and scurried to a maintenance shack. Inside, Sangasu and four other Vhelopsi waited. The other teams had already gathered their supplies and left.

Sangasu handed Rolstrun a small package. "Be careful with it. Don't let it drop."

Rolstrun gingerly tucked it into the front of his coverall, wondering how something so little could do as much damage as the Faeorn claimed. He and the others picked up various tools and exited the building. They strolled across the compound to their assigned generator, trying to appear like they were heading to a maintenance task.

Kaieli - 56 de Eyedar, 1075

Inside the processing plant, the three Faeorn triads waited in the infirmary. Kaieli had worked mostly with the Yoon triad and didn't know the Shun or Roon triads well. She nodded to them. Three of the five tall, colorful Volkerns towered over the tiny, pale Faeorns.

"Where are Flo'kik and Tre'nok?" Kaieli asked.

"They will be here soon." Vy'shol's dark blue skin was paler than normal. "They can't leave their posts until your people attack."

Kaieli's mouth tightened with worry, hoping the two Volkerns could reach the processing plant in time. Each of the refugees carried a small bag with another larger one slung over their backs, representing all they owned. It didn't look like much to Kaieli, but she doubted the Scourge allowed their slaves many personal possessions.

"Are you ready?" she asked Vy'shol.

Her eyes were wide, and her hands trembled slightly. She nodded. "There is no going back for any of us after this. No matter our status, or how valuable we are to the Scourge, the commander will kill us. None of our kind have ever openly resisted the Scourge's rule."

"Then we must pray our plan works."

"It will. It must." Mei-Ying Yoon said.

The male and gomale Faeorns slipped out of the infirmary. Kaieli peeked around the curtain. The Faeorns, along with Sorlenda and several other mechanically inclined women, moved through the machinery, stopping every so often as if they were adjusting it.

In a short time, they would all be free, or dead. Either way, they'd escape the clutches of the Scourge.

Blazel - 56 de Eyedar, 1075

Blazel walked with Rizelya to the staging field, where Graak and the team of Gryphons waited for them. He winced as Rizelya's grip on his arm tightened. Blazel rolled his shoulders to release his own tension. His pulser banged against the canister on his back.

On his other side, Aistrun strode, clenching and unclenching his jaw. If their plans worked, he and Chariel would reunite again before the sun set. She'd been working with Kaieli in the slave camp for nearly three lunadars to purge the malignant magic from the nucla. Finally, the scouts observing the enemy compound sent word the Faeorn had completed their sabotage of the invader's ship, and the Posairs could retrieve their people.

The team selected for the rescue mission strode behind them, also wearing a poison canister and carrying a pulser and packs of poisoned ammo. Each person wore a determined expression. They only had this one chance to free their people and allies.

Tuueek lifted his head feathers at Blazel's approach and resettled his wings. He led the team of the ten largest Thunder Wings in the flight. They towered over the thirty small owl-type Gryphons led by Baekeek. Kaaik, leading the larger hawk and falcon-type Gryphons, nodded to Blazel as he walked by. Taking so many Gryphons to the battle was a huge risk, but the mission wouldn't succeed without them.

After lunadars of mounting the Gryphons and settling into harnesses, Blazel's team was ready to leave within a few milcrons. Blazel stood next to Graak with a hand on his shoulder. "Today we get our people out of the clutches of the invaders. The timing of this operation is critical. Let's review, so everyone knows what is happening. Rizelya and Glork's team will destroy the control beacon."

Rizelya raised her helbraught in acknowledgment, as well as her team members Leistral, Raeleen, and Maellyn. They would need their helbraughts in addition to the other weapons.

"Laynar," Blazel continued, "your crew and Baekeek's are in charge of taking down the energy dome. Once it's down, you'll lay waste to the processing plant and any other buildings you can."

Thanks to Maheli, they knew how to destroy them. Laynar nodded. By the time they finished attacking with Laynar's fire, Saffren and Dehali's ice, and Grazeen's rot, hopefully none of the buildings would remain standing or usable.

"Shaydan, you, Kaaik, and Delestrun's people have the most difficult task ahead. Your job is to release the captives inside the compound and lead them to safety. We must ensure we also rescue our allies, the Volkern and Faeorn."

He'd assigned Ambrelya to their team because she'd become a crack shot with the confiscated and converted invaders' weapons. Candriel, Gehan, Kami, and Tami would create hardened air-shields to protect the escapees while they climbed onto the waiting Gryphon's backs.

"My team, consisting of Graak, Aistrun, and Broogk, will provide the distraction and cover for the men and Vhelopsi inside the crater to escape. Tuueek," Blazel nodded to the Thunder Wing leader, "your team's job is to steal the scout ship our allies want while demolishing the other one. Make it look like you're tearing it apart without doing too much damage. Our allies need to be able to use it later, but we don't want the Scourge to know it's still usable."

Tuueek dipped his head. *We have the schematics and have practiced with the other ships. We can do this.* He dropped his beak in a grin. In their practice, the Thunder Wings had successfully destroyed all the invader's ships, except the mother ship and the two scouts.

"From here on, we only communicate in mind-speech. We don't want to tip off the Scourge until we're ready. All right, people, stay safe and bring our friends home!" He leaped onto Graak's back, buckled in, and gave the order to launch.

As Graak climbed, Blazel lowered his goggles from where they rested on the top of his head and fitted them over his eyes, blessing Maellyn for developing them.

They soon approached the crater, and the tingle of Graak's magic passed over Blazel as Graak shifted the light waves around them to make them invisible. Blazel could still see the others through the wavy haze, but anyone not on a Gryphon and wrapped in their spell wouldn't be able to see them.

A few measures from the compound, Laynar's group zipped ahead, and a Posair and a Gryphon pair flew to their stations at each of the large towers. Groups of Vhelopsi wandered nonchalantly toward the structures without getting too close or drawing the attention of the Scourge.

Shaydan's team drifted toward the ground, landing near the processing plant, while Rizelya and Glork hovered directly over the control beacon. Red and orange flames danced over Rizelya and Leistral's helbraughts, while Raeleen's glowed a dark amber and Maellyn's turned a deep sepia-brown.

Graak, Broogk, and their group continued flying until they floated over the crater.

Ready! Laynar called.

A few moments later, Rizelya and Shaydan informed him their teams were in place.

Okay, Graak, Blazel said, a grin spreading across his face. *Let's get our people out. Now!*

Rolstrun - 56 de Eyedar, 1075

Rolstrun glanced up, but he couldn't see if the Posairs and Gryphons had arrived yet. He and the Vhelopsi reached their assigned generator and started placing the small packages of explosives on the base. Rolstrun maneuvered around the corner, avoiding contact with the fence. As he crouched to affix the charge, he heard someone call his name in mind-speech.

Rolstrun! It is you.

He peered through the metal mesh, trying to see who called to him, but the energy field obscured his view.

It's Eiden. It's almost time. Are you ready to get out of there?

He nodded, unable to speak. Rolstrun blinked at the sudden moisture filling his eyes.

Freedom was close.

A loud screech split the air, accompanied by the order, *Now!*

Above him, Gryphons suddenly emerged. Rolstrun bleated a startled grunt when Eiden, along with a woman with green hair and a Gryphon, appeared on the other side of the fence.

"This is Grazeen and Korrik," Eiden quickly introduced her companions. "Step back," she ordered.

Eiden and Grazeen lifted their helbraughts, already glowing with their magic. Streams of yellow and green light sped toward the generator. Korrik flared, a nimbus of fire radiating from him. It melded with the women's magic to surround the device.

Rolstrun grabbed Sangasu. "It's going to blow!"

Their team of Vhelopsi ran several feet away and hunkered down with arms covering their heads and faces buried between their knees.

Boom!

The generator exploded. Everywhere its debris hit the energy field, the women's magic spread, dissolving the field as it raced upward and outward. Rolstrun rose from his crouch, craning his neck toward the next generator in line. It had also exploded. Yellow, orange, and green magic expanded from it, meeting and blending with Eiden's and Grazeen's. Their magic extended farther and farther until it reached the top of the energy dome. The energy flickered, then died.

Rolstrun jumped up, cheering. The energy dome was gone!

A moment later, the beacon controlling the explosive device in his arm disintegrated. "Thank you, Warrior!" Rolstrun sobbed. He could finally leave.

A squadron of soldiers ran toward them. Eiden and Grazeen pulled out weapons that appeared like they once belonged to the enemy, shooting at the approaching invaders. Korrik tossed extra weapons to the Vhelopsi, who grinned and started firing.

Rolstrun didn't need any weapons other than what he'd been born with. He reached for the magic denied to him for so long. Fire prickled under his skin as it responded. A few moments later, he lifted his muzzle and howled. He ran—flexing his claws to release the venom—to the nearest enemy. He slashed the soft flesh of the invader's throat and ripped into its body. Rage, bottled up over the lunadars of mistreatment, erupted. The

Scourge had terrorized him for over four lunadars. Now, it was their turn to feel terror. He turned to face his next foe.

"Rolstrun! Rolstrun!" Eiden called his name.

He shook his head to clear the red haze. Only bits and pieces indicated where invaders had existed only a few milcrons ago.

"It's time to go." Eiden, already mounted on Korrik, held out her hand to him.

He glanced around. Only Sangasu remained alive of the Vhelopsi on his team, and he sat straddling another Gryphon. Rolstrun took Eiden's hand and swung onto Korrik's back.

He was free!

Rizelya - 56 de Eyedar, 1075

Rizelya and Glork took their positions above the energy dome. Shortly, explosions rocked the generators, collapsing them. Magic raced throughout the energy field, and within moments, the dome protecting the compound evaporated. As soon as it did, she directed her magic through her helbraught toward the now unprotected tower holding the control beacon. At the same time, Leistral, Raeleen, and Maellyn released theirs.

The streams met midair, twisting together, becoming stronger. Rizelya tilted her head to the side to protect her eyes from the bright light. She poured more magic into her helbraught and sensed her pack do the same. Maellyn's lava added an additional level of heat to Rizelya's normal fire. The tower slumped, metal dripping as they turned it into slag. They continued to pour magic into it until nothing remained but a molten heap.

Kaieli! Rizelya called. *The control beacon is down.*

In response, fire bloomed in the processing plant. Loud clanks and screeching metal added to the din. A large group of people raced from the building.

"Glork!" Rizelya thumped his shoulder. A squadron of invaders tromped into view, raising their weapons to shoot the fleeing people.

Cowards! Glork snarled. He screeched in anger, flaring as he dove. His heat washed harmlessly over Rizelya.

She snatched the canister's nozzle. When he flew over the soldiers, she opened the valve. Mist streamed out, covering most of the soldiers. Ambrelya fired, striking down those who escaped the mist with her projectiles. Raeleen and Maellyn killed more invaders with the poison spray.

Glork suddenly swerved, tossing Rizelya against her harness as he avoided projectiles from the soldier's weapons. They overflew the processing plant as a cloud of black smoke billowed out. Rizelya put a hand over her mouth, trying to block the noxious fumes and coughed. A familiar figure ran from the building.

"Glork! There's Kaieli!" Rizelya pointed. Her heart plummeted as a soldier sighted his weapon at Kaieli's retreating back. But before he fired, a Vhelopsi tackled him, slitting his throat with her sharp nails. Glork dropped down and crouched in front of Kaieli. She jumped onto his back.

"Hurry!" Rizelya yelled, and waved at the Vhelopsi who had saved Kaieli's life. She ran toward them, then jerked as a projectile slammed into her. Blood drenched the ground from the fatal wound. Rizelya swore as she switched weapons and fired her pulser at the invader. She grinned with satisfaction when purple blood poured from his eyes.

"Did we get Chariel and the others?" Rizelya asked as Glork launched himself back into the sky.

We did. Kaaik retrieved Chariel. We have our allies, too. Well, most of them, he added sadly as soldiers surrounded several Vhelopsi, cutting off their escape.

Rizelya had emptied her tank and ran out of poison cartridges during the fighting. It was time to leave, between the Scourge organizing and the Posairs beginning to lose people. As Glork circled the compound, a few small groups of Vhelopsi still fought against the invaders, soon succumbing to the greater numbers. In the center, soldiers herded about fifty Vhelopsi toward the cage formerly holding the Posair's children. She breathed a sigh of relief and offered a prayer of thanksgiving when she didn't see any recaptured Posairs.

The bodies of Posair, Vhelopsi, and even a few of the hairy Hap'thez lay scattered on the ground where they'd fallen. One dead Gryphon sprawled awkwardly near a burning building with his wings broken and a gaping hole in his side. Tears streamed down her face, fogging her goggles.

Glork leveled out and headed deeper into the Barrens and back to the plains. Ahead of them flew a long line of Gryphons, all of them loaded with people. Although they'd lost more people than she'd hoped, they had saved even more.

Now all they had to do was shove the Scourge off their planet.

Blazel - 56 de Eyedar, 1075

Graak dipped and swerved as the big weapons on the crater rim roared. He dropped lower, and Blazel ordered the release of the poisoned mist, targeting the guards on the mobility devices first. He shuddered when the invaders tumbled to the ground, shrieking in agony.

Below him, the men in the crater shifted into their warrior forms. Blazel looked away as they tore into their guards, all control and sanity gone. He didn't blame them at all. The Scourge had held these men captive the longest, and they'd suffered the worst. Blazel switched to his projectile weapon and fired at the invaders on the outskirts of the melee. The Vhelopsi snatched any dropped weapons and turned them against their former captors.

A small squadron of soldiers changed targets and shot at the Gryphons. Graak zipped above the crater rim, avoiding their projectiles. The height allowed Blazel to witness Tuueek leading the Thunder Wings into a dive to attack the two scout ships.

A phalanx of invaders raced from the nearby mother ship, shooting as they ran. The projectiles bounced off Gehan's invisible shield of hardened air. The commander strode from the ship, his face contorted in rage. He recovered and shouted orders at his men. Another barrage of projectiles smacked against the shield, harmless.

The Thunder Wings hooked talons on the ship's rim and, with a concerted heave, they attempted to lift it off the ground. The ship seemed to be heavier than the Gryphons had expected.

Heave! Tuueek cried. *Heave!*

The strong downdraft of their wings knocked the nearby soldiers to the ground. The Gryphons lifted the ship a few more feet, and with another surge of effort, they rose above the massive mother ship. Gehan directed her Gryphon closer to the Thunder Wings, and she released a burst of magic at them. Suddenly, the Thunder Wings flew as if the ship weighed nothing. Gehan followed closely behind. Blazel guessed she had formed a cushion of air underneath to support some of the weight. Her Talents had grown tremendously, like most of the women fighting in this war. The Thunder Wings soared higher with their prizes, and chunks of metal rained on the compound.

Graak dove toward the crater again. Only bits and pieces remained of the guards. The men, coming out of their berserk rage, looked stunned as they gazed at the carnage. They weren't the first to lose control and allow rage to overtake them. Blazel had witnessed it many times. He'd even fallen to it a time or two. But their inattention could kill them.

"Hurry!" Blazel yelled. "Get your asses moving." He pointed to the crater rim, where a large force of invaders gathered and would be within firing range shortly.

A big man with grimy, strawberry-blond hair waved at Blazel. He shouted orders, and the men stopped gaping and dashed across the crater bottom, toward the northern pass. Numerous Vhelopsi ran with them.

Blazel's team dove at the invaders going down the side of the crater in the strange contraption. Broogk flared, and several Reds added their fire to his stream of magic. The metal on the conveyance glowed red, and the soldiers screamed in pain until the Posairs fired projectiles into the crowd. The soldiers in the next machine returned fire, and a Gryphon screeched as he spiraled downward and crashed in a heap. Both he and his rider lay motionless.

Meanwhile, Blazel's squad of Gryphons dropped into the crater, picking up as many of the men as possible. But there weren't enough Gryphons for everyone. Some men and Vhelopsi would have to make the run to the northern pass. As soon as the Gryphons took off again, Blazel pumped his hand, and they climbed, winging out over the Barrens, leaving the compound—and its terror—behind.

Chapter 28

Rizelya - 56 de Eyedar, 1075

As Glork flew away from the slave camp, silent tears slid down Rizelya's face. "Thank you, Glork," she said, patting his shoulder where his feathers intermingled with his fur. "Because of your help, we finally freed our people from the invader's evil clutches. It couldn't have happened if the Goddess hadn't sent Chariel the vision that led to us reestablishing our friendship."

It's a pleasure, Glork purred. *Now comes the hard part. Throwing the ugly creatures off our world. Although depriving the invaders of their food source and their forced labor brings our goal closer than ever.*

"May it happen, soon," Rizelya prayed.

The area established along the Storengher River to receive the escapees came into view. Already, friends greeted each other or shared a moment of grief. Rizelya grinned when Aistrun unbuckled his harness and leaped off Broogk before his paws touched the ground. He raced to Chariel, sweeping her off her feet and swinging her around in a circle. They were laughing and crying and kissing. Rizelya understood their reunion. She'd felt the same way after being separated from

Blazel for only a few short days, not lunadars like Aistrun and Chariel.

After they landed, Rizelya and Blazel hurried to help the rescued people unbuckle the unfamiliar harnesses and dismount from the Gryphons. As soon as she released Kaieli, Rizelya wrapped her heart-sister in a hug, crying and laughing.

"I'm so happy you're away from the invaders."

"Me, too," Kaieli said. "Let me introduce you to my team."

"Follow Dehali," Rizelya said, after the introductions. "She'll take you to where you can bathe and change into fresh, clean clothes."

"A hot bath? Clean clothes?" Maheli asked. "Tell me I haven't died and gone to the Mother's Womb. I've been dreaming of a hot bath for two chedans. And I'm so ready to remove and burn these ugly coveralls." She plucked at the awful fabric. "Lead on, Dehali. Lead on and don't dally!"

Without a backward glance, the women rushed to the two large tents where teams had set up heated tubs.

Blazel touched her arm. "Our new allies wait for us."

Her face flushed in embarrassment. She stepped quickly to the waiting Gryphons and their passengers.

"My deepest apologies," Rizelya said as she unbuckled the harness on the first Gryphon.

"It is good to see a happy reunion of friends." The pale blue Volkern gracefully threw a leg over the Gryphon's back.

Rizelya gaped at his height. He and the other Volkern stood over seven feet tall.

Hairan stood next to another Vhelopsi. They bowed as Rizelya and Blazel approached. "This is Sangasu," Hairan said. "He remained behind to protect our people and to help yours." While Hairan's skin and hair were a golden hue, Sangasu's coloring was a bronze shade.

Rizelya tilted her head to the new Vhelopsi. "We appreciate your assistance. Hairan, the camp for your rescued people is north of here, as you requested. It's within walking distance."

"Thank you. Graak tells me we saved over one hundred of my people. We don't know yet how many men escaped the crater. We never believed so many of us would be freed from the Scourge's whip."

The tiny, delicate Faeorn stood in three groups of three, holding hands. The tallest of them was nearly Rizelya's height, although the others averaged about four feet tall. In one group, the female's belly bulged in the advanced stages of pregnancy. Their wide purple eyes stared at the Posairs surrounding them.

The pale blue Volkern stepped forward. "I am Tre'nok. This is Vy'shol, My'shel, Flo'kik, and Ze'lek." He introduced his Volkern companions. He then indicated the group of Faeorn with the pregnant female. "This is the Yoon triad, and the other two groups are the Shun and Roon triads."

"Thank you for helping our people." Blazel bowed with a gesture of thanks. "Come, let me introduce you to our Supreme Alphas and the Gryphon prince."

Blazel ushered them to where Histrun, Moraak, and Keshanal stood in front of a large white tent.

"Welcome," Keshanal said. "The Barrens is an inhospitable place. We can speak now or after you've had a chance to clean up."

Vy'shol's eyes lit up. "Ooh, a bath would be lovely." She slapped a hand over her mouth as Tre'nok glared at her. Then he smiled.

"Yes, it would be more civilized to converse when clean. The machinery to pump and recycle the water on the ship broke down, providing only enough water for drinking." He glanced at the Faeorn, a grin playing across his lips, and shrugged. "Sabotage."

"Very well," Keshanal said. "We shall speak later. Rizelya, please show them where they can wash up."

Rizelya nodded. "This way." She took the two Vhelopsi, the Volkern, and the Faeorn to a different section of the river from where the Posair men and women bathed. Keshanal had made arrangements to provide their allies with clean clothing. Hairan's wife, Zebba, had helped with the sizes needed. Once the refugees had washed away the Barren's grime and dressed, Rizelya led them back to the commanders' tent.

Inside, Histrun and Keshanal sat on chairs at the opposite end of the entrance. Moraak sat on his haunches with his tail curled around his feet. Luxurious rugs covered the dirt floor. Empty camp stools formed a semicircle in front of the leaders.

"Please sit," Keshanal said, beckoning the group into the tent.

While everyone found a seat, Rizelya observed the Volkern. Now clean, they appeared regal. Subtle patterning of whorls and spirals decorated their face around their eyes. Although Rizelya couldn't detect any obvious signs of gender, as they moved and talked, she discovered she could differentiate between the genders. Vy'shol and My'shel were female, and she'd bet Tre'nok and Vy'shol were mates.

"What can we expect from the invaders after this coup?" Histrun leaned forward with his hands clasped between his knees. "Will they leave now that they don't have anyone to mine the nucla for them and we've destroyed their processing equipment?"

My'shel quietly translated for the Faeorn.

Tre'nok shook his head sadly. "No, they will not. You have rebelled and refused to fall under the Scourge's subjugation. The commander's slaves have escaped. He cannot allow the affront to go unpunished. He can't return to his home without proof he conquered this world."

And what would be his proof? Moraak asked.

The Faeorn's eyes widened, and they made warding gestures with their hands when they heard his voice in their heads. The Volkern looked at each other.

"Ah, a telepathic species." Tre'nok smiled. "We have encountered only a few in our travels with the Scourge. It's interesting that I hear you speak in my language, rather than your own. Fascinating—"

"Commander Ke-ke-tak needs slaves," Flo'kik interrupted, refocusing the conversation. "His hold would need to be filled with people from this world." He studied Moraak with a tilt of his head. "The commander would take your people as curiosities. He doesn't know about your telepathic ability and that you are a sentient being rather than simply a beast, as he now believes. It would make you even more valuable to the collectors. And now, no one can tell him otherwise." He chuckled as he spread his hands, indicating his fellows.

"If he doesn't return with slaves to add to the food supply, he will lose status," Tre'nok said. "There were rumors he would soon make a bid to challenge the throne. But if he returns without captives, and with the news you resisted his subjugation, he most likely will lose his life. Although, the nucla is extremely valuable. It might save him, if it worked." He chuckled. "Kaieli's people did an excellent job of cleansing most of it."

Vy'shol looked thoughtful. "There aren't many slaves left, less than a hundred Kaigor and about 250 Hap'thez, plus however many Vhelopsi didn't make it out." She glanced over at Sangasu.

"Thankfully, not a lot. We estimate fewer than a hundred."

"Those who remain," Tre'nok said quietly, "won't last long, only about ninety days. There are too few slaves and too many invaders. When you freed your people and Vhelopsi, you gave the Scourge a crushing blow. They won't have any food for the return trip unless they capture your people."

"Not if we can help it." Histrun sat back in his chair, running a hand through his beard. "Ninety days, or a lunadar and a half, of food. It sounds like they are desperate."

"He is," Tre'nok agreed. "Enough to do something drastic." He paused, taking deep breaths and gazing at the tent's roof.

Vy'shol touched his arm, bringing his attention to her. "Tell them, Tre'nok," she urged. "They need to know the danger."

Tre'nok sighed. "While the Faeorn reprogrammed the navigation system, they found an unwelcome surprise. If Commander Ke-ke-tak can't subdue this world, which we believe he can't, he will destroy it. He has a bomb aboard the mother ship capable of blowing this planet to bits. Once it's armed, it takes three days for it to be fully operational."

Keshanal gasped, placing a hand over her heart. "No!"

Moraak's tail thumped, and his head feathers rose. "Impossible!" he sputtered. "Nothing could be powerful enough to destroy a world."

Rizelya's heart plummeted, and she clutched Blazel's hand. Even with help from the Gryphons and their new allies, her people could still perish. Was this what the Goddess warned about in Chariel's prophecy?

Histrun's face blanched as he shook his head. "We must ensure he doesn't arm it. Somehow." Bleakness and despair filled his voice.

The pregnant Faeorn jabbered something in her language.

Tre'nok's eyes widened before bursting into laughter. "Mei-Ying says the bomb uses nucla, and they replaced it with the treated nucla. It has just enough power to make the commander believe it is charging."

Oh ho, Moraak laughed. *Good job, Yoon triad.*

"How many people does he have left?" Keshanal asked.

"While you have succeeded in causing damage," Flo'kik answered, "you've only killed half of his force. He still has about a quarter million soldiers."

Rizelya slumped against Blazel. So many invaders! Even with the Gryphons and Vhelopsi, the invaders outnumbered the Posairs more than three to one. They may have just leveled a crushing blow to the Scourge, but they hadn't won the war by any means.

Keshanal's eyebrow rose. "How could so many fit on one ship?"

"The soldiers travel frozen," Tre'nok said. "They stack the sleepers one on top of another so they take little space. When the Scourge arrive at the target planet, they revive the soldiers. The Scourge carry their riding beasts across space as embryos and grow them to adulthood planet-side. They grow quickly."

We are badly outnumbered. Moraak's feathers flattened against his head. *Even with my flights, the additions from the northern keeps, and the Vhelopsi, we number less than eighty thousand. We must be creative in how we fight.*

"You have an advantage," Hairan said, rubbing his chin. "Your people are fighting for freedom, as are mine. The Scourge don't understand how much this motivates us to fight even against extreme odds. This is your home. Use your knowledge and familiarity with it against them."

"Yes, yes," Histrun agreed, nodding. "Thank you for the reminder."

"Speaking of home," Tre'nok swallowed hard and blinked his eyes. "Were... were you able to save the scout ship?"

Moraak dropped his beak in a smile. *Yes. It needs repairs. Even though the Thunder Wings tried to be careful, they did some damage.*

Tre'nok slumped in relief. "Oh good. No disrespect, but we really didn't want to be marooned on this planet."

"Where will you go?" Keshanal asked, concern in her voice. "Surely after this you can't return to your home world."

"No, we can't. Thanks to the Faeorn, we have a planet hidden from the invader's instruments. It's a refuge for many of the slave species. Some of our family is waiting for us there."

"But we won't leave until after you vanquish the Scourge," Vy'shol added. She gestured to the other Volkerns and the Faeorn triads. "We are obligated to help you accomplish that feat. Kaieli and her team made our own escape possible. Whatever assistance you need, we're at your disposal."

Histrun nodded to them, then turned to Hairan. "And what will your people do?"

"When we escaped with your people, we signed our own death warrant." Hairan leaned forward slightly. "We found in your people a kindred spirit. Too many of us escaped to return with the Volkern on the scout ship. We formally seek refuge with you."

"It is granted," Histrun said. "Welcome to Lairheim."

"I'm sure you're anxious to check on your people," Keshanal added. "Go, join them, eat, rest. And we'll discuss how we can win against such great odds in the morning."

After they left, no one in the tent moved or said anything for a long moment.

"Two hundred and fifty thousand invaders!" Histrun swore, slamming his fist onto his lap. "Goddess help us."

Rolstrun - 56 de Eyedar, 1075

Rolstrun couldn't believe he was riding a legendary Gryphon. He'd talked to them during the escape runs, but had never believed he'd actually ride one. He glanced down. Black smoke billowed from the processing plant. An explosion blasted, and a moment later, Korrik fought to remain upright as the shock wave hit them. A huge hole appeared in the side of the building.

The machinery inside was melting into slag. Even if there were people to mine the nucla, the invaders couldn't process it into their fuel cubes now.

Rolstrun held his breath. He searched the ground for running figures and fell into a panic when he didn't see any.

Kaieli! Kaieli! he shouted, terrified.

Rolstrun?

Tears trickled down his face at the sound of her mind-voice.*Yes! Yes, I'm here!* he replied.

The Gryphons got us out in time. All of us.

Rolstrun breathed deeply. She was safe.

Korrik banked, flying over the empty slave pens. Bits of torn fabric and other trash waved pathetically in the light breeze. He'd found love in that dismal place. But if he had the magical strength, he'd raze it until no sign of it remained.

The Gryphon soared higher, and Rolstrun shivered in the cold air. He huddled closer to Eiden.

"Thank you, Korrik, Eiden," he said. "Thank you for rescuing me." His body shook, this time from relief. Sobs broke through. He didn't care. He'd survived.

After a while, he raised his head, curious about how far they'd flown from the crater. Below, the Storengher River sparkled in the sunlight. He frowned. "Where are we going? I didn't think the base camp was located next to the river."

To the secondary camp. Histrun will debrief you there.

A bit later, Korrik gradually lost altitude. They landed in a wide field bounded by the river on the east and with two dozen tents set up on it. Someone helped him off Korrik and led him toward a tent. When he entered, joy swept through him. Kaieli, Chariel, Maheli, Bohandran, Calistrun, and the last of the captives busily scrubbed the dirt off their bodies. A pile of the awful orange coveralls sat to the side. He added his to it.

He winced as the brushes found old whiplash wounds. When he examined his skin, he scowled. It would take multiple washings to clean off the ingrained dirt and grime. Rolstrun hurried through the drapery sectioning off the rear of the tent. Steam enveloped him and he groaned with pleasure at the big soaking tubs. He climbed into the one his friends lounged in, letting the heat melt away his tension. A soft hand slipped into his. He opened one eye, and smiled at Kaieli, before closing his eyes again, drifting into a doze.

Much later, cleaned and dressed in familiar clothing, Rolstrun felt like a normal Posair again. Kaieli joined him a few milcrons later. Her cheeks appeared sunken, and her eyes looked hollowed from the ordeal. But to him, she'd never been more beautiful. She stepped into his arms, and he breathed in her fresh scent.

"Thank the Mother we're out of there," he said. They stood embracing while the rest filed out. He didn't have the energy to do anything else.

"Ahem," Dehali said, poking her head through the tent opening. "The food is getting cold."

Now that she mentioned it, Rolstrun could smell the luscious scent of good food. Taking Kaieli's hand in his, they left the bathing tent and joined the others at a large table set under the stars. He hadn't realized it had grown dark.

Kaieli glanced around. "Where are our allies?" she asked Dehali.

"They've also bathed and dressed in fresh clothes. The Volkern, Faeorn, and the leaders of the Vhelopsi are speaking with Histrun, Moraak, and Keshanal. They seemed quite pleased to be rid of those orange coveralls."

"No one looked good in that garish color," Kaieli agreed with a small laugh. "Did Bethlyn or Faelyn have a hand in preparing our meal? These are all foods easy on poor, abused stomachs."

Dehali nodded. "Bethlyn did."

Kaieli cleared her throat, and when she had everyone's attention, she said, "Eat slowly. Don't gorge. It will only come up again. Our bodies aren't used to so much food at a time anymore."

Calistrun covered his mouth, his cheeks bulging with food. He slowly chewed. Rolstrun grinned. His friend had always loved food.

Rolstrun took a bite of mashed tuber, moaning quietly as the flavor exploded on his tongue. He savored every bite, reacquainting his taste buds to flavors other than sand and watered-down soup. Propping his elbow on the table, he held up his head with his hand, blinking his eyes to stay awake. He must have fallen asleep at some point, because the next thing he knew, he jerked awake when someone nudged him.

Blazel stood over him. "Come on, you'll sleep better on a cot than here."

Blazel led him to a tent where soft snores already floated in the air. An empty cot waited for him next to Kaieli's. Rolstrun slumped onto the cot while Blazel helped him out of his boots. He remembered a time when he'd helped Blazel with his boots. So much had happened in the intervening lunadars. Rolstrun curled onto his side, facing Kaieli.

Would she stay with him now they were free?

Free.

He breathed in the word and let it fill him. Then reality hit him. The invaders were still here. Until they were gone, none of them were truly free of their tyranny.

Kaieli - 57 de Eyedar, 1075

Kaieli slowly awoke and listened to the quiet and the river rushing by. The spring of a cot underneath her and the warm blanket over her reminded her she no longer slept in the invader's compound. Tears streamed down the sides of her cheeks unheeded.

She was free.

Finally, she dried her face and blew her nose. Other sounds overrode the birdsong. She might be free of the invaders, but they still threatened her world. She had work left to do.

Kaieli threw off the blanket and sat up. She smiled at Rolstrun curled on a cot next to hers with his head pillowed on his hands and a snore buzzing from his lips. She kissed him lightly, not wanting to wake him.

Outside the tent, she followed her nose to where a pot of porridge simmered over a fire. Another fire held a large pot of boiling water. A stack of bowls and mugs sat on a table, along with a jar of taevo leaves. She picked up the jar and opened the lid, breathing in the luscious smell. Kaieli's mouth watered as she measured leaves into a pot and poured hot water over them. While she waited for the taevo to steep, she dished out a bowl of porridge. She sighed with pleasure as the taevo slid down her throat.

Kaieli spooned the last bit of porridge into her mouth as a woman with a large bosom, chestnut-brown hair, and blue-gray eyes bustled into the mess tent. She wore healer green and seemed familiar.

"Oh good, you're awake," the woman said with a smile.

Kaieli still couldn't place the woman. She drew her eyebrows together in puzzlement.

"You don't recognize my new svelte figure." She laughed as she posed. "I'm Bethlyn. Working at the war front has done wonders for me."

Kaieli remembered Bethlyn as being on the plump side with wide hips. "You look wonderful! I can't say the same for me. Gauntness isn't a good look for anyone, especially me."

"We'll get some good food in you and let you heal from the Barrens dust, and you'll be back to normal. Are you up for a bit of work? We could use your healer skills."

"Who needs healing?" Kaieli doubted she had the energy reserves to do a major healing. Even though the pain in her chest had eased, it would take time for her body to heal from being overtaxed, underfed, and in constant terror.

Bethlyn crossed her arms. "No, no, nothing like that. We have enough healers until you're rested. Besides, you don't have a full team. Jaelena left this morning to join her children at the Sanctuary. But, don't worry. We have a couple of teams working on purging the nucla poisoning from the prior captives."

Kaieli's eyebrows rose. "How? It doesn't work without Gray Talent."

"Once the Supreme knew how important they were, she sent several priestesses with secondary Gray Talent to join our healing force. While most have minor Talent, it's sufficient for doing the healing. Your method is brilliant." Bethlyn paused, uncrossed her arms, and looked away. She took a deep breath and turned back to Kaieli. "I need your help to make suicide pills. We refuse to give the invaders any more captives... or food sources."

Kaieli shuddered. Although not specifically forbidden, the Goddess frowned on suicide. Life was a gift to be treasured.

"It's a last resort," Bethlyn hurriedly added, "to be used only if the Scourge captures someone. Your Volkern friends suggested it, so any surviving invaders wouldn't have any food on their journey home."

Kaieli's memory served up image after image of the invaders sucking their victims' bodies dry and the terror frozen on their faces. She saw again people crammed into the Malvers' monster corrals, screaming as the monsters attacked. Kaieli shuddered as she remembered the euphoria on the invader's faces before killing the monsters and finishing off the Posairs themselves. She'd witnessed firsthand the terror any captives would experience if they were locked for lunadars on the invader's ship.

"I'll help. Do you have the necessary herbs?"

Bethlyn nodded and led Kaieli into another tent. Inside, various herbs, mortars, and pestles covered a long table. Faliciden sat at the table, crushing herbs, while Faelyn mixed them together. Kaieli silently took an empty seat, and she and Bethlyn rolled the mixture into small pills. When they filled a tray, Maheli came in and used her fire Talent to quickly dry the pills.

The quiet work relaxed Kaieli, and the tension in her soul began to melt. She glanced over at Faliciden, Faelyn, and Maheli. The strain was also easing from their faces. The four of them had spent the longest time in the slave pens. Outside, someone shouted, and they all jerked with their eyes widening. They hunched in their seats, waiting for the crack of a whip or the sharp command of an invader. It took several milcrons before Kaieli realized it wasn't coming.

She took a deep breath and let it out slowly. Then another one... and another, until she felt steady again. "It's okay. We're safe." Kaieli said it as much for herself as for her friends.

She slowly leaned forward, reached for the mixture, and rolled it into a log. A few moments later, the others return to their tasks. Their faces were as wet with tears as her own.

Time. It would take time for the shell shock of captivity to wear off.

In the evening before dinner, Kaieli slipped away from the tent and headed to the riverbank. Everything smelled fresh and clean from the afternoon rain. It felt strange to be able to choose what she wanted to do and when. Choosing where to walk didn't seem like much, but making the choice assured her she truly was free.

Two tall shapes appeared ahead of her in the growing dark. They resolved into Tre'nok and Vy'shol, also walking along the riverbank. They held hands, and Vy'shol laughed softly at something Tre'nok said. Kaieli had never seen them together like this before.

When they noticed her, they pulled up short and dropped their hands.

"It's just me," Kaieli called softly, and quickened her steps to reach them.

A flush covered Vy'shol's face as Tre'nok calmly and purposefully took her hand in his again.

"It is strange to be open with our affections," Tre'nok said. "We couldn't let the Scourge know about our relationship, otherwise they would have used the other to punish us. This is the first time in our lives we have been able to walk together as mates and enjoy the evening."

"Thank you for this gift." Vy'shol gave her a shy smile. "It is something I wish to continue to enjoy."

A sweet bell pealed, startling them.

"It's only the dinner bell," Kaieli explained when her heart quit trying to climb out of her throat. "It's calling the community to share food and company."

"Let us go and partake." Tre'nok gestured for her to lead the way.

As she walked back to the camp, Kaieli reflected that the Volkern and Faeorn had never experienced freedom before this. While for her and the other Posairs, it had been a right they'd taken for granted. She'd never treat it that way again. Freedom was too precious of a gift.

After dinner, Rolstrun took her by the hand and led her into the dark. The nearly full moon of Chelar, the smallest moon, provided plenty of light as they strolled along the river. They hadn't gone far when Rolstrun guided her to a lone tree. Its roots gripped the riverbank, and the grass under it smelled sweet. Rolstrun smiled shyly as he led her to the blanket already laid out in the soft grass. They sank onto it.

"Kaieli, you make my heart full, my soul sing." Rolstrun trailed kisses along the side of her neck. "Even though it was a horrible experience, I'm so grateful you were in the slave pens with me. Without you, I would never know the happiness I do now. I love you."

His lips captured hers in fierce need, stealing her breath away.

A long time later, they cuddled with the blanket pulled over their nakedness. Kaieli considered how she felt about him. She leaned over. "I love you," she whispered. She scowled when Rolstrun didn't respond. Then she heard his deep breathing. He'd fallen asleep. She watched him, memorizing his features in peaceful repose. Their people still had battles to fight before their world was truly free.

Blazel - 58 de Eyedar, 1075

Blazel accompanied Histrun and Keshanal as they walked through the secondary camp. They stopped often to visit with the former captives. Tears flowed freely down Keshanal's cheeks as she listened to horror story after horror story. Blazel surreptitiously wiped at his eyes. If the evidence wasn't before his eyes, he wouldn't believe the atrocities an intelligent species could commit against another.

Bethlyn joined them inside the Alpha's tent at the end of their tour.

"What can we do to help these poor people?" Keshanal asked, slumping into her chair. "They have suffered so much."

"They should stay here, in the secondary camp," Bethlyn said. "It's restful here and far from the Barrens. They need time to heal from the nucla poisoning, and they can't do that at our base camp. It's too close, and the dust is always blowing."

"The stuff is nasty and gets everywhere." Blazel grimaced. Until dinner last night, he hadn't realized how gritty everything at the main camp tasted.

"In addition," Bethlyn continued, "these people endured the deprivations of the Scourge and the awful slave compound for over half a year. They need time to recuperate and begin to heal from their ordeal. I've asked for more priestesses to join us here to help with the former captives' mental and spiritual healing."

"I agree," Keshanal said, resting her chin on her elbow. "We shouldn't subject them to more fighting until they recover, not only from the terror they suffered but also from being underfed and overworked."

"Alphas!" a scout shouted. An owl-type Gryphon entered the tent, with Moraak following a moment later. "A force of five thousand invaders are on their way across the Barrens, riding their lizard mounts."

Histrun swore. "Damn! I'd hoped to have more time until they hit back. Blazel, you and Rizelya's battalion stay here to protect our people in case any enemies slip past us."

Blazel grimaced, not liking being shunted out of the fighting.

"Moraak," Histrun said. "Time to return."

The enormous Gryphon dipped his head. "Not only because of the Scourge, but another sandstorm is brewing. We need to reach the main camp before it hits. Otherwise, it'll be too dangerous for us to fly."

Within half an octar of the Alphas departure, winds whipped through the camp, although not as strong as nearer the Barrens. Blazel, along with a group of men, rushed around the camp, securing tents. Rain pelleted them as they finished with the last one. By the time Blazel ran into the tent assigned to his pack, his clothes were soaked.

Two days later, the storm ended. Curious, Graak and Blazel flew over the Barrens. Blazel whistled when they reached the remnants of the enemy's force. While their camps suffered little damage, the sandstorm had devastated the invaders. The storm had hit the Scourge in an open area with only a few petrified boulders providing shelter against the sandstorm. Thousands of corpses, with the flesh scoured from the bones, littered the sands. Cuts covered the few dozen lizards wandering the black sands toward the crater.

Some invaders survived, Graak said. *I see a trail.* He swooped lower, following it until they found more invader corpses.

Blazel's nose crinkled at the dry husks. "The storm didn't kill those. Their fellow soldiers did."

Graak continued slowly flying, passing over more bodies, until the compound came into view. *Based on the tracks, I estimate fewer than a hundred survived.* He spiraled higher, turning back toward camp.

"Great Warrior, so many dead!" Blazel swore. "May the Goddess continue to send such storms to whittle away the overwhelming numbers of our enemy."

May she do so, Graak agreed.

Chapter 29

Blazel - 8 de Hondar, 1075

Over the next two chedans, Blazel split his time between fighting the enemy and checking on the newly freed captives. Rolstrun, Bohandran, and Maheli had been the first to see him as more than a lone rogue wolf and befriend him. He enjoyed renewing and deepening their friendship.

Rolstrun wept when he recounted the first time an overseer beat him with a nucla treated whip and his fear he'd never shift again. "But now, most of the nucla is gone," he said. He shifted into his warrior form and howled.

Blazel winced at the pain tingeing Rolstrun's howl. He remembered the inner fire sweeping over his muscles when shifted after he'd stayed too long in his wolf form.

"It gets easier," he assured Rolstrun and the others.

Fear haunted Bohandran's face as he shared the story of how the commander killed Nederposan after the first attempt to free the children.

On the way back to the main camp, Blazel allowed the tears to flow. He pulled off his goggles and wiped them away. "Graak, you didn't meet them before all this happened. They were such fierce fighters. Rolstrun was my first friend."

*Hey, I thought I claimed that honor!** Graak objected.

Blazel patted Graak's neck, smiling. "You're my first Gryphon friend. Rolstrun was the first Posair male to treat me as a fellow fighter and worthy of friendship. Maheli gave me my first set of red leathers."

*I understand it hurts to see them like this. But I don't believe they are broken, especially not Rolstrun. He's stronger than you give him credit. Time will heal their wounded souls.**

The next day, Blazel and Graak had barely touched the ground when a group of twenty warriors approached them.

"Blazel, we want to fight," Bohandran said, his hands clenched in tight fists.

"I—we—need to regain our self-confidence." Rolstrun twisted his hands together. "After being slaves for so long, we need to prove to ourselves we're still warriors. Please, Blazel, let us fight."

Blazel held up his hands. "I'm not the one you should ask. You should speak to Histrun."

"But Histrun isn't here," Bohandran said. "You are. And while Histrun is the Supreme Alpha, you're the battle commander."

"I'm Naila's second."

"But you can make this decision. I'm sure they'll uphold it."

Blazel hesitated. He didn't want to be responsible for them if they weren't ready.

*They aren't broken,** Graak reminded him, his mental voice directed only to Blazel. *As warriors, the only way for them to heal their terror is to fight the Scourge who caused it.**

*Are you sure?**

*I am.**

Blazel studied each of the men closer. While a certain frailness hung about them, so did inner strength. He nodded. "Don't make me regret it. Graak, can you ask for more Gryphons to join us? We have more fighters to haul back to base camp."

*Already done.** Graak warbled. *They'll arrive shortly.**

"Go get your belongings," Blazel said.

"It won't take long." Rolstrun gave a wry, sad smile. "We don't have much. The Scourge took everything we had."

Blaze smiled. "Not everything. You're still alive."

A half octar later, several Gryphons landed in the field. Blazel helped Rolstrun and the others to mount, then climbed on Graak's back.

"I hope I made the right decision," he said as they flew toward the main camp.

No matter what happens, you did. They need to exact their revenge on their former tormentors.

After that, Histrun allowed any person who chose to fight to join the war host, where they were assimilated into the battalions and fighting-packs.

Blazel - 10 de Hondar, 1075

Even after the sandstorm destroyed the Scourge commander's force, he continued to send troops to hassle the Posairs.

Blazel and Rizelya worked with their battalion to practice using the new weapons whenever they weren't fighting. They wanted to ensure everyone became proficient in switching between the poison canisters, the converted enemy weapons, and their traditional helbraughts.

"We need more," Rizelya complained to Histrun. "While the women can easily direct their magic through the pulsers, the men can only shoot the projectiles. And Maendy's crew has only given us a limited amount of ammunition."

"While we're formidable and powerful in our warrior form," Blazel added, "we can't hold it in a sustained battle. We know the commander will throw all his forces at us. The winter storms, both rain and sand, are the only thing stopping him now. The men need more than simply their fangs and claws if we hope to win against the Scourge's greater numbers."

"Yes, this is a problem." Histrun rubbed his chin. "I fully expect the Scourge to attack us en masse when spring arrives. Maendy is working as fast as possible to produce more ammo, anticipating the final battle. I'm not sure what more we can do."

"Can the Faeorn help?" Rizelya asked. "They are masters with machines, or so Kaieli tells me."

Histrun shrugged. "I'll ask them."

Several days later, Histrun called Blazel and Rizelya, along with their squad-pack, to the field near the command tent. When they arrived, the Faeorns and Tre'nok waited by a table covered with a cloth. Blazel lifted his eyebrows when he saw Maendy standing next to it, grinning. Moraak and Graak looked on with curiosity.

Tre'nok stepped forward. "The Faeorn do not like making weapons. They prefer to make machines to improve people's lives, not take them. But the Scourge never asked them their preferences, and so they've become very good at developing weapons."

The tiny Jei-Yan removed the cloth. Several pulsers lay on it. They didn't appear much different from those Maendy had converted. "We fix," Jei-Yan said. He pointed to Maendy. "She help." He gestured at the weapons, added more, then looked to Tre'nok to translate.

"The Faeorn made Maendy's conversions more effective," Tre'nok said. "The pulsers now integrate your magic, including the men's latent abilities. They hope your people can use these to eliminate the Scourge on your planet."

"What they did was bloody brilliant!" Maendy gushed. "We're experimenting with how to make the helstrim more sensitive to allow the men to use their Talents with the helstrablades, or even helbraughts."

"This is amazing news," Histrun said. "Thank you, Jei-Yan and Pei-Yoon." He walked to the table and examined the weapons. "How does it work?"

Maendy handed Blazel a pulser. "Before you pull the trigger, access your magic, like you do to shift. Instead of directing it to your body, focus it through the weapon. At first, this will be a conscious effort, but with practice, it will become instinctual."

"I don't have to think about what I'm doing," Rizelya added, "every time I use my helbraught. If this works, we'll add the same training we do with young Reds to our sessions."

"It works," Maendy huffed. "Go ahead, Blazel. Try it."

Blazel raised the weapon and sighted on the target. As he squeezed the trigger, he connected with the well of magic within him. Something tugged on his magic, drawing it out of him. He directed it toward the weapon in his hands. Fire streamed from the pulser instead of a projectile. He whooped with joy.

Aistrun and Jaehaas stared at the burning target.

"Hey, let me try!" Aistrun reached for the weapon. Blazel handed it to him.

When fire shot from the pulser, Aistrun nearly dropped it. He stared at it, shock and disbelief on his face. "I've never used my magic like that before. Amazing!"

Jaehaas tried it next. Bronze light zipped from it, covering the target with mud. Jaehaas scowled. "How will mud kill an invader?"

Blazel shrugged. "Suffocate it?"

"Wait," Jei-Yan said, smiling.

The mud began to drip, taking bits and pieces of the target with it. A few moments later, the mud gushed, and the target disintegrated. Jaehaas made a face, turned his head away, and handed the pulser back to Blazel. "Oh, that be disgusting. I'll stick to my fire arrows. The death they cause be cleaner."

With the proof the men could use the weapon, Histrun had Maendy's team of helstramiesters flown to the base camp. They established a forge on the outskirts, and worked with the Faeorn to convert the confiscated weapons to use the Posairs' magic.

The men had plenty of practice using the new weapons. True to Tre'nok's prediction, the Scourge commander dug in his heels. Whenever the weather cleared of sand or rain storms, he threw his forces at the Posairs, attempting to crush them. However, this had the unintended consequence of helping the Posairs. After each battle, they added more Scourge weapons to their stockpile.

It also gave the Vhelopsi more weapons to use. The Vhelopsi hadn't been enslaved as long as the Volkern or Faeorn, and remembered their own martial training. Many times, their savage bravery turned the tide of a battle.

"We want to prove we are capable and valuable," Hairan explained to Blazel after a particularly nasty battle. "We live here now, and are fighting for this world as much as you or the Gryphons."

"I'm happy you're on our side." Blazel wiped the sweat from his face. "I'm not sure we'd be pushing the Scourge back without your additional forces."

"Let's not forget the Volkerns," Rizelya added as she cleaned the purple blood off her helbraught blade. "Their long history with the Scourge gives them insights into their battle strategies, allowing Histrun and Naila to form more effective counter strikes. Because of them, we've lost far fewer people than we would have otherwise."

And us, Graak warbled. *Without us, you'd already be dead, or slaves.*

"Thank the Goddess she sent Chariel that vision!" Blazel patted Graak's shoulder. "She spoke truly when she said without allies, we'd all die." He glanced at Hairan. Even with the Gryphons, the Posairs would be hard pressed to win against the Scourge. "Did the Goddess foresee our alien allies when Chariel spoke her prophecy?"

"I believe she did," Rizelya said. "She brought us what we needed to prevail over the Scourge's madness."

Rizelya - 15 de Ahdar, 1076

The new year arrived and with it, spring. Rizelya celebrated that she and those she loved still lived. While many Posairs died in the constant skirmishes with the Scourge, the enemy lost even more. Between the new weapons, both the pulsers and Blazel's poison, the Vhelopsi fighters, and the information the Volkern provided, the Posairs won most of the battles.

Rizelya stood in the warm sunshine, breathing in the scents of spring. While she enjoyed the warmer days and the end of the winter storms, she dreaded the coming battle. How many of her friends would survive? The Scourge would soon run out of food, making the commander even more desperate to conquer the Posairs.

"Time to go," Blazel said from behind her, slipping an arm around her waist. "Soon, this will be over one way or another."

"The only acceptable way is the defeat of the invaders," Rizelya ground out. She turned around and kissed Blazel deeply. "One day, we'll discover how it feels to live a normal life together."

He chuckled. "We certainly haven't experienced anything close to it since meeting. I've never experienced a 'normal' life. I'm looking forward to spending whatever that means with you."

Are you coming, Graak interrupted. *We're ready, just waiting on you two.*

Rizelya sighed and stepped away from Blazel's embrace. She hurried to Glork and climbed on while Blazel mounted Graak. The scout team lifted off. Histrun wanted an assessment of the invader's forces.

Rizelya watched the land pass below them, drinking in the sights of spring. Bright green grass waved in the breeze on the plains. Pink, white, and purple flowers dotted the landscape. All too soon, they left the abundant life and flew over the wastelands of the Barrens. Random groups of petrified wood boulders punched through the black sand, which stretched for a hundred measures. Rizelya imagined the vast forest it once had been and the life it supported. Was this where the Malvers clan lived?

When they approached the crater, Rizelya's skin tingled as Glork cast his invisibility spell. She gaped at the invader's compound. The Scourge hadn't made any repairs to the damage from their raid. The derelict generators—now piles of slag—still stood, marking the dysfunctional energy field's perimeter. Only a burned-out shell remained of the processing plant. Huge holes gaped in the sides and roofs of more than half of the slave's and soldier's housing, making them unusable. She searched for any of the remaining slave species.

Rizelya pointed at the handful of the ugly Kaigors wandering the grounds. "Now we know why the invaders attacked their fallen comrades and ate them. The Scourge are starving."

Blazel grunted in agreement. "It won't be long before the commander makes one last push to annihilate us. Graak, fly over the mother ship. Something's happening."

This is bad, Graak said, hovering over the ship.

Soldiers streamed from the ship, marching to gather in front of a raised platform. There were far fewer than she expected. Between the weather and the Posairs' more effective weapons, including Blazel's poison, the Posairs had cut the invader's force by a third to a half. A Scourge dressed in gold-trimmed robes—Commander Ke-ke-tak, she assumed—strode onto the dais.

Rizelya glanced at the lime-green Volkern sitting behind Aistrun on Broogk, glad now Blazel had insisted on brining Flo'kik with them. The translator's face paled, and his eyes widened at the commander's speech.

The soldiers below them thrust their weapons into the air and roared.

Aistrun's face grew grim as he listened to Flo'kik.

They're getting ready to march on us, Aistrun said. *All of them.*

We expected as much, Blazel said. *The scout Gryphons will stay here and watch the hoard's progress across the Barrens. We need to return to warn Histrun and Moraak.*

Rizelya thanked Maellyn again for her goggles as the wind from Glork's speed slammed into her.

The final battle had arrived at last. Her people would either push the invaders off their world, or die trying.

Rizelya - 15 de Ahdar, 1076

The battle leaders met in the command tent to discuss plans now they knew the full host of invaders marched toward them.

Histrun leaned over the map of the Barrens, studying it. "With as large of a force as they have," he observed, "it will take them at least two days to get here."

Moraak pointed to a spot a few measures into the Barrens. *I suggest we meet them here, where devastation has already claimed the land. The open ground provides us with an advantage, and my Gryphons can provide aerial support.*

Naila tapped an area on the map. *When they reach here, we should send a team to double back and take out any soldiers left at their compound. They should also wait to ambush any survivors who may return.*

All the different plans and scenarios swam through Rizelya's head by the time they broke for lunch. Organized chaos reigned as people scurried around camp, preparing for the last battle with the invaders. Gryphons dove, picking up a load of supplies to take to the chosen battlefield.

Blazel plunked a quick kiss on Rizelya's cheek. "I have to run. I hope we made enough poison." He ran across the camp to his testing tent, now the poison processing plant. His team, along with Margandy and Laynal, worked to fill as many canisters and hollow cylinders with the poisonous mixture as possible.

Jaehaas galloped off to help the other centaurs and Haaslair people to ready the horses, in case the fight went against them, and the Posairs needed to run. Most of the support personnel would remain in the base camp, but also prepared to retreat deeper into the plains if necessary.

"Rizelya!"

She turned at her name being called and gave a glad cry. "Kaieli, what are you doing here?"

"I'm joining the healers for the battle." Kaieli gestured to Faliciden and Faelyn, who waited a few paces away. "We have to do our part to end this war. We can't allow the memories of the Scourge to continue to terrorize us. This is our way of fighting back."

"Be safe," Rizelya hugged Kaieli.

The three healers jogged to the waiting Gryphons, who would ferry them to the selected site. Bethlyn and over two dozen other healers sat atop Gryphons, who had packs of healing supplies for the infirmary tied onto their backs. As soon as the new arrivals settled, the Gryphons leaped into the air.

Rizelya rushed to join the team transferring the Volkerns and Faeorns to Posanreande Keep, where Histrun had hidden the scout ship. Rizelya smirked at the irony of it. The keep had been the first to fall to the invaders. When she arrived, a heavy weight lodged in her stomach. The keep felt forlorn and abandoned. Could it ever be re-inhabited? Most of the prior Posanreande citizens had died in the slave camp.

"Oh, no!" Jei-Yan cried, slipping off the Gryphon carrying him and his triad.

Pei-Yoon buried its head in its hands, shaking with sobs.

The scout ship truly appeared damaged beyond repair. After a moment, the Faeorn recovered and rushed to it, climbing over it. Mei-Ying, heavy with late pregnancy, lumbered inside. A few milcrons later, she came out, smiling and shouting.

"Mei-Ying says the gigantic ones were brilliant," Tre'nok translated. "The damage appears worse than it is, but it will still take much work for the ship to be space worthy."

Mei-Ying chattered at him, and he turned back to the Posairs. "She is correct. There is too much work to do to sit here and talk. May your Goddess watch over you and grant you victory over your enemy." Tre'nok bowed, then he and the other Volkern joined the Faeorn in repairing the ship.

Rizelya and the others had work of their own and returned to base camp.

'Two days' echoed in Rizelya's mind as she helped tie a pack onto the waiting Gryphon. In two days, they would either be free of the invaders or dead. She wanted to spend the time making love to Blazel, not in this frenzied activity. Even though exhaustion pulled on her, when Blazel joined her in her cot late that night, she enthusiastically made love with him. The quiet sounds of lovemaking filled the tent as others also affirmed they were alive.

By noon the next day, the Gryphons had conveyed the last of the supplies to the battle site, and began moving people. As commanders, Rizelya and Blazel flew to it in the first wave.

Rizelya surveyed the area. Moraak had chosen well. The wide expanse of black sand glittered in the sunlight. On slightly higher ground, boulders of petrified wood sheltered the fighters' lean-tos from the wind and provided a modicum of shade. Across from them, in the direction the invaders would come, lay only flat, black sand. The Scourge would have nothing to fall back on or to hide behind.

Dust rose on the horizon, kicked up by the invader's mounts. Soon. They would arrive soon.

The healers walked through the camp, passing out small pills to each fighter—Posair, Vhelopsi, or Gryphon.

Kaieli handed a young woman a pill. "Here, keep this with you. Take it only if you are captured."

"Will it hurt?" a young woman asked, her voice shaking.

"No," Kaieli assured her. "You will only go to sleep and never wake up."

When Kaieli gave Rizelya hers, she held up the pill between her thumb and forefinger. It seemed strange something so small could be so deadly. Rizelya shivered as she tucked it into the inside pocket of her jacket. Although she didn't want to have to take it, it was much better than the other option. She would gladly swallow it if she were unlucky enough for the invaders to capture her.

By the time the Scourge marched into the area, darkness embraced the pseudo-valley. The sounds of them making camp echoed across the sands.

Rizelya wandered through the Posair encampment, stopping to give encouragement or share a laugh with the people under her command. She joined her friends as they huddled around a tiny fire, sitting in front of Blazel. He put his arms around her, and she snuggled against his chest, grateful for his warmth. Aistrun and Jaehaas sat alone. Chariel had stayed in the secondary camp, and Wisah was still in the Sanctuary. Rizelya wondered what she'd learned from the ancient tome Rizelya had discovered. Eidstrun slung an arm over Leistral's shoulders, and she leaned into him. Sometime during the past lunadars, they'd become partners. Dehali laughed quietly at Tami's joke, while her twin, Kami, blushed furiously.

Rizelya turned away, gazing at the stars, wondering what had happened to Keandran, the missing member of her original squad-pack. She rarely thought about him, but the impending battle made her feel nostalgic. She hoped the scoundrel had found peace.

A strident shout floated through the dark, reminding them their enemy camped close by. The friendly chatter died, and their faces turned bleak. One by one, or in pairs, the group broke up to find their bedrolls. Rizelya lay in Blazel's arms, unable to fall asleep. She prayed this wouldn't be their last night together.

Chapter 30

Rizelya - 18 de Ahdar, 1076

A gentle shake woke Rizelya from a fitful sleep. Instead of her normal nightmares of the Malvers' monsters, she'd dreamed of being eaten by the Scourge commander. She rubbed her eyes and face, shaking off her dread.

"It's time." Blazel handed her a cup of hot taevo and a cold meat roll when she sat up. She gulped down the food, quickly rebraided her hair, and grabbed her helbraught and other weapons. She gave a wan smile to Aistrun as he stretched. "Stay safe, Wolf." She patted his arm.

"You too, Little Red." He kissed her on the cheek, then trotted toward the Gryphons.

Blazel came up behind her and wrapped his arms around her. Rizelya turned around so she could gaze into his face. Tension pulled his mouth into a tight line. She rose onto her toes and kissed him.

"Watch out for yourself," he said, his voice husky. "I won't be able to guard your back. I want us to grow old together." As Naila's second, he and Graak would fly above the battle and direct resources to where they were needed. He pulled her tighter against his chest.

Holding hands, Rizelya and Blazel quietly joined their squad-pack. Besides their traditional weapons, those riding Gryphons carried a poison canister and a new pulser. Leistral and Eidstrun stood together, fingers entwined. Dehali stood with Kami and Tami. Eiden held hands with the young man, Leistrun. Rizelya smiled sadly, recalling his first fight with the monsters. They'd encountered the first control-janack during that battle, and here he was now, a full warrior.

Gehan, Maellyn, Grazeen, Raeleen, and Saffren stood proudly, holding their helbraughts, with their team of warriors behind them. Rizelya smiled at Laynar, who had become not only a good friend but also a reliable platoon alpha. Her little sister, Laynal, bounced on her toes. The young never feared death.

Rizelya studied each loved one's face, burning it into her memory. How many of them would survive the coming battle?

Blazel - 18 de Ahdar, 1076

Tremors of apprehension ran through Blazel's body as he and Rizelya walked to the front lines. This battle would determine if the Posairs remained free or if the Scourge would enslave them. He'd seen the condition of the escaped captives, and Rolstrun had shared some of his nightmarish experiences. Blazel vowed that as long as he still had breath and energy, he would fight this pestilence on their land.

His command would be pivotal in ensuring his people's freedom. The responsibility made him nervous. Rizelya squeezed his hand and gave him a reassuring smile. He gazed at the friends waiting at his side. Over the lunadars, Aistrun and Jaehaas had become like brothers to him. Worry weighed on his heart. How many of them would survive this conflict? Blazel breathed deep, willing the moisture gathering in his eyes to evaporate. Rizelya brusquely brushed tears from her face.

Graak drifted down to the empty space in front of them, followed by Glork, Broogk, and the other Gryphons. The fighters hurried to their mount's sides.

Mount up, Blazel ordered. He climbed onto Graak's back, fastened the harness, and pulled his goggles over his eyes, adjusting the strap.

When everyone nodded in readiness, Blazel gave the signal, and Graak and the Gryphons ambled forward to form a long line facing the black sand. The Haaslair archers, including Jaehaas and the few other centaurs, nocked arrows and held their bows ready. Behind them, the Posair and Vhelopsi fighters, using the converted pulsers, chambered their cartridges. A ripple passed through the waiting people as men shifted to their warrior form. Helbraught blades glowed as women fed magic into them.

Blazel glanced at the pile of boulders towering over the battlefield. From there, Histrun, Naila, and Moraak had a commanding view of the battle and would relay information to Blazel about where to redirect troops or any changes in strategy. Reserve fighters waited in the makeshift camp, along with the healers and the minimal support crews. If the fight went against them, a flight of Gryphons would evacuate the commanders and any survivors.

The sun rose at their backs, highlighting the line of invaders waiting across the black sand. Their commander rode a huge sheezet. It pawed the air restlessly. He didn't make any long speeches or demands for surrender. His translators were all gone.

Blazel narrowed his eyes and glared at the commander. He resisted the urge to reach for Rizelya's hand. His stomach clenched as he lifted his arm.

Ready... now! Blazel dropped his arm.

The Gryphons leaped into the air. As soon as they were away, the archers released their arrows. Screams sounded as the arrows found targets. Graak beat his wings, fighting to gain altitude as the enemy returned fire. Projectiles whizzed past them. Blazel sensed a fire-shield form around him, none too soon. He flinched as a projectile smashed into the shield in front of his face.

Be careful, my boy. Naila's mind-voice reached him. *I'll shield you as long as I can.*

Graak finally flew out of range of the weapons and wheeled above the fighting. From this vantage point, Blazel stared at the mass of soldiers. His heart slammed into his toes. Hearing about the numbers wasn't anything like seeing how badly the invaders outnumbered them. He swallowed, forcing his fear to cower in the back of his mind.

Rostrun - 18 de Ahdar, 1076

Rolstrun waited with the rest of the fighters in the first wave. Ahead of him, Maheli fed magic into her helbraught as she grinned. She, like the other Reds who had been captives, reveled in having a helbraught back in their hands. Myndera's helbraught crackled with fire magic.

Blazel gave the signal, and Rolstrun reached for his magic, letting his body change into his warrior form. He stretched to his new full height of nearly nine feet and shook the last of the tingles of the shapeshift from himself. Next to him, Alestrun and Calistrun shifted, along with Bohandran and the rest of the former captives from Strunland Keep. They'd refused the new weapons when Blazel offered them. They wanted—needed—to use their warrior's gifts to take their revenge on their former captors.

The first time Rolstrun fought after being rescued, he reveled in tearing out the invader's throats. Their screeches of terror as his claws plunged into their soft bodies, and their purple blood soaking his fur, had satiated some of his need for vengeance. Each time he fought the invaders, the hole inside of him that said he wasn't a warrior filled a little more.

Rolstrun flexed his claws, activating his venom. A tingle of fear raced up his spine as the Gryphons at the front of the line launched into the sky, and the fighters around him began to run. Soon, he'd clash with his enemy. Whenever he faced a

Scourge soldier for the first time in battle, terror raged through him that he'd be captured again. This time, he had recourse.

Tears had streamed down Kaieli's face when she gave him the suicide pill. She still hadn't told him she loved him, but as she'd begged him to stay safe and to come back to her, love shone in her eyes. As he ran toward the enemy, he thought of her. They were so close to living their dream of being together. He clashed with an invader, anger driving his claws through the tough skin and into its heart. They wouldn't stop him from being with his love, with Kaieli, any longer.

Rizelya - 18 de Ahdar, 1076

At Blazel's order to launch, Glork bunched his hindquarters and leaped into the air. Rizelya wrapped a shield around herself and the Gryphon. Within moments, he flew into range over the mass of invaders. She gripped the nozzle of her canister and opened the valve, raining death to those below. Once she emptied it, she unhooked her pulser, shooting the poisoned cylinders into her enemies. When those were gone, she switched to her helbraught. Even though the pulser could use her magic, she much preferred to wield her helbraught. After all the years she'd used it, it felt like an extension of herself.

Glork swept and dove at the soldiers, the harness keeping her safely on his back. Behind her, her team kept pace. All their practice paying off in the chaos of this monstrous battle.

After several octars, Glork soared above the fighting, and Rizelya glimpsed the hoard seething beyond the current battleground. She gasped in dismay. Even with Blazel's poison, the additional Vhelopsi fighters, and the Faeorn's conversion of the pulsers, the situation still seemed hopeless. The Scourge so outnumbered her people.

In a moment of quiet, Rizelya took stock of the people she loved who fought in this battle. Below her, Maheli, Rolstrun, and the others in the Strunland guard-pack savagely attacked a larger group of invaders. She lost sight of them as Glork's spiraling flight took them over the green healers' tents, where Kaieli worked to heal the wounded. Rizelya knew her heart-sister would work until she dropped.

High in the sky above her, Blazel directed their troop's movements while Histrun, Naila, and Moraak watched from their perch. The commanders changed their strategy as the battle ebbed and flowed.

After she and her crew grabbed a fresh supply of poison and projectiles, Glork flew back over the fight. Rizelya's heart leaped to her throat. Laynar's squad struggled against multiple mounted invaders. *Leistral, Dehali, go help Laynar,* she ordered.

They saluted, and their Gryphons zipped to the knot of fighting. Leistral and Morru dove at a lizard. It reared, tossing its head, trying to skewer Morru with its sharp horns. Morru flared, his fire engulfing those below. The beast squealed, pawing at its burning head, then galloped away. As the flames spread, it dropped to the ground, rolling over and squashing its rider. Morru followed the beast and flew closer to the writhing creature. Leistral leaned over and stabbed it with her helbraught, putting it out of its misery.

Target the lizards! Rizelya ordered. *Fire makes them go mad. Let them kill the invaders for us.* While she hated to use the creatures, she would to protect her people.

She contacted Blazel and told him of this new strategy. He and Graak would pass the word to the other Gryphons. *How are we doing?*

We're barely holding our own. Blazel's voice held pride. *More Scourge soldiers are dying than our people. Sorry, gotta go.* He broke off contact, but Rizelya could still hear the mind-echo as he shouted directions to another team.

She hung on as Glork dove to assist Leistral and Dehali in their attack on the lizards. They fought one skirmish after another, moving across the battlefield to where the ground forces most needed help. She and Glork, along with Leistral and Morru, flew over a clump of invaders, spraying them with poison or shooting at them with the poisoned cylinders. Their efforts allowed the fighters on the ground to prevail against the greater forces. Then, they'd head to the next swarm, their higher position breaking it up.

A few times, her team arrived too late to help their people, other than to keep the invaders from eating or capturing them. Each time they did, bile filled Rizelya's throat, but it made her even more determined to win against the enemy.

Another swarm caught Graak's attention, and he swerved to fly over it. Rizelya focused her rage on the soldiers below her.

The day wore on with no end in sight.

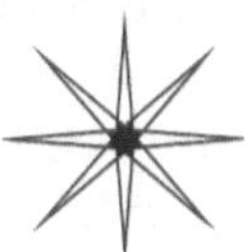

Blazel - 18 de Ahdar, 1076

The first wave of Posairs broke against the invaders' force. Blazel smiled in satisfaction as Rizelya's squad released their canisters of poison and death rained on the Scourge. She and Glork beelined toward the commander even though a squadron of thirty soldiers surrounded the commander. The soldiers shot a barrage of mixed types of projectiles at Rizelya and Glork. Before they reached the commander, Glork zipped away, avoiding the volley. Their flight carried them over another area of the fight.

Blazel kept an eye on the enemy commander. The Volkern had informed the command team, if the Posairs killed the commander, it would throw the soldiers into chaos until another officer took charge. And that could give the Posairs an advantage to defeat the Scourge. Tuueek and his Thunder Wings dove at the commander. Four invaders, inside the circle surrounding the commander, dropped to one knee, lifting a large tube to their shoulders. Blazel swore.

Pull up, Tuueek! They have a projectile launcher.

Damn! I thought we had destroyed all of those. Tuueek back-winged, trying to stop his downward flight.

The tube spit out its payload in a shower of sparks and smoke. The large projectile sped toward Tuueek. "Come on, turn, Tuueek, turn. Get out of the way!"

Tuueek's bulk worked against him, and he was too slow. The projectile grew inexorably closer.

A blur zipped between Tuueek and the projectile just as it exploded. Blazel held his breath. The air cleared, and the blur resolved into Dukaaik with Shaydan on his back. The falcon-type Gryphon's speed and nimbleness had saved the Thunder Wing. Shaydan saluted, and Blazel saw the faint outlines of a fire-shield protecting the larger Gryphons.

As he congratulated the pair, Graak pointed out a small squad of Vhelopsi surrounded by invaders. Blazel scanned the available fighters and sent the Thunder Wings to help them out.

A boom shook the air, and Graak suddenly dipped as a large projectile soared an arm's length above Blazel's head. They'd flown too far away for Naila to shield them. Another missile arced toward them, but Graak flared, burning it up before it exploded. Ash blew into Blazel's face, coating his goggles and making him cough. He dug into a pocket for a rag and wiped away the dirt. He swore as another projectile sped toward him.

The damned invaders are targeting us, Graak grumbled.

They must realize we're directing the fighters. Blazel gripped the harness as Graak swerved.

The Posairs gained ground as they pushed toward the projectile launcher—the commander had long since moved— and the fighting distracted the invaders. Tuueek dove, snatched the launcher in his talons, and ripped it to pieces.

Go, Tuueek! Blazel cheered.

Orders flowed from Histrun and Naila as the battle continued to rage, with Blazel passing them on to the various battalion alphas. His prone riding position hampered Blazel's view. Frustrated, he cut the strap on Graak's harness so he could sit up to better direct his fighters. He hung on with his legs and one hand as Graak dipped and dived, trusting if he fell off, Graak would catch him.

Over and over, Blazel directed the ebb and flow of the battle. He closed off his heart as he sent some people to their deaths, even as he saved others. He'd grieve later. The thought of the bomb capable of blowing apart his planet pushed his decisions. He must ensure his and Graak's races survived. The sweet face of his mother floated in his mind, as did the faces of all the mothers and children he'd met. They deserved to live in a world free of the invader's terror. The cost of a few lives was worth it if thousands more lived.

Rostrun - 18 de Ahdar, 1076

The berserker red haze slid over Rolstrun's vision. He howled and welcomed the rage, tearing into the soldiers in front of him. Like a whirling cyclone, he twisted and spun, using his teeth and claws to kill the invaders. At some point, the insanity left, leaving him drained and exhausted. Rolstrun was swiping with his claws one moment, and the next, the magic fled from him and he could no longer able to hold his warrior's form.

But he and his pack-mates were too deep into the battlefield to pull out. He picked up an invader's abandoned weapon lying nearby. When it ran out of ammunition, he searched for a new weapon.

"Rolstrun!"

He glanced up. Blazel and Graak hovered overhead.

"You and your squad-pack can head back to camp. Rest up."

"But..." Rolstrun protested, then looked around. The fighting had turned and left him and the Strunland guard-pack in a pocket of quiet.

"Go! Hurry, before you can't get out of here," Blazel warned, then he and Graak flew off.

Maheli jogged past Rolstrun, her face coated in purple blood and black grime. "You heard him. Let's go!"

Myndera, Calistrun, and Alestrun stumbled toward the camp ahead of Rolstrun. However, ten of their number had fallen during the battle.

Rolstrun's feet dragged, and he could barely put one foot in front of the other. He leaned against Alestrun for support as they trudged back to camp. He blinked in a daze at the setting sun blazing the sky orange. They'd fought all day.

His leg hurt, and he lifted a surprised eyebrow at the long gash on his thigh. He didn't remember receiving it. Alestrun held his side, blood seeping through his fingers. Ahead of him, blood covered Calistrun's upper back, and Myndera's arms were scratched and bleeding. None of them had come out of the fight without injuries.

They shuffled into their campsite, collapsing on the ground. A few milcrons later, Kaieli and Faliciden hurried to them and examined the team's wounds. Kaieli called for a stretcher when she lifted Alestrun's shirt.

"Is he going to be okay?" Maheli asked as men carried Alestrun to the infirmary.

Kaieli nodded. "He should be. It's a deep enough wound that we need to watch him, especially here in the Barrens." She grimaced, as they all did, at the reminder of the nucla poisoning they'd all suffered.

She bent over Maheli, and bronze light streamed from her hands to seal the cut on Maheli's forehead. Faliciden worked on Calistrun and then Myndera. Kaieli dropped to her knees next to Rolstrun, *tsking* as she carefully peeled back his pant leg.

"It isn't too deep," she said. "I can easily heal it. You'll be ready to fight again tomorrow."

"Do you think we'll still be fighting?"

"I'm sure of it." Kaieli healed his wound and sat back on her heels. She looked as exhausted as he felt. "We have lost so many people, and our infirmary is filled with wounded. But the reports I've heard say we're winning."

"That's good." Rolstrun gathered her in his arms. She dropped her head on his shoulder, letting him hold her. After a few milcrons, she struggled out of his arms and onto her feet.

"Someone will be by soon with food, water, and taevo," she told Rolstrun and the others. "Eat, sleep."

"Aren't you staying here with us?" Rolstrun asked.

She shook her head. "No, I have to get back to the infirmary. We have too many injured. Stay safe." She kissed Rolstrun before hurrying to the healers' tents.

Rizelya - 18 de Ahdar, 1076

The day progressed to evening, and still Rizelya and Glork fought. He used his talons and flame to attack the invaders or their mounts, while she streamed fire through her helbraught, or stabbed and sliced enemies with its blade. She felt drained, and it was getting harder to push her magic through her helbraught. She'd run out of poison and ammunition a couple of octars ago and hadn't been able to replenish them. Her legs ached from gripping Glork's back for so long. She wished she and Glork could leave the field and rest.

Rizelya, Blazel shouted, *there!*

She followed his directions to a pocket of soldiers surrounding a small group of overwhelmed fighters. Aistrun and Broogk sped forward. Broogk flamed, lighting several invaders on fire while Aistrun leaned over and swiped his helstrablade. A burning soldier lost his head. As Glork dropped lower, and Rizelya swung her helbraught at another invader. He ducked the attack and fired his weapon. She missed the block, and a projectile pierced Glork's wing. He screeched in pain.

Rizelya! Blazel called to her, breaking through the battle fog. *Take Glork to the healers. Stay back there and rest for a while. You're not doing any good as exhausted as you are.*

She tilted her head and searched the sky, finally spotting him and Graak flying above her. Ash caked his face and blood trickled from a cut on his cheek. Otherwise, he seemed hale. Glork soared higher above the battlefield. Gryphons flew fresh troops into the battle while the exhausted first wave stumbled off the field. She suspected this had happened several times already.

Glork whimpered in pain, and his wing beats faltered.

Rizelya patted his shoulder. *Okay, Glork, let's go. Blazel, have you rested?*

SSHe didn't answer. He and Graak had zipped to another part of the fight.

Leistral, you're in charge of our squad, Rizelya said as Glork winged toward the camp. She grimaced when he whimpered with each wing stroke.

When they landed, someone helped Rizelya unbuckle the harness. She slid off Glork's back, whimpering when her numb feet touched the ground and the blood started flowing again. By the time she stood on her own, a healer was working on Glork's wing.

"Are you hurt?" the woman helping Rizelya asked, her voice a bit loud.

Rizelya realized the healer had asked the question a couple of times already. She shook her head. "No, just tired."

"A hot cup of taevo will revive you. Come along, dearie, and we'll get you one. And some food. I'm sure you haven't eaten for octars and octars." The woman kept up a monologue while pushing Rizelya onto a camp stool and handing her a steaming cup of taevo and a plate of food.

Rizelya balanced the plate on her lap and sipped the taevo. Warmth oozed down her throat and seeped from her stomach to her aching limbs. She suspected the healer had placed a healing spell on the taevo. It helped revive her enough so she could eat.

Chapter 31

Blazel - 18 de Ahdar, 1076

The day became evening, and still they fought with the Scourge. The mass below Blazel surged in several knots of fierce activity. He now appreciated Histrun's wisdom of holding back reserve fighters. There seemed to be no end to the number of invaders. He kept watch, and when one group flagged with exhaustion, he directed another platoon to replace them. But Naila had only trained him to be her second, which left no one able to take his and Graak's place. They only took brief breaks to relieve themselves, refill water canteens, and grab some food. They refused to stop and sleep, even when directly ordered to by first Histrun, then Moraak.

Night fell, and still the battle raged, eerie in the light of glowing helbraughts and the flash from the invader's weapons. How many of his people had the enemy taken captive under the cover of darkness? Blazel patted his pocket where the death pill rested. He hoped anyone captured had the courage to take it and deprive the invaders of a food source—and avoid the terror of captivity. He'd seen the faces of those they rescued. Even though they tried to put up a brave front, horror lurked behind their eyes.

Dawn arrived with little fanfare, just a brightening of the sky. Graak spiraled higher and caught a thermal, allowing him to glide in lazy circles and rest somewhat. Riderless lizards wandered deep in the Barrens. The commander in his gold-edged robes stood out, one of the few invaders who remained mounted. The Gryphons' fiery attacks on the sheezets had decimated the beasts.

Blazel looked around, orienting himself on where the night battle had taken them. He smiled in satisfaction. They'd achieved one of their objectives of pushing the Scourge deeper into the Barrens and back toward the crater—and their ship. Far more dead soldiers scattered the battlefield than Posairs, Gryphons, or Vhelopsi.

In the areas cleared of fighting, teams of warriors and healers moved the injured off the field quickly before the tide turned and swept them up. Other people gathered the fallen weapons of both the Posairs and invaders. After witnessing many men, too exhausted to continue fighting in their warrior forms, pick up abandoned weapons and turn them on their former owners, Blazel ordered the scavenge. He didn't want their enemy to do the same thing with the helbraughts, even if for the invaders, they could only use the sharp blades.

Below Blazel, a large force of soldiers surrounded a knot of Posanlair fighters. As he sent reinforcements to them, an enormous warrior morphed back into a man with a bushy red beard—Kederposan. After having been a captive for so long, he'd fought in a berserker rage. Mutilated bodies sprawled around him.

A soldier thirty feet away lifted his weapon, aiming at Kederposan. Blazel frantically searched for someone to help. *Morru!* he screamed for the Gryphon. But before Morru took two wing beats, Kederposan crumpled to the ground, his chest riddled with holes. A dozen more Posairs fell before the reinforcements reached them. Hairan's squad arrived from the left, shooting the invaders with the confiscated weapons, while Laynar's came from the right, using helbraughts, magic, and warriors. Caught in the middle, the group of soldiers succumbed to the onslaught.

Rizelya - 19 de Ahdar, 1076

Someone shook Rizelya awake. She groaned. Her body ached from head to toe. Grit filled her eyes. She hadn't had nearly enough sleep.

"It's time to rotate," a young woman said.

Rizelya pried her eyes open to full sunlight. "Has the fighting stopped at all?"

"No, ma'am."

Rizelya glanced at the empty bedroll next to hers. "Did Blazel take a break?"

"I don't think so." The girl held out a cup of taevo and a meat roll.

Rizelya took the offered food and sat at the cold fire ring to eat.

Her heart lifted when Aistrun, Leistral, and Eidstrun joined her with their breakfast. They appeared as exhausted as she felt. She hadn't seen any of her squad since returning last night with Glork.

"Morru's in the infirmary," Leistral said. She winced as she sat, putting a hand over the bandage on her forearm. "The projectile only grazed me, but lodged into Morru's shoulder."

A few moments later, Dehali, Kami, and Tami arrived, followed by Saffren, Maellyn, Grazeen, Gehan, and Raeleen. They all suffered cuts and bruises, but nothing seemed serious. Rizelya grimaced as her movement pulled on a few of her own.

"Leistral, let's check on our Gryphon friends." Rizelya used her helbraught to push to her feet. "The rest of you, meet us at the ammunition station, then we'll find out where Histrun wants us since we're grounded today."

She and Leistral tromped to the Gryphon infirmary. The walk loosened Rizelya's muscles. Her legs ached from gripping

Glork's belly all day yesterday. Numerous Gryphons lay curled on blankets while several healers moved about, tending to their wounds.

Glork gingerly held out his wing. Next to the metacarpal bone of his left wing, a large hole still oozed blood. *Sorry, Rizelya.* Pain laced his voice. *I'm out for at least another day. Morru also needs another day to heal.*

She patted his other shoulder and stroked the soft feathers of his head. "You just rest and heal. I'll check on you when I can."

Rizelya joined her squad at the ammunition tent. They all needed to resupply their poison spray and ammunition for their pulsers.

The woman in charge of munitions shook her head. "We're out of the spray. We should receive more later today."

Rizelya shrugged. The spray worked best from the air. "Our Gryphons are recovering from injuries, so we're fighting on the ground."

The woman leaned over and placed a pile of cartridge magazines on the table. "Here, take these, although they aren't the poisoned cylinders."

"They'll work." Rizelya and her team grabbed several magazines each, stuffing them in pouches around their waists. They still possessed their tried-and-true weapons of helbraught, teeth, and claws, which worked better in close quarters than the pulsers did.

Armed, they trotted to the battlefield, which was now much farther into the Barrens. During the night, the leading edge had moved several measures south, toward the crater. Posair, Gryphon, Vhelopsi, invader, and sheezet bodies littered the ground.

The fighting surged from one area to another. In an area where the fighting had passed, groups of warriors and healers checked their people for survivors, carrying off any who still lived. Two Thunder Wings hovered nearby. A healer bent over a downed Gryphon, and a moment later, she waved at the Thunder Wings. They flew over, slipped a sling under their injured comrade, and gently lifted him off the field.

Rizelya searched for, and found, Histrun and Moraak on the tall pile of boulders of their command center, where they watched the progress of the fighting. Moraak stood intently gazing over the battle, his talons curled around the edge, his tail thumping the rocks behind him, his wings slightly outstretched for balance. As Rizelya drew closer, she could hear his commands.

Split them up, Moraak ordered. *Drive them toward Saehala's pack.*

Rizelya stopped at the base of the boulders and waved at Histrun to catch his attention. "My squad is grounded. Where do you want us?"

Histrun studied the field a moment, then pointed to the far southeast. "There. Candriel needs help. The Strunhelos contingent is getting trounced." He whistled, and several Gryphons flapped over, one for each of her squad-pack. "They'll take you and drop you off."

A chair sling dangled below the lead Gryphon's belly. Rizelya wriggled into it and thumped him on the chest to let him know she was ready. Her stomach clenched as he rose high over the battle, and she gripped the straps tighter. A few moments later, he hovered over the thick knot of fighting. Rizelya eased to the sling's edge and jumped off, feeding fire magic into her helbraught. The invader she landed behind didn't even notice her until she severed his head.

Aistrun fought at her side. Leistral and Eidstrun fought as a precise team. She used her helbraught to drive the soldiers she faced into Eidstrun's claws. Saffren and Maellyn's ice-and-lava technique worked just as well on invaders as it did on Malvers' monsters.

Rizelya threw up her helbraught, blocking an invader's knife, and sensed another one swinging toward her from the side. The enemy in front of her suddenly opened his mouth, gagging on purple blood from an ice spear penetrating his throat. Rizelya gave Gehan a nod of thanks before spinning to parry the second one's strike.

A swath of dead soldiers marked their passage as they worked their way to Candriel's pack. Rizelya bit back her grief when Tami jerked, blood blossoming on her chest. A moment later, the light went out of Tami's eyes as she died from the projectile wound. Dehali screamed and slammed a wall of hardened air into the invader. He flew several feet, landing on his back. He didn't have any time to recover before Dehali jumped on top of him, stabbing him repeatedly with her helbraught.

With the addition of Rizelya's squad to Candriel's, they now outnumbered the group of invaders, and slowly made headway in cutting them down. When Saehala's pack arrived, they crushed the remaining soldiers between them.

Before they'd taken more than a few breaths to rest, more enemies streamed toward them.

Rizelya whirled to block a slashing knife, then stabbed the invader in the gut. Her world became block, slash, strike, parry. She passed the point of exhaustion and kept fighting. More soldiers always took the place of the slain. Rizelya gasped at a sharp pain in her leg, blinking in surprise at the knife sticking from her thigh. She swung her blade down, lopping off the hand attached to it. She bent over and pulled the knife out. Blood gushed from the wound, and pain washed over her. A projectile whizzed by her head. She thrust at the soldier, sinking her helbraught deep into his belly.

And she was back in the flow of block, slash, and strike until her leg gave out, and she crumpled to the ground. She lay there, panting, tears rolling down her face, unable to stand. The pain she'd been holding off crested over her, drowning her in wave after wave.

Rolstrun - 19 de Ahdar, 1076

Early the next morning, Rolstrun's squad-pack was rousted out of bed. After a hurried meal of a meat roll and taevo, a team of Gryphons ferried them to the fighting. Rolstrun lamented he hadn't found Kaieli before returning to the battle.

They flew over a group of Vhelopsi overrun by soldiers. Rolstrun dropped, shifting into his warrior form as soon as his feet touched the ground. His pack-mates tore into the enemy from behind. The Vhelopsi rallied, and they crushed the invaders between them.

Throughout the day, Rolstrun's squad-pack and the Vhelopsi squadron fought together. The Vhelopsi acted as bait to draw a squad of invaders to them, while the Posairs ambushed them. But a particularly fierce skirmish late in the afternoon separated Rolstrun's squad-pack from the Vhelopsi.

Rolstrun grimaced when a large squadron of soldiers surrounded them. Maheli fought in a tight group with several other women, their helbraughts flashing in the sun, and streamers of fire flowing in the wake of their blades. An invader in silver-edged robes pushed forward, his soldiers letting him through until he faced Rolstrun and Calistrun. The officer smirked, recognizing them even in their warrior form, and pulled a whip from his belt. Suddenly, Rolstrun was back in the crater, helpless again as the overseers whipped him into submission. The whip cracked, and he cowered, backing away. The tip caught Rolstrun across his upper arm, and the next whiplash opened a slash in Calistrun's shoulder.

"Fight! Damn you, Calistrun, fight!" Myndera screamed. "We aren't slaves anymore." She raced toward them, flames shooting from her helbraught. She jerked as a soldier shot her in the back and another projectile caught her in the side. Myndera crumbled at Calistrun's feet, and he immediately shifted into his natural form. Light flashed as the officer drove his knife into Calistrun's side. He fell over Myndera and gathered her in his arms.

The fire of nucla poisoning rushed through Rolstrun's body from the treated whip, and he lost his hold on his warrior form. He tried to shift to his wolf form, but the nucla poisoning denied him access to even that. Rolstrun faced the officer alone, without any weapons. All around him, his pack-mates engaged with the soldiers, trying to protect Calistrun.

Myndera's helbraught caught Rolstrun's eye. He couldn't use it to focus his magic like she had, but it had an extremely sharp blade on the end of it. The officer drew back the whip, and Rolstrun dove for the helbraught, rolling to his feet and blocking the whip with the weapon. The officer sneered at him, brandishing his long knife with his other hand.

He sprang. Rolstrun leaped out of the knife's path, swinging the helbraught. He hadn't ever used one before, and it felt awkward in his hands. He thrust the blade at the officer, who sucked his stomach in to avoid the blow, and slashed the whip across Rolstrun's chest. Rolstrun gritted his teeth at the searing pain and swung the helbraught again. This time, the tip slid along the invaders' ribs. The officer stepped forward, jamming his knife into Rolstrun's chest. Rolstrun brought up the staff end and slammed it into the invader's stomach. Rolstrun spun the weapon around and decapitated his enemy.

Suddenly, his legs wouldn't hold him up, and he couldn't move his arms. He crumbled to the ground, unable to move as the fighting surged around him. He finally managed to turn his head. Myndera's dead eyes stared at him as darkness descended on him.

Blazel - 19 de Ahdar, 1076

Blazel wearily scanned the battlefield. He reached under his goggles and rubbed his bleary eyes. "I'm so tired," he said to Graak. "I can't tell which squad-packs are fighting anymore. Your long-distance vision is better than mine. Can you tell?"

They are starting to look all the same to me, too. Graak sounded bone tired. He'd flown high above the roiling mass of people and invaders to float on a thermal. Around them, other Gryphons would climb into the upper atmosphere, drift for a few milcrons, before diving to enter the fray again.

This was the fifth time in the last octar Graak had needed the rest. They'd have to stop soon. Blazel yawned, his jaw cracking. "Graak, let's—"

There! A group of our people are in trouble. They're surrounded. He snapped his wings back and dove.

The wind of Graak's passage burned Blazel's face. He reached out to Naila. *Who do we have available for reinforcements? We have a squad who needs help.*

Laynar's fighting-pack can be there shortly, Naila told him.

Tell them to hurry. Oh, Sweet Mother, it's the former Strunland guard-pack captives! None of them have any of the new weapons.

Blazel reached for his pulser before remembering he'd run out of ammunition a while earlier. Graak flared, hitting the outer circle of invaders, and climbing quickly, not wanting to hit their own people. As he circled back around, the reinforcements arrived. A wall of fire slammed into the soldiers, while men in their warrior forms slashed throats with their claws. Helbraught blades flashed in the dying sun. Purple blood mingled with red as it pooled on the ground. Laynar's team finally broke through the invaders and reached the guard-pack.

Only a few continued to fight. Blazel recognized Calistrun's reddish-gold hair as he sat slumped over the still form of his love, Myndera. Blazel searched for Rolstrun, praying he wasn't one of the fallen. The bodies were too jumbled together from his angle on Graak's back to make out individuals.

The last of the invaders fell to Laynar's blade.

Laynar! Blazel called. *Where's Rolstrun? Can you see him?*

Laynar plodded through the killing field, stopping every few feet to turn a body over. When she reached Calistrun—who by the grace of the Warrior still lived—she squatted, talking to him. Calistrun pointed a bloody, shaky finger. She hurried to a Posair lying next to a decapitated Scourge officer. She bent over, then slowly stood, shaking her head. *He's dead.*

"No! Sweet Goddess, no!" Grief threatened to overwhelm Blazel. He slumped over Graak's shoulders. Rolstrun had been his first Posair friend. His goggles fogged as tears streamed down his face. He remembered Rolstrun's friendly acceptance of him, helping him to wash the accumulated swamp grime from his tangled and matted hair. And now he was gone. How many other friends and loved ones had died?

"Graak, we need to go find our friends." His voice broke, and he took several deep gulps of air. "I need to find Rizelya. I have to know she's still alive."

We have our duty to direct the battle, Graak reminded him. *It grieves me your friend Rolstrun is dead, but many others depend on us to stay alive.*

"I know. Some of those are our friends. Just overfly the battlefield, will you? We haven't done that for a while. We can gauge the battle while searching for our people."

Graak soared higher and flew over the numerous battles raging below them. Blazel gaped at how far their forces had driven the invaders into the Barrens. The movement of mounted men racing along the outside edge of the fight caught his attention, and Graak adjusted his flight path toward it.

Blooms of fire arched over the heads of the fighters, striking the few remaining lizards. Blazel breathed a sigh of relief when he spotted Jaehaas with the other centaurs. Jaehaas fired his last arrow, slung his bow over his shoulder, and reached behind him, pulling a pulser from his back. He and the other centaurs shot at the soldiers as they jumped from their dying beasts, mowing them down before they could rejoin the fight. Some of the tightness in Blazel's chest released.

Graak circled toward the southeast. *I think Rizelya and her squad were last fighting in this direction.*

"Thank you." Blazel patted Graak's shoulder, glad he still had one of his oldest friends with him. The loss of Rolstrun was hitting him hard. Other people had died in this war, but none of them had been his friends. He'd had so few during his life, he cherished every one of them.

Fires blazed where the Reds and Gryphons burned the enemy, creating a thick layer of smoke and dirty ash. Blazel coughed as they flew through it, then wiped his goggles clean. Mangled and twisted bodies, some burned beyond recognition, lay scattered where the fighting had moved on. Red and purple blood soaked the black sand-glass. Blazel noticed with satisfaction that more black robes littered the ground than the bright colors of the Posair and Vhelopsi clothing.

As they approached the last place he'd seen Rizelya, Blazel searched for her. He found Candriel, and then Leistral and Eidstrun, but not Rizelya. Fear slid up his spine.

There she is! Graak cried, pointing a talon at a figure lying crumpled in a pool of blood. A massive pile of invader bodies lay strewn around her. Aistrun stood over her. He bled from several wounds and was using her helbraught to drive away a lone soldier. Otherwise, they occupied a quiet pocket.

Blazel's heart thudded in his chest. She wasn't moving.

"Rizelya!" The word tore from his throat.

Graak dove, flaring to kill the invader attacking Aistrun, who took a moment to salute them.

"Is she alive?" Blazel shouted.

"I think so," Aistrun called back.

"Graak, we have to save her."

No, Blazel. Sadness filled Graak's voice. *We must stay here and protect those still fighting. I've sent for a team of healers to retrieve her.*

"Please, Goddess, she has to live." Blazel wiped moisture from his cheeks. "The invaders will pay."

Yes, we will make them pay. There! That group needs help.

Blazel clenched his jaw and made a fist. As Graak flew in the direction of the conflagration, Blazel glanced over his shoulder. A Gryphon landed next to Aistrun and Rizelya. Blazel had to believe she was still alive. He couldn't lose her after losing Rolstrun.

Kaieli - 19 de Ahdar, 1076

The healers' tent filled to overflowing with the injured and dying. Kaieli, Bethlyn, Faelyn, Faliciden, and the other healers worked unceasingly, keeping their patient's life and limbs intact. When their patients stabilized, a team flew them to the base camp, where their wounds wouldn't fester from the black dust.

Several times over the past two days, Kaieli had to hold in her grief when news reached her of a friend or loved one dying in the battle.

Kaieli sat back from her patient and dropped her hands into her lap. She'd finally closed the deep wound in his arm. She stood and stretched, went to the other side of the tent where they stored the lengo root and mixed up a poultice. As she placed it on the man's wound, she blessed Blazel for bringing the root to them. It meant the difference between a patient losing a limb or keeping it.

She squeezed the man's hand, then threaded her way through the many cots to the table holding enormous urns of taevo. Copious amounts of it and stimulants kept her and the other healers functioning when they would have collapsed octars ago.

She slumped on a camp stool, leaning her elbows on the table as she sipped, her eyes heavy. *When will this sea of misery end? So many people are dead already.* She raised her head at the commotion of another wounded warrior being brought in. Wearily, she put her cup down and hurried to the new patient.

Blood poured from a gaping hole in his side, and a bleeding head wound made his reddish-gold hair even deeper red. She gasped when his head lolled to the side.

"Faliciden, help me! It's Calistrun," she called. Pale intestines slipped from his abdomen.

"We found him next to Myndera and Rolstrun," the man carrying the stretcher told her.

Kaieli frantically searched the other wounded being brought in. Fear tore through her when she didn't see any others. "Where... where are they?"

The man shook his head. "They didn't make it."

"No!" she sobbed, her knees buckling, and she dropped painfully to the ground. Tears blinded her and guilt overwhelmed her. *How can he be gone?* She'd let him go into battle without telling him she loved him, and now she never could tell him. She'd never be able to know what their relationship could have grown into.

Faliciden grabbed her by her shoulders and shook her, grief and pain also shining in her eyes. "Kaieli, you have to hold it together for a little longer. I need you to help me save Calistrun. We'll lose him if you don't."

Unable to stop crying, Kaieli pushed to her feet and bent over Calistrun. She used the last of her strength to work with Faliciden to put Calistrun's intestines back where they belonged. They then closed the small holes perforating them, cleared the infection, and knit the muscles together before closing the wound. His head wound proved to be shallow and easily healed.

Calistrun woke up as they loaded him on a stretcher to be flown to the base camp and weakly gripped Kaieli's hand. "He died saving me," he croaked. "I'd frozen at the sight of an officer with his whip."

"Hush now," she whispered, tears streaking down her face anew. "Save your strength."

She buried her head in her hands, sobbing as they took Calistrun away.

Faliciden hugged her. "I know you loved him. He loved you, too. I could see it in his eyes. You're done for a while. Go rest. We'll call you if we need you."

Kaieli stumbled to the empty cot near the door set aside for the healers. She pulled the rough blanket over her head, curled into a ball, and let the grief take her.

Awhile later, a ruckus disturbed her as someone shouted for a healer, drawing her out of her misery. She didn't want to leave her safe cocoon, but when she heard Rizelya's name, she threw off the covers and hurried outside.

Blood covered Rizelya from many wounds, and she hung on to life by a tenuous thread. The most serious injury was the gash in her thigh. It oozed green pus mixed with blood. *I'm not losing another beloved!* Kaieli bent her head, pouring healing energy into the wound, but it resisted her magic, making it impossible for her to heal Rizelya fully. Kaieli wept with frustration as she applied lengo root poultices to it.

Bethlyn approached the cot where Rizelya lay pale and barely breathing. "She needs to be evacuated, Kaieli. She'll heal better away from this damned black sand."

"No!" Kaieli whirled around, anger burning her face. "She stays with me!"

Bethlyn stepped back from the force of Kaieli's fury.

Kaieli softened. "Please, Bethlyn. Let her stay here. After Rolstrun, I want—need—her to be close so I can be sure she still lives. She's my heart-sister."

Bethlyn nodded once. "Don't neglect our other patients. The battle still rages."

Kaieli bowed her head. "I won't. Thank you, Bethlyn."

Throughout the long night, more injured streamed in. In the precious spare moments she had, Kaieli returned to Rizelya's cot, changing the lengo root poultices, and praying. Hope filled her as Rizelya continued to cling to life.

Blazel - 19 de Ahdar, 1076

The fighting raged on. Blazel had long since passed the point of exhaustion. He and Graak were flagging. "I can't focus any longer," he said. "And you can't keep flying."

I think I'm flying in my sleep, Graak mumbled. *We need a break. Kaaik and Delestrun can cover for us while we rest.*

Graak's flight wobbled and dipped as they flew back to camp, now nearly twenty measures away from the fighting. He landed, flapping his wings for balance as he tumbled forward.

Blazel slid to the ground, gasping at the pins and needles shooting up his feet and legs. When he could stand, he pulled the harness from Graak's back. Graak's head already rested on his fore talons, and soft chirrups escaped him as he snored.

Blazel patted his friend, and staggering with fatigue, he weaved through the camp, searching for Bethlyn.

"Blazel, you look like crap." She scowled at him, her arms crossed over her chest. "When was the last time you slept?"

"The night before the battle started. Do you have something to keep me and Graak awake, aware, and functioning? The stimulant in taevo is no longer working."

"You'd be better off catching a few octars of sleep."

Blazel rubbed his eyes and face wearily. "I know. But our people depend on us. We have to continue fighting. This should be over soon. We just need to get through the next day or so."

Bethlyn shook her head and rolled her eyes. "Histrun and Naila have already asked me for this. I figured you'd be coming around soon. Follow me." She led him to a table and gave him a small tin.

Blazel flipped open the lid and looked at the long capsules inside.

"One of those will give you energy for four octars," Bethlyn explained. "Don't take more than four in a sixteen-hour period. I gave you enough for you and Graak for two days. Expect to crash for a couple days afterward. This takes a toll on your body."

Blazel kissed her on the cheek and tucked the tin into the inner pocket of his jacket. "Have... have you seen Rizelya? Is she alive?"

Bethlyn nodded. "She's still unconscious and in critical condition, but Kaieli saved her leg with the lengo root."

Blazel slumped in relief. "Thank you, Goddess!"

Bethlyn patted his shoulder, pointed out Rizelya's cot, then returned to her work.

Blazel hurried to it, and Kaieli joined him.

"How is she?"

"Alive. She should pull through."

"I know you'll do everything you can for her. I'm so sorry about Rolstrun."

A sob racked her. "I won't let her die, Blazel." Kaieli's voice broke, and she sniffed, dashing tears from her eyes. "I promise." She hurried from Rizelya's cot, using a corner of her apron to dry her eyes.

Blazel gazed at Rizelya's pale face. She'd lost so much blood. Her shallow breathing assured him she still lived. He bent and kissed her forehead. He'd come so close to losing her. Blazel brushed away the tears in his eyes and left to find some food. She and everyone else he loved depended on him to win this battle.

After a quick, hot dinner and a short nap, he and Graak took back to the air. Blazel swallowed a capsule, grimacing at the bitter aftertaste. He gave Graak one too. A few milcrons later, the heaviness in his limbs and the fog in his mind lifted.

Blazel - 20 de Ahdar, 1076

Pride filled Blazel. Between the Posairs' magic, the poison spray, the converted weapons, and the new ammunition, Blazel's people continued to prevail over the greater number of the invaders. By now, he included the Gryphons and Vhelopsi as part of his people.

Throughout the day, the Posair army pushed the invaders farther into the Barrens, leaving a trail of bodies in their wake. Blazel smirked in satisfaction as he and Graak overflew the carnage. The enemy soldiers made up most of the corpses.

In the dying light, Blazel scanned the fighting. He estimated about a quarter of his people had fallen in the battle, while less than five thousand invaders remained. Somehow, the commander survived to direct his troops.

"We did it!" Blazel whooped, thrusting his fist in the air. "Although, I didn't really believe we could defeat them," he confessed. "There were so many of them, and so few of us."

But we had the greater advantage, Graak said, skimming over the battlefield. *We were fighting for our home and for our people's survival.*

Over the course of the battle, Blazel's people continued fighting when they probably should have surrendered. While in the same circumstances, the invaders gave up. "Yes, there is power in defending your home, rather than trying to conquer a world. And we've had allies to fight on our side."

Yes, the Vhelopsi have helped tremendously.

"I was actually thinking of you." Blazel caressed the soft fur of Graak's shoulder, where it blended with his feathers. "We couldn't have defeated the Scourge without the renewal of our ancient alliance with your people."

No, you wouldn't have. He paused, and warmth filled his voice. *It's a good partnership.*

A scout zipped to fly next to them, panting hard. Blazel recognized him as one of the scouts sent to the compound.

We did it! the scout crowed. *When we arrived, we only found a skeleton crew left by the invaders. Our force easily took them out. We control the enemy's compound!*

"Excellent!" Blazel surveyed the field again.

Moraak, Histrun, he called and passed on the information. *We should send another contingent of fighters and Gryphons under cover of darkness to augment those who wait at the mother ship. We can finish this.*

Agreed, Histrun said.

In less than an octar, a flight of Gryphons, carrying a battalion of fighters, silently winged toward the crater.

This war would be over soon.

Blazel - 21 de Ahdar, 1076

As daylight crept across the sky, Blazel sagged with exhaustion against Graak's back, and took out another stimulant for himself and Graak. They had to see this through to the end. Graak flew higher to catch a thermal where he could float and rest while still watching the battle's flow.

Blazel, look there! A group is trying to escape. Graak pointed to a small group of twenty invaders breaking away from the main fight and running deeper into the Barrens. Instead of fleeing toward the crater, they ran toward the northern guard fortress.

"Crone's fires," Blazel swore. "They're not finding a stronghold." He searched for the closest Gryphon team. *Kaaik, Delestrun!* he ordered. *Go stop them.*

Graak sent a mental image to Kaaik of the escaping invaders. Kaaik let out a screech, and he and four other Gryphons dove at the group. Delestrun leaned over Kaaik's back to swipe his claws across the back of a soldier. Shaydan sent out a pulse of magic from her helbraught, forming a fire-shield around the invaders. Gehan lifted a converted weapon, shooting a stream of yellow-green light from it. The light split into five cold-air spears, each one impaling an invader and instantly freezing them. Kaaik climbed and dove into the frozen soldiers, who shattered into bits at the collision. Gehan and Kaaik repeated the technique twice more. By then, the team had killed the other soldiers.

As the morning progressed, Blazel grinned. Less than a thousand invaders lived. Finally, the commander shouted an order, and the soldiers broke away from the fighting and ran toward their compound.

Blazel let them run. They wanted them to leave in their ship. He and Graak joined the fighters following the line of retreating invaders. Every so often, a Gryphon dove, and a bolt of fire slammed into a running soldier, or a Red would lop off an invader's head with her helbraught. Other times, Gehan or another Yellow would shoot cold-air spears into an invader. The Posairs continued to harry the Scourge's retreat, cutting their numbers down even more.

The pile of petrified boulders where Blazel had first met Kaieli came into view. "Graak," Blazel croaked, his voice nearly gone. He'd lost his mental voice an octar ago. "Tell our people inside the compound to get ready. We're almost there."

Graak complied.

A few milcrons later, only two hundred and fifty Scourge passed the ruined fence and raced through the dilapidated compound toward the mother ship. The Posairs, including Blazel and Graak, followed closely behind them.

As soon as the retreating invaders reached the ship, the waiting Posair force exploded into view above them. The commander shrieked in anger.

Graak and Blazel dove toward him. He ducked, and Graak's talons raked across his back as Blazel's helstrablade cut deeply into his feeding appendages. Purple blood oozed from the wounds. Graak wheeled about for another attack.

The commander stood his ground, a small pulser in one hand and a whip in the other. He fired. Graak flared, burning the projectile to useless slag. The commander swore—they didn't need to understand his words—and continued to shoot. All his projectiles slammed uselessly into Graak's flames, until finally the pulser clicked, empty. He tossed the useless weapon aside and opened his arms in invitation, his whip held out at his side.

Graak streaked toward him. The whip cracked, and Blazel flinched as the tip caught his cheek. The commander swung the whip again, and Graak screeched in pain as it lanced across his chest. He pulled into a steep climb.

The commander ran up the ramp and into the mother ship, followed by twenty of his men. As soon as they entered, the hatch slammed closed. A few milcrons later, the engines roared to life. The Gryphons scattered, leaving an open path out of the Barrens and out of their atmosphere.

The Posairs erupted into cheers as the ship continued to climb, while the Gryphons added their warbles and screeches to the cacophony.

"We did it, my friend!" Blazel excitedly croaked. "They're gone! Our home is safe."

Graak circled the empty compound, his eyes trained on the ship. *Yes, we did. Let's go back and tell Moraak and Histrun.*

Blazel pointed at the ship zooming across the sky, a red comet returning to the heavens. "I think they know. The whole world knows!"

We need to give them our final report.

Final report. Blazel let the words replay in his head. The war was finally over.

When the fighters eventually calmed down, Blazel and Graak led them back to camp. On their way, they killed any marooned invaders and picked up any Posair or Vhelopsi survivors they found. They would have three days to find out if the Faeorn had disabled the bomb.

In the meantime, they would celebrate.

Chapter 32

Kaieli - 21 de Ahdar, 1076

The morning of the fourth day of the final battle, exhausted fighters stumbled out of the battlefield and back to the battle camp.

Kaieli's heart raced as Aistrun staggered into the healers' tent. Blood and grime still coated his face. Although numerous cuts and scrapes covered his arms, none were deep enough to warrant a healing. She glanced at the cots filling the infirmary where fighters clung to life, like Rizelya.

"Hey, Kaieli, is Rizelya okay?" Worry etched Aistrun's face. He and Rizelya had been best friends since childhood. "She isn't... she isn't..."

"She's still alive. You can see her. But first, let's wash your wounds so they don't become infected." Kaieli dipped a rag into a bucket of water and wiped the dirt from the cuts and scrapes, adding a tiny burst of energy to cleanse them. She led the way to Rizelya's cot. "What's happening with the battle?"

"We've won! The invaders are retreating." He grinned tiredly. "Blazel and a platoon are following them to ensure they leave." He paused. "I'm... I'm sorry to hear about Rolstrun. I really liked him." He put his arms around her and pulled her to him.

"Me too." Kaieli blinked her eyes, willing the tears back. A black wave of grief threatened to swamp her, but she pushed it aside. Too many injured still needed her skills. They reached Rizelya's cot, where she lay unconscious. A thin trickle of pus oozed from her thigh, but her breathing was steadier.

Aistrun slumped onto the stool next to Rizelya's cot and took her hand. "She looks so fragile, so tiny. She was always so full of life. I called her Little Red because even as little as she was, she had the power to make you pay attention to her. I knew then she was an alpha." He bowed his head over Rizelya's hand, quietly weeping.

"She's going to pull through, Aistrun. I promise." Kaieli patted his shoulder. He reached up and squeezed her hand. She changed the lengo root poultice on Rizelya's leg, then was called back to work.

Later, a Red stuck her head into the healers' tent. "Blazel just sent word. The invaders are leaving!"

Kaieli, and every able-bodied or awake person, raced outside and gazed toward the crater. The ground under Kaieli's feet vibrated, and a few milcrons later, the humongous mother ship rose above the crater, dwarfing the sun. It gained altitude, turning into a red comet as it sped away from their world.

"Whoo-hoo!" Kaieli cheered with the rest, as elation momentarily replaced her grief. *It's finally over! Rolstrun would have loved this.* The smile slid from her face, and her shoulders slumped. Kaieli turned her back on the cheering crowd and returned to work.

Later in the evening, Kaieli checked on Rizelya. She still hadn't regained consciousness, but the lengo root had done its job, and Kaieli could finally heal her heart-sister. As she stood at the foot of the cot, she wished she could heal her own heart as easily.

Rizelya groaned and rubbed her eyes. A few moments later, she carefully lifted the blanket and heaved a sigh.

"Yes, your leg is intact." Kaieli placed her hands on her hips and glared at Rizelya. "You're a stubborn woman. I don't know how you continued to fight after getting that wound, but they say over twenty dead invaders were piled around you. No, don't sit up. You lost a lot of blood." Kaieli pushed Rizelya back onto the cot.

"Are we still fighting?"

"No. The Scourge are speeding out of our atmosphere."

"How many have we lost?"

"Too many." Kaieli slumped onto the edge of the cot. "Kederposan, Bohandran, and Myndera are dead. Laynal—she was so young, too young to be fighting a war—as well as Tami."

"I saw Tami die."

"Oh, Rizelya, Rolstrun... Rolstrun's gone," Kaieli wailed. She couldn't stop the torrent of tears. She crawled onto the cot with Rizelya, who pulled her close.

"I loved him, Rizelya," Kaieli sobbed. "But I never told him."

"I know you did, Dear Heart. It shone clearly from your eyes that time the two of you met us in the Barrens. I'm so glad you found someone to love."

"I didn't think I'd ever fall for a man because I preferred women. But when he stood up against the commander to protect our people, something changed. You never saw the change in him. He wasn't the stuck-up boy we knew. He became an alpha, a leader." For a long time, Kaieli lay curled up with Rizelya, reliving her memories of life and falling in love with Rolstrun in the midst their captivity's horrors.

Blazel - 21 de Ahdar, 1076

By the time Graak reached the battle camp, he could barely beat his wings. Tuueek and another Thunder Wing flew under him, supporting him between them. Blazel lay in a stupor across Graak's back. Before leaving the compound, Blazel had fixed the harness and buckled himself in. A few times on the return flight, he jerked awake as he slipped, and the harness was the only thing keeping him from falling to his death.

Graak collapsed as soon as he landed, his head resting on his forepaws, and his tail curled around him.

"Sleep, my friend," Blazel croaked, patting Graak's neck. "You've earned it."

You too, Blazel. This has been an exceedingly long four days. I'm glad it is over. We won! The tip of his tail flicked once. *I think I'll sleep right here. I'm too exhausted to move.*

Blazel fumbled with the buckles, but someone's hands helped him undo them and supported him as he slid off Graak's back. His knees gave out under him, and the strong arm around him kept him from crumpling on the ground. He tilted his head to find Histrun holding him.

"You did well, boy," Histrun said, smiling. "We couldn't have succeeded without you and Graak."

Blazel blushed from the praise.

Histrun half carried him to a healer's tent with an empty cot, and Blazel crumpled onto it. Histrun pulled a blanket over him and patted him on the shoulder. "You rest now. We can take care of it from here."

Blazel was asleep before Histrun reached the tent flap.

The next morning, the sounds of tents being taken down and the shouting of orders jolted Blazel awake. He groaned as every muscle in his body hurt. His limbs felt heavy with fatigue. Tears pricked his eyes, and although he blamed them on his aching body, he knew better. Grief overwhelmed him now he could finally process all the deaths he'd witnessed in the past four days.

The quiet in the tent assured him he was alone, and Blazel allowed the grief—and the tears—to flow. Names and faces flashed in his mind of those they'd lost. Bohandran, Myndera, Laynal—oh, sweet Goddess she had been so young— Kederposan, and so many more, Posair, Gryphon, and Vhelopsi. He sobbed, remembering Rolstrun falling under an invader's knife. Finally, his sorrow abated. He still had work to do and a life to live.

Rizelya! His eyes flew open. The last time Blazel had seen her, she lay close to death. He grit his teeth against the pain and lethargy and forced his body to move. Beside his cot, a bowl of water, a towel, and a set of clean clothes waited for him. After cleaning off the worst of the battle grime, Blazel flung back the tent flap and stared.

It wasn't morning, but early evening. He'd slept the entire day! The camp appeared completely different. People had already taken down and packed most of the tents, with only one straggler besides his still standing. Gryphons ferried people and supplies back to the base camp in the plains. Histrun and Naila walked through the camp, giving orders or stopping to give a gesture of comfort.

Blazel rushed—a shambling walk was the best he could do—to the tent.

"Kaieli? Bethlyn?" he called as he stepped inside.

Kaieli hurried toward him. Her hair hung limp, and the vibrancy he'd noticed, even while she had been a captive, had disappeared. Grief lined her face, and she looked ten years older. Panic gathered around his heart. *No, Rizelya can't be dead!* Then he remembered Kaieli and Rolstrun had become lovers, perhaps as close as he and Rizelya.

He took the two steps separating them and enfolded her in his arms. "I'm so sorry, Kaieli. He was a good man. A good friend." He didn't care that her tears soaked the shoulder of his shirt or that his added to the moisture. They stood grieving together, a quiet eddy formed around them amid the chaos of the tent being torn down.

"Where's Rizelya?" he asked, finally stepping back from Kaieli.

"Here," Rizelya answered from the shadows by the tent door. "I wouldn't let them take me to the base camp without seeing you first." She held out her arms.

He sank onto the cot with her, holding her in a crushing embrace. "I was so terrified when I saw you lying in a pool of blood. I thought I'd lost you." He shuddered, and a sob broke from him.

"Shh... I'm still here. You can't get rid of me so easily."

The warmth of her arms pulling him close assured him he wasn't alone.

Later, after they both had eaten, Aistrun carried Rizelya to Glork. Blazel wasn't steady enough yet to carry her. He climbed onto Glork's back behind Rizelya to ensure she stayed on. It felt strange to straddle a Gryphon different from Graak, but

Graak was still too exhausted from their extraordinary flight for anyone to ride on him, even Blazel. Their squad-pack joined them, and they flew to the base camp together.

As soon as he saw Rizelya installed in the healer's tent, Blazel stumbled to his tent and collapsed.

The surviving war host carried the dead Posairs, Gryphons, and Vhelopsi from the Barrens and to a site near the river, inside the plains where life reigned. No one wanted their loved ones to cross the veil in that dead, empty place. The pall of smoke wafted over the base camp as massive funeral pyres—each holding numerous people—burned day-in-and-day-out. The final battle had cost the Posair dearly. Over thirty-five thousand people, including Gryphons and Vhelopsi, died to free their world.

Blazel woke from his exhausted sleep two days after returning to the base camp. He scrubbed his face, grimacing at the stubble scratching his hands. After cleaning up and eating, he hurried to the healer's tent where Rizelya recuperated.

Bethlyn chuckled. "You're finally awake, huh?"

Blazel grimaced. "You did warn me the stimulant would take its toll on me. But it was worth it to end the Scourge's invasion."

"Yes, it was. We all appreciate your dedication." Bethlyn patted his back and pointed out Rizelya's cot before scurrying to attend to a patient.

Blazel appreciated the subtly guidance. Because he'd been in such a daze when they'd brought Rizelya in, he didn't remember where her cot was located. Joy filled him when he reached Rizelya's cot. She reclined on it with her leg resting on several pillows, and her color had returned to normal. A wide grin lit her face when he approached her.

"You're awake!" She held out her arms to him.

He enfolded her in his arms and kissed her.

"I was getting worried about you," Rizelya said, running her thumb over the palm of his hand. "You slept so long."

"Not sleeping while fighting for three-and-a-half days wears one out." He shrugged. "I'm fine, now."

"I'm so relieved the war is over, and we can resume our normal lives."

They spoke quietly together, dreaming of ridding their world of the other menace plaguing it—the Malvers' monsters.

A few octars later, Aistrun came in. "Hey, you're both awake and looking good!" Instead of clapping Blazel on the back, Aistrun pulled him into a rough hug.

"Did we miss Rolstrun's funeral?" Blazel asked, suddenly afraid he'd slept through it.

Aistrun shook his head. "No, it's tomorrow afternoon. Blazel, we're done removing our dead from the battlefield. Although we don't want to, we're burning the invader's remains. While there isn't anything living in the Barrens, it doesn't seem right to allow the Scourge to pollute the land further. There's so many corpses, we need every able body to help."

"Sure, I'll help."

"So will I." Rizelya grimaced as she attempted to move her leg.

"No, you don't," Blazel ground out.

"Hey, Little Red, you stay there," Aistrun shouted at the same time.

To stop Rizelya's scowl, Blazel kissed her. Smirking, he strode from the tent with Aistrun. "Has Graak recovered yet?"

Aistrun nodded. "He and Broogk are waiting for us. They'll work with us, since we can cover more area than those walking. Here, you'll need this." He handed Blazel a cloth to put over his mouth and nose as they grabbed a converted weapon.

The sun glinted on Graak's sandy brown feathers and brown fur. Blazel's steps lightened. Extreme fatigue had dulled Graak's feathers and fur by the end of their marathon flight.

"Graak!" Blazel flung his arms around his friend's neck, eliciting a startled squawk from Graak. "You ready for another adventure?"

"I could use more rest, but burning invader corpses won't be too taxing." Graak crouched, inviting Blazel to climb onto his back.

Blazel raised his eyebrows at the new harness.

"You ruined your old one," Aistrun explained.

As they reached the battlefield, Blazel scrunched his nose. "What is that stench?"

"Scourge." Aistrun positioned the mask over his mouth and nose. "It only gets worse."

Blazel affixed his own mask, then directed his magic through the weapon, shooting fire at a mass of ugly black bodies. Graak flared, adding his flames. Soon, only ash remained to mingle with the sand-glass.

They flew over the spot where Rolstrun and the Strunland guard-pack had perished. Grief washed over Blazel. *Too bad we can't erase the grief and horror inflicted by the Scourge as easily.*

Kaieli - 25 de Ahdar, 1076

The pall of dark, acrid smoke hazing the sky fit Kaieli's spirit. For the past two days, the funeral pyres had constantly burned, sending their dead to the womb of the Mother.

She trudged up the knoll between Rizelya and Blazel, and toward the pyre holding Rolstrun, Myndera, Bohandran, and the other former captives who died in the fighting. A glance at Rizelya's leg assured Kaieli the wound was sufficiently healed for Rizelya to walk, or rather limp, on it.

Below the hill, the bright spring green plains grass spread like a welcoming blanket. Yellow, pink, and lavender flowers dotted it. Kaieli barely registered the beauty. What beauty could there be in the world without Rolstrun's love and laughter? How could she go on without him? She sniffed and dashed away a stray tear. She didn't even possess any mementos of their life together to remember him by.

Maheli limped up the hill, with Alestrun and Calistrun on either side of her. Kaieli scowled at Calistrun. Even though he shouldn't be out of his sickbed yet, she understood his need to attend the funeral of his friends and pack-mates. Noriana, Nelieh, and Anyola trudged behind them. Faliciden and Faelyn, already crying, stumbled up the knoll, followed by Loshera and Chariel, dressed in priestess white.

The crater still held malignant magic they needed to clear, plus that found in the swamps. But with Rolstrun gone, Kaieli couldn't fathom adding a new male into their tight-knit group. If she didn't understand how important it was, she wouldn't ever merge her Talents again. It just wouldn't be the same without Rolstrun.

Loshera led a short but eloquent eulogy, remembering the good things about of their friends, before she nodded to Rizelya and Maheli to light the fire. Tears streamed down Kaieli's face as the flames consumed Rolstrun's body. Resentment filled her as Rizelya stood hand-in-hand with Blazel.

As the fire died, Kaieli turned her back on it. She had work to do. Hundreds of injured, many of them with mortal wounds, still waited for her help. She slogged toward the healers' tent.

A shadow fell across hers. She glanced up, frowning to discover Tre'nok and Vy'shol blocked her way. They held hands, openly displaying their affection now.

"I am very sorry about Rolstrun's death," Vy'shol said. "Our deepest sympathies."

Kaieli swallowed hard and blinked, trying to keep the grief from overspilling—again.

"We've almost finished the repairs on the scout ship," Tre'nok grinned, bouncing on his toes. "We will be able to leave soon."

Vy'shol tentatively took Kaieli's hand. "Come. We have other news. We want you to be there when we tell your leaders."

Kaieli allowed them to pull her to the command tent. When they entered, the other Volkerns and the three Faeorn triads, as well as Hairan, Zebba, and Sangasu, stood to one side of the tent. Rizelya, Blazel, Aistrun, Chariel, and Jaehaas occupied the other side. Graak, Glork, Broogk, and several other Gryphons sat behind Prince Moraak. They'd rolled the tent's sides up to provide more room, but even so, the tent felt crowded.

Histrun slumped in his chair and had aged noticeably during the past lunadars. Keshanal perched on the edge of hers, her eyes bright, watching everyone find places.

"So, what news do you have for us?" Histrun asked.

Tre'nok rocked on his heels, his hands behind his back, and a huge grin on his face. "The long-range sensors on our scout ship are working again. The Scourge left this planet's solar system this morning."

A brief smile crossed Kaieli's lips. The invader's terror was over.

Moraak ruffled his head feathers. *And do you know if your sabotage worked?*

"The Faeorn are extremely good at what they do," Tre'nok assured him. "The Scourge will never make it home. When they activated their jump drive, the hidden program overrode the one they entered. The scout ship's sensors verified this. It will take them to a system far, far away. Hundreds of light-years from their destination. The Faeorn calculate the commander had enough fuel for a single jump—and their calculations are never wrong. Their life support systems will shut down in a few days. We also confirmed Commander Ke-ke-tak did not share the coordinates of this planet with anyone back on his home world. You are out of danger. No Scourge will come to seek revenge."

A slow smiled crossed Histrun's face. "It also means your people, and your rebel planet, are safe."

Tre'nok inclined his head. "It does. Our people have waited for over four hundred cycles to throw off the yoke of slavery. We thank our Gods the Scourge came to this planet."

Will you be able to free the rest of your people? Moraak asked.

"Many, if not all. The Scourge have become complacent in guarding their long-term slaves, believing we are now so used to it we will not rebel. They don't know how wrong they are. Thanks to you, we have enough fuel for several trips between our home worlds and the rebel planet. The Scourge's supply is running out with only enough for a few cycles. Once it is gone, they will be grounded and incapable of star flight."

Tension eased from Kaieli's shoulders, and she sighed deeply. The news released her fear the invaders would return and recapture her. Her ordeal was truly over.

"Won't they just mine the nucla from somewhere else?" Histrun asked.

Tre'nok shook his head. "No. In the four hundred cycles they have been in space, they discovered the mineral on exactly two planets. Their home world and this one. It is good for us that it's such a rare substance."

Keshanal sat with a hand covering her mouth, deep in thought. Concern clouded her eyes. "But what about the bomb? Did they activate it?"

Kaieli had forgotten about the hidden threat.

Vy'shol's eyes lit up. "Oh yes."

She sounded more excited than Kaieli expected. The Volkerns would still be on the planet when, if, it went off.

"It was amazing to see the mighty Thunder Wings carry it out over your ocean, where they dropped it. The water will contain any radiation it emits."

Kaieli hadn't known that had happened. She'd been too wrapped up in her grief to notice much around her.

Histrun leaned forward, his elbows on his knees. "How sure are the Faeorn that it won't be a danger?"

Tre'nok smiled. "Very sure. The Yoon triad has a powerful motivation to protect their babies. They will be the first Faeorn born free in many, many generations. Our future children will also be born free. That miracle would never have happened if your people were not so brave. We have much to thank you for."

"And we you," Keshanal said with a nod. "Our people and world are free because of your help."

The tent broke into jubilant cheers.

Rizelya caught Kaieli in a hug, then Blazel spun her around. Aistrun hugged her next, and when he put her down, she glanced over to see Rizelya and Blazel kissing. Longing and grief washed over her. As tears slid down her cheeks, she slipped from the tent and returned to work—the only thing keeping her sane.

Rizelya - 25 de Ahdar, 1076

The survivors celebrated the defeat of the invaders. People brought out instruments they'd hauled with them over long distances. Rizelya clapped with the others when Blazel grabbed his flute and joined the impromptu band on the platform above the dance square. Histrun ordered the wine casks broached and hailed the Volkern and Faeorn as heroes. The Vhelopsi took a turn singing, and Rizelya cried at the haunting sounds that spoke of the longing for freedom and home.

Rizelya ignored the twinges of pain in her leg caused by dancing. She wasn't about to let it stop her from enjoying the evening. The last celebration she'd attended had been nearly a year ago, right after meeting Shaydan. So much had occurred since then. As Aistrun whirled her around the dance area, they spun by the band, and Blazel caught her eye and winked. Rizelya threw her head back, laughing with the joy bubbling through her. Her relationship with Blazel was the best thing to happen to her in the past year.

Breathless and needing to rest her leg, Rizelya bowed to Aistrun, found a mug of wine, and wandered to the tables, humming with the music. Her joy dampened when she saw Kaieli sitting alone on a bench at the edge of the festivities. Kaieli leaned her back against the table and drank from her cup. A flagon of wine dangled from her other hand. Rizelya plopped next to her.

Kaieli turned bleary eyes to Rizelya. "Rolstrun would have loved the singing and dancing, and become roaring drunk." She lifted her cup in a salute and chugged the contents.

"Yes. Yes, he would," Rizelya agreed. She'd liked Rolstrun.

Kaieli's cup slipped from her hands and clanked on the ground. She stared at it for a long moment, then twisted around on the bench. She stretched out an arm on the table, rested her head on it, and closed her eyes.

Soon, Kaieli was snoring softly. Rizelya gazed at her friend and gently brushed the curls back from her face. She understood the overwhelming grief. If it had been Blazel instead of Rolstrun, she'd be in the same state. She guarded

Kaieli's sleep until Blazel finished his set with the band and came looking for her. He sighed sadly, gathered Kaieli in his arms, and carried her to her cot.

"While I understand her pain," Blazel said, catching Rizelya's hand in his, "I'm extremely grateful I didn't lose you."

Rizelya squeezed his hand, then lifted it and kissed it. "I'm happy we both survived."

Their mood somber now, they returned to the festivities, refilled their cups, and toasted Rolstrun.

"Come on, this is a celebration of life." Rizelya pulled Blazel to his feet. "Let's dance."

While dancing, the Volkern couple, Tre'nok and Vy'shol, swung around and danced near them. The two couples weaved around each other, switching partners and back, following the dance's pattern. At the end of the dance, they left the dance floor together.

"You are Kaieli's friend?" Tre'nok asked.

Rizelya nodded.

"We are very worried about her." Vy'shol's hands twisted together. "She is so sad. We know she and Rolstrun became close."

"They did." Rizelya smiled. "Although we are no longer lovers, she is still my heart-sister. I'll watch over her and make sure she's okay."

"Thank you." Tre'nok inclined his head. "We are quite fond of her. Her courage prompted us to help your people. We are grateful now that we did. Our ship is repaired, and we plan to leave in the morning. Will you make sure Kaieli comes to the ceremony? I'm afraid she won't attend on her own, and we have a gift for her."

"I will."

The Volkerns moved away to converse with Histrun and Keshanal.

Rizelya and Blazel returned to the dance floor and celebrated far into the night. The stars were fading when they finally fell into their cot.

Rizelya - 26 de Ahdar, 1076

Forewarned about the ceremony, Rizelya dressed in her cleanest clothes. Then she went to the healers' tent, where a long line already waited. People held their heads and rubbed their bleary eyes from far too much drinking. She skipped the line and slipped into the tent. Her eyes watered, and her stomach clenched at the pervasive stench. She was glad she hadn't drunk too much the night before and didn't need the noxious hangover brew.

"Hey, Faliciden, can I have a cup of that brew for Kaieli? She'll need it."

Faliciden dipped into the huge pot, filled a mug, and handed it to Rizelya. She walked to Kaieli's tent and shook Kaieli awake.

She blinked her eyes, and with a groan, eased into a sitting position.

"Here," Rizelya said, holding out the steaming mug. "Your head will feel better after you drink this."

Kaieli wrinkled her nose. "What are you doing here?" She grimaced, then gulped down the mug's contents.

"You need to hurry and dress. The Volkerns and Faeorns are leaving this morning. They asked for you to attend. They would be heartbroken if you weren't there to send them off. You were the one to befriend them and urge them to join us."

Kaieli rubbed her eyes. "You're right. I do want to see them before they leave. We wouldn't have saved so many without their help." She stood and rummaged in her trunk.

While Kaieli dressed, Rizelya trotted to the mess tent and brought back a pot of taevo for them both. She poured two cups and handed one to Kaieli. They sat on camp stools, sipping their morning taevo. It reminded Rizelya of when they'd done the same last year before the control-janack appeared and the Scourge invaded their world. She sighed, missing her simpler life.

As Kaieli sipped her drink, tears ran down her face.

"What's wrong?" Rizelya leaned forward and placed her hand on Kaieli's knee.

"I was just thinking I never had a chance to share morning taevo with Rolstrun."

"How are you holding up?"

"The grief of his passing presses on me, sometimes suffocating me. But I'm better today than yesterday. Someday, I'll wake up, and the hurt will be a dull memory."

"You still have me. Lean on me whenever you need to." Rizelya patted Kaieli's knee and put down her cup. "Histrun and Moraak are making a big deal of the Volkern leaving. They have a ceremony planned, and you have an important part in it. Come on, it won't do for you to be late." Rizelya tucked Kaieli's arm in hers, and together, they left the tent. Blazel waited for them outside and fell into step behind them as they headed to the field where the scout ship rested.

It seemed like everyone in the war camp had gathered to watch the proceedings. Blazel moved ahead of the women, forging a path for them. Finally, they arrived at the front—after a few elbows in their ribs and stomping of toes. Rizelya rubbed her forehead where some man, much taller than herself, had accidentally rammed her head with his elbow.

Histrun and Keshanal wore elaborate red robes gilded with silver and gold. Chariel, resplendent in her white priestess dress, stood to one side of them. A beautiful gold collar gleamed on Moraak's chest.

"I feel so under dressed," Kaieli sighed, looking down at her work clothes.

"You're fine," Rizelya assured her. "Nobody else has any finery. I don't know where they hid those away. I certainly didn't bring any formal clothes with me."

The Volkern paraded from the ship. Tre'nok wore an ensemble of deep yellow, which contrasted beautifully with his pale blue skin. The fabric shone and rippled with his movements. Gold flourishes painted his face highlighted his features and natural swirls. He'd replaced the small ring in his nose with a larger one set with rubies. A matching ring decorated Vy'shol's nose. She'd painted her face with similar gold patterns, and her dark red clothes complemented his. The other Volkern also wore brightly colored outfits and painted their faces, each design as individual as the Volkern themselves.

The Faeorn wore short tunics and tight breeches in shades of purple, matching their eyes. Mei-Ying's pale hair had been elaborately braided and piled on her head.

The four hundred surviving Vhelopsi stood to one side, wearing borrowed Posair clothing. When they'd escaped the invader's compound, they had only carried the clothes on their backs—and those had been the awful orange slave coveralls. Rizelya wasn't sure she could start a new life with nothing. Histrun and Hairan were discussing settling the Vhelopsi refugees in the abandoned Posanreande Keep.

Histrun and Moraak gave speeches, extolling the courage and bravery of the Volkerns and Faeorn and welcoming the Vhelopsi, reminding everyone they had sacrificed everything to help the Posairs. Rizelya smiled at Kaieli's furious blushing at the frequent mention of her name. Rizelya rolled her eyes whenever they mentioned her. She hadn't done anything to warrant the praise, unlike Kaieli, who deserved it, and much more.

The dignitaries exchanged gifts. Kaieli moved to leave, but Rizelya caught her hand, stopping her. Based on Tre'nok's comment the night before, the ceremony wasn't over.

"Healer Kaieli," Tre'nok said, stepping forward. "We have a gift for you. A small token of our gratitude. Your bravery in the face of such horror and difficulties inspired us to find our own courage. Without you, our people could never hope to be free. Our children's children will remember your name."

When Kaieli didn't move, Rizelya nudged her forward.

Tre'nok placed a garment into Kaieli's hands, made from the same finely woven fabric the Volkerns wore. It shimmered with bronze and silver. Next, he offered her a delicate egg as long as her arm. Intricate carvings covered its surface, showing strange, beautiful beasts hiding amid flowers and trees. He pointed to a spot on it.

"It's Rolstrun," Kaieli whispered, tears flowing down her cheeks.

Tre'nok ducked his head shyly. "I began this carving on the journey here. The animals and plants are from my home. I hope you will gaze upon it with fondness and forgive us for the wrongs the Scourge forced us to perpetrate on you."

"It's gorgeous," Kaieli breathed, taking the gift carefully. "I shall treasure it always. You're already forgiven."

"Then we shall leave you in peace and pray the Gods grant you a long and prosperous life." Tre'nok crossed his hands together, placed them on his chest, and bowed. The other Volkerns and Faeorn did the same.

Without any other farewells, they turned and filed into the scout ship. Tre'nok, the last to enter, had one foot on the threshold when a distant boom sounded, and the ground rolled under Rizelya's feet. Kaieli flailed her arms, trying to keep her balance while also protecting the precious gift. Rizelya reached out and steadied her, knowing it contained the only likeness of Rolstrun Kaieli possessed.

Tre'nok stopped and turned around. "The bomb. See, your planet survives." He tilted his head and smiled. "But quite a few fish did not. Take care, Kaieli." He disappeared into the ship, the door sliding shut behind him. A blast of steam jetted from the engines.

Everyone stepped away quickly. The ship rose above the ground, then zoomed diagonally across the sky. Rizelya watched it vanish over the horizon.

Kaieli hugged the egg to her chest and hurried to her tent.

"Form a hunting party," Histrun ordered. "After the feast last night, we could use some fresh meat. The Volkerns mentioned there would be a bounty of fish floating on the surface of the ocean soon. Everyone else, go to work cleaning up. We'll head home tomorrow."

A cheer rose at his announcement, and the crowd dispersed.

Blazel - 26 de Ahdar, 1076

Elation coursed through Blazel. The invaders were gone, and their world was safe. He looked around the crowd, which included Gryphons and Vhelopsi. If they hadn't joined the

Posairs as allies, they'd be experiencing a much different outcome. His thoughts took him back to Chariel's prophecy that had sent him and the others into the Deep Mountains searching for the Gryphons. The line, *"Long-lost allies to fight once more. Ancient enemies coming into the light. A menace comes. No allies, the enemy wins, and all die,"* replayed in his mind.

The menace referred to the Scourge, didn't it? They would have all died if they hadn't allied with not only the Gryphons but also the Vhelopsi, Volkern, and Faeorn. "Chariel, is the prophecy..."

A haunted look filled her eyes, and she shook her head.

His elation dampened, suddenly feeling their peace would be short-lived.

"Hey, Blazel," Aistrun said, punching him on the arm lightly. "Get a move on it. Let's go hunting."

Fresh fish sounds good. Graak dropped his beak in a grin. His head feathers danced as he shook his head. *I'm tired of dried meat.*

Glork and Broogk bobbed their heads in agreement.

"Me too," Blazel said. "I'd like to do something besides fight for a change." He kept his worry to himself and resolved to enjoy the respite for as long as it lasted.

Rizelya agreed. They mounted the Gryphons, and in a few milcrons, they were aloft and winging east over the plains. Horses raced the Gryphon's shadows, and Rizelya laughed with joy. Blazel joined her. Soon, the ocean came into sight.

Instead of a clear expanse of blue and the expected bounty of fish, strange creatures flew on the horizon. As they drew closer, a tremor shook Graak from head to toe. Blazel squinted, trying to see them better.

"What's wrong? What are they?" Blazel's stomach dropped in foreboding.

A big problem, Graak replied. *They are beasts we thought long extinct. They were the Malvers' mounts during the Great War.*

"Does this mean..." Aistrun gulped, "those are Malvers riding them?"

I can't see them clearly. Glork's head feathers stood on end. *And I should be able to. I don't like this at all.*

How could so many Malvers survive all this time? Graak shook again, and if not for the harness, Blazel would have fallen off his back.

"We know at least one of them survived." Fear filled Rizelya's voice. "The woman who keeps haunting my dreams."

Blazel narrowed his eyes and followed the creature's trajectory. "If they continue in the same direction they are now, their flight path will take them to the black castle Graak and I found in the southern swamp. That thing was pure evil. We need to return quickly and warn Histrun and Moraak."

The fish were forgotten as the Gryphons sped back to camp. A part of Blazel's mind jabbered in terror. They'd seen what the Malvers could do in the form of the Malvers' monsters while locked behind a magical barrier. What terrors would their ancient enemy enact now they were free?

Epilogue

The Supreme sat at her desk, staring at the thick book Wisah had brought to her over two lunadars ago. She'd needed to gather her strength to open it. The magic within it pulsed in sync with her heartbeat. The book was ancient, even older than the Great War. It came from a time when people with Black Talent walked the earth, and men wielded the same kind of magic as women did. Why did it surface now?

A spell bound the book closed. The magic in it must be terrible to warrant such protections. With trembling hands, she traced the sigils and spoke the chant of a spell passed from Supreme to Supreme. She sensed a click, and the book fell open. Leaning forward, she peered at the script. It swam before her eyes, and she mumbled another spell. The words flowed into place, and she began to read.

Her assistants came in and dropped off food and taevo for her. She sipped on the taevo but didn't eat, the story too fascinating to stop reading for even a moment. Finally, in the early morning octars, she sat back in her chair and rubbed her eyes.

She now knew what had gone wrong with Shandir's spell at the end of the war. She'd designed it to cleanse all death magic from the land and render its users powerless. But somehow Malviana, the leader of the rebel Malvernlair Clan, found out about the spell and twisted it. The combined magics resulted in killing every living organism in a one-hundred measure radius of the blast zone. Malignant magic flooded the area and fused with the molecular structure of the rocks—the only thing left in the Barrens. The epicenter created the crater known as Shandir's Misery.

The book speculated that Black Talent could undo this wrong. But the Malvers had systematically sought out and killed everyone with Black Talent until it was now extinct. The Supreme rubbed her temples, a headache blooming behind her eyes. Even a thousand years later, no one was born with Black Talent. There must be a reason this book revealed itself now. But she couldn't find the link.

The Supreme stood and stretched, her old bones creaking from sitting for so long. She shuffled to her quarters, opened her hidden safe, and removed the gold and silver coffer. Using her seal of office, she unlocked it and slowly tipped back the lid.

A small portrait of a beautiful young woman with black hair and yellow eyes, her cheeks glowing with health, and a mischievous smile curving her lips, stared at her. She picked it up to reveal another one showing a mature, thin woman with charcoal-gray hair, pale gray skin, and black eyes lacking the whites. Looking at them, the Supreme hardly believed the portraits were of the same person. The first depicted a young Malviana, and the second one showed her after she'd used death magic for decades.

The Supreme carried the two pictures back to her office and placed them on her desk. Flipping through the book, she found the entry she wanted. She'd always wondered what had turned Malviana to proscribed magic. She read the entry again, glancing often at the young woman. It was a testament to Malviana's will to live that she'd endured the evil wrought on her by Mordar. Did the sweet, young woman survive somewhere inside her still, or had her experiences destroyed her? The Supreme contemplated the story and the picture, praying for a way to reach beyond Malviana's evil.

As the morning light filtered through her curtains, the Supreme's head drooped, and her chin rested on her chest in the uneasy rest of the old. A shock tore through her mind, jerking her awake. She sent out her senses and cried out. Somehow,

Malviana had shredded the magical barrier surrounding the Malvers' island.

A cackle reverberated through the psychic plane. A stab of pain pierced the Supreme's head, and she slumped back in her chair, her face slack, and her limbs convulsing. She gathered her will around her. She must survive this attack.

The Malvers were no longer in exile. They were coming to Lairheim with vengeance in their hearts.

WHAT TO READ NEXT

Rizelya, Blazel, and the team fights their final battle with the Malvers in *Exiles' Vengeance*, the exciting conclusion in the completed Legends of Lairheim series!

You can purchase this, and all my books, directly from me at *Shop.ToraMoon.com* or at your favorite retailer.

A relentless enemy returns...
A final battle begins...
A world on the brink of transformation...

As Lairheim recovers from the Scourge invasion, the Posairs face an even more formidable foe in their ancient enemies, the Malvers, led by their queen, Malviana.

Rizelya creates the Black Weave, a blending of Talents and Gryphons. With its power, she seeks to destroy the Malvers' monstrous abominations and protect her people. As her powers grow, she wrestles with her new role and an uncertain future.

Blazel, joining the Black Weave team, discovers latent magical abilities, becoming a Black Talent and a crucial asset in the battle. Yet, the struggle between his desire for peace and the necessity of war tests his resolve.

White Priestess Wisah discovers she's the next Supreme, the Goddess' avatar. Unusual sigil magic gives her the power to wield the Unmaking device—the only power capable of destroying Malviana. Torn between duty and love, she must reconcile her destiny as a leader with the call of her heart.

Queen Malviana, driven by a dark desire to resurrect her beloved, leads her Malvers army north toward the Sanctuary and her ultimate vengeance. But first, she must eliminate the one person with the power to defeat her.

Will Rizelya, Blazel, and Wisah save Lairheim, or will Malviana plunge it into darkness?

Friendship and unity clashes with greed and the lust for power, testing the Posairs' and their allies' resolve. Be prepared to be immersed in this breathtaking tale of magic, courage, and the enduring strength of love.

Exile's Vengeance is the final book in the epic science-fantasy series, Legends of Lairheim, where the line between hope and despair is razor thin.

Discover the thrilling end of the Lairheim saga today!

APPENDIX

CAST
POSAIRS

(IN ALPHABETICAL ORDER)

Adriandran - (A-dri-an-dran) Andranlair Clan Alpha

Aistrun - (Aye-strun) Co-squad-pack Alpha with Rizelya; Strunland Keep; Rizelya's squad-pack

Alestrun - (Ale-strun) Strunland guard-pack at crater

Ambrelya - (Am-brel-ya) Red; Haasneh Keep

Anyola - (An-yo-la) Red; Posanreande Keep

Aradehan - (Ara-de-han) Dehanrandean Keep

Baerenposan - (Bear-en-po-san) Posanreande Keep

Beladi - (Bell-ah-de) Double Red with Yellow; Strunlair Clan Alpha

Belistril - (Bell-ih-stil) Red and Brown; Haasneh Keep Alpha

Bethlyn - (Beth-lyn) Brown, healer; Strunhelos Keep

Blazel - (Blay-zel) Born and raised in the Sanctuary, no clan affiliation (main character)

Blenora - (Blen-or-ah) White Priestess; Sanctuary; Blazel's mother

Bohandran - (Bo-han-dran) Strunland guard pack alpha at crater

Bolstrun - (Bol-strun) Strunhelos Keep Alpha

Bren - (Br-en) Red; Strunell Keep

Brendel - (Bren-del) Red; Dehanlair Clan Alpha

Calistrun - (Cal-ih-strun) Strunland guard-pack at crater

Candriel - (Can-dree-el) Red; Strunhelos Keep

Celedon - (Cel-eh-don) Guard at the Sanctuary; Ledonlair Keep

Chariel - (Char-ee-el) Gray, also known as the Gray Oracle; The Sanctuary

Dehali - (Dee-haa-lee) Red and Yellow; Strunland Keep; Rizelya's squad-pack

Delestrun - (Del-eh-strun) Strunlair Keep

Detheren - (De-ther-en) Red; Posanreande Keep

Dreana - (Dray-an-a) Young girl; Posanreande Keep; Jaelena's daughter

Drustrun - (Drew-strun) Strunell Keep

Eiden - (Eye-den) Yellow, twin to Eidstrun; Strunland Keep

Eidstrun - (Eyed-strun) Strunland Keep; twin to Eiden; Rizelya's squad-pack

Faelyn - (Fae-lyn) Brown; a healer; Strunland guard-pack at crater

Faliciden - (Fa-leh-si-den) Green; healer; Posanlair Keep

Farikeistan - (Far-ih-kei-stan) Keistanlair Clan Alpha

Gehan - (Gay-han) Yellow and Green; Strunven Keep

Grazeen - (Gray-zeen) Green and Brown; Strunven Keep

Hadronan - (Had-ro-nan) Ronanlair Clan Alpha

Halistrun - (Hal-ih-strun) Legendary hero from the Great War

Histrun - (His-strun) Supreme Alpha; Strunland Keep, Rizelya's father

Jaehaas - (Jay-haas) Centaur, Haasneh Keep

Jaelena - (Jay-lee-na) Yellow; Posanreande Keep

Jorstrun - (Jor-strun) Strunland Keep

Joydan - (Joy-dan) Red; Strunhelos Keep Alpha

Kaidel - (Kai-del) Red; Haaslair Clan Alpha

Kaieli - (Kai-ee-le) Brown and Blue; Strunland Keep; heart sister to Rizelya

Kami - (Cam-ee) Yellow and Green, identical twins to Tami; Strunell Keep

Keandran - (Kae-an-dran) Originally from Andranlair, transferred to Strunlair Keep; Missing

Kederposan - (Ke-dare-po-san) Posanreande Keep Alpha

Keshanal - (Khe-shan-al) Supreme AlphaRed and Brown

Kolhaas - (Kol-haas) Haaslornas Keep Alpha

Kothera - (Ko-ther-ah) Red; Keep Alpha Posanreande Keep

Laean - (Lay-an) Red; Strunland guard-pack at crater

Laenstrun - (Lay-en-strun) Strunheim Keep

Larenposan - (Lar-en-po-san) Posanreande Keep

Layhalya - (Lay-hall-yah) Red and Green; Strunheim Keep Alpha

Laynad - (Lay-nad) Red; Strunhamde Keep Alpha

Laynal - (Lay-nal) Red and Yellow; Strunheim Keep, younger sister of Laynar

Laynar - (Lay-nar) Red; Strunheim Keep, granddaughter of Layhalya

Leistral - (Lay-ee-straal) Red and Green; Strunland Keep; Rizelya's squad-pack

Leistrun - (Lay-is-strun) Strunland Keep; Rizelya's squad-pack

Loshera - (Lo-sher-ah) White Priestess; Posanreande Keep

Maellyn - (May-lyn) Brown with Red; Strunven Keep

Maendy - (May-en-dee) Brown and Red, with some Yellow, Helstramiester; Strunven Keep

Maheli - (Ma-he-lee) Red; Strunlair guard pack alpha at crater

Margandy - (Mar-gan-dee) Green; healer

Melidehan - (Mel-ih-de-han) Dehanlair Clan Alpha

Metherposan - (Me-ther-po-san) Posanreande Keep

Molstrun - (Mol-strun) Strunland guard-pack at crater

Myndera - (Min-der-ah) Red; Strunland guard-pack at crater

Nadandran - (Na-da-an-dran) Andranlair Keep

Naila - (Neigh-la) Red and Yellow; Strunland Keep Alpha; Rizelya's sister

Nederposan - (Ne-der-po-san) Posanreande guard-pack Alpha

Nelieh - (Nay-lee-eh) Red; Posanreande Keep

Nestrun - (Nay-strun) Strunlair Clan Alpha

Noriana - (Nor-ee-an-ah) Blue; Posanreande Keep

Paena - (Pay-na) Red; Posanreande Keep

Raeleen - (Ray-leen) Brown with Yellow; Strunven Keep

Rizelya - (Rha-zeel-yha) Red and Brown; Strunland Keep (main character)

Rolstrun - (Rolstrun) Strunlair guard-pack at crater

Saehala - (Say-hall-la) Red; Strunven Keep Alpha

Saehalstrun - (Say-hal-strun) Strunven Keep Alpha

Saffren - (Saff-fren) Blue with some Green; Strunven Keep

Serenposan - (Ser-en-po-san) Posanreande Keep

Shandir - (Shan-deer) Legendary hero from the Great War, a White Priestess; the huge crater in the south is named after her, Shandir's Crater, also called Shandir's Misery.

Shaydan - (Shay-dan) Red; Strunell Keep

Sorlenda - (Sor-len-da) Brown; Posanlynde Keep

Tami - (Tam-ee) Yellow, identical twin to Kami; Strunell Keep

Telekhaas - (Tel-ek-haas) Haasneh Keep Alpha

Teleposan - (Tel-eh-po-san) Posanlair Clan Alpha

Treana - (Tray-an-na) Young girl, daughter to Jaelena, Posanreande Keep

The Supreme - White; the Posairs' spiritual leader; The Sanctuary

Voledon - (Vo-le-don) Ledonlair Keep

Wisah - (Wee-sah) White and Grey with some Blue; The Sanctuary; Naila's daughter, Rizelya's niece

Zehala - (Zay-hal-ah) Red; Naila and Rizelya's mother, DECEASED

Zehana - (Zay-han-ah) legendary alpha from the Great War

THE GRYPHONS

Baekeek - (Bea-keek) Silent Prowlers

Broogk - (Broo-gak) Wing second to Graak; Thorn Claw

Daelaak - (Day-laak) Gold Wing; the eldest son of king Zorlaak; in line to inherit the crown

Dukaaik - (Du-Kaa-ik) Razor Beaks

Glork - (Glor-k) Brown Feathers; partners with Rizelya

Graak - (Grr-aak); Flight leader; Thorn Claw; partners with Blazel

Kaaik - (Kaa-ik) Brown Feather

Keeru - (Kee-ru) Thorn Claw

Korrik - (Kor-rik) Gray Feathers

Moraak - (Moor-aak) Prince; Gold Wing; in line to inherit the crown

Morru - (Mor-rue) Dark Talons

Sheekeek - (Shee-keek) Silver Beak, a mystic

Tuueek - (Tuu-eek) Thunder Wing

Zorlaak - King of the Gryphons; Gold Wing

THE HORSES

Brishna - (Brish-na) Rolstrun's mare

Caela - (Say-la) Leistral's mare

Chaezreen - (Chay-zreen) Chariel's mare

Gemmy - (Gem-mae) Rizelya's pack multa

Jezhan - (Jay-zhen) Aistrun's gelding

Julay - (Ju-lay) Dehali's mare

Kressy - (Kress-ee) Rizelya's multa

Kymaya - (Kai-may-ah) Rizelya's mare

Lighzel - (Lie-zel) Blazel's mare

Luchen - (Lou-chen) Eidstrun's gelding

Tejen - (Tee-jen) Wisah's stallion

ALIENS

VOLKERNS

Flo'kik - male

My'shel - female

Tre'nok - male

Vy'shol - female

Ze'lek - male

VHELOPSI

Hairan Aziru - (hi-ran ah-zee-rue) male; prince

Sangasu Musa - (san-ga-su moo-sue) male

Zebba Azirubi - (zeab-ba ah-zee-rue-bee) female; mate to Hairan

YOON FAEORN TRIAD

Jei-Yan Yoon - male

Mei-Ying Yoon - female

Pei Yoon - gomale

THE SCOURGE

Commander Ke-ke-tak

Mo-de-tak

SLAVE SPECIES

Volkern

Faeorn

Kaigor

Hap'thez

Gheethong

Coufrish

Vhelopsi

The World

The main continent is called Lairheim. The Barrens is an area of desolation, with only petrified wood and sand-glass in it. It covers a hundred-mile radius from Shandir's Crater, which is in the center of the isthmus between the main continent and the sub-continent. After the Great War, travel south of the Barrens became taboo, and so no one knows what the area is like. The sub-continent is believed to be covered by one huge swamp and is located south of the Barrens.

No one sails the oceans anymore because of the sea monsters created during the Great War. There is limited travel along the coasts.

The Provinces

There are eight provinces, each divided into eight territories. Each clan takes the name of the Province.

Strunlair

Ledonlair

Andranlair

Posanlair

Haaslair

Dehanlair

Ronanlair

Keistanlair

Days and Time

Milcron - equivalent to a minute.

Octar - roughly equals an hour. There are 16 octars in a day.

Chedan - roughly a week, consisting of eight days.

Lunadar - a month consists of eight chedans, or 64 days.

A year is eight chedans, or 512 days.

Measure - term for distance, a little less than a mile (5,000 feet).

The Months

Ahdar - Month one; Spring

Neydar - Month two; Spring

Sandar - Month three; Summer

Drudar - Month four; Summer

Godar - Month five; Autumn

Rokdar - Month six; Autumn

Eyedar - Month seven; Winter

Hondar - Month eight; Winter

The Moons

Kelar - the largest moon takes 64 days for a full cycle, measurement of a month.

Zelar - the middle-sized moon takes 32 days for a full cycle.

Chelar - the smallest moon's cycle takes 8 days, measurement for chedan, or eight-days.

Magical Abilities of the Women

There are eight types of magic, called Talents, worked by the women. Men exchanged the ability to do magic (except very basic skills) for the gift of shapeshifting into their warrior form when the Malvers' monsters appeared after the Great War. Hair and eye color indicate of the type of magic the person uses. Hair color indicates the person's major Talent and the eye color their secondary Talent. The darker the hair or eye color, the more powerful in that Talent the person is. A woman with fire magic is called a Red, one with water is called a Blue, and so on. Hair color pales with age.

The Powers

Whites - have shades of white hair. Priestesses — mind and soul workers, spiritual leaders. (Unseen in men.)

Grays - have shades of gray hair. Priestesses — also mind and soul workers but they work more with the transitions of the soul. This is a rare Talent. (Unseen in men.)

Reds - have shades of red hair — the fire workers and warriors.

Yellows - have shades of blond hair — the air workers.

Blues - have shades of blue hair — the water workers.

Greens - have shades of green hair — earth workers, plants, and are healers.

Browns - shades of brown hair — earth workers, animals and minerals/metals, and are healers.

Blacks - shades of black hair (extinct) — can work all types of magic.

Gryphons

Gryphons live in flights of several generations. Most flocks can be mixed bird-type species; except the three flights a Gryphon must be born into.

The flights are:

Gold Wings (must be born into—the royal house)

Black Feathers

White Feathers

Gray Feathers

Brown Feathers

Red Feathers

Thorn Claws

Thunder Wings

Razor Beaks

Dark Talons

Silent Prowlers (must be born into—owl types)

Silver Beaks

Green Talons (must be born into—they have poison sacks on their talons)

GLOSSARY

angulete - (an-goo-le-te) a flying serpent found in the swamps, a twisted, venomous beast

baethor - (bae-thor) a predator found in the Deep Mountains

billocks - (bill-ox) a wild, large herd beast and resists domestication

brecha - (bray-cha) one of the symbiotic pair of monsters collectively called the Malvers' monsters

dojee - (doe-gee) a toxic vine found in the southern swamp

dracur - (dray-cur) a flying reptile found in the southern swamp

ducorn - (dew-corn) a type of antelope with two twisty horns

helbore - (hel-bore) a toxic plant found in swamps

helbraught - (hell-brac-kt) the magical halberd type blades the women use to fight the monsters; the wooden staff is the height of the woman with a 16"-24" inch blade made from helstrim attached to the end

helstrablade - (hell-stra-blade) knives made from helstrim but not keyed to any type of magic

helstramiester - (hell-sta-my-ster) masters of the helstrim alloy

helstrim - (hell-strim) a special alloy that accepts and holds magic used to make helstrablades and helbraught blades

jallopitar - (ja-lop-ih-tar) a reptilian swamp predator

janack - (jan-ack) one of the symbiotic pair of monsters collectively called the Malvers' monsters *jedash* - (jay-dash) a bushy plant resistant to monster toxins and cools the area around them

jelehan - (jay-lay-han) a throwing game using sticks of varying lengths with colored bands

kehani - (kay-han-ee) the flowers of the kehani tree are sacred to The Goddess and are used by the priestesses in the temples as perfume and incense

keshe - (kay-she) a strategy board game. It can be played with as few as two players or up to ten players; the more players added, the more complicated the game becomes

lengo - (len-go) a sweet-smelling herb found in the swamps; the leaves stop bleeding and the boiled roots fight infection, especially when caused by swamp creatures and Barrens dust

marsh ragtile - a fruit tree found in the swamps where there is fresh water and no malignant pools of magic are around

molktaak - (mole-ka-ta-ak) a Gryphon ceremony that transfers memories

mookti - (mook-tee) an early ripening spring berry that is sweet, dark purple, and grows in small clusters

multa - (mul-ta) a pack animal with cloven, platter-like feet able to carry heavy loads

narhili - (nar-hee-lee) also called narhili beasts, predators that live in the swamps during the day and hunt the surrounding area at night

oyt - a nonsensical term used to activate the fire arrows

paether - (pae-ther) a canid-like predator found in the northern part of Lairheim *sabertiger* - a large white and black striped feline that lives in the Deep Mountains

sheadash - (shea-dash) a type of white stone that repels and negates any malignant magic. The Malvers' monsters can't cross it and so it is used for buildings and roads

skeaeter - (skae-ter) a large insectoid carnivorous predator

sheezet - (shee-zhet) the Scourge's lizard mounts

snelks - (snell-ks) a grub which eats rotten matter

solanar - (sol-an-nar) plant found in the swamp with poisonous berries

taevo - (tay-vo) a stimulating drink made from the leaves and berries of the taeve bush

STAY IN TOUCH!

Sign up for Tora's newsletter to keep in touch with what's happening in the world of Tora. Receive exclusive extras, news, and discounts on my books, products, and art. I have lots of ideas and always have a project—or three—in progress.

ToraMoon.com/subscribe

Also By Tora Moon

Legends of Lairheim (Epic Science-Fantasy)

Ancient Enemies (Book 1)
Ancient Allies (Book 2)
The Scourge Incursion (Book 3)
Exile's Vengeance (Book 4)
Redemption - A Novel

The Sentinel Witches (Urban Fantasy)

Crossroads to Destiny (Book 1)
Descent Into Darkness (Book 2)
Well of Sorrows (Book 3)

Indie Author Guides

Business & Accounting for Authors
Business Plans for Authors

To get an up-to-date listing of all my books or to purchase visit
ToraMoon.com

THANK YOU!

I hope you're enjoying discovering the world of Legends of Lairheim world and Rizelya and her team's story.

If you have a moment, please help others enjoy these books too by leaving a review on my shop or the retail site where you purchased this book, review it on a blog, share it on your social media, or even just tell your friends about it.

Reviews help other readers choose what to read and authors depend on reviews to get the word out on good books. Honest reviews and genuine word-of-mouth recommendations make all the difference.

I'm not asking for one of those awful book reports we did at school. Leaving a review will only take a minute: it doesn't have to be long or involved, just a sentence or two that tells people what you liked about the book. This will help other readers know why they might like it, too, and help me write more of what you love. But please, no spoilers!

The truth is, VERY few readers leave reviews. Please help me by being the exception.

ABOUT THE AUTHOR

Tora Moon writes Goddess fantasy and science fiction, skillfully melding different sub-genres to create unique, memorable stories. Her completed series, The Legends of Lairheim, combines elements of epic, paranormal, and science fiction into a breathtaking tale of magic, courage, and the enduring power of unity.

Her series, The Sentinel Witches, blends her love of urban/ magical realism, mythology, and portal fantasy—and skates close to the edge of thriller and horror. Throughout all her works, you will find Tora's love of Goddess mythology as she weaves aspects of these into her stories.

As Tora-Iresh'nai Moon, she writes about Goddess Spirituality and shares her nearly fifty years of experience of connecting with the Goddess and the Feminine Divine.

Tora is also an artist who explores drawing and watercolor painting. Her current passion is creating and coloring mandalas inspired by the Goddess. Tora also expresses her creativity through various handcrafts.

You can find out more about Tora, her books, and her art at: ToraMoon.com